A Kingdom of Wicked Souls
Dark and Twisted Tales
Book Three

Jay R. Wolf

NIGHT MUSE PRESS

A KINGDOM OF WICKED SOULS

Copyright © 2025 by Jay R. Wolf

First Edition: All rights reserved.

No part of this book may be reproduced in any form or by any electronic or mechanical means, including information storage and retrieval systems, without written permission from the author, except for use if brief quotations in a book review. This book is a work of fiction. Names, characters, places and incidents either are the product of the authors' imagination or are used fictitiously. Any resemblance to actual events, locales, or persons, living or dead is purely coincidental.

Print ISBN: 978-1-960411-16-7

Published by Night Muse Press

Cover Art by Maria Spada

Character by Art Kalynne Art

Editing by Claire M. Knight / Jay R. Wolf

Formatted by Jay R. Wolf

❀ Created with Vellum

To the brave souls who've been waiting for the spice – congratulations, your patience has paid off. May this book make you question your life choices, consider a cold shower, and want your very own hook-handed pirate.

CONTENT WARNING

This book is intended for a mature audience (18+). It contains explicit sex scenes, considerable profanity, nudity, violence, death, hook play, and torture.

PROLOGUE
ARIE

"Are you ready?" Tink asked. Her wings fluttered—wings that looked far better than when Wendy had broken them.

A warmth spread through me, something I'd learned came from the bond I now shared with Tink. At first, I thought being tied to a fairy would be a terrible idea but now... now it was as if the bond completed what's always been missing.

I didn't know how to answer Tink. *Was* I ready to face off against dozens of Neverbeasts? Not entirely, but I forged on anyway. For my sister, the one person in this damned world that gave me a reason to fight. For Ulrich, and Pascal who came into my life when I didn't know I needed them. And my crew, who stuck by me through the good, bad, and deadly.

There were far too many people counting on me. I had no choice but to be ready.

I led the way with my head high and uncertainty in my heart. We still had no idea where Jameson was and whether Pascal would be able to hold his own against Wendy. He had no choice, *we* had no choice—but to win.

Though no matter what I did, or thought, Ulrich's final

words to me rang through my mind. Words that left me breathless and confused.

I will do whatever it takes to prove to you I'm not the bad guy.

How could a simple sentence threaten to bring me to my knees?

I gripped Slayer tighter in my hand and led my group toward Wendy's homestead. The grounds were bedecked in ivy and lush gardens with towering cypress trees and stone archways. The villa itself was grand in stature, a white and stone building that loomed over us with its expansive windows and turrets. From the exterior, it reminded me of a castle depicted in one of the fairytale books from my library on the *Betty*.

The *Betty* that was no more.

My ship had been destroyed and my friend . . . I swallowed down a sob. Hector was gone but what we did here today would ensure his death wasn't in vain.

With that in mind, I focused on the present.

"You okay?" Frankie asked as she approached. My beautiful sister. I hated that we'd been dealt such a shitty hand by our parents' murder. She deserved so much better. No matter how hard I tried though, the visions of her hiding under her bed as our fathers' slaughtered bodies lay in the adjacent room would haunt me for the rest of my life.

"Are you?" I asked.

She shrugged. "I'm ready for this to be over so we can find out who killed our fathers. I'm ready to be done fighting because all it has brought me is death, pain, and an anger that never seems to end."

I nodded. "Once all this is over, we'll find a quiet place to live where nothing, but the bugs will harm us."

Frankie chuckled. We stayed quiet for a while before I said, "Can you imagine what our fathers would say if they saw us now?"

Malakai and Viktor were always pushing the two of us to explore the joys of the world, to never get caught up in the chaos it inflicts. And yet here we were, wrapped in all its destruction.

"They wouldn't recognize us." Frankie sighed. "I miss them."

"I do too."

Frankie pulled something out from under her shirt—a necklace, and not just any necklace, but the one I'd given her as a child. She pulled it over her hand and handed it to me, tears forming in her eyes.

"You gave this to me before you left, a memento to remember that everything was going to be okay. I want you to—"

"Don't you dare." I turned toward her and pushed her hand back. "Don't you do this, Frankie. Everything's going to be okay. So you best put that back on before I do it myself."

Frankie shook her head. "Fine."

I pulled her into my arms, squeezing her tight. "We're going to be okay, Frankie."

She pulled out of my grasp and cleared her throat, putting on her mask of indifference. "Of course we are."

We continued forward, getting closer to the villa until we passed through the gardens. There were no Neverbeasts roaming the grounds. That didn't mean there weren't any lurking in the shadows.

"Does anyone see *anything*?" I asked.

"No," Keenan replied. "Do you think Wendy has ordered them inside?"

Marian shook her head. "Some maybe, but she'd want more patrolling and keeping watch."

"Are you certain this is going to work, Cap?" Keenan asked.

"Are you doubting me, Keenan? After all this time."

"Never," he said immediately, his gaze nothing but serious.

A warmth spread through me and I blinked back tears. "Okay then, let's find some beasts."

As if my words called them out from the shadows, a deafening roar sounded from nearby.

Neverbeasts emerged from all over the villa. I raised Slayer and pointed it at them, ready for their attack. We had to keep these beasts distracted and away from Wendy. No one was sure how long it would take for Pascal and Ulrich to reach her and end her before the beasts ripped us to shreds, but we had to do whatever we could to buy them time.

Marian had been pretty certain my magic would be able to hold them off, so without a second hesitation, I dug into the well of my most sacred power, the magic gifted to me by my birth father: King Rylan. The raging river of mermaid magic swirled and surged inside me.

While it was new to me, it didn't take much to call it to the forefront. I pushed aside the call of the sea witch and dug into the half of me that could control these beasts. Holding out a hand, I pulled on the expanse of energy and everything in me. I commanded them to stop.

It took a couple tries, considering there were far more of them than I'd ever been able to control before. At least Chimera was gone and there wouldn't be another witch to stop me.

The beasts roared in frustration as they came to a halt. Confusion and aggression radiated off them, but I continued to keep them at bay or our plan would fail. The Lost Boys and my crew would work to tie up as many of the beasts as they could. Now that we knew they weren't just beasts but cursed people, no one wanted to harm them more than necessary.

My grip remained firm on the Neverbeasts, but something shifted. A wave of foreign energy pulsed through me. I gritted my teeth, bracing myself as the pressure built, my instincts screaming for release—for control. A cry threatened to rip from my throat, but I bit it back as the power pushed through me, then I heard something—unfamiliar voices. They were faint and distant, like whispers in my mind. As they grew louder and more persistent, I realized that the voices were coming from inside me; it was the Neverbeasts calling out from my own mind.

Please help us.
Free us, Atlantean Princess.
Save us like you did Marian.
You have the power within you.
You can do this.

They continued begging for me to release them from their bond to Wendy, pleading for mercy and freedom.

"I'm not so sure about that." I called out. How was I going to free dozens of beasts all at once? It had taken so much time and *energy* to free Marian and the second I started to free all these people, Wendy would know, and my strength would be barely hanging on.

But I didn't give two shits what Wendy thought or what happened to me. I trusted Pascal and Ulrich to get the job done.

If I could sever all these bonds like I'd done Marian, perhaps we could end this now. I'd been worried about it before, about the consequences, but if it worked maybe the beasts would take our side. We could stop Wendy before anyone else I loved got hurt.

The pleading grew louder and more persistent as the beasts bared their teeth at me—the beast and human halves at odds with one another.

Okay, yes, I'll try. I thought.

"Arie, are you okay?" Frankie asked.

"Stay. Back," I said through gritted teeth. My strength dwindled with each passing second. "None of you touch them."

"I thought you wanted us to tie them up?" Keenan argued.

I shook my head and gritted my teeth. "Trust. Me."

I'd severed Marian's bond with the trident, well the one inside my mind anyway. This time I had the real thing. Perhaps this was the key I needed. With newfound vigor, I grabbed hold of the necklace around my neck—the hidden trident—and dug deep into the well of my power. My muscles ached and my head pounded, but I pressed on.

I closed my eyes and searched for the connection between me and the beasts. Seconds grew into minutes before I found dozens of yarn-like strands. Each one of them was dark and dripping with black ooze. I clutched the trident in my hand and picked up a strand. Darkness swam through me, invading my body and mind as I struggled to snap the stands in half. My head throbbed, threatening to crack and I cried out.

I couldn't do this.

Fight, Pirate Queen.

Clutching the trident tighter in my head I focused all of my energy into it, each fiber of the string easing the darkness within me.

As the last tendril broke free, I let go of the trident, the magic dissipating as I dropped to my knees. I gasped for breath and tried to steady my racing pulse.

Slowly, the beasts retreated, vanishing into the crabgrass.

We owe everything to you, Arie Lockwood.

You have our eternal gratitude.

Thank you.

"You're welcome."

Marian's jaw dropped. "Did you just . . ."

I nodded, struggling to rise but the air shifted, sending an icy chill through the gardens and a deep fog descended around us faster than an oncoming storm, obstructing my vision with a thick, black veil.

I was completely blind.

Before I could find a place for cover, I was met with a sharp, intense pain in my shoulder that sent me reeling backwards. My vision blurred with a mix of fear and anger as I touched the arrow lodged into my flesh. My knees buckled and I gritted my teeth against the pain.

Was this it? Had fate finally caught up to me and this was how it ended? *With a fucking arrow?*

I grabbed a hold of the arrow's shaft and just as I was about to pluck it from my shoulder, a familiar face appeared in front of me.

Jameson.

A wicked smile played on his lips as he stalked forward.

"And here I thought it would be much harder to take down the mighty and dangerous pirate queen."

I bit back a groan as I struggled to my feet. "Is this your doing?"

"Consider it my little going away present," he purred, circling me like a predator eyeing its prey. "You didn't honestly think I'd let you waltz in here and disturb all Wendy's fun, did you?"

I clutched Slayer tightly and braced myself for what was to come.

"You're too late. I've already broken the bonds. Now all that's left is to end the two of you."

"Yes, yes, you'll stab me with your little dagger and feed me to the sharks. But I don't think you're in the position to do much right now." He leaned closer and flicked the arrow.

I groaned, pain radiating through my arm. "If you were trying to kill me you did a piss poor job of that."

The fog around the two of us thickened as muffled shouts rang out around us.

"Kill you?" Jameson threw his head back and laughed. "I

have something far more entertaining planned for you. The mistress is waiting for you after all."

"The mistress?" I asked.

Suddenly, flecks entered my vision, the once pristine gardens around me a dizzying blur of colors and shapes as tears welled in my eyes. A searing heat shot through my veins from the wound, a sharp throbbing ache. I screamed.

Dropping to my knees, panic coursed through me at the sight of thin black lines spreading out from the wound like poisoned roots digging into the soil. Tendrils of dark blood oozed out like a slow-moving river, pooling onto the ground beneath me. Time slowed down and everything around me faded away into a distant hum. All I could focus on were those writhing lines crawling across my skin and the thick, syrupy blood that refused to stop flowing.

"Sleep tight, pirate queen. When you wake up, a whole new adventure begins."

I

No Way Out
ULRICH

I will kill them all.

The thought ripped through me like a tempest, fierce and unrelenting. My nails bit into my palm, the sting grounding me against the storm churning in my chest. The cliff beneath my boots felt as unstable as the rage boiling under my skin, the jagged rocks below a cruel reminder of how far I would fall if I didn't keep myself in check.

Below, waves thundered against the shore, violent and ready to swallow me whole if I took one step forward. They mirrored the riot in my heart, each crash pounding as fiercely as the blood rushing in my ears. The salty spray reached me even here, sharp and biting against my face, but it was nothing compared to the fire that consumed me.

They had taken her.

Every soul who played a part in that betrayal would pay. I'd make sure of it. My fist trembled with the weight of my promise, my knuckles turning white as I clung to the only certainty I had left: getting Arie back. I swore to the abyss that I'd stop at nothing to get her.

I ran my hook over my beard, a dark smile twisting my lips. Funny, how things changed.

It seemed like yesterday she was nothing more than a thorn in my side. A rival. A woman who haunted the same waters I did, hunting the same monsters and chasing the same gold. The bounty boards had never been big enough for the both of us, and yet she'd made room—with fists and a wicked grin that promised trouble.

We had clashed again and again, and each time I expected her to come for my throat, to finally put an end to me. I never saw it coming when she saved my life instead.

I still remembered the sirens—their claws, their songs, the way they dragged my men and my ship into the depths of the sea. How certain I was that my end had come, until it hadn't. Arie had come to my aid without hesitation.

Me. She'd saved me.

Something shifted after that day. Something I couldn't name, something I couldn't stop. I'd tried to ignore it, tried to shove it down where it wouldn't claw at me. It worked, for a while. Until it didn't.

And then I'd lost her.

The memory hit like a blade between the ribs, sharp and merciless. I ground my teeth, trying to bury the ache. But it didn't matter. None of it mattered anymore. She was gone, and I...

I would burn the world to bring her back.

The wind whirled around me, carrying the scent of salt and sea. In the distance, storm clouds gathered and I let out a sigh. If Arie were here she'd be able to calm the skies with her gift. A sea witch, Arie could command the sea itself. A power I once thought was dangerous and full of darkness.

How times have changed.

Now I knew that Arie was a goddess in her own right. A savior the Seven Seas needed.

She was a force to be reckoned with.

"How did Jameson get the upper hand on you, Arie?" I murmured into the wind.

"Magic."

Spinning around, a figure emerged from the shadows of the forest. His wild, blond hair whipped against his face and his green eyes blazed with as much anger as I carried. A long-jagged scar crossed over the other eye.

"Pascal," I said. Still trying to get used to the fact that not long ago he'd been King Roland's right-hand man—The Wizard. No thanks to Wendy.

Wendy who was finally dead. One more villain laid to rest thanks to Arie freeing the beasts and Pascal.

"Whatever happened doesn't matter right now. We know that she will fight every second which means we need to find her." Pascal stopped short of the cliff.

"Did you find anything to help us?" I asked.

"Marian and Tink found a mirror," Pascal replied

"A mirror?"

"Apparently. It's some sort of magic portal Wendy had. I've seen them before. Twin mirrors that were created by the gods to allow certain people to travel from one realm to the other. How Wendy managed to get her hands on one is beyond me, though I suspect it's whoever she's been working with."

Hurt flashed in Pascal's face for a split second before his anger returned. The scar that covered his face had been a stark reminder of the pain Wendy inflicted on him. She had been his friend—our friend—and she betrayed us in the worst way possible.

"So, what are we waiting for? We need to get to that mirror." I pushed past Pascal, but he grabbed my arm.

"I'm sorry, Ulrich," Pascal frowned. "Someone smashed the mirror to pieces. Tink says the magic is beyond her skill set and can't be fixed."

This meant they could be anywhere in the Seven Seas right now. How were we going to find her?

Pascal grabbed my shoulder and squeezed. "We'll figure this out, Ulrich. She's a survivor and whoever took her obviously needs her. I have a suspicion as to who it might be but it's too soon to tell. Let's head back and regroup."

I took one final look at the sea and prayed to the gods Arie would get through whatever was coming her way.

2

CHAINED
ARIE

I WAS COMPLETELY, AND UTTERLY, FUCKED.

The air was stale and musty, and the walls of the tiny room were damp with mold and mildew. I tried to move, but a sharp pain in my left shoulder brought me back to the reality of what I'd been through. The sudden attack, the swiftness of Jameson's arrow as it plunged into my shoulder, and the mercilessness of his cold, dark eyes.

I'd been so sure that our plan would work. Had assumed I'd accounted for all variables and would be above reproach. But I was proven wrong in the most brutal way imaginable. The weight of my naivety sat heavy as the chains that bound me to this shit hole of a prison dug into my wrists and ankles.

I was really tired of being thrown into a cell. Once I murdered the person who put me in here, I vowed to choose death before ever being put back in a cell.

The second Jameson killed Giles back in Neverland, I knew he was up to something. I'd kept myself sharp and my awareness open as we made our way to Lily's Cove. I knew he was out there, waiting to strike but I thought I'd had the upper hand. I had the trident, a band of pirates, and the Lost Boys at my back.

I'd even managed to sever the bonds of the Neverbeasts. Yet, he still managed to find a way to stop me with a simple fucking arrow to the shoulder.

He'd mentioned bringing me to a mistress, as had Wendy stating the mistress wouldn't be pleased if I was harmed. Now that I thought about it, Ursa had even mentioned someone. I'd once thought it was Wendy but now I wasn't so sure.

You may have bested me, but you'll never stop her.

Had she been talking about this mistress?

Silver moonlight peeked through the barred window of my cell, casting an eerie glow on the damp stone walls. I sat up, and instantly regretted it as my world spun. I placed a hand on the wall to ground myself and gritted my teeth at the pain.

Where in sea's sake was I? I took measured steps, my feet chained together. I paused at the window and peered out to a sprawling city.

I sure as hells am not in Neverland anymore.

Buildings spanned as far as my eyes could see but there was a stillness to the darkness that sent a shiver down my back. Two soldiers stood guard on one of the rooftops nearest me with swords at their sides as they conversed.

I narrowed my eyes, taking in every detail—the crisp lines of their coats, the gleaming buttons polished to perfection, the way they stood with rigid, practiced posture. No, these weren't Kingsmen. Their uniforms lacked the golden medallion, the proud dragon crest that marked Khan's soldiers. And yet, they were too refined, too polished to belong to any of the usual mercenary bands. Their boots were free of mud, their gloves unstained, their presence exuding an air of quiet authority. These men weren't just disciplined—they were trained for something more. Something deliberate. Something dangerous.

So where was I?

It hit me then: Jameson was a member of the Brotherhood,

which meant . . . *hells*, was I in Chione? I'd never been to the capital of the Enchanted Realm, mostly because it was thousands of miles away from where I'd grown up. How had Jameson managed to get me here so quickly? There was no way I'd been unconscious for that long. Had the arrow been laced with some sort of drug?

With a heavy sigh, I slumped to the floor and pressed my back against the wall. I took in a breath, trying to clear my mind and think of a way out of this mess. I had to survive, had to get back to my crew and my sister.

Did Pascal manage to stop Wendy? Were they even alive?

Was Ulrich all right?

Rather than the residual annoyance I usually felt for Ulrich, sorrow crept into my chest. The last thing he said to me came to the forefront: *You may say that you're broken, Arie, and that's fine because I accept that. I accept all of you. And I will do whatever it takes to help you put those pieces back together. I will do whatever it takes to prove to you I'm not the bad guy.* And then he was gone, leaving me breathless and unsure of everything.

Now I was halfway across the world in chains with no allies.

I focused my energy on the bond between me and Tink, reaching for the fragile thread that tied us together. A wave of relief surged through me as I felt it—thin, distant, but still there. It was a web of light stretching across the vast distance between us, barely holding, frayed at the edges but unbroken. I tried to pull more from it, to grasp onto something stronger, but the power I drew from it was weak, flickering like a dying ember.

Still, at least I knew she was alive.

I exhaled, pressing my fingers against the cool metal of the railing as I stared out at the city, wishing it were Neverland's cliffs instead.

There was a time I had feared a bond like this—feared the

idea of being tied to someone else, bound for life in ways I couldn't control. I had spent years believing that to be free meant belonging to no one. That attachment only led to chains, to suffering, to something that could be ripped away.

But now?

Now, it was starting to grow on me.

The bonds I had forged weren't shackles—they were lifelines. And as much as I hated the vulnerability of it, I couldn't deny the way it settled into my bones like something I had always been meant to carry.

I tried again, closing my eyes, focusing on Tink's presence. If I could push a little harder, maybe—

Nothing.

The connection was too thin. Too weak.

A flicker of frustration burned through me, but I forced myself to let it go. We were too far apart. I couldn't reach her. Not yet.

Which meant I'd have to get myself out of here.

My heart leapt to my throat as I searched my clothes. *No.* Slayer was gone. Without that dagger by my side, a part of me was missing. It had been an ever-present companion for so long; its absence was a physical ache in my chest. I clutched my neck and more dread filled me. The trident was gone, too.

What would King Rylan think of me for losing the trident to the Brotherhood?

My father had entrusted it to me, and now it was in the hands of the enemy. Did they know what they held? Did they know they had the key to Atlantis in their hands?

Boots scuffed along the floor, pulling me from my sulking as keys rattled and murmured voices sounded from down the hall. I rose to my feet, refusing to let them believe I'd been bested more than I already had by being in this damned place.

The door unlocked with a loud click and sunlight flooded

the room. I quickly brought my arm up to shield my eyes, blinking hard against the sudden brightness.

"Thank you, Gregory. Please see to it that she is fed the moment I leave."

"Yes, your Majesty."

The door closed and a soft glow from a candle filled the space to reveal one of the more regal looking women I'd ever seen. If we were in Chione, then this was Queen Gemma.

The firelight danced across her face, highlighting her pale complexion and the deep shadows of her eyes—eyes so dark they teetered on black. Her long dark hair was pulled back into an elegant bun with a crown of deep obsidian that contrasted well against a black dress with ornate silver embroidery.

She smiled, one that didn't quite meet her eyes. "Apologies for the extreme measures." She pointed to her wrists and looked down at the chains combining mine. Not before looking me up and down as if to size me up, her brow lifted slightly. "But I've been told you're a rather good escape artist."

I narrowed my eyes at the woman, taking in her appearance and the cold detachment in her voice. "Who are you and what the fuck do you want?" I demanded, my own voice rough.

The woman's smile grew wider, but her eyes remained unreadable. "You have quite the mouth on you. Though I'm pretty certain you know exactly who I am."

I held her gaze, unbothered by her attempt at intimidation as I waited for her to get on with it. I knew who she was, or at least I had my suspicions. If I was in Chione, and I had a rising suspicion I was, then this was the queen who ruled it.

She was the one who'd been dealing this deck from the beginning.

First, my mother, by signing her up for this mission that got her killed by her own daughter. Then King Roland, who had an ongoing alliance with her, and for all I know has been in on this from the start. Next, Jameson, who came aboard my ship with false intentions. And finally, Wendy. They were all connected in an elaborate web of villains and bargains

But through all that, the worst was the thought that this woman could have been the direct cause of Viktor and Malakai's death. So, it made sense that she was the one behind my kidnapping. She may have been watching me, studying me for years while my good-for-nothing mother helped her until her much deserved demise, but she didn't *know* me or the tricks I had up my sleeve.

Gemma may have been the queen in this game, but I was the ace in the hole, and I had no plans of folding.

This was all speculation, of course, but something told me I was on the right track.

"Are you prone to not answering questions, Queen Gemma?" I asked.

The smile slid from her face and her jaw ticked. *Yep, I guessed right.*

"I'd suggest you treat a queen with a bit more respect."

She had to know I was baiting her, feeling out her control and how much she would let slide. Sure, it was stupid and dangerous, but I needed to know exactly what I was up against. I only knew what Marian had told me, and it wasn't much.

I'd wanted to get more information once Wendy was taken care of. If only Jameson hadn't ruined that for me.

When King Roland had me, I'd known his reputation and the things he was capable of. With this queen, I knew next to nothing— I needed more. Who she was, what made her tick, every possible weakness, if I were going to make it out of this alive.

"I respect only those who've earned it," I sneered.

A flicker of anger came and went on the Queen's face.

A short fuse. Noted.

"You do realize you're the one sitting on the stone floor of *my* prison, yes? I'd think you'd be a little more understanding and willing to hear what I have to say if you want to get out of here."

"What. Do. You. Want." I snapped.

"It appears you have the same fiery attitude as your mother. Pity." She clicked her tongue. "Well, seeing as you're not ready for civility. I'll come back when you've decided not to continue acting like a child." She turned and strolled to the door before stopping short and looking back at me. "Oh, and I'll be sure to tell Gregory you're far too tired for dinner tonight."

"Why thank you, your regalness." I bit out. A grin crept to my lips as the door slammed shut. The lock clicked into place and unintelligible murmurs sounded from behind before I was once again surrounded by silence.

I was certain if Keenan were here, he'd be rolling his eyes and telling me how reckless that was.

I didn't give two flying shits. Recklessness got me answers I needed. Sometimes that recklessness came in handy, and I had a feeling I wasn't going to last long here without pulling out all the stops.

My stomach rumbled and for a moment I regretted poking the monster. But that didn't last long, not when I remembered where I was. What the Queen had done.

Marian had told me she knew of Malakai and Viktor and all signs of their death pointed to the Brotherhood. The band of assassins who dwelled in Chione's dark streets, sworn to serve the Elders who in turn worked for the Queen. If it was in fact a member of the Brotherhood who murdered them, then by all rights, Gemma was the one truly responsible. She was the one who plucked their strings and directed them to do as she pleased.

Gemma had done me a favor by bringing me here. Now I

just needed to find a way to get to her without being chained and locked up like an animal.

Just when I was about to let my thoughts drift elsewhere, a knock came to the door. I jumped and whirled to see the door shimmer. A man with rich dark skin and eyes stepped through. Shaggy auburn hair reached past his chin where even more hair cascaded down, ending at his chest. A dark cloak hung off his sloped shoulders and worry lined his worn expression as he surveyed me.

"Arie," he said with a nod.

Instantly my gaze sharpened on him, suspicion's claws dug into my gut. He knew my name. "Who are you?"

"A friend," his voice rumbled. "Someone who knows quite a bit about you and would like to help you escape."

A friend who knew me but I knew nothing about. I had no idea who this man was or what his intentions were. Did his offer have something to do with the Queen? I took a step back and studied him. His demeanor held an air of authority and something about him sent a wave of unease through me.

I raised an eyebrow. "Why? What's in it for you?"

"We don't have a lot of time before the guard returns. Let's just say our interests are aligned when it comes to the Queen."

Despite my suspicion, my curiosity was piqued. "So you've come to free me then?"

The man leaned in closer. "It isn't that simple I'm afraid. You'll have to stay here for a while. Play the part of the good little pet and—"

I threw my head back and laughed. "You can't be serious?"

He *was* working with the Queen. She'd expected me to be civil and I was anything but, not when it came to those trying to harm me.

The man's eyes widened as he shifted his gaze from me to the dark hall. "Keep your voice down. For you to survive the false Queen, you need to play nice, if only until the annual masquerade ball."

"Wait, what?" *False queen and a ball*? Was this man out of his mind?

"There will be more time to explain later. Are you capable of playing along?"

It seemed like a particularly cruel twist of fate that I'd been forced to go through this all over again. Play nice and do what I was told just like when King Roland had Frankie. Only this time, my friends and family weren't here to bargain with—but *my* life was.

I refused to hope he was actually offering me a way out—a man who I didn't even know. He didn't seem fond of the Queen—at least had that going for him. At this point, what other choice did I have? Still, something didn't feel right.

"And why would I believe anything you say when I don't even know who you are? For all I know this is some elaborate trick set up by the Queen herself."

He nodded, as if he expected the skepticism. "My name is Kaelryn, you can call me Kael. I'm from a village outside of the city, working as a consultant of sorts to the Elders. After word spread that the Queen managed to imprison Arie Lockwood, the monster hunter and sea witch, I took it as a sign."

I stifled my laugh. "A sign? From who, the gods?"

"One day when this is over, I'll explain to you why it's a good choice to put a little faith in people."

"Well, that's not cryptic or anything."

"I understand the hesitation," Kael said. "If you change your mind, just call out my name three times and I'll be here."

Something sparked in the air before the door shimmered again and Kael disappeared, leaving me shrouded in darkness once more. I stood for a while, mulling over Kael's words. Could I trust him? Did I have any other options? I knew I couldn't stay here for long. The longer Gemma held me captive, the more information she could glean from me, and the harder it would be to escape. I wouldn't risk that but at the same time, I couldn't outright trust a stranger who claimed he wanted to help. I'd been burned far too many times for that.

I paced the cell, trying to formulate a plan. When my stomach rumbled again, I knew I couldn't afford to dwell on my situation any longer. I needed to keep my strength up and my senses sharp if I was going to survive this. Which meant taking whatever opportunities presented themselves, no matter how small, or risky, they might be.

With a deep sigh, I leaned back against the cold stone wall and closed my eyes. It was time to rest, to conserve my energy for the battles to come. But even as I drifted off, I couldn't shake the impending doom that lurked over me, or the thoughts of what was happening in Neverland.

3
PENANCE
ARIE

Days passed in a blur of questions. Where were my friends? Were they safe or had my capture abandoned them to their fate? What was Gemma planning to do with me, why was I being held prisoner? Every answer seemed farther away than the next.

I paced back and forth in the cell, searching for any weak point in the walls or a way to get these damn cuffs off. But nothing worked, no matter how hard I tried. These cuffs, whatever Gemma had done to them, were far more powerful than any I'd been subjected to in the past. King Roland's cuffs snuffed out my magic, but these made it feel like I had no magic at all.

Despair crept over me as I sat down on the cold floor and my gaze drifted toward the barred window.

Heavy footfalls of what I presumed were guards sounded from behind the door. A metallic rattle of keys echoed off the walls before the door flung open and golden light flowed in. The silhouettes of the two figures standing in the doorway cast long menacing shadows onto the walls.

"You've been summoned by the Queen," the one on the

right said. He stood head and shoulders above the other. Nearly as big and furry as a Sasquatch, he had unkempt dark hair, a long beard, and a crooked nose. His plated armor clinked as he motioned toward the door.

Before I had a moment to think of a response, the smaller one with short blond hair and stubble along his jaw, yanked me forward.

"Come, you don't want to keep her waiting," Sasquatch said as he moved in front to lead the way.

Short-Round pushed me forward and shoved me out the door. I stumbled, nearly crashing into the adjacent wall.

"That's an interesting way to treat a lady," I murmured.

"A lady," Short-Round said as he looked up at Sasquatch. "Do you see a lady here?"

Sasquatch shook his head. "All I see is a bitch who needs to learn a lesson or two."

Anger whirled through me as Short-Round pushed me forward again. I bit my tongue from lashing out. I'd done enough of that when the Queen first came to see me. I wasn't going to survive if I let my mouth run wild with every scathing thought. My brain seemed to agree because I said nothing more until we stopped at a giant door.

The door stood imposingly tall, stretching nearly twice the height of the two guards. It appeared to be made of thick, dark wood and was studded with iron fixtures. The enormous hinges clanked loudly as they swung.

The opened door revealed a lavish throne room. Large and intricate vases lined the walls, filled with colorful flowers. Vines laced with dark red flowers cascade down every pillar, and I could have sworn some of them moved upon our entry. A long luxurious rug sat across the walkway as we made our way to a giant throne with an ornately carved backrest and gilded armrests. Above the throne, silk curtains draped between two large pillars. Queen Gemma stepped out from the shadows wearing a flowing emerald dress and a diamond-studded crown.

She watched me with a piercing gaze as she moved to the chair and sat. My heart pounded in my chest. I tried to steady myself and stand before the ruler with as much dignity as my chains allowed.

"You two may leave." The Queen waved the guards away.

They turned and left without a word until I stood alone with Gemma. It was odd her guards abandoned her safety so willingly and unease crept over me. Granted, I had no weapons of any kind but that didn't matter either. My chains may be keeping me from using my magic, but they wouldn't stop me from choking the life out of her.

What kind of powers did Gemma possess? I pushed aside the panic building in my chest and tried to remember that I may be magicless and weaponless, but I wasn't helpless.

Gemma stared at me for a few moments before finally speaking. "I hope you're ready to be more amicable this time. I'd hate to have to punish you for disobedience."

If only I had Slayer.

I said nothing and nodded. Once again not trusting my mouth to say the right thing.

"Do you know why you're here?"

There were a dozen ways I could have answered that question. But I wasn't sure how much to reveal. I liked knowing—at least for the moment—that I had the upper hand in terms of knowledge. She wanted my powers, her greedy ambitions the most likely reason my mother turned into a violent and deadly monster and had been the sole reason Pascal had to endure Wendy's torture.

For all I knew she'd been the one to teach Wendy, had been a mentor to her. It would explain how Wendy went from being friends with the Lost Boys to wanting to destroy them.

But as far as being in the Enchanted Realm, I could only guess it had something to do with the Celestial Plains, and the souls my mother had been unsuccessful to gather. She wanted Pan and would go to great lengths to get him.

"I'd imagine it has something to do with why you sent my mother after me."

"Your mother was weak." She spat. "But I suppose you already knew that. I truly didn't think you had it in you to kill your own mother. Though I admit, I was pleasantly surprised to see you rise to the occasion. Which is part of why you are here."

"What do you want with me then?"

"In a few moments the Elders of the Brotherhood will walk through those doors."

The Elders—my heart sped up and blood pounded in my ears. Someone in the Brotherhood had been responsible for my fathers'—Viktor and Malakai—deaths. This could possibly be the only chance I had to figure out who ordered the hit. Whether it was Gemma or an Elder of the Brotherhood. I was going to find out one way or another.

"They believe you're here to repent for the misdeeds you've caused across the Seven Seas." Gemma continued.

What? I had to bite my tongue from doubling over in a fit of laughter. She had to be joking right? I was a pirate, sure, but I was also a monster hunter. I protected the seas and the people who sailed it. How was that a crime?

"Misdeeds?" I asked.

"Did you not pillage and steal from naval captains and innocent merchant ships?"

Only when they were firing at me or when I needed more supplies. We never killed anyone unless provoked. Usually, missions to board a ship were done with stealth and precision, and yet I doubted she really gave two shits about any of that.

"I did what was necessary to protect the seas."

Queen Gemma raised a brow. "I believe you think you were doing the right thing. It's admirable, the work you do, but now," a sinister glint came into the Queen's eyes, "now, you'll work for me, doing something bigger than slaying sea monsters. I need the Elders to understand this."

"Why."

Gemma stood from her throne and walked to me. "Don't worry about the why right now. All you need to do is work with me in a civilized manner, and I will ensure your time here isn't entirely unpleasant. Keep your mouth shut during this meeting and let the Elders see that you can take orders like a good little soldier. Do this, and I'll allow you to stay out of those dungeons. I'll help you find what you seek."

I fought off the laughter building within me. She really had no idea who I was if she expected me to fall in line. Did she honestly think I'd believe she'd help me with anything? I'm sure she would so long as I did what she asked and there was no way in all the Seven Seas I'd align myself with someone like her. While I didn't want to risk becoming another name on the Brotherhood's target list, it was possible that the person responsible for Malakai and Viktor's death was *here,* within my reach. Which meant I'd have to be compliant long enough to get my answers.

The doors opened again with a loud creak, and three men draped in long robes of red and gold entered the room. They moved with an air of confidence and authority that had my stomach twisting in knots.

"Bow before the Elders, pirate," Gemma hissed.

She expected me to bow before men?

Play along, Arie. A voice rang out in my mind and reluctantly, I obeyed, bowing and trying with all my might to hide the rage on my face. These were powerful men who did not take kindly to defiance or insubordination—something that would no doubt be part of this journey with Queen Gemma. But for survival, it was my only option and so I chose to play along, at least for now.

"Gentlemen, good to see you. Shall we take this to the meeting room?"

The men nodded in unison, their eyes never fully reaching my own as they turned toward another door. As we walked, I couldn't help but feel like a lamb led to slaughter—or in this case, a pirate led to the plank.

We walked in silence until reaching another large wooden door. Gemma retrieved a small key from her pocket, unlocking the door with a soft click. The three men wasted no time entering the room, and I followed closely, unsure of what to expect.

The room was large, with bookshelves lining every wall and comfortable armchairs scattered throughout. Stained-glass windows reflected an array of beautiful colors along the floor that reminded me of Seven Falls—of Ulrich. The air was thick with the leather-bound books and smoke from a crackling fire that burned in the hearth. This was definitely a place I could get lost in.

The men settled into chairs behind a long rectangular table.

Standing before the Elders, I scrutinized them. The ones who decided the fate of two of the best people I'd known. The fire in my heart was no longer simmering, it blazed with passionate hatred. I was determined to find out which one of them had ordered the hit on my family and then make them pay for the destruction they caused.

Gemma took a seat at the head of the table. "Miss Lockwood, we—"

"Captain," I said and could have slapped myself from speaking out loud. I needed to keep my composure if I wanted to make it out of this. Hadn't I learned that in the time I'd been in King Roland's dungeons, or as I was forced to look upon his notorious guillotine?

Gemma's jaw ticked.

"The Brotherhood does not recognize false captains. Sailors do not steal, murder, and attack those of innocent intent," The Elder closest to Gemma said. He lowered his hood to reveal a head of short white hair and deep-set eyes that appeared almost green in the light.

"As I was saying," Gemma said before I could say something else to further anger the grumpy old man. "You are here before the Brotherhood to answer for the crimes you have committed."

They kept talking about my crimes and yet had anyone done anything about the ones they carried out on a regular basis? Hypocrites—all of them.

I kept my gaze fixed on the Elders, trying to ignore the anger bubbling inside of me.

"However, we are willing to give you a choice," Gemma continued.

One of the Elders, a man with greying dark hair and wrinkles near his eyes, shot the Queen a look. She simply raised her hand. "While the Elders may advise me, they do not have the final say here. I do. And I am willing to give you a chance to repent for your sins and start anew."

"Your Majesty," the man scoffed. "We didn't agree to this."

"No, Elder Wulf, but you know why this is necessary."

Wulf.

I had heard rumors about a powerful figure on the east side of the Enchanted Realm. All I knew was that his name was Wulf, and he held numerous churches in the city under his control. He seemed to be everywhere, and everyone spoke of him with fear. He was a monster worthy of slaying. I'd once heard someone refer to him as the Huntsman.

"What are you proposing then?" The Elder next to Wulf said. He slipped a hand over his head, pulling his hood down in the process. There was nothing special about this man's features, a bland face with a thick mustache and small beady eyes that seemed to look everywhere but at me.

"Elder Sinclair, we all know what Arie is." Queen Gemma gestured toward me. "She could be good for us."

"That's precisely why this is a bad idea," Elder Sinclair said. "How do you propose we keep her in line? Torture could be effective, but given that . . ."

I listened as Wulf and Sinclair went on about all the ways they'd love to string me up and slice into every bit of my skin until I was broken into millions of pieces. Perhaps Gemma wasn't the only one who taught Wendy a few things.

Though all I could picture were Malakai and Viktor. Of me walking into the house to find them both sitting in their chairs and . . . lifeless. Which one of these Elders had given the order to execute them while my sister cried in the next room? Blood boiled beneath my skin and my palms hurt from digging my nails into them. My good sense slipped and before I could think better of it, I opened my mouth.

"Which one of you did it?" I snarled.

The men across from me all shot me a look.

"Excuse me?" The Elder between Wulf and Sinclair asked. His white hair hung well past his shoulders and his eyes were so dark they were nearly black.

"Which one of you gave the order?"

Wulf and Sinclair looked at one another as though I'd said the strangest thing they'd ever heard. The one on the left, the one furthest from Gemma, stared at me with narrowed eyes. He lowered his hood, revealing blond hair and a pair of striking blue eyes. His face was handsome for an Elder, and he seemed far too young to be sitting with these other men. But he was no different. I could see it in his gaze. It was the same one I looked at every time I stepped in front of a mirror. The look of death, of someone with nothing to lose.

"Was it you?" I hissed at the blond. "Did you kill them? What could they have possibly done to any of you?"

"What are you talking about, girl?" Wulf snapped and turned to Gemma. "Are you going to let her speak to us like this?"

"Fucking tell me!" I shouted, my words echoing off the walls as my pulse picked up. "Who ordered the hit on my fathers, Malakai and Viktor?"

Wulf threw his head back and laughed.

He fucking laughed.

"That's what this is about? *That's* what you're so upset over? It's time to grow up and learn that life isn't some perfect fairy tale. Death is inevitable. Haven't you learned that by now?"

Hells, I really wished I had Slayer so I could slice that grin right from his face. Perhaps my hands would be more . . . satisfying.

"So, it was you then?"

Wulf shook his head. "I do wish it had been."

"Shut up, Wulf." The white-haired man said.

"I will do no such thing, Ranta. She's chained. What could she possibly do to me? Besides, if she wants to live, she'll be a good girl and mind her own."

Wulf's eyes trailed up and down my body before he licked his lips. A shiver rolled down my spine and I fought to keep myself rooted in place. I wanted to lash out, to scream and slice him to pieces the same way he'd threatened to do to me.

Just because I was chained and powerless, didn't mean there weren't other ways to attack.

"You're right," I said through gritted teeth. "But while you think you can speak to me this way, threaten torture and dismemberment, and treat me as inferior, it doesn't make any of that true. I want answers, you want my compliance. If either of us are to get what we want, you will provide what I need."

I didn't think—I didn't give myself the time. I lunged, pushing off the ground with as much force as I could muster. My body flew forward, chains flailing, and before anyone could stop me, I landed a punch square to Wulf's jaw.

The other Elders gasped and jumped to their feet. Wulf staggered backwards, hand clasped over his bloodied nose as his eyes filled with a mix of fury and fear.

The blond man jumped over the table and pinned me back.

"You're a brave girl, I'll give you that," the blond Elder said, looking at me with newfound respect.

"Brave?" Wulf's muffled voice made his words lack the punch I'm sure he'd intended to have. "I'll have you nailed to a cross while the people of this kingdom spit on your bones. Then we can see how brave she is."

"That's enough, Wulf. Robin, hold her still." Queen Gemma strolled over to a table and pulled a small wooden box from the drawer. She turned and walked over to me.

"You see, I was really hoping it wouldn't come to this. Striking an Elder is one of the highest offenses in Chione."

Wulf lowered his hand slowly and the blood from his nose dripped down his lips and chin. His face twisted into a sinister grin as a cold darkness took over his gaze. His eyes were sharp and filled with fury, but also something else.

I knew hitting him was not going to earn me any favors, but at that moment, I didn't give a shit. I didn't care what happened to me so long as the one who killed my fathers paid for what they did.

"You don't know our customs and laws but as we stated you're here to atone for the crimes you've committed." Gemma said as she set the box down behind her and held out a rounded necklace—no, not a necklace. A collar.

"Stop, what are you doing? What is that?" I thrashed against Robin's hold but I barely budged. Hells, he was strong.

The second the collar clicked into place everything went dull. The heavy metal felt like an icy vise around my neck, squeezing tighter with each breath. Sparks of pain shot through my head as I frantically tried to unclasp it from my throat.

My magic, which was always strong and vibrant as the waves crashing at my bare feet on a beach, was gone. Not out of reach and unusable like with the chains on my wrists, but *gone.* As in, not there, as if never had been. I felt nothing, not even Tink's connection.

I was powerless and . . . hollow.

Is this what it felt like to be purely human? I swallowed down the panic that rose in my chest.

"Robin, it appears our guest is not ready to mingle within the castle. Take her back to her cell and let Gregory know he has a patient."

"As you wish, Your Majesty."

Patient? What did that mean? I opened my mouth to ask, but Robin wrenched me from the room and back toward the halls.

"Keep that Atlantean mouth of yours shut and move. You've already made this much worse for yourself than it needed to be."

I huffed. "Like you give a damn."

He didn't say another word as he brought me back to my cell. Darkness swallowed me whole as the lock clicked into place behind me.

"You have allies in this place, Arie Lockwood. I suggest you remember that before signing your own death wish."

And then he was gone.

Allies? Hadn't Kael said the same thing? Or this was all some elaborate ruse to keep me off my game. Robin was a damn Elder after all, there was no way he was an ally. Perhaps I could ask Kael—not that I trusted him either but he was all I had.

I waited a bit longer to ensure Gregory wasn't coming before I said three words I would possibly regret later.

"Kael, Kael, Kael."

4

NEVER BREAK, NEVER SURRENDER

ARIE

My fingers trembled as I tugged at the cold, unforgiving metal collar around my neck. It's grip served as a constant reminder of just how fucked I really was. I'd been stripped down to the barest form of myself, reduced to a magicless prisoner in the hands of the enemy.

The sun had finally set and still there'd been no word from Kael. Had he intended this all along? Was this part of the queen's plan? To make me think there was hope?

I'd forgotten what hope felt like a long time ago. Hector's face flashed in my mind and my throat tightened. I missed his and Nathaniel's comic relief. But mostly I just missed *him*. My friend. I swallowed down the sob and sighed.

My thoughts were drowned out by a light tap on the door and seconds later Kael stood before me, his eyes darting between me and the door to my cell.

"It's about time," I snapped.

"One has to be careful when walking the halls of the castle. There's no telling who might be within its shadows. Now, tell me why you've called upon me."

I spilled everything, what had happened and what Gemma said. Every detail laid out excluding the death of my fathers. I didn't trust him enough for that. I wasn't even sure I trusted him enough to walk my dog, but the fact that he showed up counted for something.

After a few moments of silence, I said, "Kael, did you hear me?"

He jumped at my words and nodded. "Yes, of course. You want out of here and you need my help to do so."

"That's not exactly what I said."

I had no intention of escaping just yet. There were far too many plots unraveling for my liking and I needed information. I needed to know who the Elders were, what the Queen had planned, and an ally who could provide it to me.

"As I said before, you must play along until the masquerade ball. Leaving before then is . . . is that a collar?" Kael's eyes widened and purple flecks flickered in the irises. Something that could have been anger flashed across his face before his gaze darted to the door once more.

I tugged on the collar, the metal digging into my reddening skin. "Apparently, it's the Queen's way of ensuring the castle's safety. But none of this is why I called you. I need information."

Kael's eyebrows shot up. "Information? Are you mad?"

It was a possibility.

"How much do you know about the Elders of the Brotherhood?" I asked.

Kael froze. His eyes darted to the cell door and his voice lowered to a whisper. "Well for starters, I know asking questions about them is dangerous. They have eyes and ears in every part of this kingdom and if the wrong person hears—"

"Are you the wrong person, Kael?" I asked as I rose to my feet. The long, tarnished chains clanked and scraped against the cold stone. "Are you going to turn me in for asking questions?"

Kael waved his hands in front of him. "Never. You have my word. I will tell no one."

"Good," I said, "then all you need to do is help me gather information. Once I have what I need, then and only then will I be ready to go along with whatever plan you've concocted."

"That's a lot to ask, Arie Lockwood."

It was, but there wasn't much of an alternative here. Though, I was putting a lot of pressure on someone I barely knew. There was danger hidden in the walls of this castle, and I was asking this man to risk his life for me. The least I could do was offer him something in return. "I'll be in your debt. One favor of any kind so long as it doesn't end in my demise, or anyone else I know."

Kael paced the cell and mumbled to himself. Finally, he clasped his hands together and nodded. "Deal."

He cleared his throat, a thin sheen of sweat appearing on his forehead. I clenched my jaw and steeled myself, as determination rose within me. No matter what Queen Gemma threw my way, I would face it head-on.

"Before you go, any chance you know how to get this thing off me?" I pointed to the collar. "At least until the guards come back?" I said and sat back on the cold floor.

A distant caw echoed through the damp, stagnant air, sharp and cutting against the steady drip of water from the ceiling. I tensed, my body instinctively reacting to the sound. Kael went rigid beside me, and my nerves stood on end. Before I had time to comprehend what was happening, Kael was gone, vanishing into thin air like smoke just as a flutter of massive wings sent a gust of wind through the iron bars of my window, rattling them like the chime of a death knell. The scent of damp feathers filled the tiny cell as talons scraped against the stone ledge outside. Slowly, I turned, my pulse quickening.

Morrigan.

The massive raven perched just beyond the bars, its beady, intelligent eyes boring into mine. Ebony feathers gleamed in the dim light, and the wicked curve of her beak twitched, as if waiting for something—watching, always watching. A chill slithered down my spine. She was a harbinger, a messenger of death, bound only to one man.

Jameson.

The moment the thought formed, heavy boots echoed down the hall, deliberate and unhurried. A slow-building storm rolling toward me.

The bird didn't move as the door groaned open, the scent of steel and damp leather washing over me before Jameson stepped inside. His presence filled the space like a slow-building storm. His face was an unreadable mask, but I could see the truth beneath it—the darkness simmering just below the surface, the weight of choices made long before this moment. He took his time surveying me, his gaze calculated, assessing, like he was already planning the next move in a game I hadn't realized we were playing.

Rage flared hot in my chest, searing away the ache in my limbs. I surged forward, only to be yanked back by the chains at my wrists. "You," I spat, my voice venomous. "You traitorous, spineless bastard. I should've let you die in Neverland."

A flicker of something crossed his face—amusement, maybe. But it was gone before I could place it. He took another slow step forward, arms loose at his sides, utterly at ease despite the fury radiating from me.

"I am, and forever will be, a member of the Brotherhood," he said, voice steady, unwavering. "You knew that." His head tilted slightly. "After all, Hank warned you, didn't he? Told you to watch your back around me. But you never listened. You were too busy worrying about everyone else—too busy playing hero." He tsked, shaking his head. "And look where that got you."

I clenched my jaw, bile rising in my throat. He was right, but I refused to give him the satisfaction of admitting it.

Jameson exhaled through his nose, his expression hardening. "Now, get up."

I stayed where I was, pressing my back against the cold stone. "I think I'll stay right here. I've grown rather fond of the rats and the piss-stained floors your queen calls a prison."

His lips curled at the edges, but there was no humor in it. Something cold. Something final.

Jameson's heavy grasp clamped onto the chains around my wrists, and he wrenched me forward with a force that sent me soaring through the air. I landed with a thud, unable to escape his vice-like grip as he dragged me across the cold prison cell. I cried out and thrashed, but my body was helpless as it bounced along the hallway.

Where was he taking me? I wasn't about to give the Queen, or anyone, the satisfaction of playing along. I wasn't some pawn. Ursa, Roland, Wendy. They all tried to play me and work me like a child's toy. No one was going to pull my strings this time, not if I had anything to say about it.

We reached a winding staircase that seemed to stretch on forever. He hauled me up each step, the jagged edges cutting painfully into my skin as I protested. He didn't stop until we reached an abandoned chamber. All that occupied it was one lonely stone slab that sat in its center; nothing else remained beyond its cold walls and arched ceiling high above.

"Get on the table."

"Screw you." I spat.

Jameson grabbed a fistful of my hair and lowered his face to mine. "Keep fighting, pirate queen, it will only make this more fun for me."

We stared at each other, neither of us daring to look away. I wasn't going to let myself be subjected to whatever was about to happen without a godsdamn fight.

I lunged toward Jameson, aiming to break free from his grasp. But he twisted my arm behind my back and forced me down onto the cold stone slab. The impact knocked the breath out of me, leaving me stunned as he towered over me.

He chuckled darkly. "I told you, this will only make it more fun for me. Though the same can't be said for you." His voice dripped with malice, sending a shiver down my spine.

Panic surged through me. My mind raced, searching for any possible escape route, but I was cornered with nowhere to run.

His hand closed around my throat, cutting off my air supply. "Get up there."

I hoisted myself up, shivering as I laid down. Before I could even gather my thoughts, thick leather straps sprung from different parts of the table and wound tightly around my limbs, pinning me to it like a helpless moth caught in an invisible web. Fear surged through me, and I tried with everything I had to take deep breaths in an attempt to calm my racing heart.

I also had to remember that this was their plan. If they couldn't get me to work with them willingly, torture was the next best step. But would I survive it?

The bastard said nothing as his lifeless eyes bore into mine. He reached behind him and pulled out a dagger. He pushed the blade into my exposed skin, and I cried out. He slowly traced a line up my arm, adding more and more pressure until I could feel the warm blood trickling down my skin. He twisted it in his grip, making sure each time he drew it away from me, that it left behind a trail of blood.

"Stop," I cried. "Why are you doing this?"

Jameson stepped back and looked me over. His eyes traveled up and down my body before finally meeting mine again. "I was told you needed to understand the gravity of the situation here, Lockwood. You will either submit and play the part the Queen needs you to play, or I will spend the next several days torturing you until you understand that you have no other choice.

My body trembled and I pressed my lips together. While I falsely assumed this had something to do with my monster of a mother . . . I still refused to bend in any way.

Jameson lashed out, his hand striking my cheek and I grunted.

"Come now. You can scream and squirm all you want," he said, a hint of amusement in his words. "I won't tell."

I bit my tongue until I tasted blood and thrashed as Jameson continued to work the blade up and down my skin. I was in and out of consciousness as the torture he inflicted grew more brutal. Question after question and still I refused to say anything. Though after some time I'd relented to the pain, my screams echoing off the walls until my throat was raw, and my head pounded.

By the time my torturer returned me to my cell, I was barely conscious. Only the door closing with a deafening slam gave me any indication the torture was over. My body was weak and battered and my broken mind teetered on insanity. But I'd survived.

Darkness encompassed me again, and held me prisoner as I lay there, trembling in a pool of my own sweat. I could still feel the sensation of the blood trickling down my skin and my body ached from where Jameson had cut into me. I was exhausted, and terrified to close my eyes for fear that he would return and continue his torment. My eyes, however, had other plans and after a few minutes I succumbed to darkness.

Days, and several visits from Gemma's torturer, later, the heavy wooden door creaked open, a single beam of light cutting through the darkness of the cell. I squinted against the sudden glare, my eyes eventually settling on Jameson's hulking figure in the doorway. My heart jumped as he stepped inside, but my body refused to move. His large hands snatched me up by the arm.

"Time for today's . . . session," he rasped. I struggled against his iron grip, but it only tightened as he dragged me to my feet.

"Let go of me, you bastard!" I screamed, though I had no energy left to try and pull myself from his grip. He laughed before delivering a powerful backhand across my face, sending a wave of pain flooding through me and filling my mouth with the metallic burn of blood.

"That's no way to speak to your only companion," Jameson taunted. He dragged me from the cell, and I dug my heels into the ground for purchase but nothing gave. I prayed and pleaded to the gods to end my life right then and there. I couldn't survive another round of his torture, and he knew it.

My body still ached from the beating it had already endured, and my ribs protested with each breath.

Jameson grabbed me by the shoulders and propelled me into the room, pushing me until I stood in front of the table. The smell of iron was overwhelming as my eyes settled on its surface stained with blood—*my* blood.

"Time for a new game today," Jameson said with far too much excitement. He took a step forward and I threw everything I had left into a punch that he deflected with ease.

"Feisty today, I see."

"I swear when I get out of here, I will bleed you dry and throw your body to the fucking wolves."

"I very much doubt that." He laughed and lunged forward. He grabbed my wrists and secured them to a set of manacles that hung down from the ceiling. *Where the hells did these come from?*

I thrashed and bucked, and even then he managed to easily overpower me as I was left dangling, toes barely brushing the floor. Panic rose in my chest like bile. I tugged uselessly at the manacles and blinked back the tears forming in my eyes. I was completely at his mercy now, unable to defend myself in any way.

A sinister grin split Jameson's face. "Thought you might enjoy a little . . . sensory deprivation."

He placed a thick, heavy blindfold over my eyes, plunging me into darkness. My breath came in short, sharp gasps, my chest heaving.

"Fuck you," I hissed

"Remember, no one will hear you if you scream."

The crack of a whip sounded as it exploded across my back like a flash of lightning, setting every nerve in my body alight with agonizing pain. I screamed until the sound echoed around me, torn from my throat until it was raw and hoarse.

"It's time to think about what you want to do, Arie. Continue this never ending pain, or understand that the Queen is merciful and she will end your suffering here and now. "

"Piss . . . off," I said breathlessly.

Jameson's breath blew in my ear as he said, "See this is the issue. All your defiance and unwillingness to cooperate is something that can't continue."

My limbs trembled as the relentless onslaught continued without mercy; leather tearing skin at every stroke, accompanied by the sickening crack of flesh being broken and reshaped. I felt a deep agony in my wrists and shoulders, muscles pulled to their limit in my suspended state. Unable to bear anymore I surrendered to darkness, my body reduced to nothing more than a ragdoll of mutilated flesh.

When Jameson's voice finally broke through the fog I had sunk into, his words were almost gentle. "Have we learned our lesson yet?"

I didn't respond. I wouldn't give him the satisfaction. I had no intention of breaking. Ulrich, Frankie, my crew—someone would come for me. I considered calling Kael again but thought better of it. I couldn't run from Gemma, not when she'd been in control since the beginning. She'd only find some way to hurt someone else I loved.

No. I had to stay, had to endure every bit of unrelenting torture inflicted on me. Because . . .

Because this was my punishment. For Hector, for Frankie, for Malakai and Viktor. All this was because of who and what I was. The daughter of a sea witch and the King of Atlantis.

Maybe it was better that my family forgot about me and leave me to my own devices.

I kept my mouth shut. I wouldn't answer his question, I wouldn't allow him to hear the ache in my voice or the fear laced within every word. I would rather die.

He sighed. "Very well. We'll continue this lesson another time." He ran his fingers down my cheek but I flinched away, not wanting him to feel the dampness lining my face. No matter how hard I tried I couldn't hold back the tears that spilled or stop myself from begging for it to end. But this was his game and he wasn't ready for it to be over.

The door opened and closed with a finality that made me sag in relief. How long had I been here? What time was it? Pain and delirium distorted reality, blurring together in an endless sea of anguish.

Sometime later, the door opened again and a hand grasped my chin, tilting my face up. I stiffened, bracing for more punishment. But the voice that spoke was not Jameson's. It was soft and smooth as velvet.

"I must admit I'm rather impressed you've lasted this long."

My heart leapt. Queen Gemma? Was this some sort of trick—some sick joke, maybe?

Gentle, cool hands tended to my wounds, applying a salve that soothed every bit of my skin. I whimpered in relief, leaning into the comfort.

"This salve was crafted by the giants themselves—so potent that men once waged wars to claim it. It is said to heal even the deepest wounds, no matter how dire."

"Why are you doing this?" I asked. She'd been the one who wanted me to suffer, hadn't she?

The blindfold gave way and I blinked until the Queen's face came into focus. "You've endured enough punishment. So, you'll be joining me for dinner. I'd like to have a fresh start."

Dinner? A fresh start? I stifled a laugh. First she throws me inside a prison cell, then forces me to be in the same vicinity as my father's possible killer, then subjects me to Jameson's torture, and now she wants to have dinner with me? This was definitely some sick, cruel joke. I knew what she wanted from me, or at least I suspected, and I'd do whatever I could to refuse. There was no way in all the Seven Seas I'd ever help her get into the Celestial Plains or help her kill Pascal's father. She had to know that.

"Unless you'd like to go back to your cell?"

I hesitated, my brain stuck between going back to my cell to face the devil I knew or going to dinner with the one I didn't. I just had to be smart. Malakai and Viktor had taught Frankie and I how to play with half truths. Perhaps now all I had to do was play along and buy myself time to figure a way out. I needed backup . . . I needed to *heal*.

Finally, I nodded.

"Good, come with me."

I moved with laggard steps, the salve Gemma had used

dulled most of my pain but I knew the scars left behind would never fade.

The Queen led me through the tunnels before ascending more stairs until we were on the main floor of the castle. Gemma stepped through a large door and into a lavish dining room where the walls were lined with gilded mirrors, and light from the chandeliers twinkled against tapestries. The table was set with fine bone china, delicate crystal chalices, and intricate silverware. Platters of food covered the middle of the table, from succulent roast meats to fruits glistening with glazes and syrups. Every part of my body ached, but it wasn't enough to dull the roaring hunger in my stomach. Gemma wasted no time in helping herself to a plate of food and motioned for me to do the same.

We ate in silence. It was by far the best food I'd eaten since Neverland. I shoveled more food in, chasing it down with wine so I could shove in more. *Gods, this was good.*

Gemma drank wine from a chalice and eyed me over its rim as if she were judging me. Well, I was certainly judging her. She had so much power, so much at her disposal and instead of using that to help those who needed it, she chose herself. It was a bold move as a leader and I wondered what her people really thought of her.

"You're a brave girl, Arie," she finally said. "I admire you and what you are fighting for. You fight to save the ones you love—just as I do." Her voice was soft but her words were strong and powerful. She looked away from me, her gaze settling on something far away. "I know what it's like to have someone taken away from you—to feel helpless and powerless in the face of tragedy. And yet despite all that, you still have the strength to stand up and fight another day."

"If you admire what I fight for, then why throw me to your hound?"

"Knowledge, of course, and I gained plenty."

Plenty? I hadn't given her monster anything. I'd kept quiet. *Hadn't I?* There were times I'd lose consciousness, was it possible that I'd also lost chunks of time? What had I said under so much duress?

"I wanted to see if you'd break and if all the things I'd heard about you were true."

That's what this was about? Several days of torture and all she wanted was to know how long it would take for me to break? I placed my fork on the table, the food turned to ash in my mouth, and wrapped my arms around my stomach.

"You're strong and you have a lot of fight in you. But most importantly I know how much you want to find the person who killed your fathers." Gemma's gaze flicked to mine. "Vengeance is what keeps us going in the wake of tragedy. The idea of finally stopping the one responsible is all that matters to people like us. You and I are more alike than—"

"I am nothing like you," I hissed. "I don't kill innocent people and take their souls. I'm not trying to kill a god and bring back loved ones from the dead." I bit my tongue. A statement like that was sure to get me thrown back in the cell.

Rage came and went on Gemma's face before she cleared her throat. "I see you know quite a bit about me. Even if it is misconstrued."

I snorted. "Misconstrued?"

"I take souls of those who have committed crimes against this realm. Those who are weak and intolerant of law and order. It was *your mother* who decided to take any soul she could get her hands on. Not I."

"You really expect me to believe that?"

Queen Gemma sighed and placed her goblet on the table. "No, I don't. But what I do expect you to understand is that I am not a monster like your mother was. I have been trying to restore balance to this realm for years now, but it isn't easy. There are powerful forces at work that try to stop me from doing so. From doing what is necessary."

"Do you think I like ruling with an iron fist? Or that I enjoy taking lives? Of course not. But sometimes it is necessary to keep peace and order."

I crossed my arms and stared at her. She was right—sometimes harsh measures were needed to maintain peace and order, but there was never a reason to take an innocent life.

"You're right," I said finally, my voice low and steady. "Sometimes harsh measures are necessary, but when those measures start affecting people who have done nothing wrong then something needs to be done. Whether you want to admit it or not, Your Majesty, my mother's actions aren't just her doing. You're the one who sent her to do your bidding. The blood of the innocent lives she took are also on your hands."

We stared at each other, neither one wavering until a servant came and stood beside me.

"More wine?" she asked and I absentmindedly nodded. Then, they walked over to Gemma's and collected her's before the Queen spoke again.

"You are ever the hero, Miss Lockwood. Saving your sister from King Roland, saving Captain Hook from sirens, killing your own mother to save countless lives. All I have ever wanted to do was to bring back those I love most. I'd think someone in your state would understand that."

The servant returned moments later, carefully placing the chalice in front of me.

"Thank you," I murmured and returned my attention to Gemma. "My fathers are gone. The only thing I can do now is find the person, or *people*, responsible." I squeezed the chalice with trembling fingers, its cool metal sending a shudder through me. The Queen watched with curious eyes as I raised it to my lips and drank from it. As the sweet liquid touched my tongue, I let out a sigh. It was delicious and better than anything I'd ever tasted. I threw my head back, drinking in every drop in hopes of steadying my nerves.

The chalice clanked on the table and instantly I felt woozy. It had been quite some time since I'd tasted something so good.

"And I'd like to help you with that."

"Why?" I raised a brow. "You expect me to believe you had nothing to do with it? I know it was someone from the Brotherhood."

"This is why you need my help. Think of it as a way to apologize for what comes next."

My head spun and my vision blurred. Not only was it the best tasting wine I'd ever had, but it was also the strongest. How could one drink make me feel like this?

"And what's that?

Gemma took another drink before speaking. "I'd love to tell you, but I'm afraid you won't remember by tomorrow anyway."

My stomach twisted in knots and my heart thudded like a drum in my chest. I fought to stay conscious but Gemma's words seemed hollow and distant, as if she were speaking from across the room rather than a table. My eyelids fluttered heavily and it was all I could do to keep them open.

"I don't usually like to use magic like this, but as you can see, time isn't on my side and I am growing increasingly impatient with this self-righteous act of yours. Thankfully, drinking the tonic will get better and won't feel like this the next time you drink it. But I needed to act fast."

What was she saying? I strained against the ringing in my ears, trying to focus on every word, but something was very wrong.

"What . . . d-did you . . ."

The Queen shouted, and suddenly, strong arms grabbed me from behind, crushing my body against an unyielding chest. I struggled, but my limbs turned to lead and no sound other than a faint gasp left my throat.

"We'll speak in the morning when you're feeling better."

"Y-You bi . . . bit . . . ch."

The Queen laughed as my lips refused to form the words as the entire room faded to black. Again.

5
A CAPTAIN'S CURSE
ULRICH

We only had a few days left before our departure and we were still behind in terms of repairs. I wasted no time in rushing to get the ship up and running, but with every stitch and hammer blow, my heart weighed heavier.

Was Arie all right?

My attempts to figure out the extent of the curse from the previous captain's logs were met with frustrating failure. If we stayed too long, there was a possibility we would miss our chance at retrieving Arie from her captors—an unacceptable outcome.

The crew sensed the weight of my mood and kept their distance. It was for the best. I was beyond angry, hell-bent on getting off this damn island. My temper flared at the slightest thing, I'd shattered more glasses than I could count, and I barely had the energy to eat.

Frankie and Ace had taken it upon themselves to keep up the spirits of the crew. To which I was very grateful.

It was only when Ace took out his guitar under the twilight sky I found a way to calm the rage boiling beneath my skin. Even just for a moment.

Tonight, the crew had seemed more grim than usual. Ace sat atop a barrel under the shelter we'd made on the sandy beach. The instrument sat propped on his lap as his nimble fingers danced over the strings, coaxing out a haunting melody that weaved around Frankie's captivating voice. Something I hadn't known her to possess.

There seemed to be a lot about Frankie I didn't know. She mostly kept to herself, but there were times when I caught glimpses of something . . . calculated beneath the surface. Like how she always positioned herself with her back to a wall, near exits, never fully exposed. The way her gaze flicked across a room, not just looking but assessing, cataloging threats with quiet precision. It was subtle, the kind of thing most wouldn't notice. But I did.

Arie should have been here with us, singing and boasting about our victory over Wendy. She'd go on and on about the legendary battles at sea or better yet, cracking jokes with Nathaniel and trying to school me in a game of cards.

But she wasn't. And the mood of the crew certainly reflected that. Even through the chatter and music the weight of our mission pressed down on us all.

My sadness must have been quite apparent because Nathaniel placed his hand on my shoulder. "We'll get her back."

I looked up into his reassuring gaze and nodded even if every part of me worried that Arie might never return to us. But I knew no matter how long it took, I would find my way to her. To those eyes that were a mixture of vulnerability and bravery, to the voice that sometimes shifted from fierce and bold to tender and soft. Something about the combination stirred something deep inside me. I promised her I'd do whatever it took to give her the chance to know the real me, the person beneath the facade, and that was not a promise I intended to break.

"She cares about you, you know." Nathaniel smiled, though it wasn't like the usual one that brightened his face. Hector's death had taken the light from him more so than anyone else.

"Do *you* believe that? After what happened?" My tone turned serious.

Nathaniel shook his head. "You're not at fault for what Wendy did or for the *Betty* and Arie knows that too. Hector and I knew what we were getting into when we joined Arie's crew. It was only a matter of time before one of us . . ." He cleared his throat. "Stop sulking. It's not a good look on you."

I forced a laugh and left the crew to their own devices as I made my way back to the *Jolly Dutchman*.

I slipped into the captain's chair behind the desk, grateful to simply be away from the company of others. The emptiness was familiar, and I welcomed it. I needed a few moments alone to rest and clear my mind even though Nathaniel's words echoed in my head. It was a much-needed reminder of why I was here and what we were trying to achieve. I reached for the nearest journal on the desk.

It was heavy with the weight of the days, thick and full like an ancient tome. I ran a finger over the top page, tracing each letter as if they were rare and delicate artifacts revealing what secrets lay on each page. The words spoke about adventures at sea and exciting places they had been; about storms so fierce they rocked the boat for days on end; and creatures that defied all-natural logic. Each turn of the page offered a wondrous escape from reality as I devoured each word hungrily, exploring a world of possibilities not bound by fate or human limitations.

It didn't take long for that to change.

Entry 782

I miss the land, the feel of the sand between my toes and the warmth of a woman in my bed. I miss Sandra's special ale and not being surrounded by angry pirates all the time. The moon and scorching sun are my only companions in this hell I call home. Not even my crew can bring a smile to my face anymore.

The timeline didn't add up. Like a book with torn-out pages, there were gaps—obvious, gaping holes where events should have been. One moment, everything was clear, the story unfolding as expected. Then pieces went missing, details smudged out like ink washed away by the tide. Which would make finding out how to end the curse that much harder. Where had they gone? None of this made me feel better about sailing a cursed ship, but what choice did we have?

I flipped through more pages, the captain's desperation bleeding through their words as the journals crept on.

Entry 795

I'm out of options. Out of ideas. The crew grows more hostile by the day and I'm afraid they will turn on one another—on me. We still have no leads on how to break the curse. The witches of H'ijal had been an upsetting waste of time. They did nothing but sacrifice the weakest of my crew to a god who had scorned me long ago. I suppose next we could try...

Is this what we were about to face? No options and an unbreakable curse. The writing went on and on about the captain's failed attempts. I tossed the journal aside and opened a new one. As my eyes glanced over the words a chill ran down my spine. There was no longer an entry number, just words meshed together sporadically.

I killed Adonis today. My hands have been covered in blood many times, but never from someone I cared for. But I had no choice. He broke the rules. No one breaks the rules, not even me. The curse doesn't allow us to.

I flipped to the next page.

After centuries of being forced to endure this hell of an existence, I knew one day hope would guide us to our destination. Finally, our search has brought us to our sanctuary. Finally, we have reached the isle of Never.

I stilled. How was that possible? Neverland was supposed to have been hidden from outsiders, especially pirates. While he'd obviously found Neverland considering where his ship was, I didn't understand how he managed it? It also didn't explain how they'd gotten past the wards. Rumor said mermaids helped the curse ship find their way in, but they weren't around anymore to ask.

I closed the book with a sigh. Hours passed as the night crept on and I was still no closer to finding out what the curse was or any theories on how to break it. Maybe there were more journals somewhere else on this ship? I slumped back in my chair and rubbed my eyes, exhaustion creeping in like a tide. There wasn't much more to be gleaned through the journals tonight and we had a long journey ahead of us. With luck, we'd be out of here and on our way to Arie in a few days.

The door flung open and crashed against the wall behind it as Pascal burst in. His eyes were wild with terror, and Tink clung to his shoulder, her tiny form trembling. My stomach sank as I waited for one of them to speak.

Pascal turned his head to Tink and nodded. "Go ahead."

Tears streamed down Tink's face as she looked over at me. Her twinkling voice trembled. "It's Arie."

I clutched the desk to keep me grounded and pressed my hook its the wood. My body vibrated with a mixture of anger and fear.

"Is she . . ." I paused, unable to get the words out. Arie had to be alive if Tink was still breathing. They'd bonded to one another to save my life. If one died, so did the other, and while she looked pale and scared, she seemed otherwise intact. Maybe because the two of them were so far apart, it would take longer for Tink to die.

Tink shook her head. "The connection between us . . . it's gone."

"What the hells do you mean it's gone?" I said with much more bite than I'd intended. "How is that possible?"

Tink's eyes widened. "I don't know, I can't feel her anymore. She's still alive, I swear it, but something is blocking our connection."

My veins pulsed with rage, and I let out a primal scream, unleashing the fury that had been building inside me. With one sweep of my arms, I sent the items on the desk crashing to the floor. Books, scrolls, pens, and ink scattered everywhere. My anger lasted only a moment before I gathered myself.

"We need to leave. Now," I snapped.

"The Queen needs her," Pascal said.

I snarled at him, unleashing the barely contained fury." If I have to take a rowboat and brave the sea monsters alone to get there, I will. We get her back before—"

"We can speculate as to what she wants, but Queen Gemma will need Arie alive. We have time, Ulrich."

My hand shot out over the desk, grabbing Pascal's shirt as I pressed my hook to his cheek. "Do you really think the Queen is going to keep her alive after she's done with her? We. Leave. *Now*." shoved Pascal

Tink hovered between me and Pascal. "You can't take on the Brotherhood and the Queen on your own, Ulrich. That's a sure way to get both you and Arie killed."

I let go of Pascal, my breath coming in shallow, jagged bursts, my heart pounding in my chest. The hot rush of anger pulsed in my veins, but it was no longer a fiery blaze—it was an out-of-control wildfire. I clenched my teeth, trying to wrestle the storm back down, to think clearly.

After some effort, I said, "Then you'd better figure out a way to get this ship ready. I'm not waiting any longer. Either fix the ship or send me to the Enchanted Realm. Curse or no curse, I'm going after her."

Tink regarded me for a moment before speaking. "Fairy dust has a healing quality. If I put enough energy into it, I could repair some of the sails and damaged masts, but it will leave me depleted and unable to produce more for quite some time without Arie."

Having to sit and wait while the Brotherhood did the gods only knew what left me more on edge than I'd ever been. I had to keep it together.

"Get with Smith at first light and see what needs to be finished."

"And what about the curse?" Pascal asked.

"I haven't found anything on how it started or how to break it. But there's also nothing that says it's the actual ship that's cursed. For all we know it was only the crew. Unless you see another ship, this is our only option." That and hope to the gods we aren't too late to save Arie.

"All right then, we'll get to work at first light," Pascal said before turning and leaving with Tink still clinging to him.

With a growl of frustration, I made my way over to the window and gazed out into the night. I thought about Arie, and wondered if she was looking at the same moon as me, questioning if or when her friends would come to her aid.

"I'm coming for you Arie. There's no hells-damned curse large enough that can keep me from you. And by the gods, I swear to make those who have harmed you bleed for what they've done."

I promised to have her by my side while we killed every last one of those who have wronged us. Because now I understood, now I knew what I'd done to Arie the day Hector died. I'd held her back, and had I trusted her, had I done what she asked, none of this would have happened.

Never again would I hold her back.

6
REUNITED
ULRICH

WE'D FINALLY MANAGED TO GET THE *Jolly Dutchman* sailing, and had gone several days without issue, not even the curse had made itself known. Though we were racing against time, and I worried we wouldn't make it before the curse reared her head.

Whenever that was.

The sea breathed like a sleeping god—a deceptive calm that set my teeth on edge. Salt-stiffened sails snapped taut above as our shadow cut through water shimmering with bioluminescent plankton. I leaned against the starboard rail, fingertips brushing against Arie's dagger.

I wished more than anything we had our Sea Witch to guide us.

Someone shouted from above, pulling me from my thoughts.

Someone groaned behind me, and I turned to find Smith. He was doubled over, clutching his side, sweat pouring down his face. There was no blood on his hands or open wounds that I could see but something was wrong.

Nathaniel and I rushed to his side, Smith's eyes were wide

with fear as he coughed and wheezed before lifting his shirt, revealing the skin beneath.

A large, inky bruise bloomed on his ribs.

"Captain," he rasped, clearly in pain.

"Stay with us, Smith," I urged, gripping his shoulder reassuringly. "Find Doc."

Doc had insisted on coming with us, fully aware that stepping onto the Dutchman meant sealing his fate alongside ours. It didn't stop him—his mind was made up. I might not have remembered much from my childhood, but the one constant was Doc and his six brothers always looking out for me and Clayton.

He had been there when Pascal whisked us away to Neverland, a steady presence when everything else was uncertain. And every time we tried to drag the past back into the light, Doc shut it down, brushing it aside with that same gruff certainty. *The past belongs where it was left,* he'd say. *Keep looking back, and you'll never move forward.*

I used to think he was just being difficult. Now, I wasn't so sure.

"Ulrich, there are others," Frankie said quietly behind me.

Glancing around, I saw that several crew members showed similar symptoms, feverish sweats with dark spots on their body. Panic started to settle in my chest, but I pushed it away.

"Find anyone who's affected and bring them below deck," I instructed.

"Do you think . . .?" Frankie's voice trailed off, but I knew what she was about to say.

"Let's focus on helping them for now," I said firmly, trying to quell the rising fear in my own heart. Finding Keenan I said, "My quarters."

He nodded, barked an order for someone to man the helm, and followed.

I threw open the door to my quarters and slammed it behind Keenan. An overwhelming sense of anger washed over me, consuming me in its violent grasp. I hoped we would have been able to reach the Enchanted Realm before the curse made itself known. With how fast it just spread, I wasn't sure we had time to figure out a plan, let alone make it another league. We could use the row boats and pray to the gods that the sea was good enough to get us there. Unless they were touched by the curse as well.

I was going to have to look through the journals again; there had to be something I missed.

"What the hell is happening, Ulrich?" Keenan asked, his voice filled with a mix of fear and confusion.

I shook my head, unable to answer as I paced the room. My mind raced with questions and possibilities.

"We have to find out more about this curse," I said finally, turning to face him. "We need to know what we're dealing with before we can make any decisions on how to move forward. We can't let this spread further or put anyone else in danger."

"While I agree with that assessment, how are we going to do that? None of those logs you read gave any information worth using."

"We'll just have to keep looking."

Several days passed, and the curse was spreading more and more, curling its fingers deeper into the crew. It started small—sickly pallor, coughing fits, a few aching bones—but it didn't take long for the symptoms to worsen. At least a dozen of the crew had started showing signs, their once-strong bodies weakening, eyes dulling with an unnatural sheen. The fever set in next, burning hot against their skin one moment, freezing cold the next. Some of them trembled uncontrollably, while others barely had the strength to stand, their limbs shaking with exhaustion.

Worst was the change in their eyes. There was a flicker of something dark in them—something hollow, like the curse was slowly taking over their very souls. It was random on who it affected. Not like a sickness that's contagious, but more like luck of the draw.

I didn't need to look at the infected to know it was only a matter of time before the rest of us fell victim to it. The air felt thicker, like it was suffocating, and I could hear the rasp of breath, labored and uneven, in every corner of the ship.

I could feel it creeping up on me as well, a gnawing chill settling into my bones.

With everything I had, I hoped I hadn't made the wrong choice in sailing this ship. The guilt of that thought weighed heavily on me as I paced along my desk.

Moments later, Pascal barged into the room carrying a tattered leather journal and he thrust it toward me. "I found this in one of the old crew member's quarters. It doesn't say how they were cursed but it does suggest that it starts with the crew members getting sick closer to the red moon, and then fully takes effect when the red moon is at its peak."

He handed me the book and I quickly opened it to find the entry Pascal had mentioned. The ink was faded and worn, but I could still make out most of the words.

The devil's prediction was correct. The closer the red moon draws, the more people aboard the ship become afflicted with a mysterious malady. Deep purple bruises spread like ink on their skin, fevers boil beneath their flesh, and body aches that leave them limp and useless until they become a former shell of themselves, mindless, undead workers. Captain roars orders in a delirious stupor, while I fear for us all as the curse takes hold. We will soon be consumed by it.

I closed the journal and peered up at Pascal. "How long do we have?"

"It's hard to say but judging by that journal," he replied. "I'd say seven days. Ten if we're lucky."

I glanced back at the journal and nodded. It didn't provide us with much information but at least we had a time frame.

Though I had no idea what to do when it finally started. I worried for my crew, for Arie's, for the fractured family we'd made against all odds. I was acting captain and I'd done a piss poor job in Arie's absence. But we all knew what we signed up for. I just hoped it hadn't been for nothing.

"We need to prepare for the worst," I said, my voice low.

We we're at least five days from the ports of the Enchanted Realm. If the winds blew in our favor, it was possible we could make it there sooner. We had to come up with a plan if we didn't make it. Five days to the port of Chione didn't leave us much time to find Arie and figure out how to save our ship and its crew.

Thankfully, I had one.

"Where's Tink?"

"Last I saw she was with Doc." Pascal replied.

I stood from my chair and made my way to the door before stopping and turning to the two men. "Search through the rest of the quarters. If we're lucky, we'll find another journal." The men nodded as I left.

I quickly made my way down the stairs to where Doc and Tink were treating Smith. Tink had already spread a silvery dust all over his body in an intricate pattern, humming softly while Doc worked.

"What is that you're doing?" I asked cautiously so as not to startle her.

Tink paused and looked up at me with wide eyes, then smiled warmly. "It's a healing spell," she explained as she continued to work her magic. Her voice was like twinkling bells. "It won't cure him, but it will stall the pain and break the fever."

"Hopefully it will buy us time," Doc said.

Smith's eyelids fluttered open, and he squinted as his pupils adjusted to the light. His breathing was shallow and fast, and there was a pinkish tinge to his normally pallid complexion. He twitched slightly before settling back into unconsciousness, his expression was tense and pained—it seemed that the curse was only getting worse.

My heart ached as I watched my friend. Smith had been by my side for many years, my knees threatened to buckle at the thought of losing him.

"Tink, I need to speak to you alone, please."

Tink eyed me for a moment before nodding and motioning for me to follow her. We made our way to a room in the far back of the ship, one for food and water storage. I shut the door behind us. "Whatever I say to you must stay within these walls."

Tink narrowed her eyes on me but gave a quick tilt of her head.

"Good," I said and explained what Pascal had found.

Her eyes widened. "Will we even make it there by then?"

"I don't know but we have to try." I paused and sucked in a deep breath. "There's something I need you to do for me, Tink."

She looked up at me and smiled. "Anything."

"I need you to promise me that if we don't make it to the Enchanted Realm that you will do whatever you can to save Arie. Even if it means leaving us behind to succumb to the curse."

Just then, chaos erupted on the main deck.

"Enemy ship!"

The words had scarcely escaped the crewman's lips when the sharp, metallic clang of the warning bell pierced the stillness of the night, shattering the eerie quiet that had settled over the ship. I snapped upright, every muscle in my body tensed like a drawn bowstring as I ran. I pushed past the crew and looked out at the horizon.

The moon cast a ghostly silver sheen over the rolling waves, highlighting a shadowy silhouette that emerged from the swirling mist. A sense of dread tightened in my stomach, a visceral knot of unease.

Not just any ship.

A *warship*.

Damn it.

I ran back to the main deck. "Positions!" I barked, already moving. The crew scrambled into action, boots hammering against the deck as men climbed the rigging, readied the cannons, and armed themselves for whatever fresh hell was about to befall us.

I turned toward the helm, my heart a hammer against my ribs. Arie wasn't here.

She should be standing beside me, dagger in hand, eyes burning with that fire she always carried.

"Recognize the flag?" Nathaniel shouted from the main mast.

Not yet. The warship cut through the water with the precision of a blade, its torches burning in the dark, casting jagged shadows across the deck.

Then I saw it.

A crimson banner emblazoned with a golden crest.

My stomach dropped.

King Roland's colors.

I cursed under my breath. King Roland's naval fleet was the

strongest in the seven seas, and we were no match for them. Had he come in search of Pascal or Arie? They'd managed to escape from him before we left to take on Ursa so maybe this was his way of getting back at us.

I had to think fast. Our crew was skilled, but our ship was smaller than theirs and lightly armed. A direct assault would be suicide, but perhaps if we boarded their ship, we had a chance.

"Nathaniel, drop the sails," I shouted, my hand and hook gripping the wheel tightly as I steered us toward the warship.

"*What?*" came the incredulous reply from above.

"Just do it!" I gritted my teeth in frustration.

As soon as our sails were down, we slowed. The distance between us closed rapidly and before we knew it, we were within shouting distance of each other.

The warship crept closer, the sea churning as if in anticipation. I clenched my fists, waiting for what came next.

"Hook!" Nathaniel shouted from above. "They're flying a white flag!"

What?

Eyes narrowed, I looked again.

A stark *white flag* fluttered against the night sky, lifted high above the enemy ship.

A surrender?

"Hold fire," I called, jaw tightening. "But be diligent. This could be a trap."

The warship pulled alongside us, and as it did, a figure stepped to the rail. The torchlight caught his face.

My eyes widened.

Clayton.

My *brother*.

For a moment, I couldn't move. Couldn't think.

The last time I'd seen him he'd decided to return to Khan. He hadn't exactly been forthcoming with why he'd wanted to, but here he was, standing on the deck of the King's warship, looking straight at me. I wasn't sure if I wanted to embrace him or punch him in the godsdamned face for being on one of Roland's ships. But a part of me was relieved to see him anyway.

Clayton's face was all sharp angles and shadows under the torchlight—too much like mine and yet not. His hands rested casually on the warship's railing; posture relaxed as if we were meeting at a damned tea party instead of a standoff in the middle of the sea. The wind whipped strands of his dark hair around his face as he called out. "Hello, brother."

My fists tightened at my side. What in the hells was he doing on Roland's ship and how had he found us?

"You've got three breaths to explain why you're sailing under a tyrant's banner before I tell my crew to light the cannons, brother or not."

"It's not what it looks like," Clayton said. "Though I can understand the confusion. King Roland and I have come to an . . . agreement. Now, can I come aboard so we can talk?"

The crew murmured behind me, waiting for my command. I didn't give one, still gripping the railing as if letting go would send me flying across the gap between our ships.

I turned toward the others. "Let him on."

Clayton stepped onto the *Jolly Dutchman*, his sharp eyes sweeping across the deck, taking in the crew, the rigging, the newly polished wood beneath his boots. A low whistle escaped his lips.

"You've upgraded," he mused, running a hand along the railing. "I thought the old ship was great, but this is something else, brother."

"What the fuck is he doing here?" Frankie came up beside me, anger roaring off of her in waves. I'd almost forgotten they had been close before he'd decided to go back to Khan.

Clayton's expression dropped and he rubbed his chest. "Frankie."

"I thought you had better things to do than sail on ships. Turns out that wasn't it at all, was it? Was it me?"

I rolled my eyes. We didn't have time for this shit.

"It's not like that. The second I left and went to King Roland, I had a plan to help, to stop whatever was coming. Roland may be a pain in all of our asses, but he wants Gemma dead just as much as we do. He was reluctant to help, especially considering Arie took his prized possession. We know who has Arie—I swear to you, I'm here to help." He didn't need to say anything, we all knew he meant Pascal, but that didn't stop Clayton from looking in his direction.

My patience frayed. "Tell me what the hells you know about Arie's abduction."

Clayton met my glare, then sighed and crossed his arms. "It's Queen Gemma. She has her. Her and the Brotherhood of Assassins."

Frankie rushed up to him and shoved him. "I swear to all the gods, Clay, you better be telling the truth."

I froze, every muscle locking in place. Murmurs rippled across the ship, but I tuned them out, my mind focusing on the single name that had just been spoken. It sent a bolt of ice through my veins. Gemma.

That godsdamned snake in a crown.

We'd all suspected she was involved somehow, especially after what happened with Wendy. Jameson was a member of the Brotherhood and thanks to Tink's bond with Arie, we knew Jameson had taken her north. And the only place north of Neverland was the Enchanted Realm. And Gemma—she was the one pulling the strings behind the Brotherhood. But hearing it confirmed by Clay, having the truth laid bare in front of me . . . it was enough to make me want to scream.

"Are you certain?" I asked.

Clayton's gaze remained fixed on Frankie, his face swimming with emotions I didn't care to name. "Word spread like wildfire that a woman fitting Arie's description had been taken by the Brotherhood. It didn't take much to put the pieces together. King Roland and Gemma had sprung an alliance years ago that had something to do with Arie's mother but recent events have left that sour. He's furious with her. That's when I knew I had to act. I asked for a meeting, and we agreed that Gemma is the root of all our problems. He's got a bounty on her head, and I've come to collect."

Something in my chest twisted.

I searched his face, looking for any sign of deception. I found none.

The years with me at sea had changed him, but he was still my brother and I trusted him.

Clayton's voice was steady as he continued. "I know where she is, Ulrich. And I know how to get to her much faster."

A dangerous hope ignited in my chest. I exhaled, nodding once. "Then let's get her back."

"Why the hells should we trust you?" Frankie snapped.

Clayton's expression grew serious. "You trusted me once. I'm sure you can do it again."

Frankie threw her head back and laughed. She drew her sword and moved fast. She had him pinned against a crate in seconds. "Don't think I won't gut you where you stand. I don't care if my captain is your brother."

"Frankie," I warned. "Let him go."

"No, he left us to go plan shit with one of our many enemies. With the man who kidnapped me and forced my sister down this path. I want Gemma dead if she is responsible for any of this but we don't need him."

I stepped up to Frankie, placing a firm yet steady hand on

her arm. "We need all the help we can get to find your sister," I said, my voice low, calm. "If he wants to help, let him. Watch him like a hawk if you have to, but don't let your anger cost us a chance to bring her home. Let him go."

Her jaw clenched, but after a tense beat, she shoved him aside. Clayton barely caught himself before scrambling to his feet.

"Let me prove myself to you, Frankie. Please." His voice wavered, raw with something dangerously close to desperation. "I still care—"

Frankie didn't let him finish. She spun and drove her fist into his jaw with a sickening crack.

Clayton groaned, staggering back as he clutched his face. Before he could say another word, a woman from the other ship stood at the rail.

"Who is that?" Frankie's face turned a bright shade of red.

"Frankie," I hissed. "Will you let me handle this please?"

Everyone else around the Jolly Dutchman remained silent, their hands hovering over their weapons. Nathaniel had climbed down from the nest to stand beside Frankie.

"Let them figure this out, *darling*. It'll be okay." Nathaniel flung his arm over Frankie.

Clayton's gaze flicked to Nathaniel and Frankie, his expression unreadable—but I knew my brother well enough to recognize the brief flicker of something sharp beneath his cool exterior. Jealousy. It was gone as quickly as it had appeared, masked beneath that easy smirk of his, but the tension in his shoulders remained.

He didn't comment on it and instead turned his attention back to me. "She's here to help," he said simply.

The woman moved with an eerie grace, her bare feet soundless against the plank as she crossed from her ship to mine. Moonlight caught in her long, inky-black hair, the strands shifting like liquid shadows down her back. She was tall and willowy, her deep brown skin glistening with the faint sheen of salt water, as though the sea itself clung to her.

Her eyes—gods, her eyes—were a storm-tossed blend of silver and blue, shifting like the tide as she took in the crew. They lingered on me, something ancient and knowing swirling in their depths, before flicking to Clayton with a smile.

She wore a dark, flowing garment that shimmered when she moved, its fabric cut in a way that hinted at scales beneath the surface. A necklace of seashells and bone rested against her collarbone, and at her hip, she carried a curved dagger with an iridescent blade.

The scent of brine and something darker—something old—rolled off her, thick as the mist curling around the ship's hull.

"Captain Hook," she purred, voice smooth as a lullaby sung beneath the waves. "It seems the sea has finally brought us together."

Keenan narrowed his eyes, stepping forward with the quiet authority that had made him my most trusted second. "Who are you?" His voice was even, but there was something else beneath it—something sharp. His gaze swept over her, searching. "You look . . . familiar."

The woman's lips curled, revealing a hint of amusement. "I go by many names," she said, her voice a rolling tide of silk and smoke. "But many know me as Calypso."

A hush fell over the crew, broken only by the scattered murmurs of disbelief.

"She's like Arie," Clayton said, watching me carefully.

Calypso tilted her head, her silver-blue eyes flashing. "You could say we are *family*."

"The fuck you are," Frankie snapped, stepping forward like she was ready to swing. "I'll be damned if some prissy bit—"

Nathaniel clamped a hand over her mouth before she could finish. "Quiet, woman. Let her speak."

Calypso turned her attention to him, slow and deliberate, a wicked smile teasing at the corner of her lips. "Well, aren't you handsome," she mused, licking her lips.

Nathaniel hesitated just long enough for Frankie to elbow him in the ribs. "If what you say is true," he said, rubbing his side, "then where the hell have you been? Why are you just now crawling out of the shadows?"

Calypso exhaled through her nose, her expression unreadable. "Because that is how it was meant to be," she said simply, her voice carrying the weight of something ancient. "I am not a mermaid, nor a sea witch like Arie, but a Nereid."

A sharp intake of breath came from somewhere behind me.

"A sea nymph," Keenan whispered.

And suddenly, the air around us felt heavier, as though the sea itself listened.

Calypso's gaze swept over the crew, her expression unreadable as the ocean's depths. "I am the answer to many of your problems," she said, her voice like the pull of the tide—steady, inescapable. "But for now, there is only one that matters, and that is reaching the Enchanted Realm."

I studied her, my grip tightening on the hilt of my sword. "And how exactly do you intend to do that?"

She stepped closer, the scent of salt and something wild clinging to her like a second skin. "I may not be a sea witch, but the ocean bends for me all the same." She raised a hand, fingers curling as if calling something unseen. The air shifted, a strange energy humming in the space between us. "I can push the winds, hasten the currents. What should take you days will take hours."

The crew murmured among themselves, some excited,

others wary. Keenan exchanged a glance with me, his jaw tight. Something about this felt like tempting fate.

I exhaled sharply, weighing the risk against the urgency thrumming in my chest. Arie was out there. Every moment wasted was a moment too long.

"Do it," I said. "But, Clayton, you need to stay on your ship. Meet us in the Enchanted Realm as soon as you can and—"

"I'm not leaving you. I've already instructed the crew to meet us there."

Frankie bristled at Clayton's words. A large part of me was glad to hear that my brother was back with me even if I doubted his motives.

Calypso smiled, a slow, knowing thing, before she turned toward the sea. The wind picked up, the sails filling as if the ship had taken a deep breath. The *Jolly Dutchman* lurched forward, cutting through the water at a pace no ordinary vessel could achieve.

I watched the horizon, jaw set.

We were coming, and not even the godsdamned sea could stop us.

7
FORGOTTEN
ARIE

Bells sounded from somewhere in the distance, startling me as I shot upward. I was covered in velvet sheets and surrounded by plush pillows. The walls surrounding me were painted an inviting shade of blue and the sun streamed through the windows, bathing the room in a soft morning light. I felt anything but comfort in my surroundings. Fear pulsed through my veins. Where was I? How did I get here? I tried to pull on my memories, but everything was . . . blank. What was the last thing I remembered?

I tugged and tugged on the strands of memories. Nothing came. Hells, I couldn't even remember my name. Panic nearly choked me as I shot out of bed and raced toward the door—a door that was locked.

My heart raced as I moved from the door to the windows, all sealed tight with no hope of escape. I opened my mouth to scream when something on the far end of the room caught my eye.

"Thank gods you're okay. Are you hurt?" A strange man rushed forward and I jumped back, grabbing hold of the closest thing to me: a candelabra.

"Stay back!" I cried out. "Who are you?"

The man narrowed his eyes on me. "What's wrong? It's me, Kael."

"I don't know you." Hells, I didn't know anyone. Did I have a family? Were they somewhere in this place locked behind doors too?

Kael drew in a harsh breath and cursed. "She got to you, hasn't she?"

Confusion swam through me. "What do you want with me? Why have you locked me in here?"

Sadness swept over Kael's face before he stepped back. "Stay safe, pirate queen. We will figure this out."

The air around Kael shimmered and sparked before the man vanished in thin air. I screamed, dropped the candelabra, and climbed back into bed, wrapping my arms around my legs. Despite the warmth of the velvet sheets, I shivered with fear and uncertainty. What was going on? Who had locked me up and took away my memories? And why did this Kael call me a pirate queen? It made no sense.

As I hugged myself tighter, the door creaked open, and a woman entered. She was dressed in a long, flowing gown and had a serene smile on her face.

"Good morning," she said softly. "I hope you slept well."

I glared at her, trying to keep my fear at bay. "Who are you? What do you want? Why am I locked in here?"

The woman approached me slowly, as if I were a wild animal that might attack at any moment. "My name is Gemma, I am the Queen of the Enchanted Realm. You're only locked in here for your safety."

My safety?

"What happened to me? Why can't I remember anything?"

The Queen clicked her tongue. "You poor thing. You'd

come so far to train with the Brotherhood and, due to an unfortunate accident, you hit your head quite hard."

I reached to the top of my head, searching for any signs of head trauma but there was nothing.

"The healers were able to take care of the wound, but they said memory loss was a possible side effect."

"I'm sorry, I don't understand. What's the Brotherhood?"

"They're the men and women who guard the realm from those who wish to harm it. They protect this city and all who live within its walls."

And I was here to join them? Why did that sound . . . *wrong*?

I shook my head, and before I could speak, two women waltzed into the room. The one who carried a tray of food had tanned skin and wore her hair in twin braids. She looked strong and delicate at the same time, like she spent her afternoons working in the fields and evenings on her knees at prayer. Her tunic was long and dark blue. It made me think of a night sky filled with stars. The woman who carried clothes had pale skin and wore her hair in a tight bun at the top of her head. Her tunic was cream-colored and loose, hanging off a thin frame.

"Ana and Cala have agreed to see that you are taken care of." The Queen grabbed a chalice off the tray and held it out. "It's a tonic for the head injury. It may not bring back the memories as soon as you'd like, but it will in time."

I hesitated, eyeing the chalice suspiciously. But the queen's kind smile and gentle tone made me lower my guard. I took the chalice and drank it down, as a warm sensation spread through my body.

The queen clapped her hands, beaming. "Good, now that you're finally awake, Ana and Cala have volunteered to help you dress and take you down to the training yards. I'm sure it will be good to get out and perhaps it will help jog your memory."

As the queen turned to leave, I leapt out of bed. "Wait, please, I don't even remember my name."

Something flashed in the queen's eyes I couldn't decipher. "It's... *Rose*. And do not worry, we will chat again soon."

With that, the Queen left me with Ana and Cala, each taking one of my hands. They led me into a dressing room and helped me change into a light blue tunic and trousers. As we walked through the palace, they pointed out different rooms and explained their uses, but all I could think about was the name the Queen gave me.

I'd hoped my name would have jogged my memory, but even that had little effect.

Ana and Cala dragged me outside and down to a beautiful courtyard before stopping at the training yard. It was full of men and women practicing with swords and shields, and others with bows and arrows. A few used their own bodies as weapons, flipping and spinning through the air in a graceful dance of speed and agility. I watched them in awe, mesmerized by the power they possessed. As we walked closer, I could hear their shouts of encouragement to one another as they sparred or cheered for a successful hit.

It was clear that these people had trained hard to become so skilled. Even though I couldn't remember my past, excitement stirred inside me; as if something deep within recognized these warriors and wanted to join them. Perhaps the queen was right, and I was here to train with them.

"This must be Rose." A tall man with long blond hair and deep blue eyes walked over, bringing with him a gentle but unmistakable fragrance of wet earth and freshly fallen leaves.

"It is," Cala said. "Rose, this is Commander Robin, he is also one of the Elders."

She gave far too much emphasis on the commander's name. Like the man was more of a god than a simple man.

"I'll take it from here, thank you ladies." Robin gestured for me to follow, as he led me through the thick of the training. When we reached the middle, surrounded by swinging swords and tumbling men, he stopped and turned to me.

"The training season has already started, but Gemma says you seem ready to get back into things." He gave me a once over and I straightened my shoulders.

I opened my mouth to speak but he cut me off. "I didn't say you could speak, recruit. This is my yard, and these are my men. Do anything to jeopardize that or get in anyone's way and you'll wish you'd never stepped foot in this city. Understand?"

Something deep within me twisted at being talked to like that. Anger boiled up from within and the confused part of me wondered why. I must have known this was what I was getting myself into when I signed up. Right?

Still, I didn't say anything. Just stared back at him as his eyes narrowed. "Good," he said and continued to walk. "You'll be answering to Tibault. He will make sure you get caught up to the others."

"May I speak, Commander?" I asked.

He sighed but nodded.

Swallowing, I worked up some courage and said, "I woke up with no memory of who I am or how I got here. Which means I also don't know *why* I'm here. Maybe it would help me understand if you told me a bit about the Brotherhood or why I'm here."

A flicker of annoyance crossed the commander's face, causing his brow to furrow and his lips to purse. "All Queen Gemma said was that you lost someone special to you. That you came to seek revenge, but let me tell you this, recruit. The assassins and what you learn here will help you unlock far more than revenge. We are the guardians of the realm. Each member, finely tuned to lethal precision, dedicated to eliminating any threats that may arise. When you join us, you forfeit everything else in your life for the cause."

His words were delivered with a rehearsed tone, lacking any emotion. *Interesting*. I stuck that tidbit in the back of my mind.

"The queen said you're her guards."

Robin shook his head. "We are more than that. We are assassins, masters of shadows and death. Our enemies never see us coming until it's too late."

Shivers rolled down my back.

Another man approached and laughed. "Always so poetic, Commander." His gaze fell on me. "We kill people with the pointy end of a blade and sometimes the blunt end too."

"Frederick, aren't you supposed to be with the Elites?"

Frederick ran a hand over his dark hair and flashed a charming smile. "I just wanted to say hello to our newest member. Well, that and to tell you Elder Sinclair is looking for you."

Robin looked at me and then Frederick. "See to it that she meets Tibault." And then he took off in the opposite direction.

"You want to know more about the Brotherhood?" Frederick asked once Robin was far enough away.

Frederick led me to a nearby corner of the training yard. Two men fought with blades, their feet light and almost silent as they moved.

"Captain Tibault." Frederick cleared his throat. "The commander wanted—"

A small knife *whooshed* between us and I squeaked.

"What the fuck?" I snapped.

The men abruptly stopped and turned to me.

The blade quivered in the wooden post behind us, its edge kissing the place where Frederick's ear had been moments before. Tibault strode forward, his weathered face carved into lines of displeasure that made Robin's stern aloofness look playful. Moonlight glinted off the silver scar bisecting his left eyebrow—a mark I recognized from nowhere and everywhere all at once but couldn't place.

"Language," he said, yanking the knife free. Sawdust drifted down like cursed snowflakes. "Or do you plan to scold our enemies to death?"

Frederick chuckled nervously, but my hands were already curling into fists. Muscle memory flexed beneath my skin like a caged beast stretching awake. "I'd prefer steel over screeching," I reply, chin lifting.

Tibault's nostrils flared as he circled me, his boots crunching gravel in the silence between us. "You smell of brine and blood," he muttered. "Not flowers."

Before I can ask what that meant, he barked at the sparring men. "Swords! Now!" They scrambled back like startled crows as metal sang through air—a practice blade hilt slamming into my palms before I had fully turned.

"Defend," Tibault growled, already swinging.

Steel clashed in a shower of sparks that stung my cheeks. My knees bent low as though some phantom warrior puppeted my limbs, guiding my movements with an instinct I didn't fully understand. The shock of each impact rattled my teeth, but it didn't slow him. Tibault's strikes came fast and ruthless, meant to maim rather than test, each blow vibrating up my arms like a war drum sounding in my bones.

And yet, I moved as if I had trained my entire life for this.

My body knew what my mind had forgotten.

While my muscles coiled and released with precision, my blade met his with unerring accuracy. I pivoted, ducked, and countered without hesitation. I gripped the hilt of my weapon with the confidence of someone who had done this before—countless times, in countless fights.

Which meant I had.

I was exactly where I was supposed to be.

I had come here for a reason, seeking the Brotherhood, drawn to them before I remembered why. And if my instincts still carried the weight of the warrior I once was, then I had no doubt—I belonged here.

Sweat dripped down my face, but I refused to falter.

"Too slow," he snarled as his elbow cracked against my ribs.

Pain bloomed hot under my tunic—and something else *answered*. A ripple beneath flesh that tasted of midnight oil and iron chains in moonlight—

My next parry came faster than breath should allow.

Tibault's blade flew wide as I twisted inside his guard, edge grazing his throat before skittering away—controlled? Accidental? Even I didn't know until I saw the thin red line welling above his collarbone.

The yard stilled so completely I heard Frederick swallow three paces away.

Tibault touched the cut slowly, his blood black as ink in shadowed daylight. When he smiled it transformed him into something feral—a wolf welcoming winter's hunger. "Well now," he rasped, eyes gleaming with cruel approval . . . and deeper suspicion. "Seems Her Majesty forgot to mention you'd done this dance before."

My sword arm trembled not from exertion but revelation: These lethal steps feel less like memory and more like a resurrection.

"The next few days will be to test more of your skills. Keep sharp and you'll do just fine here," Tiabult said.

I sighed. This was a test, and one I apparently passed. Thank all the gods.

I'd lost track of the days as they flowed together in a monotonous rhythm. And yet, after several days of rigorous training, I still failed to remember anything about who I was or where I came from. The Queen had ordered tonics for me twice a day, and even that refused to jog my memory.

"Rose," Tibault called for me during an early morning session. "You've done well these past few days, and Queen Gemma has decided it's time to put what you've learned to the test. Take the rest of the day and I'll send Frederick to come fetch you when it's time."

"All right," I said and left the training yards. As I found my way through the castle, a familiar voice stopped me. "Rosie, wait up!"

I whirled around to find Frederick hot on my heels. He'd been my sparring partner the last few days when Tibault had been busy with other trainees. Frederick had a massive head of dark red hair and freckles that covered every inch of his face and arms. There was something so familiar about him, something that made me comfortable to the point where I could let my guard down. A part of it anyway.

"We have the day off, are you really going to sulk in your room?" He asked.

What else was there to do in this place? I didn't know Chione, the main city of the Enchanted Realm, and hadn't been able to leave the castle grounds without a guard questioning me every time. Sometimes this place resembled more of a prison than a sanctuary. Apparently recruits weren't allowed to wander.

"I was actually headed to the library."

Frederick raised a brow. "The library? On a day like this? Come now, Rosie, let's do something fun!"

"Don't call me that." I hissed. Not only did the name Rose

not feel right but having him call me *Rosie* made it worse. "And I'm not going anywhere with you."

Frederick had become somewhat of a friend, if you'd call someone forced to fight against every day, a friend. Someone who never let up and handed you your ass most days.

"Come now, Rosie Posie, what are you afraid of?"

I scoffed. "I'm not afraid."

Frederick hooked his arm through mine and turned me back toward the training yard. "Then let's find some mischief to cause. Go get changed and meet me back here in an hour."

He led me down into the city, the scent of damp stone and lantern smoke thick in the air. The streets pulsed with life, even at this hour laughter rang out from dimly lit doorways, mingling with the occasional clatter of dice on wood and the lilting notes of a lute played by a street performer on the corner.

Frederick moved through the streets with purpose, his boots near silent against the cobblestones. We turned down a narrow street, its buildings leaning so close together that the sky above was little more than a sliver of darkness between the rooftops. Somewhere in the distance, a bell tolled the hour.

My gaze caught on something farther ahead. As we moved closer, it came into view. Perched along the crumbling edge of a stone wall sat a massive raven. Its feathers gleamed an unnatural black beneath the moonlight, its beady eyes fixed intently on me. It didn't move, didn't so much as twitch, but something about the way it stared sent a shiver down my spine.

I slowed. "That's a big damn bird."

Frederick barely glanced at it. "It's just a raven."

"It's watching us."

"Ravens watch everything."

I frowned, but before I could comment further, he pressed a hand to my back, guiding me forward. "Come on. We're almost there."

I cast one last glance at the bird, a strange unease curling in my gut before I followed Frederick deeper into the city.

Apparently, mischief was apparently a pub called Eddard's with big burly men playing cards and drinking themselves into a stupor.

We stepped through the door into a cavernous room paneled with deep walnut wood. Light from the fireplace illuminated an assortment of worn and creaky chairs surrounding a long bar where drinkers perched on stools, chatting and laughing. The air was heavy with the smell of tobacco smoke and strong ale, mixed with cinnamon and nutmeg.

The atmosphere was thick with camaraderie and laughter; two things I hadn't experienced much of since waking up in a strange bed without my memory. I noticed Tibault across the room with a few other members of the Brotherhood, but he didn't even glance our way as we found a small table in the corner.

Frederick waved toward a woman carrying a tray of ale. She walked over, sending me a glare before setting the mugs down on the table.

"Thank you, Darla." Frederick smirked.

"Anything for you, Freddy." Darla traced a finger over Frederick's shoulder. She flicked her hair over her shoulder and shot me a warning glare before retreating behind the bar.

Frederick chuckled, his gaze never leaving Darla. "Thank the gods for women like her."

I rolled my eyes and took a sip of ale, its warmth spread through my body.

"So what do you want to do?" Frederick asked.

I shrugged. "I don't know. That looks like fun." I pointed

toward a group of men huddled around a table playing a card game.

He laughed at my expression before reaching into his pocket and pulling out a few coins which he tossed onto the table with a flourish. "Let's join in then."

I didn't know how to play cards—at least, I didn't remember if I ever had—but Frederick seemed to have it all figured out. He moved through the game with effortless ease, his fingers shuffling the worn deck like a magician weaving spells. When he noticed my hesitation, he leaned in, voice low and smooth as he explained the basics—what cards were good, when to bluff, when to fold, and most importantly, how to read the people sitting across from you.

At first, I fumbled. My fingers hesitated as I tried to make sense of the suits and numbers, of the quiet strategy that ran beneath every exchange. But then, something happened. The movements started to feel familiar, like muscle memory buried beneath the surface, waiting to be unlocked. My fingers stopped faltering when I placed my bets. My eyes instinctively flicked to the players instead of the cards, searching for the tells Frederick had pointed out—the nervous twitch of a lip, the restless drumming of fingers against the table, the way someone's breathing changed when they were sitting on a good hand.

I found myself surprised by how easily I slipped into the rhythm of the game. It was like I had been playing for years instead of mere minutes. With every round, my confidence grew. My bluffs became sharper, my risks bolder, my victories more frequent. Laughter and groans of frustration filled the air as I raked in another pile of coins, my opponents shaking their heads in mock despair.

"You're sure you've never played before?" one of the men muttered, eyeing me with suspicion as I collected my winnings.

Frederick chuckled, his eyes gleaming with amusement. "Maybe she has a knack for it."

Or maybe I had done this before. Maybe, in another life—before the stolen memories, before the Brotherhood, before the bloodshed—this had been second nature to me.

Before long, the entire table cheered me on, treating me as if I were an old friend rather than a newcomer with gaps in her past. The warmth of their camaraderie curled in my chest, a welcome contrast to the cold weight of uncertainty I carried.

Frederick clapped me on the back with a huge grin on his face as we both revelled in my success. However, we'd started to attract quite the crowd, one that had caught the attention of Tibault and the rest of the Brotherhood.

"Is this what you call resting, trainee?" Tibault raised a brow.

I stilled, unsure if this was him being serious or not. "I—"

"It is when you're as good as Rosie is. Pull up a seat Tibault and let the lady take your money."

I covered my laugh with a cough, bringing my mug to my lips before darting my eyes from Tibault.

Hells, the man was gorgeous. He certainly looked like he belonged in the middle of the forest or on the plains of a farm. A man who'd worked hard every day of his life. It was his face though that captivated me the most. His eyes were an intense green, the kind of green that made you think of spring and leaves and life. A sharp nose led into a strong square jaw that had a hint of stubble. His lips, though thin, had a hint of fullness to them, and when he smiled, they lifted on one side in a smirk. I wondered what he'd be like in bed.

What? I did *not* just think that. Yet, there was something about him that seemed familiar. How was I still unable to remember anything after days of tonics and rest?

"This *lady* needs to sober up and get ready to prove herself useful to the Queen. Or is someone second guessing their desire to join the Brotherhood?"

Everyone around the table shot me a look and I wanted nothing more than to crawl under the table and scurry out of the room. Before I knew what happened, the challenge bubbled within in me and my mouth moved without a second thought.

"Sounds like someone's not up for the challenge." I said, tossing a couple coins into the pot in the middle. "Pity, I do enjoy a good ass kicking."

I shook my head slightly. Where was all this coming from?

"Hell, I fold . . . again." The man to my right, Todd, placed his cards on the table and took a long swig of his ale. "You can take my spot, Tibby. If I don't get home, the misses will have my ass on a platter."

"Yeah, *Tibby*, have a seat." I grinned.

"Maybe another time." Tibault plucked the cards from my hand and threw them onto the tale. "Time to go."

A wave of seriousness washed over Tibault. The other Brothers all had their masks of no emotion on. Not a single one of them budged and I rolled my eyes. "Frederick, make sure my winnings find their way to my room will you, and if any of it's missing, I know where you sleep." I winked before turning and pushing past Tibault and his bully brigade.

"I like 'em feisty." Frederick called back, causing all the men I'd just been schooling in poker to laugh.

"You're supposed to stay within the castle grounds, Rose," Tibault said as we made our way outside. The night air was crisp and a blanket of stars was scattered across the sky. How long had we been there? And why didn't I feel as drunk as I should have felt? *Was I someone who drank often?*

"I've been cooped up for days. I needed something to do besides sit in the library and read or train on the fields."

Tibault's face softened and he put a hand on my arm.

"Rose, I understand your need to explore, but you also need to be aware of the dangers. You are a recruit, an important piece to the Brotherhood and if anything were to happen to you . . ." His voice trailed off as he looked away from me.

I was important to the Brotherhood? Why? It's not like I was anything special. Sure, I was skilled with a knife and I had a helluva punch, but that was about it. Still, the way he looked at me, it was like standing before your father as he scolded you for forgetting to feed the chickens.

"I'm sorry," I said quickly, feeling guilty for causing Tibault undue stress.

"It's all right." He smiled but it didn't quite reach his eyes. "Now come on, we have somewhere to be."

"I thought I was supposed to be resting?"

"You were to rest until I came to get you. It's time to prove yourself."

We made our way through the winding streets until we came to a small bakery in the corner of town. The lights were still on even though it was late, and Tibault motioned for me to go inside. A small bell tinkled overhead when Tibault closed it behind him.

"Isn't it a bit late to be here?"

"Not for what's hidden beneath the surface."

"What's below the surface exactly?"

Tibault grinned. "The Pits."

8
WELCOME TO CHIONE
ULRICH

THE ENCHANTED REALM LOOMED AHEAD, RISING from the mist-thick waters like the ribs of a long-dead beast. Cliffs jutted from the sea, their jagged peaks clawing at the low-hanging clouds. The sky was covered in shades of violet and deep indigo, stars swallowed by the heavy gloom that hung over this cursed kingdom. The air reeked of damp earth, salt, and something else—something ancient.

The Jolly Dutchman skimmed across the waves, gliding too smooth, too fast. The wind wasn't natural—it had a pulse, a will, pushing us toward the shore with unseen hands. A gift from Calypso, or so she claimed. I didn't trust her, and I knew if Arie were here she'd feel the same way.

I turned my attention back to the land before us.

Arie was here. Somewhere in that tangled wilderness of stone and shadow. And so was Queen Gemma.

My fingers tightened on the wheel, the rough grooves of the wood digging into my palms. For weeks, that woman had her hands on Arie. For weeks, Arie had been trapped, alone, and I had been stuck in Neverland and helpless on the goddamned sea. A familiar rage curled in my chest, hot and suffocating, but there was something else beneath it, something colder.

Fear.

I tried to drown it in anger, but it clung to me, whispering of all the things I might be too late to stop.

Behind me, the low hum of voices twisted into the wind. Clayton and Calypso, standing close—too close—near the mast. His body angled toward her, the easy way she leaned in. The way they spoke in hushed tones like there were secrets worth keeping between them.

Something about it set off alarm bells in my mind. I was still mad at him for going back to Khan, but that didn't stop the worry building in my chest now that Calypso had her claws in him.

Frankie, arms crossed tight enough to crack her own ribs, watched them like a cat waiting to pounce. The muscles in her jaw twitched, her narrowed eyes flicking between them with a sharpness that could cut glass.

"She's too pretty," Frankie muttered, loud enough for the whole damned ship to hear. "I don't trust pretty women who talk in riddles."

Calypso's lips curled at the edges, something like amusement sparking in her storm-blue eyes. "I could make myself ugly, if that would help."

Frankie snorted. "That's not the point."

Clayton scrubbed a hand down his face, his patience fraying at the edges. "For the love of the gods, Frankie, must you pick a fight with every person you meet?"

Frankie turned her glare on him, slow and deliberate. "Not every person. Just the ones who piss me off."

Nathaniel, lounging nearby like this was all a game to him, muttered, "So, all of them."

A headache pulsed behind my eyes. "Enough." The word

came out sharp, cutting through the tension. "Save the bickering for later. Not when we're sailing into the unknown."

Silence settled over the deck, but the weight of it didn't lift. The mist coiled around us as we neared the shore, thick as a breath, wrapping its fingers around the ship's hull.

"Frankie, go tell the crew to make themselves scarce for a while but to stay close. There's no telling when we'll need to leave in a moment's notice. We'll also need to ensure those who are infected stay on the ship. I don't want to draw too much attention here. Tell Doc to keep an eye on our crew while we're gone, and that I'll check on him when I can."

Frankie nodded and pulled Nathaniel along with her.

The *Jolly Dutchman* groaned as it kissed the dock, timbers shuddering like a beast reluctant to release its prey. Ropes tightened, sails rustled, and the sea hissed against the hull as if whispering a warning.

Before us, Chione rose from the mist—a city of salt-rusted spires and crumbling bridges strung with flickering witchlights, their sickly green glow barely piercing the thick, damp air. The scent of brine and burnt offerings clung to the wind, laced with something acrid, something old. Magic. And not the kind that welcomed strangers.

The docks teemed with bodies—sailors barking in tongues that twisted between human speech. Cargo was unloaded in frantic bursts of movement even at the late hour, crates thudding against warped planks slick with brine and gods knew what else.

I waited for Frankie to return before we made our way off the ship. The boards groaned under my boots as I stepped onto the dock.

Calypso drifted ahead, her cloak rippling unnaturally around her ankles. Even here, where monsters walked freely, she carried an air of something other, something untouchable.

"Mind your tempers," she purred over her shoulder, voice smooth as tide-worn glass. "Unless you fancy spending your first night here pickled in a slaver's barrel."

Frankie scoffed, shouldering past a hulking fur trader whose foxfire-yellow eyes tracked her with lazy amusement. "Says the woman who smells like trouble wrapped in silk," she muttered, fingers twitching toward the dagger at her hip.

"Calypso and I will meet up with you once my ship has arrived," Clayton said. "Thanks to Calypso's magic it won't be here as fast as we made it, but it will get here faster than normal."

I watched as the two of them took off in another direction and returned my gaze to Chione. The city coiled upward, its streets winding like a serpent into the heights. Moss-slick stairs glistened underfoot, leading past overhanging balconies draped in bright orchids.

Vendors hawked horrors disguised as delicacies—glowing eels writhing in brine-filled jars, skewered songbird hearts still pulsing faintly on sticks. A hunched woman ground something dark and glistening beneath a mortar, her hollow gaze flicking up as we passed.

I resisted the urge to rest my hand on my cutlass.

This city was alive in a way that felt wrong—like a creature that never slept, only waited, hungry and patient.

And somewhere in its depths, Queen Gemma had Arie.

"Hook," Nathaniel said, breaking through my thoughts. "What's the plan?"

"We could stay on the ship, scout for information," Frankie suggested.

"No," I snarled, "I refused to wait any longer to find your sister, or did you forget why we're here?"

I knew it was wrong to say and yet the words still flew from my mouth. Frankie's expression darkened but Pascal stepped in before anything happened.

"We can't go after Arie tonight," he said. "Not without knowing exactly where she is and what we're up against. I know a safe place for us to stay tonight that will give us the information we need."

"Tink," Pascal continued, peering over his shoulder to Tink who fluttered behind him. "You're going to need to stay inconspicuous here. These folks aren't used to seeing a fairy flutter about."

Tink grinned. "That won't be a problem."

A bright light swirled around her and seconds later...

What the hells?

Tink, her petite frame mirroring Pascal's stature, stood with her wings seamlessly folded into her back. The delicate, iridescent appendages vanished entirely, leaving no trace of their existence.

"Whoa." Nathaniel's jaw dropped. "Damn, Tink, you're even more gorgeous than I thought."

Tink giggled. "Thanks, big guy. It only works outside of Neverland; a little trick I learned from a witch many years ago." Her voice had gone from twinkling bells to a soft, lilting cadence, no longer carrying the ethereal chime of fairy magic but something entirely human. It was strange, hearing her like this—grounded, real, almost ordinary.

"That's amazing." Keenan circled Tink as though she was a specimen ready to be examined.

Nathaniel whispered something into Frankie's ear that sounded a bit like him calling dibs, but I couldn't be certain.

"There's an Inn just up ahead where we can stay," Pascal interrupted. "It's where I stay when I come in search of Lost Ones."

We traipsed through the dimly-lit city, guided by Pascal.

The old buildings stood like sentinels along the narrow streets, their wooden walls and clay brick illuminated by several lamps.

After a while we finally stopped in front of a small, but sturdy, building made of dark wood with red shuttered windows, a faint light visible from where we stood. A creaky wooden sign hung above the entrance, its letters slightly faded but still legible: The Hunter's Inn.

"Seems like as good of a place as any," Keenan commented, eyeing the Inn with an approving nod.

"Let's hope so," I said. The smell of cinnamon and freshly baked bread wafted through the air, tempting my empty stomach and reminding me it had been too long since I'd eaten.

"Smells heavenly," Frankie murmured, her eyes lighting up at the prospect of food.

The door creaked as I opened it, revealing a cozy, rustic room with wooden walls and floors. Flickering lanterns hung from the ceiling, casting shadows across the walls. A wave of warmth rippled through the air, accompanied by the soft humming of conversations and laughter of the few people sitting around a small fireplace.

"I swear to the almighty gods, Hans," a woman shouted, "if you touch one more piece of my apple pie, I will cut your fingers off and feed them to the wolves." She appeared through a set of double swinging doors sporting dark hair in a tight bun, arms heavy with a platter of miniature pies. The light illuminated her stocky frame and something shiny in her hair. *Was that a hilt of a knife?*

She looked up at me for the briefest moment and placed the platter on the desk. "Welcome to the Hunter's Inn, how many rooms will you be needing?" She turned around to grab a few keys from the wall behind her.

"Hello, Gretel," Pascal said.

Gretel paused and whirled around to stare at him. Her eyes widened and jaw slacked. "Petey, is that you?"

Pascal nodded and approached the desk.

"I-I don't believe it. You're alive?"

"As alive as one can be." Pascal shrugged.

Gretel reached forward and traced a finger down the large scar that marred Pascal's face. I waited for him to flinch or pull away from her touch, but he never did. I'd never seen Pascal allow someone to touch his face like that. She was at least four inches taller than him and by the looks of her, could take on just about any one of the pirates on the *Jolly Dutchman*.

Gretel pulled her hand away and then shoved him before grabbing his shoulders and pulling him in for a hug. "Petey, you slippery eel! I thought for sure Davy Jones finally caught up with you. Where on earth have you been hiding all this time?"

Pascal laughed as Gretel released her hold. "It's a long story and I'm afraid we're on borrowed time." She narrowed her eyes but before she could say anything Pascal added, "We'd appreciate it if you could keep our presence here discreet."

Gretel gave a stiff nod, anger flashing in her eyes and then gone the next minute, replaced by a warm inviting smile that reached her bright eyes. "You know you can always count on . . . *Bells*?" Her gaze flicked to Tink.

Tink beamed at Gretel. "The one and only."

"Good to see you still remember how to use that little trick I taught you." Gretel gave her an approving look.

Tink twirled. "It comes in handy every now and again."

I narrowed my eyes on Gretel. Did that make her some sort of witch or sorceress, or something else? Someone who could play with illusions like that. I'd have to keep that in mind. Witches weren't known for their generosity or helpfulness. Not any of the ones I'd known anyway.

"Good, and yes, you can all count on my discretion as well

as Hansel." Gretel stuck out her hand and held out four keys. "We only have four rooms available at the moment."

"That will be fine, thank you," I said.

"What brings you all to the Enchanted Realm? It's a pretty dark time in the city."

Pascal nodded. "I'd actually like to speak to you and Hansel about that. Tomorrow?"

"Breakfast starts when the crows howl," Gretel said and directed us up the wooden staircase to our rooms.

"Crows howl?" Frankie whispered behind me.

"These ones do," Gretel quipped, apparently having excellent hearing from where she led the way. "If you're going to be staying for a while and want to lay low, stay as far away from the castle as possible. There's a ball happening in a few days and people from all over the Seven Seas will be showing up to celebrate. That also means the Brotherhood will be on watch more than usual. Oh, and welcome to Chione."

The stairs creaked under our feet as we made our way to the second floor. My room was the first on the right, and I unlocked the door to reveal a cozy space with a small bed, a table, and a window that overlooked the street below.

I collapsed onto the bed, exhaustion finally catching up with me. My mind raced with thoughts of Arie, the curse, and all the men we'd left behind. For now, however, all I could do was rest and gather my strength for the battle ahead.

The scent of spiced honey and crisping bacon pulled me from the depths of sleep. My body ached from days at sea, muscles stiff as though they'd been carved from driftwood. Sunlight streamed through the warped panes of my window, casting long, golden fingers across the wooden floor. For a moment, I let myself lie there, inhaling the warmth of fresh bread and roasted coffee, the kind of morning that belonged to someone else—to a man without ghosts at his heels.

The murmur of voices drifted up from below, threaded with laughter. It was a sound I hadn't heard in too long. My crew, my family, reveling in something as simple as breakfast. It twisted through my chest, made my ribs feel too tight. They deserved this moment of peace, even if it wouldn't last.

I forced myself up, dragging a hand through my hair before slipping on my boots. My coat hung over the chair by the small wooden table, still damp from the sea wind. I left it. No need for extra weight when I had another to carry.

Finding Arie.

Every second wasted was a second closer to whatever fate Queen Gemma had planned for her. I needed to move. I needed to find her.

I crept down the stairs, footsteps light, keeping close to the wall. If I was careful, I could slip past the dining hall and into the streets before anyone noticed—

A hooded man stepped through the entrance.

I stiffened, hand instinctively drifting to my cutlass, but before I could speak, Gretel called from across the room.

"Took your damn time getting here, Robin."

The hooded figure at the entrance hesitated for half a breath, then reached up and pushed back his hood revealing a head of blond hair and sharp green eyes.

The name whispered through my mind, tangled with a thousand rumors. Some painted him a hero. Others a menace. But the man before me . . . there was something dark in the way he carried himself, something coiled beneath the easy smirk. A blade hidden in silk. A man who had seen too much and done worse to survive it.

I kept my expression neutral, but instinct kept my spine rigid, my hand never straying far from my weapon.

A firm clap landed on my back, jolting me forward a step. Keenan.

"Bloody hell," I muttered, shaking him off as he grinned.

"Relax, Hook," Keenan said, guiding me toward the table. "Come eat. We need to talk about next steps."

I cast one more glance at Robin, meeting his gaze across the room. A blur ran past me and threw their arms around him. "Hood!"

Robin stiffened for a moment before relaxing. "What are you doing here, killer?"

Killer? How the hells did Frankie know this guy? This girl had many secrets. I peered over at Pascal but he simply shook his head and returned to his plate of food.

Frankie beamed at him before letting him go, her face darkened. "We're hoping you can help us."

"Everyone sit down, we have a lot to discuss." Pascal motioned toward the table.

The table was alive with movement—clinking mugs, the scrape of knives against plates, the low hum of conversation laced with the occasional burst of laughter. A fleeting moment of peace in the heart of a city that never slept easy. But tension coiled beneath it, an undercurrent of urgency that none of us could shake.

Pascal leaned forward, resting his forearms on the table, his expression grim. "We're looking for a friend of ours," he said, voice steady. "Fiery red hair—"

"Big attitude," Frankie added, shoving a piece of bacon in her mouth. "Real pain in the ass. Also my sister."

I exhaled slowly. "She's reckless, stubborn, and has a heart too damn big for her own good." My fingers curled against the rough wood of the table. "She was taken by an assassin and we believe he's given her to Queen Gemma."

Hansel went rigid beside Gretel, his fingers whitening around his mug. A heavy silence stretched between us, thick with unspoken tension.

Robin, however, only arched a brow. "I know of who you speak."

Something about his tone made my skin prickle.

Frankie narrowed her eyes. "You do?"

Robin leaned back, dragging a hand through his light hair. "Well for starters, I didn't know you had a sister. And secondly, relax, love. No need for dramatics." His green eyes flickered to me, assessing. "Yes, of course I know of the notorious Sea Witch. She arrived in the city several days ago, give or take a few, and is under constant guard by Gemma. But she's no longer Gemma's prisoner. She's been working with the assassins."

"Shit," Gretel muttered.

Frankie's face paled. "She wouldn't."

Robin shrugged. "Maybe she wouldn't. But it sure seems like *Rose* would."

I stiffened. *Rose?* The name felt wrong, like a misfitting piece in a puzzle that should never have existed.

Tink, who had been unusually quiet, suddenly sat up straighter. "Rose?"

Robin nodded. "That's what they call her. Not Arie. I think the Queen has her under some sort of influence. Doesn't remember anything. She'll be at the Pits tonight."

My stomach twisted.

Something dark curled in my chest, something that felt an awful lot like rage. *Arie, lost in someone else's hands. Someone else's control.*

And worse—Robin spoke of it like it was inevitable. Like it was expected.

I clenched my jaw, fingers curling into a fist beneath the table. *Like hell.*

Tink inhaled sharply. "That's why I still feel her, but it's distant. Like there's a wall between us. It has to be magic. A spell or enchantment."

I frowned, ignoring Tink's comments. "What the hell are the Pits?"

At the same time Frankie said, "Godsdamnit."

Yes, Frankie and I definitely needed to have a chat.

Hansel sighed, rubbing a hand over his face. "A fighting ring. People place bets, make gold, and prove their strength." His tone was even, but his eyes flicked toward Robin, searching.

Robin remained unreadable. Unbothered. *Too* unbothered. Like a man who had long since accepted the ugliness of the world.

"The Queen enjoys her theatrics." Robin bit out.

"Sounds like you don't like this place," Keenan chimed in, oblivious to the shift in the room.

Robin's expression didn't change, but something behind his eyes sharpened—something old and bitter.

"He has good reason," Gretel snapped, her voice cutting through the air like a blade. She stood abruptly, moving toward Robin, and placed a hand on his shoulder. "I thought after what happened they wouldn't have rebuilt so soon. I'm sorry, friend."

What happened?

Her words sent a ripple of unease through me. They spoke of something dark, something heavy that the rest of us weren't privy to. I didn't like that. I didn't like *him*.

Gretel squeezed Robin's arm.

Something inside me snapped tight.

I shot up, already reaching for my cutlass. "Then we need to go to her . . . *now*."

Robin let out a low chuckle. "Easy, Captain. You charge in there now, and you won't make it past the guard. We'll go tonight." He lifted his cup to his lips, eyes glinting over the rim. "When the real monsters come out to play."

While Robin went on about how he'd be there and would ensure we would be able to get in, I seethed. Gemma had messed with Arie's mind. I wasn't sure what to expect at the Pits, but one thing was certain: I wanted to pierce Gemma through her cold black heart and watch her body burn. And I would stop at nothing to make sure that happened.

9
FISTS & FANGS
ARIE

"Why on earth would anyone name their flower shop 'The Pits'?" I asked. Unless, of course, they were secretly selling carnivorous plants that smelled like ass. I tried to imagine a shop where the flowers smell like sewage and wanted to gag.

Tibault grunted as he swung the creaking door open. With a hesitant step, I followed him inside, and instantly the air was alive with a heavy perfume of blossoms in full bloom. It wrapped around me like a warm embrace, infusing the space with not just an intoxicating scent but a myriad of vibrant colors. Moonlight filtered through the windows above, casting a delicate glow that heightened each flower.

As Tibault strode forward, a single rose caught his eye. He plucked its resting place and lifted it to his nose.

I peered around the assassin and searched for the shop's owner, but the place was empty.

"Are we allowed to be in here right now?" Once more, my question was met with silence. Tibault continued walking toward the back of the shop on light feet. He opened a door to what looked like a broom closet and motioned me in.

My heart sped up and my hand grew clammy. What was this? I didn't even know this guy. Was he trying to—

One of the walls shifted, sliding open with a soft *whoosh*. An elderly man dressed in a simple white tunic and black trousers appeared through the opening. His hair was pure white and his face was etched with wrinkles, but his eyes were sharp and clear.

"Bahir." Tibault spread his arms open and flung them around Bahir and lifted him from the floor.

Bahir laughed. "Yes, it's me, now put me down before you crush all my bones."

Tibault gently lowered him to his feet. "It's good to see you again. I'm glad this place is finally back up and running after what those damn rebels did." Something softened in Tibault's voice before he cleared his throat and gestured to me. "This is Rose, the queen's new apprentice."

Did he just say the queen? Didn't he mean his apprentice? I was going to be an assassin. At least that's what Gemma had implied. For a moment I worked through what I could remember but still everything was hazy. Like I'd spent an entire month binge drinking and was in a permanent state of drunkenness.

Sadness crept in Bahir's face before vanishing behind a soft smile. "Hello, Rose. Welcome to my flower shop, and yes, Tibault, it took time and help from the Elders, but we managed. I'm sorry I can't stay and chat, I have somewhere to be. The festivities are still going on downstairs, if you think you can stomach it. Today's flowers are tulips."

"Stomach what?" I asked and this time Tibault answered.

"You'll see. Keep close and try not to stare."

"Stare at what?"

Tibault walked through the open Bahir had come through and turned to face me. "Anything."

We walked down the winding staircase until stopping at

another room mirroring the one upstairs. Tibault approached another wall and tapped three times before it disappeared, shimmering out of sight.

A man with broad shoulders and horns coming out of his nose grunted. "Today's flower?"

"Tulips," Tibault said. The man nodded and gestured us through.

We followed the man down a narrow passageway, illuminated only by flickering torches along the walls. The sound of cheering and shouting grew louder as we descended deeper into the network of tunnels beneath the city.

As we rounded a corner, we were met with a sight that took my breath away. A vast, underground arena had been carved out of solid rock, with rows of stone benches lining the walls and a large, elevated platform at one end. In the center of the arena stood a towering cage, its mesh sides filled with snarling, fanged beasts.

Something flashed in my mind, a beautiful dark beast with elongated fangs as it approached. Its eyes glowed in the darkness. I blinked and the beasts transformed into a beautiful dark-skinned woman with a wicked smile on her face.

The woman shrieked.

Arie.

Her words were like silk to my ears.

Holy shit, it's you. Where are you? You're so far away. Hang in there, girl. The others are coming for you.

I blinked, my thoughts muddled, disoriented. I tried to focus, but the voice felt distant, like it was coming from somewhere beyond the fog in my mind. The woman didn't sound or look familiar. Not that I remembered.

Tibault snapped his fingers in my face, pulling me from my thrall. What the hells was that? And who was Arie? What did the voice mean? They were coming?

Dozens of people sat around the arena, their eyes wide with excitement as they cheered and roared.

The air was thick with a mixture of fragrant flowers and something else, a scent that was unmistakably of power and magic and. . . blood. Adrenaline coursed through me as I followed Tibault through the crowds.

We settled into our seats toward the middle of the room. Tibault wasted no time summoning a server and ordering a round of drinks, his nonchalant gesture suggesting a familiarity with this place.

But I couldn't tear my eyes away from the brutal battle unfolding in the cage. Two massive beasts snarled and lunged at each other with savage abandon. Crimson droplets flew through the ring as they fought tooth and nail, neither one gaining the upper hand.

This was . . . barbaric.

"Do people actually find this entertaining?"

"You don't?"

I shrugged, not wanting to show just how much this bothered me. "What's the point?"

"It's a test. The Brotherhood use these beasts in battle. Only the strongest are allowed to join our ranks. This is how we ensure they're the right fit.

"By forcing them to fight?"

"Yes." Tibault leaned in closer. "This is the way of the Brotherhood, Rose. This is what you signed up for. Being an assassin means you have to do what others can't. You have to be able to make the tough calls. Consider this your first real lesson."

Was this really what I signed up for? A knot of unease tightened in the pit of my stomach. As I watched the brutal spectacle play out before me, I couldn't shake the nagging feeling that I had stumbled into something far darker, far more sinister than I had bargained for.

By the fourth fight, my stomach churned so violently I had to look away, unable to watch as another creature tore and clawed at the other, a lifeless body eventually thrown from the ring.

I wanted to leave but the set in Tibaults jaw told me that wasn't an option.

Did the queen really sanction this shit? Or was this all the Brotherhood and she didn't know what was going on. Either way, something gnawed at the back of my mind but my lost memory made it impossible to know what.

"You look a little pale, Rose. Are you okay?" Tibault smirked.

"Fine." I muttered.

"Good, because the night's just beginning. Excuse me, I have to go speak to someone. Can I trust you to stay put and not go wandering around?"

I nodded, trying my best to hide just how far from fine I really was.

Tibault raised a brow, then shook his head before disappearing into the crowd.

I snapped my attention back to the cage, just in time to see one of the snarling beasts sink its sharp fangs into the other's neck. Blood spurted out, splattering against the floor and a bell echoed throughout the room.

"We have a winner!" a loud voice rang out.

Boos and cheers mixed together as the losing beast was pulled out of the cage. My heart ached for these creatures who probably had no choice but to fight for their life. Anger swelled within me and before I could think better of it, I was up and moving, my feet leading me through the crowd.

I had no desire to stay here for another second. All I wanted was to go back to my room and scream into my pillow, then pray for all the souls lost tonight.

The crowd was rowdy as ever, but I pushed through, finally spotting Tibault at the back of the arena. He was talking with a man and woman both dressed in ornate robes and hoods over their heads. The three of them slipped into a door, disappearing farther into the arena.

I thought about just leaving and heading back to the castle without telling Tibault, but something pulled me forward.

Entering the dimly lit corridor they disappeared in, a chill rolled down my back and I shivered.

Flickering torches lit the path until I reached a set of double doors. Murmured voices sounded from behind the old wood and I crept closer. A voice in my head told me to turn around, to not eavesdrop, but there was another deeper instinct, one hidden within me telling me to push on. I pressed my ear against one of the doors.

"Are you sure, Tibault?" someone asked, their voice a low grumble.

"I am," Tibault said.

"Can you keep her safe? There are things in motion and we just need a little time. With this new information, we'll have to rethink our strategy."

"We can't wait for that," the woman hissed. "The queen—"

Who were they talking about?

"The queen will do as I advise," the mystery man said. "I'll ensure she plays her part. Tibault and I won't let anything happen to her."

The woman laughed. "Like you did with Marian?"

Marian. Why did I know that name?

"Watch yourself, Gret." Tibault snapped.

"Enjoying the conversation?" A voice sliced through the tense air, and I whirled around, heart hammering against my rib cage. A man cloaked in shadow stood before me clad all in black. His grip tightened around the hilt of the sword.

"I-I was looking for the exit. Must have gotten myself turned around." My stuttered excuse fell flat.

"Or, you were trying to get inside information about the Pits. Well, it's your lucky night. We need a main attraction and you seem like the perfect candidate."

Inside information about the Pits? The words hung heavily in the air. Before I could muster a response, the room shifted as three figures materialized out of the darkness, converging on me with predatory intent.

Panic surged through my veins like wildfire, adrenaline coursing through me as I scanned the room for an escape route. But the walls closed in like a vise.

The man's blade pressed against my throat. "Come on, newbie. Let's see what you've got."

Newbie? Did these guys know who I was? I wasn't one of their beasts.

"I think you have me mixed up. I'm with the B—"

"There's no mixup. We know exactly who you are." One of the men grabbed my arm, his rough fingers digging into my skin.

I twisted my body, my elbow connecting with the man's chest, knocking him back as I broke free.

Without hesitation, I launched a swift kick toward his knee, causing him to stumble further. The other man was quick to react, lunging at me with a snarl as he aimed to grab me too. I narrowly dodged his grasp, my heart pounding in my chest.

"Enough of this." The first man snapped. A jolt of bright light struck me square in the chest knocking the breath out of me. I opened my mouth to cry out when one of the other men clamped his hand around my mouth.

A burning sensation rippled through my body as they

dragged me through the tunnels. Each heartbeat drummed out a frantic rhythm of fear and uncertainty. I had to get the hell out of here. I blinked away the spots in my vision as the burning subsided.

Finally, they tossed me into the brightly lit cage at the center of the arena, the harsh clang of metal echoing through the chamber as the door slammed shut behind me.

"Looks like we have a new contender for our main event! Tell us, what's your name?"

I rose to my feet, my knees shaking as I lifted my arm to shield the bright light above. "It's . . . Rose."

My voice sounded as unsure as I felt.

"Well, Rose. Welcome to The Pits!"

I tried to say something when a loud bell rang. The cage opened and three more people—two men and one woman—were thrown into the arena with me.

My gaze drifted toward the trio standing along the edge of the cage. The two men, their torsos bared to reveal a canvas of swirling dark ink, roared as they lifted their hands in the air. One of them flexed his muscles, the tattoos rippling and shifting with the movement. His eyes scanned the arena with a predatory gleam, until they landed on me. A smirk rose to his lips.

The man beside him pounded on the cage. His eyes glinted with a fierce determination.

But it was the woman who captured my attention the most, her presence commanding the room with a quiet intensity that was impossible to ignore. Her shoulders rolled with fluid grace, muscles coiling beneath her ink-clad skin like a lioness poised to strike.

In her eyes, fire burned brighter than any flame. As she turned to face me, a silent challenge flickered in the depths of her gaze.

I eyed them warily, knowing that my chances of survival in

this brutal game had just decreased significantly. There was no way out of this. But as the adrenaline pumped through my veins, a fierce resolve ignited within me.

My memory was hazy but there was one thing I was certain of. One thing that not even a lost memory could stop. I was a force to be reckoned with, and I refused to go down tonight.

With a deep breath to steady my nerves, I braced myself.

The woman who the announcer called the "Nightshade" lunged toward me with a wild look, swinging a fist in my direction. I dodged her attack with a swift side-step, then countered with a well-aimed kick to her midsection. The girl stumbled back, giving me precious moments to assess the situation.

The other two contenders were engaged in their own battle, locked in a flurry of punches and body slams. I needed to act fast if I wanted to survive this.

Tibault's voice roared my name, but I had to keep my focus.

The girl I had kicked recovered quickly, her eyes blazing with fury. With a primal roar, she charged forward. I had no time to evade., Instead, I braced for the impact as she closed the distance between us with alarming speed. She aimed a powerful strike at my midsection, her fist like a battering ram crashing into my ribs with bone-jarring force.

As her other fist collided with my jaw, a sharp burst of pain shot through my face and down my neck. Her blows were relentless, each one landing with precision and force.

One of the men tumbled into the woman, giving me a moment of reprieve. She shoved the man forward and turned back to me.

With a quick feint to the left, I caught her off guard and delivered a series of rapid punches that forced her back. She stumbled, dazed by the unexpected assault. Seizing the opportunity I twirled in the air, landing a kick to her face that sent her spiraling backward. My body landed on the ground with a *thud* and I grunted.

"Watch out!" A man's voice hollered at me as I turned to see one of the other contenders charging at me. At the last second, I leapt to my feet and blocked his right hook. He kneed me in the stomach and I coughed, doubling over. Gritting my teeth, I channeled pain into strength, driving my elbow into his side. He doubled over, gasping for air, and I didn't waste a moment before tackling him to the ground. Each punch leeched more blood from his face until he stopped moving. His chest rising and falling just enough to know he still breathed.

All I saw was red. The voices of the arena were a soft murmur to the blood pounding in my ears.

I wasn't going to kill anyone. Not today, not if I could help it.

The man who warned me earlier yelled at me again. "Arie! Stop! What are you doing?"

There was that name again. Why did he call me that? I turned around, looking to the crowd for the man but a brawl in the stands kept me from figuring out who it was.

A primal scream rumbled behind me and I whirled around just in time to be slammed into from the side. The final contender and I rolled to the ground. His grip was like a vice around my throat, cutting off my air supply as I fought for breath.

My nails dug into his arm and my legs kicked with a furious abandon.

Just when I felt the tendrils of unconsciousness creeping in, an ache grew in my chest. No . . . not an ache. What was that? It felt . . . like power. Raw and unrelenting power that bubbled beneath the surface.

What was this?

With a surge of newfound strength, I drew on the power as

though it was something I did every day. It came easy, like I'd done it my entire life. A burst of energy erupted from my core, throwing the other contenders off me and sending them crashing into the metal bars of the cage.

Gasps rippled through the crowd as I staggered forward, feeling the energy crackling like lightning seeking ground. The crowd feel silent, their expressions a mix of awe and fear.

I looked around the cage at the three contenders and my heart wrenched in my chest. Had I just . . . were they . . . hells, what had I done? My hands shook and I swallowed down bile. I'd only meant to knock them out but none of them moved. Their chest didn't rise.

"Arie!" The man from earlier pushed through the crowd. His long hair cascaded down broad shoulders, and a beard covered his face. Worry etched in his face as he grabbed hold of the metal bars.

"We have to get you out of here."

"Who are you and why do you keep calling me 'Arie'?" I asked.

"It's me, Hook. Er—Ulrich."

"Congratulations to our new winner!" the voice on the loudspeaker roared.

I turned around to find Tibault walking into the ring. His eyes narrowed on Ulrich and nodded to the two people in robes who grabbed him and tugged him out of the arena.

"Take your godsdamn hands off me" He roared as he tried to fend them off.

"Who was that?" I asked.

Tibault tugged me out of the ring, the crowd's applause fading into the background as people patted my back and offered congratulations. But my mind couldn't shake the image of that man.

Why did it feel like I knew him? Like our paths had crossed before, though I couldn't place when or how.

A strange pang of loss washed over me, the feeling so sudden and sharp that it made my chest tighten. I wanted to remember but the memory remained just out of reach, slipping through my fingers like sand.

As I stepped out of the Pits, cool night air hit me like a wave, clearing my head from the chaos of the fight. Tibault led me through winding alleys and dimly lit streets, my mind still reeling from the mysterious encounter.

"Who was that and why did he keep calling me 'Arie'?"

Tibault whirled around and pointed a finger at me. "What the hells were you thinking, getting yourself thrown into the pit? You could have died, Rose."

"But I didn't." Only because of that raw power that had come from somewhere deep within me. "And will you please answer my questions?"

"I don't know," Curiosity crept into the cracks of Tibault's gaze. "Thousands of people enter this arena from all over, he probably just mistook you for someone else." Tibault grabbed my shoulders, his face inches from mine. "You can't do something like that again, do you hear me?"

I nodded. Why was he so concerned about me now? Hells, he was the one who had brought me there in the first place.

We walked back to the castle in silence, which was fine. My thoughts were consumed with Ulrich and the power I'd used in the cage. I didn't quite buy Tibaults claim that the strange man thought I was someone else. The way he looked at me . . . like a man who had found his lost love. Could he have been someone from my past?

But that didn't explain who the hells Arie was and why the name felt . . . familiar.

Then the magic—the energy, the power, whatever it was—had surged through me like a current, both foreign and familiar at once. An old friend, always there, hidden beneath my skin, and waiting for the right moment to surface. And yet, when I wielded it, there was a dissonance, a whisper of something just out of reach, as if I were grasping at a memory that refused to fully form. The sensation unsettled me, but I knew I couldn't afford to dwell on it now. Answers would come in time, but at this moment, I needed rest. My body ached, my thoughts were tangled, and sleep—however fleeting—was the only reprieve I could allow myself.

10

THE LOST PRINCE
ULRICH

"You were reckless," Robin hissed, his voice a sharp whisper that cut through the air.

"I had to do something," I snapped back, jaw tight. The taste of smoke and blood still clung to the back of my throat, the roar of the crowd ringing in my ears. I hadn't meant to speak but seeing her, standing in that ring, had torn something loose inside me.

Gods, she had been a fucking *masterpiece* in the ring.

I'd foolishly hoped the sound of my voice, the familiarity of my presence, would have stirred something in her. Would have made her *remember*.

I could still see her—sharp, feral, deadly. The way she moved, her body a weapon honed by instinct rather than memory. There had been a flicker of something when our eyes met, a hesitation that told me I hadn't been wrong to try. That beneath whatever had been done to her, Arie was still in there, fighting her way back.

Robin grabbed my arm and yanked me into the shadows, his grip iron tight. "We were there to *observe*, Ulrich. You have no idea who you're messing with."

I scoffed, shaking him off as we turned down another alley. "Don't patronize me, Robin. I know exactly who I'm dealing with."

His jaw tensed, eyes flashing. "Do you? Because from where I'm standing, you just painted a target on our backs."

I ran a hand through my hair, exhaling sharply. Maybe he was right. Maybe I *had* just made things worse. But seeing her in that ring, knowing she was under Queen Gemma's spell . . .

A heavy silence stretched between us, broken only by the distant echo of footsteps approaching from the main street.

Robin exhaled through his nose, rubbing a hand over his face. He lowered his voice. "We need to be careful. If Gemma and her Brotherhood find out what we're trying to do—"

"I know," I muttered.

Robin's expression darkened, but after a beat, he softened. "She hesitated," he admitted. "When she saw you. I think you can get through to her if we try again."

Hope sparked in my chest, quick and volatile. "Then we still have a chance."

Robin didn't respond, but he didn't argue either. That was something.

I folded my arms and leveled a look at him, my voice low but firm. "Tell me something, Robin. You're supposed to be one of her assassins. An Elder, no less. But you're also working against her. How the hell are you pulling that off?"

Robin didn't answer right away. His expression darkened, a flicker of something unreadable in his gaze. He exhaled sharply, rubbing a hand down his face as if the weight of my question was just another stone added to the mountain he already carried.

"Not all of the assassins belong to Gemma," he finally said. "Just like not all the Elders think highly of her."

I narrowed my eyes, searching his face for any sign of deception. "Then why not take her out already? If you have people backing you, why the delay? Why let her go on ruling through fear?"

Robin let out a bitter chuckle. "You think it's that simple?" His voice was quiet, edged with something sharp and exhausted all at once. "You know what she's capable of. What happens in the Pits is only a fraction of the power she wields. We've been trying to find a way to counter it for years." He swallowed hard, gaze flicking toward the shadows like he could still see the ghosts of the past lurking there. "She took our loved ones. The ones she didn't kill, she turned into those monsters you saw. She has leverage over too many of us."

My jaw tightened. I thought of the soulless creatures in the pits, the twisted remnants of men and women who had once lived, fought, and loved. I thought of Arie—alone in that cursed place, believing she had no one left.

Robin ran a hand through his hair, his shoulders tensing. "The Hoods—assassins from the Brotherhood who are still loyal to me—and I have been working in the shadows, sabotaging her where we can. But as far as Gemma knows, it's the rebels causing her problems." His lips curled into something like amusement, but the bitterness in his tone undercut it. "That's why she's so desperate to wipe them out. She thinks they're the greatest threat to her reign. Not us."

"Then what's the plan?" I pressed. "How do we stop her? How do we get Arie back?"

Robin's eyes locked onto mine, and for a moment, there was a flicker of hesitation—like he wasn't sure if he should trust me with the answer.

Then—

Voices.

We tensed, sinking deeper into the shadows.

"I say we throw her back in tomorrow," one of them grunted.

My blood turned to ice.

"See if she can handle a real test," another voice sneered, filled with cruel amusement.

Robin's expression shifted—cold, controlled, but there was a flicker of something beneath it. Fury.

My fist clenched.

Robin caught my expression and grabbed my wrist before I could move. "Don't," he warned.

I swallowed hard, forcing myself to stay put. We needed a plan. Charging in without one would get us both killed.

The other one laughed. "She'd probably kick your ass, too. Did you see the magic?"

The guards' voices faded as they rounded a distant corner, leaving me vibrating with restless energy. Robin released my wrist slowly, as if expecting me to bolt after them like an untrained hound.

"I'm not waiting, Robin. I'm going after her."

Robin blocked my path, moonlight carving shadows across his scowl. "That's not going to save her. It will only result in both of your deaths. She doesn't even remember you."

"You just said—"

"That doesn't mean I believe charging in there is the answer." His finger jabbed at my chest. "One wrong move and Gemma will bury whatever's left of her mind and skin you alive. That's how she works."

I stepped into him, close enough to taste his breath—bitter ale and cloves. "Then you come up with a better plan."

Robin nodded. "There's someone who I think can help us," he muttered. "He can be a bit . . . unreliable, but he's good people."

My pulse spiked. I didn't want to trust anyone else with

Arie's life. There were already too many people involved, I would have better luck doing this alone.

"I know where your head is at, Hook. I've been there, but the best thing you can do for Arie is to do this right. You don't know the queen like I do. I can help, so let me."

I sighed, conceding his point.

"Fine. I—"

Robin lifted a hand, stopping me. His expression darkened. "It comes at a cost."

I met his gaze, unflinching. "Name it."

"Your sword," he said, voice quiet but firm.

I froze. The cutlass at my hip grew heavier, as if it knew what was coming. This blade had been with me since the day I set foot in Neverland, forged in fire and gifted by Pascal himself. Every Lost Boy had one, but this—this was mine. A part of me.

My fingers tightened around the hilt, my stomach twisting at the thought of parting with it.

For Arie, I would give everything.

"Done," I rasped before reason could claw its way back up my throat.

Robin's eyes widened, surprise flickering across his face before he nodded. "Meet me at the docks when the midnight bells toll."

I exhaled sharply, feeling the weight of my choice settle in my bones. Whatever awaited me beyond those docks, there was no turning back now.

"How are they?" I asked Doc, stopping beside him as he leaned against the ship's railing. The lantern light flickered over his face, sharpening the exhaustion in his features.

I realized this was the first moment I'd had to truly sit back and talk with Doc since my return to Neverland.

"Not well," he admitted, running a rough hand through his unkempt hair. "But they're alive—for now." His jaw tightened. "The sickness hasn't changed, but something's off. The ones who still seem healthy, if they leave the ship every few hours, they stay that way. But those already sick . . . it doesn't matter what we do." His fingers curled against the wood, knuckles paling. "The Red Moon is closer, Ulrich. We don't have much time." He lifted his gaze to mine, shadowed with worry. "Have you found Arie?"

I let out a slow breath, the scent of salt and sickness clinging to the air between us.

"I have." The words felt heavy on my tongue. "And it's . . . complicated."

Doc studied me, searching for more, but I gave him nothing. His lips pressed into a firm line, his shoulders squared with quiet frustration.

"You know, you can leave them with Keenan for a day and visit your—"

Doc threw a hand up. "No. They're better off not knowing I'm here. We don't want to put them in danger."

I sighed but I respected his answer. He was right, we didn't need to put targets on anyone else's backs. When we stopped Gemma and the Elders, we'd visit them again.

"I'm going to see someone who might be able to help," I said, gripping the hilt of my cutlass like it could steady me. I caught a glimpse of Robin on the docks and took that as my sign. "I'll be back soon to check on everyone."

"Ulrich." Doc caught my arm, his grip firm, his expression grave. "Be careful. This is bigger than we realized. You may be walking into a web of deception. The Enchanted Realm is a place of masks, and not all of them are made of silk and gold.

Keep your eyes open, or you'll end up playing someone else's game without even knowing it."

I nodded, but the tension in my stance didn't ease. I turned away before he could say anything else. The deck groaned under my boots as I made my way toward the docks, the weight of every lost second pressing against my ribs.

The midnight bells hadn't tolled yet, but Robin already waited in the shadows. His arms were crossed, his expression unreadable as the lantern light cast sharp angles across his face.

"You're early," he noted.

"So are you," I countered.

He huffed a quiet laugh before nodding toward the darkened streets. "Come on. We don't have time to waste."

I followed him, winding through the narrow alleys where the scent of brine and damp wood clung to the air. But the further we went, the more it changed—soured. The briny sharpness turned thick and putrid. A different kind of rot settled at the back of my throat, making my stomach churn.

Robin stopped at the mouth of a crumbling tunnel, half-hidden behind an abandoned cart. The stone walls were slick with moisture, the air heavy with decay.

"This is the best way in?" I muttered, holding my coat over my nose as we waded into ankle-deep filth.

Robin shot me a look over his shoulder, unfazed by the sludge soaking into his boots. "Not everyone gets to travel in luxury, Hook. Some of us make do."

I scowled but didn't argue. My days of luxury had ended long ago, but even as a pirate, I'd never had to trek through a sewer just to meet with the right people..

Robin moved ahead with purpose, his steps sure despite the uneven ground. I tried to follow his lead, but I nearly lost my footing when something—not just water—sloshed beneath my boot.

I gagged, then Robin chuckled under his breath but didn't slow. "Relax, princess. We're almost there."

After an eternity of winding through the tunnels, he stopped in front of a rusted metal door, nearly indistinguishable from the surrounding stone. Without hesitation, he knocked twice, then three times in quick succession.

A moment passed. Then another.

Shifting, I glanced down the tunnel behind us. "Robin—"

The door groaned as hidden mechanisms unlocked. With a sharp *clank*, it swung inward.

Robin stepped inside, and I followed, hesitating briefly before the door sealed shut behind us.

The change was instant.

The stench of sewage faded, replaced by the scent of burning oil and earth. The tunnel widened into a dimly lit stairwell, spiraling downward into darkness.

Robin descended first, his boots echoing against the metal steps. I followed, hand resting on the hilt of my cutlass out of instinct. The air grew warmer the further we went, the flickering glow of lanterns casting jagged shadows on the walls.

The tunnel opened up—into a city.

I stopped at the threshold, taking it in.

Buildings of stone and metal stretched across the cavern, stacked atop one another in a deliberately chaotic sprawl. Rickety bridges connected rooftops, and pulleys dangled from overhead platforms, carrying crates between levels. Lanterns flickered along narrow pathways, illuminating vendors selling goods from makeshift stalls. People moved through the streets with purpose, dressed in patchwork clothing, some armed, some watching us with wary eyes.

Robin glanced at me, smirking at my stunned silence. "Welcome to the Underbelly."

I turned to Robin. "Does the Queen know about this?"

He didn't even glance at me as he started down a narrow pathway. "No."

That gave me pause. The Queen's spies were everywhere. There wasn't a whisper in this kingdom that didn't eventually reach her ears. And yet, *this*—an entire underground city—had escaped her notice?

"How?" I asked, quickening my steps to catch up.

Robin's smirk was sharp. "Because we built it where no one thought to look." He gestured at the city around us. "It took years—me, the Hoods, and witches from the rebel groups. We laid the groundwork in the sewers, expanding passageways where we could, creating interlinking tunnels that run beneath half the capital. Each door has its own knock code, and no two are the same. It keeps out the uninvited."

I glanced back at the door we had entered through. From this side, it looked like part of the stone wall, nearly invisible unless you knew what to look for.

Robin continued, leading me down a winding stairwell that opened up to another level below. "There are entrances all over the city, each disguised. Some doors open through old grates; others are hidden behind crumbling buildings. We've got escape routes, supply lines, and safe houses all linked through this network. If the Queen's hounds ever get too close, we can vanish."

I studied him as he spoke. He wasn't just some washed-up assassin running from his past—this was *his* domain, something he had built from the shadows while the Queen played her games above.

"How do you keep it from collapsing?" I asked, eyeing the stonework.

"The witches wove reinforcement spells into the foundation. As long as the enchantments hold, this place will stand."

"And if they don't?"

Robin shot me a sideways glance. "Then we drown in our own filth."

Charming.

He led me deeper into the city, past a group of children darting through the streets, their laughter echoing against the cavern walls. A blacksmith worked in an open-air forge, the clang of metal against metal ringing through the Underbelly. A woman with a thick braid and a pair of curved daggers watched us from a balcony above, her gaze sharp as a hawk's.

"You've built an army," I murmured, taking it all in.

Robin led me through the winding streets of the Underbelly, his steps sure and measured, while I took in the sheer *scope* of what they had built. Even I had to admit, it was impressive.

"This," Robin said, gesturing at the city around us, "this is how we win the war."

I scoffed. "By living in shit?"

Robin barely spared me a glance. "By being *smarter* than her."

I frowned but let him continue.

"She controls the surface, the courts, the armies. She thrives on power and fear, always watching, always listening. But this?" He swept his arm out again. "She doesn't see *this*. Doesn't even suspect it exists. And that is why we need to tread lightly."

I could hear the weight in his voice. The truth of it. The Queen's strength lay in knowing the rebel's next move before her enemies acted. But an entire city beneath her feet? Hidden right under her nose? That was dangerous in a way she wouldn't expect.

Robin led me deeper, away from the market and toward a quieter section of the city where the streets grew narrower. The houses here were built directly into the cavern walls, their doors reinforced metal, their windows small and heavily shuttered.

He stopped at a modest iron door, rapped his knuckles

against it in a quick, deliberate pattern. A few moments later, a latch scraped open, and the door swung inward.

An older black gentleman stood in the doorway, his graying beard neatly trimmed, his warm brown eyes sweeping over Robin first before settling on me with quiet scrutiny. He was broad-shouldered, dressed in a simple tunic and dark trousers, his hands calloused from years of work. He exuded the kind of quiet strength that made a man pause before speaking out of turn.

Robin gave a respectful nod. "Kaelryn."

Kaelryn eyed me for a beat longer before stepping aside. "Come in."

The home was small but well-kept, old books and burnt wood filling the air. A single lantern flickered on the wooden table, casting long shadows across the stone walls. Various tools and vials were carefully arranged on the shelves, alongside a few rolled-up maps and loose parchment filled with scrawled notes.

Robin shut the door behind us, locking it with two heavy bolts before turning back to Kaelryn. "We need your expertise."

Kaelryn sighed, rubbing a hand over his beard. "I figured as much." He flicked his gaze to me again. "And who's this?"

Robin smirked. "Captain Hook."

Kaelryn's brow lifted slightly, as if he recognized the name. "Hmph. Thought you'd be taller."

The room felt smaller under Kaelryn's scrutiny, the flickering lanterns casting his deep-set eyes in shifting pools of shadow. He sat behind a rickety wooden table, his fingers drumming against the wood.

His gaze flicked between me and Robin, unreadable, calculating. Then, finally, he spoke.

"Payment first." His voice was gravel and smoke, edged with the confidence of a man who knew we needed him more than he needed us. "I don't do charity for just anyone."

I gritted my teeth, my fingers twitching toward the cutlass, instinctively wanting to feel its weight in my hand. The blade had been by my side for years, a part of me. Reluctantly, I unclasped the leather strap that held it in place and drew it free, the hilt cold against my palm. I placed it on the table, the metal clinking softly against the wood. Every part of me wanted to take it back, to keep it close, but I forced myself to let go.

"There. Shall we continue?" I asked.

Kaelryn's smirk was slow and sharp as he picked up the sword, swiping it through the air before setting it on the table. "Generous," he mused. "Very well. Speak."

I didn't waste time. I told him everything that had happened since we lost Arie, leaving out the curse and all the people on the *Dutchman*. He didn't need to know those things. I had no intention of asking for his help with that when the only weapon I had was Arie's dagger.

His reaction was immediate. His smirk faltered, just for a second, before something unreadable crossed his face. He exhaled sharply through his nose, leaning back in his chair.

"I've met her," he admitted. His fingers curled into a loose fist, knuckles white against the strain. "I offered her my help." He hesitated, jaw working, before shaking his head. "We'd come to an agreement, but the Queen got to her."

A slow, heavy silence filled the room.

The words *the Queen got to her* lodged themselves under my ribs like a rusted dagger. I could barely unclench my jaw to speak, my pulse hammering at my throat.

"How did you meet her, exactly?" I forced the words out, each one a knife's sharp stab in my chest.

Kaelryn shifted in his chair. "This," he lifted the cutlass, "Isn't enough payment for that story. But I will tell you Arie is the key we need to end this war. She's well known in the rebel community. Our army can stand against Gemma's but it must be Arie who deals the final blow."

I raised a brow. "She is?"

"It's true," Robin continued. "What happened to the Leviathan and the abilities she has is known throughout the Enchanted Realm. But it's more than that. She has the power to stop Gemma for good."

Kaelryn didn't respond immediately. Instead, he watched me—really watched me. His head tilted slightly, his dark eyes narrowing as if he wanted to see past my skin, past the man standing before him and into my soul.

The silence stretched too long.

"So, this is the information that cost me my weapon?"

Kaelryn laughed. "No, but I am the person who runs this city. I have the ability to send the rebel army above ground. If you're going to take on Gemma and her shadow assassins, you're going to need my help."

His gaze flicked from my face to my stance, to the way my hand clenched and unclenched at my sides. A slow frown tugged at his lips, his fingers tapping against the tabletop once more.

Then, as if something finally clicked into place, his expression shifted. "What did you say your name was again?"

I squared my shoulders, meeting his gaze head-on. "Hook," I said, voice steady. Then, after a beat, I added, "Though my real name is Ulrich."

Kaelryn's breath hitched.

His entire body went rigid, his chair creaking as he pushed back slightly. The color drained from his face, his lips parting like he wanted to speak but had forgotten how. He took a step back, then another, his wide eyes locked onto me as though I'd just grown a second head.

"Robin, do you realize who this is?" Kaelryn hissed.

Robin's brows furrowed, and his gaze flicked from me to Kaelryn and back again.

"The lost prince." The words fell from his lips in a whisper, like a prayer, like something that shouldn't exist but did.

A strange, charged silence filled the space between us, the weight of his words pressing down on my chest like a storm waiting to break.

Robin's expression morphed from one of cold resolve to something more vulnerable, his eyes widening in disbelief. His face paled, and for a moment, I thought I might have been imagining the rawness in his gaze.

"I—I never . . . I never thought . . ." His voice faltered, and his gaze fell to the table as if searching for something to hold onto. "The lost prince."

I turned to Kaelryn, confusion knotting my stomach. "What the hell are you two talking about?"

Kaelryn didn't answer right away, his gaze shifting between Robin and me, an odd glimmer of recognition flickering in his eyes as he studied me. But then he straightened, his fingers brushing a lock of dark hair from his face, his expression turning solemn. He took a breath and began, his voice calm but laced with a weight I could feel deep in my bones.

"The VonWhite family," he began, drawing the name out slowly as if savoring the bitter history that came with it. "The Royal Family. King John and Queen Sydney . . . They were loved, you know. A rare thing in monarchs, but they cared for their people—truly cared. They traveled often, venturing through the kingdom to see to their people's needs, and they were adored for it."

He paused, his voice thickening, and for a brief moment, his eyes lost focus, as if he were looking far beyond the present moment.

"They were traveling through the Enchanted Forest when

they were killed along with their two children, Ulrich and Clayton. Vanished without a trace." His voice dropped to a whisper. "At least that's what we were told."

My jaw dropped. *What in all the seven seas*? My grip tightened on the table, the rough wood digging into my palms as the weight of his words settled over me.

"Gods, you look so much like him." Kaelryn grinned for a moment before it faltered. "Queen Gemma," his voice grew colder, "she was their advisor. And after their death, seized the throne. She claimed it was rebels—traitors who'd killed them for their gold. She told everyone she would get justice for them. Which is why the war with the rebels started. A false war."

I felt a chill run down my spine. "And you never thought to question it?" I asked, my voice cutting through the thick tension like a blade. "You just let her take over?"

Kaelryn's eyes sharpened, but there was a sorrow in them that deepened the weight of his words. "We did question it. We tried to find proof, but there was nothing. No one would listen. Gemma's grip on the throne was too strong. She manipulated everything, made sure that anyone who posed a threat was silenced before they could speak. Her magic is strong and her influence even stronger. She turned the city against the rebels."

"She found a way to steal the majority of my assassins." Robin gritted his teeth.

"Yes," Kaelryn said. "And now, we've lived under her rule for far too long."

"No one had the power to take her down—not then." Robin cut in. "But now . . . now, with you back, Ulrich . . ." His voice softened, becoming almost reverent. "You and Arie are the keys. The people will rally behind you. They'll finally have someone they can believe in. Arie can take down Gemma and you can take back the throne."

The walls closed in on me, the weight of the past pressing

down on my chest, suffocating me. I'd never been prepared for this. To hear of my family's death, to hear that I could be the one to right the wrongs of a kingdom lost under the grip of a tyrant...

My memories of this place, of my birth parents had been lost to the years and Pascal's magic.

Pascal. Anger raged through me at the thought of my best and longest friend lying to me all these years, keeping such a secret from me. I'd only known Doc and his brothers. I'd thought they were the only family Clay and I had. Pascal never told me any of this.

"I—I can't do this," I muttered, shaking my head, my thoughts spiraling out of control. "I'm not . . . I'm not the prince. I wouldn't know the first thing about ruling a kingdom."

"Listen to me." Kaelryn's voice was sharp, pulling me back from the abyss of panic. "You're the one they've been waiting for. The blood of the VonWhite family runs through your veins. You're not some stranger to these people. You are the rightful heir."

"No!" I snapped, my voice rising in frustration. "I'm no prince. I'm a damn pirate."

The weight of everything—of the crown, of the kingdom, of the rebellion, of the promise that was now mine to carry—pressed down on me like a thousand tons of stone. My mind raced, and the pressure suffocated me under its tonnage.

Robin stepped forward, placing a hand on my shoulder. "Ulrich, this is our chance. We can finally take her down. You don't have to do this alone. We'll fight for you, fight for what's right."

I shook my head again, panic rising in my chest like an uncontrollable tide. "I can't. I don't know how to lead a kingdom. I don't know how to be a prince. I only know how to kill, how to pillage, and to terrorize."

How to be a Lost One.

Kaelryn studied me for a moment, then stepped back, his expression shifting into something softer, more understanding. "You don't have to know everything now. What matters is that you're here. The people need a symbol, someone to look to, someone who can show them that they aren't forgotten."

But I wasn't sure I could be that symbol. I wasn't sure I could carry that weight.

I turned to leave, my chest tight, my mind too scattered to focus. The thoughts whirled like a storm, chaos battering against my insides. As I reached the door, the sound of Kaelryn's voice calling out to me faded, lost to the storm of thoughts.

II

QUEEN'S GAMBIT
GEMMA

"Just a little longer."

The words barely carried past my lips, swallowed by the stillness of my chambers. My grip tightened around the stem of an ornate goblet bedecked in jewels. One of the gems' sharp edges dug into my palm, and then blood seeped from the wound, but I ignored it. The pain was a welcome distraction from the turmoil raging within me. I stared at the dark red liquid within, my reflection rippling in the surface, distorted, like the past I refused to drown in.

I had spent a lifetime waiting for this.

The fire in the hearth burned low, its embers pulsing with a soft glow that flickered across the velvet-draped walls. My sanctuary, my prison, a home I had built for myself across decades of careful strategy and sacrifice.

Sacrifice.

The word curled through my mind like smoke.

I had done what was necessary. I had bled for this kingdom, buried my heart alongside the ones I had lost, molded myself into something greater, something stronger.

All because a fucking god destroyed my life.

I glanced at the clock on the mantel. The hands ticked away the seconds, counting down to the moment everything would change.

Did the people of this city honestly think I wanted to rule? That I enjoyed sitting on this throne, weaving my web of power while the people whispered my name like a curse?

Fools.

I never wanted a kingdom. I wanted retribution.

But power was the only way to secure it.

The royals had been getting too close, their curiosity turning to suspicion, their whispers sharpening into accusations. They had begun to unravel the truth, to question the shadows I moved within, the deals I made behind their backs.

One by one, I unraveled their fragile dynasty, watching as their polished facades crumbled beneath my hands. It had been too easy. And when my assassins had ended them, there had been no one left to challenge me.

So, I took the throne.

Not for power, not for greed, but because it was the only way to ensure that no one could stop what was coming.

And Arie—sweet, oblivious Arie—was the key.

The pawn I had been waiting for.

For years, I scoured the land for someone like her, someone with the right blood, the right abilities—someone who could do what I could not. The Celestial Plains had been locked to me for too long, its gates guarded by a force I could not break. But with Arie . . .

With Arie, I would finally be able to breach their gates. With enough souls I could make my way inside and take back what was rightfully mine.

This time, however, I had to take extra measures. I refused to make the same mistake I made with her mother. Ursa's ambition was too great . . . too greedy in her endeavors. So Arie would continue drinking the tonics until the supply dried up. I swirled the liquid in the chalice, considering.

Her spirit and will... it reminded me of...

I shook my head. I wasn't going there.

When Jameson hadn't been able to break her, it forced my hand to something more drastic. I knew it would take a little time, but the damn pirate kept remembering things sooner than she should have. Already the elixir ran low but making more would take time I didn't have.

I suspected the resilience had more to do with the blood running through her veins than anything else. *Godsdamn fucking bitch ass mermaids.*

Hopefully, I'd have enough until the ball. The masquerade was set. The final souls would be collected. The energy gathered. Then, and only then, could I take the final step toward what had been stolen from me.

The mirror in Neverland had been damaged when Jameson brought Arie here, so my way back was compromised. I had some ideas on how to get there without it, but first I had to focus on getting the last souls. It could have been anyone really, any would suffice, but I didn't want just *any*. Those fucking Elders who thought they controlled me, who questioned my motives and moves daily.

I inhaled deeply, steadying myself before striding toward the mirror against the far wall. The gilded frame shimmered in the candlelight, its carvings twisting like golden vines, but the glass itself held no reflection—only darkness, deep and endless.

"Is everything still on schedule?" My voice was smooth, controlled, but there was an edge beneath it, the weight of decades pressing against my ribs.

The mirror rippled, sluggish at first, before a voice—velvet and amused—answered.

"The path is set, the pieces in motion . . . but the winds shift, my queen. A new shadow falls upon your destiny."

A frown tugged at my lips. "What does that mean?" My fingers grazed the frame, cold despite the firelight.

The mirror pulsed, reluctant to speak, before the voice murmured, "Someone has entered the city. Someone who could take everything away."

A chill curled through my spine.

Impossible.

I had spent years ensuring no one could challenge me. Every threat had been erased before it could take shape, every loose end tied and burned. I had woven my future too tightly for it to unravel now.

"Who?" My voice sharpened, cutting through the thick silence of the room.

The mirror darkened further, the swirling depths shifting, forming something—*someone*—just beyond reach. A phantom of an image, never quite taking shape.

Then—

A knock at the door.

I swore, my pulse stilling, the moment shattered. The mirror's surface smoothed into nothingness, leaving only darkness staring back at me.

But the unease remained.

"Enter," I called, masking the anger in my voice.

The heavy doors groaned open, and Elder Wulf stepped inside. His broad frame cast a long shadow in the dim torchlight. His eyes—sharp, watchful—locked onto me with something unreadable. Wulf had once commanded King John's army. He was and still is feared by many and had been a loyal *pet*. Until I got my claws into him. Now he was mine to use as I pleased.

"My queen," he greeted, his voice a measured rumble. "We need to talk."

I lifted my chin, forcing a slow smile as I turned to face him.

"Yes," I murmured, the firelight carving sharp angles across my face. "We do."

You always come back to me," I whispered, my voice a breath against his lips.

Wulf's fingers dug into my hips, strong and possessive, his body pressing mine against the cold marble of the vanity. I felt the heat of him, the raw need coiled in every muscle as his chest rose and fell with heavy, uneven breaths.

"Because you always call for me," he rasped.

I did.

Not because I needed him, or because I wanted him.

But because my body still remembered how to feel, even when my heart did not.

I dragged my nails down his chest, slow and teasing, watching the way his muscles tensed beneath my touch. Wulf was built for war—scarred, hardened, brutal. A blade honed over time.

But here, with me, he burned.

His mouth found my throat, lips brushing against the rapid pulse there before trailing lower, nipping at my collarbone. My head tipped back, a soft sigh escaping me, though it was more satisfaction than surrender. He wanted me breathless. He wanted to *ruin* me.

But I was already broken.

His hands slipped beneath my robe, fingers skimming the silk and baring my skin inch by inch. He exhaled sharply, a quiet curse spilling from his lips as he traced the curve of my waist, the swell of my hips.

"Do you even think of me when I'm not between your thighs?" he muttered against my skin, voice thick with something unspoken.

"Does it matter?"

A growl rumbled in his throat before his mouth was on mine, claiming, demanding. I let him take, let him pour whatever he thought this was into the kiss, but my fingers tangled in his hair, pulling hard enough to make him *hurt*.

Pain and pleasure blurred in the way his body crushed against mine, in the way his hands gripped me with bruising force. There was nothing gentle about this—no tenderness, no love.

Only need.

Only hunger.

He lifted me with ease, setting me on the vanity's cool surface, spreading my legs as he pressed himself between them. I gasped against his mouth, arching as he dragged his teeth over the sensitive skin of my throat, as his hands traced my thighs in teasing, torturous strokes.

He brushed the robe from my shoulders, then tossed it to the side. He pulled back slightly, biting his lip as his eyes trailed over my body.

I wanted this over.

Wanted the heat, the rush, the sharp edge of pleasure and then *nothing*.

He had to have sensed it—the shift in me, the impatience—because he didn't waste another breath before pushing into me with a deep, guttural curse.

I bit my lip, swallowing the sound threatening to escape as he moved, as he *took*. My nails raked down his back, drawing faint red lines across already-scarred skin. His grip on me tightened, hands holding me in place as he drove deeper, faster.

The room blurred at the edges, the golden glow of candlelight flickering against the high ceiling. My breath hitched, pleasure tightening in my spine, coiling—*almost—almost—*

I shattered.

I came with a sharp inhale, my body shuddering, back arching as heat flooded through me. Wulf followed moments later, a rough, broken groan spilling from his lips as he buried himself inside me one last time.

And then, just as quickly, it was over.

I pushed against his chest, and he stepped back, his breathing ragged, his body thrumming with the aftershocks. But I was already gone, already slipping off the vanity and reaching for my robe.

"That's it?" Wulf muttered, running a hand through his damp hair.

I tied the silk belt with a measured calm, my fingers steady. "What else did you expect?"

His jaw tightened, a flicker of something raw in his gaze. I had seen it before, had ignored it every time. He wanted more. "You always do this," he said, voice low.

"And yet you never refuse. I'm not that much of a monster, Wulf. You can say no."

Silence stretched between us, thick and tense. Then he exhaled sharply, shaking his head as he reached for his discarded trousers. I watched him dress, my expression unreadable, my mind already shifting to what came next.

"I need you to do something for me."

Wulf scoffed. "Of course you do."

I ignored the bite in his tone. "The mirror has seen someone new in the city. A threat." I turned back to face him, letting my words sink in. "Find them and bring them to me."

Darkness and something *more* flashed in his gaze, a thing I couldn't decipher. "And if they don't come willingly?"

I smiled, slow and cold. "Then make them."

Wulf studied me for a long moment, the flickering light catching in the storm of his eyes. "Who is it?"

"That's what I need you to find out."

He exhaled through his nose, rolling his shoulders before finally pushing off the bed. The sheets pooled around his waist before he stood, unabashed in his nakedness as he reached for his discarded trousers.

"You expect me to hunt someone I know nothing about," he muttered, fastening the buckle at his waist.

"You're the Huntsman, are you not?" I tilted my head, feigning curiosity. "Or have you lost your touch?"

His lips pressed into a thin line. I knew the insult would land—knew it would dig into that quiet, simmering pride of his.

Wulf had never failed me before.

I doubted he'd start now.

He pulled his shirt over his head, tugging the laces tight before running a hand through his hair. "And if I find them?"

I stepped forward, trailing my fingers over his bare forearm, the barest ghost of a touch. "I'll take care of the rest."

His eyes flickered to my lips, just for a moment, before he schooled his features into something unreadable.

"Fine," he muttered, shaking his head.

A victorious smile curled at the edges of my mouth as I stepped away, turning back to the window. The city stretched beyond the palace walls, glowing with lantern light and brimming with secrets.

Soon, I would have everything I needed.

And nothing—not fate, not gods, and certainly not some stranger in my city—would stand in my way.

12
LEARNING THE PAST
ARIE

THE TERRACE WAS STILL COOL FROM THE NIGHT AIR, the morning sun casting a soft, golden glow over the intricate gardens below. I leaned against the stone balcony, my fingers brushing the rough surface, seeking a semblance of grounding. The scent of blooming jasmine lingered on the breeze, though it did little to ease the storm raging inside me.

Who was that man? His voice, sharp and urgent, echoed in my memory, stirring something deep within my chest. *Arie.* He had called me that. But why? It felt as though there was a weight to the word, something familiar but foreign. Like an echo of a memory just beyond reach, slipping away every time I grasped for it. Perhaps he had just mistaken me for someone else like Tibault suggested.

I clenched my fists, frustration bubbling up. *Why can't I remember?* Flashes of images, fragmented and unclear, danced behind my eyes—tall, dark figures reaching out to me, a ship rocking violently in a storm, a crown, a throne, a trident. But none of it made sense. *Were they mine?*

Swallowing the rising panic, I tried to focus. I couldn't let it consume me—not yet, anyway. The fragments were there, floating just out of reach. *I knew I could remember.*

The sound of soft footsteps broke through my thoughts, and I turned just in time to see Ana stepping outside, a tray of food balanced in her hands.

"Breakfast for you, Rose," she said, setting the tray carefully on the small table before me. "And this"—she placed the small familiar chalice beside the food—"the Queen sent this."

I glanced at the chalice. The red liquid inside swirled as if it held more than its simple appearance suggested.

"Thank you, Ana" I said, my voice quiet but sincere, though it betrayed the uncertainty inside me. "Is there . . . anything else? You look like you're waiting for something."

She shook her head, a gentle smile forming on her lips. "No. I'll leave you to your meal."

I nodded absently, my mind already drifting back to the Pits, back to that man's harsh shout. His voice was desperate, urgent—*Arie.* Why had he called me that? Why had it felt like the sound of my name was supposed to spark something within me? Why hadn't it? Every time I tried to push further, to piece the fragments together, they scattered like sand slipping through my fingers.

I was so close to something. I could feel it.

I grabbed the chalice, feeling its weight, the gilded cup chilly against my palm. I pressed it to my lips, the smell faintly herbal with something else—something metallic. It was cold as it slid down my throat, smooth but unsettling.

A warmth spread through me just as the door opened again and Queen Gemma stepped into view. Her eyes, sharp and calculating, landed on me immediately, and a tight smile formed on her lips.

"Ah, Rose," she said, her voice as cold as the wind that

followed her in. "I see you've been drinking the tonic. How does your head feel, are you getting any memories back?"

I swallowed, my fingers tightening around the chalice in my hand.

"My head is fine . . . but the memories are still fragmented," I replied softly, lowering the vial to the table. "I don't remember anything, not really."

Gemma stepped further onto the terrace, her gaze shifting from me to the tray of food. "Memory is a tricky thing," she mused, almost to herself. "Sometimes it takes more than a little tonic to bring it back. Which is why I'd like you to come with me. Perhaps there is more we can do."

Her words hung in the air for a moment before I nodded in agreement. I was eager for answers, and if Gemma had the means to assist, I would follow her without hesitation.

Gemma offered me a smile, one that didn't quite reach her eyes, and gestured for me to follow.

The halls of the castle stretched before us, lined with towering windows that casted the marble floors in morning light. The flickering torches along the walls had been dimmed, allowing the natural glow to take their place. The corridors were quiet at this hour, save for the distant murmur of servants going about their morning duties.

Gemma moved with effortless grace, the train of her dark gown whispering across the polished floor. "I want to show you something," she said, breaking the silence as we approached a large set of double doors, their dark wood engraved with swirling patterns of ivy and celestial symbols.

She pushed the doors open, revealing a grand library bathed in golden light. My breath caught as I stepped inside. It was unlike anything I had ever seen—shelves upon shelves of ancient tomes stretched high into the vaulted ceiling, their spines gilded and worn with age. Chandeliers hung from above, casting flickering light over the deep mahogany tables and plush chairs scattered throughout the space. The scent of old parchment and ink filled the air, mingling with the faint hint of smoke.

Gemma strode inside, trailing her fingers over the spine of a nearby book as she walked. "This library has stood for centuries," she said. "It was once the heart of the castle, a place of knowledge and power."

I followed her deeper into the room, my fingers brushing against the smooth wood of the nearest table. "Has your family always lived here?"

Gemma tilted her head, considering her words carefully. "No. This castle once belonged to the royal family—King John and Queen Sydney," she said, her voice laced with something unreadable. "They were beloved rulers, wise and just. The people adored them and their two beautiful sons."

"What happened to them?" I asked.

Gemma exhaled softly, moving toward a tall window overlooking the sprawling city below. "They died," she said, her voice quieter now. "Years ago, while traveling through the Enchanted Forest. It was a tragedy."

I frowned, an odd sense of unease settling over me. "How did they die?"

She turned to me, her expression unreadable. "Rebels," she said simply.

Gemma was silent for a long moment, then offered me a small, measured smile. "I had been their advisor for many years before they left and after they were gone, to ensure the kingdom didn't fall, I was chosen by the council of Elders to guide us forward."

I glanced around the library, the weight of her words pressing into me. Something about this felt . . . off. There was an untold truth woven into her words, something she wasn't saying.

I swallowed, forcing myself to meet her gaze. "Their children, too?" I asked carefully.

For the briefest moment, something flickered in her eyes—something cold, something dangerous. But it was gone as quickly as it had come. "Yes," she said, turning away once more. "Without them, the royal line ended."

The words sent a strange chill through me, but I couldn't explain why.

I lowered my gaze to the nearest book, my fingers tightening around the leather binding.

She wasn't telling me everything. I didn't need memory or experience to read that.

Gemma's fingers grazed a massive tome bound in cracked leather as we drifted toward a shadowed alcove. Light filtered through stained glass above, fracturing into sapphire and crimson shards across a tapestry draped along the wall. It depicted two towering figures—a giant clad in mountainstone armor and a human knight wreathed in flames—locked in combat above a burning city, their faces contorted in rage. Beneath a bleeding sun, their armies clashed like swarms of ants devouring each other.

"The war began long before my reign." Gemma said, voice echoing faintly in the vaulted space. She plucked one of the books from its shelf. "Giants carved fortresses from living rock in the northern ranges while humans cultivated empires of steel and sorcery in the southern valleys. For centuries, they clashed over territory and power." Her nail traced an illuminated manuscript within the book—a grotesque scene of giants hurtling boulders while human mages split open the earth beneath them. "Blood turned rivers black. Entire cities became tombs."

She snapped the book shut abruptly, its thunderous echo making me flinch.

"When the giant queen perished—" Her gaze cut toward me. "Crushed beneath her own crown during a siege—the realms fell silent. A hollow peace. But fire needs no encouragement to reignite."

"King John sought peace," Gemma gestured toward a faded portrait hanging crookedly nearby—a man with storm-gray eyes and obsidian hair seated on a throne of stone. "He united fae lords and human kings under one banner . . . forced treaties between clans who'd rather feast on each other's hearts than break bread."

A bitter smile flickered across Gemma's face as she drifted past shelves lined with scrolls sealed in obsidian tubes. "His death was . . . convenient for those still hungry for glory and power." Her gown flowed against stone as she paused before a marble pedestal displaying a broken crown fused with charred bone fragments—the relic glowed faintly blue as through cursed veins pulsed within it. "The royal family's carriage was ambushed not by common rebels," she murmured, "but by noble houses who claimed John and Sydney's mercy made them weak."

My throat tightened as I stared at the jagged cracks spider webbing across that bone-white crown.

Gemma's reflection swam in the glass case as I leaned closer.

"Afterward," she continued coldly, "the realm fractured into petty squabbles that drove the realm into madness. It took many years, but I managed to bring back peace. Mostly. The rebels have always been a plague upon this kingdom. They call themselves liberators, but all they bring is chaos. Death. Destruction."

Something about her words stirred a deep, aching sorrow within me.

Gemma took a step closer, her voice softening. "And they took from you, too."

I stiffened. "What?"

Her expression turned solemn. "Your family, Rose."

I swallowed hard. "I don't remember them."

"No," she said gently. "But I do."

My breath hitched as Gemma reached out, lightly brushing a strand of hair from my face. It was a careful, motherly gesture, but her eyes were searching, her expression unreadable.

"You had parents who loved you," she said softly. "Good men. They lived a simple life, far from the corruption of the city. They wanted peace." She let the words settle before tilting her head slightly. "And the rebels slaughtered them for it."

I couldn't breathe. Gemma's words hung heavy in the air, a weight that crushed my chest and made it hard to think. I tried to picture them, tried to remember their faces or the sound of their voices, but there was nothing. Just a void where memories should be.

Shouldn't Gemma's tonic be working by now?

"Why?" I finally managed to croak out, my voice hoarse and raw.

"Because they were loyal," Gemma said bitterly. "They refused to join the rebels' cause, refused to bow to their demands. When the royal line died, many of the soldiers fled. So, they were deemed traitors and executed.

Tears pricked at the corners of my eyes as I stared at the queen, feeling lost and helpless.

"That's why you came here," Gemma continued. "So that the Brotherhood could help you."

She stepped back, her eyes gleaming in the dim light. "Would you like to see what happened to them?"

I hesitated, a thousand emotions warring within me, but in the end, I nodded. No matter how hard it would be to see their deaths, it had to be done. I needed all the help I could get to remember my past. Hopefully seeing them would jog my memory.

Gemma turned and led me through a narrow passage at the back of the library. The air grew cooler as we descended a spiral staircase. At the bottom, she pushed open a heavy wooden door, revealing a smaller, circular chamber.

In the center of the room, a basin sat atop an intricately carved pedestal, filled with water so dark it looked like liquid shadow. Runes glowed faintly along the edges, pulsing with energy.

Gemma gestured toward it. "Come closer."

I did, my heart pounding.

She dipped a chalice into the water, murmuring under her breath. The liquid rippled in the cup as she handed it to me. "Drink."

Slowly, I grabbed the chalice and hesitated. "Is it safe?"

"As safe as the tonic you've been drinking."

I closed my eyes, pressed the chalice to my lips, and let the inky liquid flow down the back of my throat.

The world tilted.

I gasped as everything melted away, the stone walls and torchlight dissolving into something new.

A small, cozy house took shape around us, its wooden beams and stone walls exuding a quiet warmth. The scent of burning wood filled the air, mingling with cinnamon and earth.

The fireplace crackled softly, drawing my attention to the mantel. A row of framed pictures stood along the shelf. Some were slightly tilted, their edges worn, but well cared for. One frame held an old, sepia-toned photograph of two little girls sitting at the edge of a wooden dock. The wood beneath them was worn smooth by time and summer afternoons. I leaned in, squinting, my fingers ghosting over the glass as if touching it might bring the moment back to life. The blonde girl held a fishing rod clumsily in her lap, her small hands gripping it with all her might. Beside her, the girl with crimson hair had her face turned away but—

A jolt ran through me.

It was me.

I opened my mouth to comment when someone with a deep voice laughed. I spun around to find two men sitting near the hearth, their laughter low and familiar, as if they had spent years sharing these moments together. They hadn't been there when I arrived, but it seemed as if they'd been sitting there for hours. One of them had dark hair streaked with silver, his eyes crinkled with warmth. The other appeared younger with golden hair and light eyes.

A deep sense of familiarity settled into my bones. My chest ached.

I knew them. Their names were lost to me though.

The way they looked at each other was nothing short of love. Joy overflowed my heart that these two beautiful men had been my family.

Before I could get the next thought out, the door burst open with a violent crash.

Men in dark, tattered clothing rushed in, their faces obscured by masks. Steel glinted in the firelight as they drew their blades, the air splitting with the sound of shouting.

The elder man pushed up from his chair, "How did you find us?" he started, but his voice was cut off by a blade driving into his stomach.

I choked on a cry, my body frozen.

The younger man lunged forward, grief and rage twisting his features, but he, too, was cut down in seconds.

The fire crackled on, indifferent to the horrors unfolding before it.

My stomach turned, bile rising in my throat as the scene burned itself into my mind, the bodies, the blood splattered across the wooden floor.

The rebels stepped back, sheathing their weapons like this was nothing more than a task completed, another loose end tied. One of them spat on the floor before turning and leaving as swiftly as they had come.

The vision dissolved into blackness, and I found myself back in the circular chamber, gasping for air. Gemma watched with a mixture of sympathy and concern.

I couldn't move.

Gemma's voice whispered beside me, smooth and cold as silk. "This is what they do, Rose. They take. They destroy."

I swallowed back the sob clawing at my throat, my hands trembling.

"You see now," Gemma murmured, her hand resting lightly on my shoulder. "Why they must be stopped."

Tears burned my eyes. I had no memories. No past. But this? This was *real*.

I could feel it in my bones.

The rebels had taken everything from me.

"Where can I find them?" I asked.

A slow, satisfied smile curved on Gemma's lips. She stepped in front of me, her sharp gaze searching my face, as if confirming that the fire had truly settled in my heart.

"So eager," she said softly, circling me. "There is something about you, Rose. Something powerful and inherited."

I shivered as the air around us shifted, a slow, crawling energy awakening beneath my skin.

"You are not ordinary," Gemma continued. "Your parents were gifted—blessed with a power older than any kingdom. And it lives in you."

I swallowed. "What power?"

Gemma reached out, her fingertips ghosting over my wrist, and a sudden pulse of cold ran through me. A thousand whispers brushed against my mind, voices clawing to be heard, to be freed.

"You can take souls," she murmured. "The living. The dead. Those who deserve punishment and those who beg for mercy. You can hold them, shape them. Make them yours."

I sucked in a sharp breath.

The moment she said it, I knew it to be true.

That hollow ache in my chest—it had been there since I'd woken up in my bed after losing my memory. Pulling. Whispering. I had ignored it, convinced myself it was nothing more than the weight of memory loss. But standing here, feeling the power hum beneath my skin like a fire finally given oxygen, I knew the truth. It hadn't been an emptiness. It had been a patient beast, biding its time. And it had shown itself during the fight at the Pits.

Flashes of that fight surged forward, unbidden and sharp. The heat of the arena, the stench of sweat and blood, the roar of the crowd pressing in on all sides. I had fought with instinct alone, muscle memory guiding my hands. But that last fight—when they had cornered me, when I had felt desperation clawing at my throat—I unleashed magic I couldn't explain. I hadn't realized what I'd done.

But now, I understood.

I swallowed hard, my heart still pounding from the weight of what I had just witnessed. The raw fury was a storm gathering inside me, ready to tear through every ounce of restraint I had left. I turned to Gemma, my voice steady despite the storm inside me. "What do you need me to do?" I asked.

"There is a rebel leader hiding in a nearby village. He is one of their strongest, their most cunning. Taking him out will send a message." Her gaze sharpened, her fingers trailing over the spine of a nearby book as she spoke, as if this were a casual conversation rather than the start of something deadly. "You'll be accompanied by the Elites—my best assassins. I want you to see what it is to wield your power against those who deserve it. Take his soul and bring it back to me."

A chill ran down my spine, my stomach souring at her words, but I nodded.

"Do Robin and Tibault know about this?" I asked.

Gemma tilted her head slightly. "No. This mission does not concern them."

I frowned. "But I thought—"

"I need you to meet Frederick at the stables at dusk," she interrupted smoothly, cutting off any further argument. "He will lead the Elites, and he will guide you."

Frederick. Tension eased my shoulders. At least it was someone I knew.

Gemma reached into the folds of her gown and withdrew a thin chain, a small purple stone set in its center. It pulsed faintly, as if it were alive, thrumming with an unseen energy. She held it out to me, her gaze piercing.

"When you take his soul," she said softly, "you must put it into the stone for safekeeping. We cannot risk it wandering. This is not simply about ending them—it is about fixing them. Containing them until they can be turned into something better."

I hesitated, staring at the necklace in her outstretched palm. The gem hummed in response to me, a whisper curling at the edges of my mind.

Something deep within me knew what to do.

"How can we fix them if they're dead?" I asked.

"Magic has a way of righting many wrongs, my dear. Do this and I will show you how we can achieve greatness. We can bring the world to a new potential, to stop the rebels and bring peace. Trust that I can do this for all of us."

I took the chain, clasping it around my neck. The moment it settled against my skin, warmth spread through me, that same aching hollowness in my chest stirring again, but this time, it didn't feel empty. It felt like a chasm waiting to be filled.

"I understand," I murmured.

Gemma's expression softened a fraction, approval flickering in her eyes.

"Good. When you return, we'll discuss this year's ball."

I arched my brow. "Ball?"

She tilted her head, studying me as if debating how much to say. "A masquerade held every year on the anniversary of King John and Queen Sydney's deaths. As a tribute to their legacy."

There was a fleeting note of something unreadable in her voice. But before I could latch onto it, she smoothed her expression into cold and practiced poise.

"It will also serve another purpose," she said. "I have reason to believe some of the Elders are working against me. They've been obstructing my orders, pushing back in ways they think I don't notice." Her eyes darkened. "But I do."

I waited, sensing there was more.

"I've uncovered evidence against Elder Sinclair and Elder Ranta—proof that they are rebel leaders. Their hands are stained with treachery, and they aren't the only ones." Her voice was low, deliberate. "All of them will be together at the ball. They'll believe themselves untouchable, free to scheme under the guise of drunken revelry. That's when they'll slip, and when they do, I need you to take them out and claim their souls, Rose. Can you handle this? Can you do what is necessary for your Queen and kingdom? For your family?"

I straightened, shoulders rolling back as if shaking off the weight of hesitation. I met Gemma's gaze without flinching. "I can handle it," I said, my voice steady. "Consider it done."

A slow, pleased smile curled at the Queen's lips. "Good."

Gemma studied her a moment longer before reaching for a decanter of wine, pouring a glass before turning back to me.

"This will not be a bloodbath, nor a reckless slaughter." She took a measured sip, her eyes glittering over the rim. "Each move must be calculated, precise. I want them removed without suspicion—quietly, methodically."

"Don't you want them to know who's responsible?"

"They'll know." Gemma paused, her face harsh in its severity. "Do not fail me, Rose."

The weight of the command settled around my neck like a noose.

"I won't."

13

BROTHERS
ULRICH

The Hunter's Inn was loud with chatter when I walked down for breakfast, and filled with the scent of roasted meat, stale ale, and the lingering aroma of cinnamon. I pushed through the crowded space to where Pascal sat in a far corner, the hood of his cloak drawn low over his face, though I could see the sharp gleam of his eyes as they tracked my approach.

I'd barely slept after returning from the Underbelly. Robin had helped me find my way back but thankfully kept to himself. I hadn't been in the mood to discuss shit with him anyway. Anger boiled in my veins, like an itch I couldn't scratch. How in hell's sake had I been born from royalty? There had to be a mistake. Pascal, my longest friend, had spent the majority of my life lying to me. Before I could spiral, I reigned in the temper and dropped into the chair across from him, exhaling slowly as I leaned back. "Tell me why you never said anything. Explain to me how I'm supposed to trust someone who lied to me about my past."

"Well hello to you too, friend." Pascal didn't feign confusion. His fingers traced the rim of his tankard, and for a long moment, I thought he might try to avoid answering. But then, he sighed. "It wasn't my secret to tell."

My jaw tightened. "Bullshit."

His lips twitched, almost amused. "Hook, my job was never to reveal the past. It was to bury it. I'm bound by my word, you know this."

I narrowed my eyes. "You need to give me more than that."

Pascal leaned forward slightly, voice dropping lower. "I've spent my long existence helping children. Doing so required wiping memories and creating new ones for those who had nowhere to go. Orphans, runaways, the lost, the abandoned and abused—I took them in and gave them a chance at a new life. A fresh start, free from whatever horrors had led them to my doorstep—to Neverland. In most cases the children find me but you and Clayton . . . someone *brought* you to me."

The flames of the candle between us threw shadows across the scarred hollow of Pascal's milky eye as he continued. "A man who worked closely with your parents. He said he'd tracked me halfway across the Enchanted Realm." His voice lowered, fingers curling briefly around his tankard. "You were both so young. I still remember the way you held Clayton in your arms and refused to let him go." His fingernail traced a groove in the wooden table, a small smile on his lips. "I didn't know why at the time, but my job wasn't to ask questions. It was to save."

I leaned closer as Gretel walked past with a tray of pies leaving a trace of cinnamon in her wake. My stomach groaned and the witch stopped in her tracks.

"Those noises aren't allowed in my inn," she grumbled, then set down two pieces of pie.

Pascal didn't hesitate to grab a piece. "You're going to want to eat that. Not only is this the best pie you will ever have, but if Gretel comes back and sees you haven't tried it . . ." Pascal let the threat hang and stuffed a piece of pastry into his mouth. Apples oozed from the side causing my stomach to howl louder.

I grabbed the second piece.

"Where was I? Pie? No . . . oh, right." Pascal thought a moment, mulling his thoughts over another bite of pie. "The man pleaded with me to protect you and Clayton. To get you as far from the Enchanted Realm and to keep the truth from you until the time was right."

I scoffed. "And who decided when that time was?" I shoved a piece of pie into my mouth and . . .

Holy mother of the gods. I melted until only a soppy puddle of Hook remained. I'd never in all my life tasted something so good. I shoveled more into my mouth.

Pascal hesitated. "I almost did back in Neverland but Arie was captured. I intended to tell you myself before someone let it slip when we arrived but it doesn't matter now."

I rubbed a hand over my face. Gods I'd hoped Robin and Kaelryn had been mistaken. That I wasn't the lost prince whose parents were. . . my stomach wrenched and an ache pounded against my chest. Is this how Arie felt when she thought of her parents? Maybe but I suspected it was worse for her. She had actual memories of her fathers, had the chance to grow up with them. I didn't remember mine no matter how hard I tried.

I swallowed a sob and cleared my throat. "Who was the man?"

Pascal shrugged but a voice from behind made me jump.

"They called him the Huntsman."

Pascal's face paled as a figure walked up beside us.

I turned slowly, my pulse hammering in my throat. The figure that loomed beside us was broad-shouldered, his presence a shadow stretching across the candlelight.

"Wulf," Pascal murmured. He looked like he'd seen a ghost.

Wulf's sharp, dark eyes scanned Pascal before landing on

me. A muscle feathered in his jaw. "How long?" he asked, voice rough as gravel. "How long have you been back?"

Before I could respond, another voice cut through the tension like a blade.

"Well, well. The Queen's hound," Robin drawled, stepping into the dim light. His expression was a mixture of disdain and cold amusement as he regarded Wulf with open suspicion. "Lurking around my men now? That desperate for scraps?"

Wulf's head snapped to him, his glare sharp as a dagger. "Watch your mouth, thief."

Robin folded his arms. "You've been the Queen's right-hand since the day the VonWhite family was killed. Since she took the throne drenched in their blood." His lips curled. "I always wondered how deep that loyalty ran."

"Don't you work for the Queen too?" I asked.

Robin ignored me and continued to scowl at Wulf.

A shadow passed over Wulf's face, a dark exhaustion that spoke of too many masks. "I was forced just like you," he muttered, voice tight. "You think I had a choice?"

Robin scoffed. "And yet you warm her bed without difficulty, don't you? You don't see me sleeping with the enemy."

A flicker of something—anger? Shame?—flashed in Wulf's eyes. He inhaled sharply, steadying himself. "I do what I must. I stay close so she confides in me. It's the only way I can keep my position, the only way I can be of use." His eyes darkened. "I've been waiting for this day for years. For you." His gaze flickered to me. "For the VonWhite children to return."

His words sat heavy in my chest. A strange sensation curled in my gut—like there wasn't a way to outrun this.

Robin narrowed his eyes. "And yet my guess is she sent you here. Why?"

Wulf hesitated. "She ordered me to kill you." His stare

stayed locked on me. "To kill the newcomers that threaten her reign."

Silence stretched between us, thick as fog.

"But I won't," Wulf continued, his voice low, urgent. "I can't. My vow to your parents outweighs Gemma's orders." His hands curled into fists. "I will stall her, delay her suspicions as long as I can—but whatever you have planned, you need to do it fast."

Robin assessed him with a sharp gaze. "And why should we trust you?"

"Because he's telling the truth," Pascal said, his voice steady. He turned his one good eye to me. "He's the one who brought the boys to me and informed the Queen they were dead."

Silence settled over the table, thick as the storm brewing outside.

Wulf exhaled, tension easing from his shoulders as if a great weight had been lifted. His gaze flickered to me, relief in his dark eyes. "The rightful heir has returned." A small, grim smile tugged at his lips. "At last, the throne can be restored."

My gut twisted at his words. I clenched my jaw. "No."

Wulf frowned. "No?"

"I won't take the throne," I said, my voice firm. Final.

Wulf's brows furrowed. "You are—"

"I don't give a gods damn who I am," I cut him off. "I'm not a king. I don't want a throne. You're wasting your time. I'm here to save the woman I love and get the hells out of here."

I stilled. *Did I just admit that? Aloud?*

Wulf studied me for a long moment, something unreadable passing over his face, but before he could say anything, the Inn doors creaked open.

A gust of wind blew in, sending the candle flames shivering.

Clayton stepped inside and my shoulders relaxed. He'd arrived. My earlier anger about him showing up on one of King

Roland's ships dissipated at seeing him. I was still upset about it but having my brother here with me again, especially with what we were facing, eased the anger a little.

His gaze swept the room, taking in Pascal, Robin, and Wulf before finally landing on me. His expression was unreadable, but there was a shark, knowing glint in his eyes.

"I won't lead, but I know someone who might. Someone better suited," I said.

Clayton strode toward us, two men flanking him. "Everything okay, brother?"

Clayton's gaze locked onto mine, and for a moment, the room faded away, a thousand unspoken words passing between us in silent conversation. We needed to talk away from everything, to figure this out together. I needed him to know that my promise to him hadn't changed.

I pushed away from the table. "Clayton, a moment please."

Clayton raised a brow but didn't argue. We left the inn, stepping into the crisp morning air. The scent of pine and damp earth filled my lungs, grounding me as we walked in silence.

The city swallowed us whole as we walked. The air was thick with the scent of damp stone and the acrid smoke of torches burning low in their sconces. Our boots echoed against the cobbled streets, each step reverberating through the silence stretching taut between us.

I broke the silence first, telling Clayton everything—how Pascal wiped our memories to protect us, how we're princes, how Gemma butchered our parents and twisted the truth to turn the people against the rebels. I told him of the Huntsman, of his confession, of how Wulf has been biding his time for our return.

"We need to stop her," I said, watching his face for any flicker of emotion, but Clayton had always been unreadable when he wanted to be. "Once she's gone, the throne will be free. And I need you to take it."

Clayton's eyes flicked to mine, but he didn't speak, so I pushed forward. "You were always meant to sit on that throne. Even in Neverland before we became pirates you were a leader. The only reason I'd taken the captaincy was because you refused. I can lead men into war but you, brother, you can lead them into something greater. A future."

Clayton exhaled, his jaw tightening as he glanced away, his hands curling into fists at his sides. For a long moment, he said nothing, and I worried he might refuse. That he'd throw my words back at me, insist I was wrong.

But he met my gaze, and in the dim torchlight, I saw something settle in him—resolve, acceptance, a flicker of the boy he used to be before our memories were stolen.

"If we do this," he said slowly, his voice steady, "we do it together. I won't let you disappear into the depths of the sea the way you always do."

A sharp laugh left me, but there was no humor in it. "I don't belong in the light, Clayton. Never have. Plus, my place is on the sea."

With Arie.

"You belong with me." His words were quiet but firm. "And if I take the throne, I'm not doing it alone."

You belong with me. The words rang in my mind, they were a mantra we'd whispered to each other in moments of comfort. Hearing them now, my throat tightened. It was like a piece of my past, a part of who I was, had just clicked back into place.

But right now, we had to focus on one problem at a time.

"Let's just get through this and then we can figure out semantics later".

He didn't argue or fight me on it. He only nodded, solemn as ever, before turning back toward the inn.

Pascal eye'd us warily as we took our seats. "Is everything all right?"

I exchanged a look with Clayton before speaking. "We need to discuss our next move."

Wulf leaned forward, his gaze intense. "I'm here to support you in whatever decision you make. The people of this kingdom have been waiting for their rightful heirs to return."

"So how do we stop a queen?" Pascal asked.

Two hours and a few drinks later we stood in the back room of the inn—Frankie, Tink, Nathaniel, and Hansel included.

Robin leaned forward, his fingers drumming against the table. "I already have something in motion," he said, his voice low, sharp. "Gemma's throwing a masquerade ball in two days. It's the perfect time to strike."

Gretel, arms crossed over her chest, gave him a skeptical look. "And how exactly do we plan to infiltrate a ball full of assassins?"

Hansel smirked from across the table. "We give them something else to focus on." He tapped the map, his finger landing on the castle's outer courtyard. "I'll take some assassins—the ones loyal to Robin—and we'll create a distraction outside the castle walls. If we mak enough noise, enough chaos, Gemma will send a good portion of her assassins away from the ballroom to deal with it."

"That's risky," Wulf muttered. "If she catches on, you'll be executed."

Hansel grinned. "Then we better make it convincing. She already blames the rebels for everything."

Robin nodded, satisfied. "With the castle's defenses weakened, Gretel and I will attend the ball. She'll expect me, but she won't expect Gretel at my side. Not when she thinks we haven't spoken in nearly a decade. I think it's time for the people to know the truth."

Gretel tilted her head, the ghost of a smirk playing at her lips. "You always did need me to clean up your messes."

Robin ignored her. "Hook, you'll be in charge of getting to Arie." His gaze flicked to mine. "We know what kind of hold Gemma has on her, so if you can get her to snap out of it, do it. If not . . ." He exhaled. "Then you need to get her out. No matter what. We'll figure out how to reverse it later."

I nodded once, my jaw tightening.

Robin gestured to Frankie and Tink, who had been listening silently until now. "You two will act as Hook's backup. He'll need cover, and the best way to blend in is with a distraction of his own."

Frankie arched a brow. "So what, we're just supposed to be his arm candy for the night?"

"Exactly." Robin's smirk was sharp. "You'll be his two lovely dates. But if things go south, make sure he gets out alive."

Tink cracked her knuckles. "Oh, I'll do more than that."

Wulf, who had been silent for most of the discussion, finally spoke up. "And me?"

Robin's expression darkened. "You're going to sit at the Queen's side. Once we make our announcement, she'll try to flee. Make sure she doesn't."

A heavy silence settled over the room. This was it. No turning back.

Clayton exhaled and straightened. "Then we have two days to prepare."

My fingers curled around the edge of the table. Two days, and then it all ends.

One way or another.

14
VELVET & VICE
ARIE

FREDERICK'S TALL FRAME CASUALLY PROPPED AGAINST the wooden stable door, arms folded tightly across his chest, and the corners of his mouth curled into that familiar, infuriating smirk. The late afternoon sun cast a warm glow over him, highlighting the playful glint in his eyes as he watched me approach.

"Surprised you actually showed up," he drawled.

"What, are you sad now that you can't have all the glory?" I shot back, tightening my cloak around my shoulders.

Frederick pressed a hand to his chest in mock offense. "I don't do this for the glory, Rosie. I do this for the *thrill*."

I rolled my eyes. "Will you stop calling me that?"

Though the way he'd say thrill sent a shiver down my back.

"Never." He winked. "Come on, we have a meeting to get to."

Two hours on horseback left my muscles aching and my body in desperate need of rest as we finally slowed before an unassuming home wedged between two larger buildings. The structure was plain—worn shutters, a door softened by time—but something about it felt . . . deliberate. Like it was meant to be overlooked.

Frederick swung down from his horse first, boots hitting the damp ground without a sound. He approached the door with the kind of confidence only someone who belonged here could muster, rapping twice in a distinct rhythm. A pause. Then the faintest creak of wood as the door cracked open, revealing a sliver of darkness.

I followed Frederick inside. The air carried the scent of old wood and smoke, a heavy quiet settling over the space. Two figures loomed in the dim light, their dark leathers melding with the shadows. They weren't just standing; they were waiting. Still, but coiled with something dangerous—something that crackled just beneath the surface.

The shorter one, a woman with a scar carving a wicked path down her cheek, let her gaze flick to Frederick before settling on me. There was no immediate recognition, but there was scrutiny—like she was trying to decide whether I was worth her attention or her blade.

Something about her scar tugged at my memory, a whisper of familiarity just out of reach. I'd seen one like it before—on someone else, or maybe in the reflection of a story told in hushed voices. My mind reached for the thread, trying to untangle it from my scattered memories.

The man beside her shifted, stepping farther into the light. He was broad-shouldered but lean, built for speed rather than brute strength, and wore his leathers with the ease of someone who had lived in them far too long. His face was sharp—angular cheekbones, a strong jaw marred by the faint shadow of old bruising, like he'd spent his life throwing and taking punches in equal measure.

But it was his eyes that stood out. A shade too light for comfort, a piercing gray that cut through the dim room like a blade seeking a weakness. They flicked to Frederick, then to me, assessing, weighing, already finding reasons not to trust me.

"She's the one?" His voice carried no inflection, no hint of what he thought about that revelation. Just a flat, unreadable challenge.

Frederick leaned against the doorframe, arms crossing lazily over his chest. "She is."

The man clicked his tongue, shaking his head as if he'd already decided this was a mistake. Then his gaze locked on me, the corner of his mouth pulling into a curl too sharp to be a smirk.

"Didn't think we'd be working with the Queen's new pet."

"Didn't think I'd be working with a secret society of glorified murderers, yet here we are," I shot back.

The man grinned. "I like her."

Frederick rolled his eyes. "Are we going to keep trading insults, Dom or are we going to discuss the plan?"

Dom nodded toward the table, where a map of the city lay spread out. "The target frequents a brothel near the docks. High-ranking rebel, and dangerous. We take him out quietly, no mess, no witnesses. In and out before anyone knows he's dead."

I leaned over the map, studying the markings. "Sounds simple enough," I said.

The woman shook her head. "It never is."

Dom's finger traced a route along the docks, but I didn't hear his words. My pulse banged in my throat as the woman shifted beside me, lantern light catching her scar again. That raised ridge of flesh . . . a milky white eye flashed in my vision.

Frederick's boot nudged mine under the table. "Still with us?"

I blink. "Sure am."

Dom's gaze sliced upward from the map. For a heartbeat too long, his gray eyes lingered on my face like he could read my thoughts. His knuckles whitened around a dagger's hilt. "We'll move soon," he said abruptly. "There's food through the doors, help yourself."

I stood up from the map with a stiff smile, feeling Dom's gaze burn into the back of my neck. It was like he was waiting for me to slip up, to show some weakness. I wasn't about to give him that satisfaction.

Frederick motioned toward the door leading to the kitchen. "Let's grab something to eat—you're going to need your strength, especially with Dom and Sienna here."

I followed him, casting one last glance back at Dom. The tension in the room still clung to me like a shadow, but I forced it aside. If there was one thing I was good at, it was ignoring the pressure.

The kitchen was warmer, a contrast to the cold tension that had wrapped around us in the meeting room. Pots and pans clattered as Frederick worked, and the scent of something hearty cooking in the oven made my stomach growl.

"Nice place," I commented, leaning against the counter as Frederick dug through a cabinet. The light from the hearth cast dancing shadows across the stone walls, making everything feel a little too . . . homey.

Frederick grinned, grabbing a loaf of bread and slicing it. "It has its perks. No one looks too closely at what goes on behind these walls. Though, I wouldn't exactly call it a *home*." He raised an eyebrow, as if waiting for me to catch the implication.

I rolled my eyes, though there was a smirk tugging at the corner of my lips. "Right. Secret society, glorified murderers, and all that."

"Exactly." He handed me a piece of bread. "Better than a cage."

I took the bread, eyeing him suspiciously. "That sounds like you've been in one."

He only shrugged, not offering more. Instead, his attention

shifted to the door where Sienna and Dom talked quietly. "About this mission..."

I raised an eyebrow, curious where this was going. "What about it?"

Frederick smirked, glancing back at me. "Brothel near the docks. You ever been?"

I froze, the question catching me off guard. I hadn't really thought about the details of the mission yet—just the target and the plan—but this was different. "No. I can't even remember if I've ever been to one," I admitted, feeling a slight twinge of discomfort. "Why?"

Frederick's grin widened, clearly amused. "Are you curious?"

"Not exactly," I said, more to myself than him.

He laughed, leaning against the counter. "You know, you might be surprised. It's not like what the stories tell you. People go for all kinds of reasons. Some for a bit of company, others for ... a bit of something else." He gave me a knowing look. "Not everyone there is a 'worker,' either."

I raised an eyebrow, not sure where he was going with that. "What do you mean?"

Frederick shrugged casually. "Brothels like this are places where all sorts of business is done. Not just the kind you're thinking of. You'd be surprised who spends time there."

I was silent for a moment, trying to process the unexpected revelation. "So, it's like a ... cover? For other kinds of deals?"

He nodded. "You'd be wise to keep your eyes open. People from all walks of life go there. It's a mix of desperation and influence."

I chewed on that, nodding slowly. "Guess that makes sense. Keep it casual, blend in, no one suspects anything."

"Right," Frederick said with a grin, grabbing a few more supplies. "And you can expect that *everything* will be kept hush-

hush, no matter what goes down inside. It's a business. You just need to do your job, and no one will bother you."

I raised my glass of water to him, feeling the faintest pulse of curiosity creeping in. "I'll take your word for it."

Frederick clinked his glass to mine before downing the drink. "Trust me, I know what I'm talking about." His eyes flicked toward the door, where Sienna and Dom were still chatting. "We'll be ready when the time comes. Just don't get too comfortable with any of it."

I didn't need a reminder. Whatever went down at the brothel, I knew it wasn't going to be simple. But I could handle myself. I just had to keep my wits about me.

Some light conversation and a full stomach later, I followed Frederick back to the main room.

"So, what's next?" I asked, glancing back at the map. The mission, after all, was the priority. Everything else would have to wait.

Frederick tore off another piece of bread, chewing thoughtfully before answering. "We wait until nightfall. Less eyes, less questions. We'll take the back entrance—most of the staff use it to sneak out for fresh air or a quick smoke. From there, we blend in, find our target, and make it quick."

I studied the map again, tracing the route he'd pointed out earlier. The brothel sat near the docks, a cluster of winding alleyways surrounding it like a natural maze. Good for cover. Bad if things went sideways.

"And what do we know about him?" I asked. "The rebel leader."

Frederick leaned against the table, arms crossed over his chest. "Name's Rian Dorne. Dangerous, careful. He's been rallying support for months, moving between safe houses. The brothel's a favorite spot of his—probably thinks it's neutral ground." He grinned. "He's about to find out it's not."

I nodded. "Any guards?"

"Always," he said, rolling his shoulders. "Two, maybe three, stationed inside. He won't make it easy, but that's why we're not kicking the door down. We slip in, get close, and by the time he realizes what's happening, it'll be too late."

I drummed my fingers against the counter, letting the plan settle in my mind. "And what if things *do* go sideways?"

Frederick gave me a pointed look. "Then we improvise."

"Great," I muttered. "Love a solid plan."

He smirked. "Welcome to the job."

I exhaled slowly, pushing away the creeping unease. It wasn't the mission that unsettled me—it was the unpredictability of it. Places like that were unpredictable by nature. And memory loss or not, I didn't like surprises, especially the life-threatening kind."

Still, I could handle it. I *would* handle it.

Frederick's gaze flicked toward me, sharper now. "Are you sure you're ready for this?"

I met his eyes, unwavering. "Always."

His smirk deepened, and he gave a small nod. "Good. Then we'd better get changed."

"Changed?" I raised a brow.

"You don't think you're going to get in and out of a brothel unnoticed dressed like that?" He gestured toward my trousers and buttoned shirt.

"Don't worry," Sienna said. "I'm sure we have something you can fit into. We leave in two hours. Bathing chambers are down the hall in the main room."

I sighed. So much for this being simple. Something told me that even in the life before my memory loss, the thought of wearing dresses made me squirm.

Several irritating hours later, I was bathed, dressed, and ready to commit murder—though not the one we'd planned.

The outfit Sienna had chosen wasn't so much a dress as a declaration, and the message was *look, don't touch.* Or maybe *touch and die.* Deep crimson silk clung to me like a second skin, the bodice tight enough that I wondered if breathing was optional. The neckline plunged scandalously low, exposing more of my chest than I'd ever deemed necessary. The slit riding high on my thigh promised ease of movement but cost me any shred of modesty.

A sheer black shawl draped over my arms, utterly useless except for the illusion of coverage. My hair, usually tied back for practicality, cascaded in soft waves down my shoulders, strands still damp from the rushed bath. My skin smelled faintly of lavender and rich, spiced perfumes—Sienna's idea of making sure I 'fit the part'.

The worst part? Finding a place to hide my blade had been a nightmare. The fabric left little room for creativity. After a few failed attempts, I managed to secure it to my upper thigh with a thin leather strap. It would have to do.

I took one last glance in the mirror and barely recognized myself. It wasn't just the outfit—it was the woman in it. The way she held herself, stiff with irritation but standing like she was ready to fight her way out. A stranger, yet someone familiar.

Was this the kind of person I used to be? The thought flickered through my mind before I pushed it aside. It didn't matter.

What mattered was getting the job done.

I stepped out, adjusting the slit of the dress so I wouldn't trip over myself.

Frederick looked up from where he was leaning against the wall. He blinked once. Then his lips curled into a slow, insufferable smirk. "Well, damn. Didn't think you cleaned up this nicely."

I narrowed my eyes. "Say one more word, and I'll test how fast you can dodge a knife."

He let out a low chuckle, clearly enjoying this. "Relax. You look the part, and that's what matters."

Sienna, fastening a bracelet around her wrist, smirked. "Just try not to look like you're about to stab someone the whole time. It ruins the illusion."

I exhaled through my nose, resisting the urge to cross my arms. The last thing I needed was to draw more attention to how exposed I felt. "No promises."

Frederick chuckled. "Let's hope the target doesn't *see through* the act before we get close enough to finish the job."

I exhaled sharply, forcing myself to push past the discomfort. The mission came first. Whatever I had to do to make this work, I'd deal with it.

I just hoped I didn't have to kill anyone *before* we got to the target.

Two hours by horseback while wearing a dress was fucking worse than anything I'd ever experienced. Sienna at least had managed to keep my hair intact and had changed my heels into riding boots courtesy of her magic.

The air was thick with the briny bite of the sea as we returned to Chione's winding alleys, the scent of salt and earth mingling in the breeze. The more I breathed it in, the more the scent wrapped around me, familiar, like something I should know, something that should stir a memory. But it didn't.

I paused for a heartbeat, trying to place it. Where had I smelled this before? Who had I been with when this scent was near? My mind raced, but the memories were elusive, slipping through my fingers.

Lanterns had swung overhead, their pale blue and green glow casting eerie ripples across the cobblestones. Frederick moved ahead, all sharp focus now, his earlier amusement long gone. Dom followed behind me, steady and unshakable, while Sienna lingered somewhere unseen, her presence a phantom weight at my back.

We hadn't needed directions to find the brothel—it had announced itself before we even laid eyes on it. Laughter spilled into the street, thick and syrupy, weaving between the low thrum of music. A fiddle, maybe a lute, something fast and meant to intoxicate. Then came the scent: perfume and sweat, spiced wine, and something heavier underneath, something metallic. The building itself was old, its wooden door carved with curling designs of mermaids and wolves locked in an embrace, worn smooth by years of passing hands.

Frederick led us around back, then slowed near a rusted grate venting steam from the kitchens, nodding toward a narrow stairwell nearly swallowed by creeping ivy. "Staff entrance," he murmured, fingers brushing the hilt of a dagger at his thigh. "Stay close."

Inside, the air changed—warmer, cloying, laced with incense and the faint burn of spiced oil. The servants' passage had been cramped, pressing in too close before spitting us out into a dim antechamber where heavy silks hung from the walls in deep purples and golds. The light was low, sconces flickering with a dull, golden glow. A girl drifted past in a gauzy robe; a gilded mask pressed to her face like it had become part of her skin. Her eyes met mine, one molten gold, the other an abyss of black. Magic swirled at the edges of her gaze, and I looked away before she could see whatever flicker of unease crossed my face.

Frederick plucked two glasses of wine from a passing tray without breaking stride, pressing one into my hand. "Smile," he murmured, his palm settling against the small of my back, the warmth bleeding through the thin fabric of my dress. "We're just another couple looking to indulge."

His thumb brushed idly against my spine, and I swallowed down the unwelcome heat curling in my stomach, forcing my focus back to the room. The main floor sprawled ahead, separated by gauzy curtains that shifted with every movement. Dom slid into the shadows near an exit, keeping watch, while Sienna slipped upstairs, vanishing without a sound.

Beyond the archway, the floor dipped into a sunken pit where performers moved in hypnotic rhythms, their bodies twisting unnaturally, guided by unseen magic. Water arced through the air above them in thin, shimmering ribbons, coiling like serpents before splashing down in perfect time with the music. Laughter rose from velvet-draped booths, where half-dressed courtesans lounged, their skin glinting with iridescent scales as they plucked fruit from silver spoons, feeding them to their clients with slow, teasing smiles.

Just beyond, the real business of the brothel unfolded in dimly lit alcoves and shadowed lounges, where bodies tangled in silk sheets, limbs entwined in pleasure and transaction alike. Some pairs sat lazily in half-open rooms, robes falling away to expose glistening skin as fingers trailed slow, knowing paths over flushed flesh. Others engaged with more fervor—pressed against walls, nails raking down backs, gasps swallowed by eager mouths. A woman with dark kohl-lined eyes sat astride a masked patron in a low-backed chair, her spine arching as he gripped her hips, guiding her in a rhythm that matched the slow throb of the music. A soft, breathy moan carried through the air, lost in the haze of incense and wine.

I had a hard time peeling my eyes from it. My focus was hazy until Sienna and Dom caught up to us near the edge of the main room. Sienna flicked a glance toward the upper levels, where shadowed figures leaned over balconies, watching the debauchery unfold below. "Looks like we have a few guards upstairs and more in the back rooms, we'll have to search a bit to find Rian," she said, adjusting the dagger at her hip. "He won't be sitting out in the open. He's too careful for that."

Dom nodded, cracking his knuckles. "We'll check upstairs. You two take the main floor and the private lounges."

Sienna narrowed her eyes. "Try not to get too much blood on the dress, hey?"

I scoffed but said nothing as they disappeared into the crowd.

Frederick and I moved forward, weaving through bodies that pressed too close, the air thick with sweat, perfume, and cloying sweet smoke—opium, most likely.

A hand shot out from the crowd, fingers gripping my waist. A drunken slur of a voice followed. "Where you runnin' off to, pretty thing?"

Instinct took over. I spun, blade unsheathed in a blink, pressing the cold steel against the man's throat. He reeked of liquor, his greasy hair falling over his sunken eyes, but instead of fear, a slow, sick smile stretched across his lips.

"Feisty," he murmured, his Adam's apple bobbing against my blade. "I like when they put up a fight."

Disgust curdled in my stomach, my fingers twitching to slice him open just to see the smile slip away—but then Frederick's arm curled around my waist, tugging me back against his chest. His other hand covered mine, easing the dagger away from the man's skin before I did something reckless.

"Not here," Frederick murmured against my ear, his voice a low, grounding thing. "He's not worth it."

The man chuckled, licking his lips as he stepped back, completely unfazed. "Shame," he sighed. "Maybe next time, love."

Frederick's grip tightened just enough to keep me from

lunging, then steered me forward, away from the temptation to paint this wretched place red. "Deep breaths," he muttered.

I placed the dagger back against my leg, wishing I could keep it in my grasp. We moved deeper into the brothel, slipping past gauzy curtains and into the dimly lit corridors where the air hung thick with incense and sin. Laughter and moans bled together behind closed doors, the muted sound of bodies meeting in hurried, frantic rhythms echoing in the narrow hall. The deeper we went, the more the air shifted—pleasure curdling into something darker.

Frederick moved ahead, his eyes sharp, scanning doorways as we passed. My fingers twitched at my side, itching to grip the dagger strapped to my thigh. I hated feeling this exposed, hated the way the fabric of Sienna's dress clung to me, leaving too much skin bare.

"Look." Frederick came to a stop at the room before a door where a guard stood outside, his voice barely above a whisper. The sounds beyond it were unmistakable—breathy gasps, a low chuckle, the rhythmic creak of a bed frame against the floor. The scent of sweat and wine spilled into the hallway through the narrow gap beneath the door.

Rian.

My pulse quickened, not with nerves, but with the slow, simmering burn of anticipation. This was the man we had come to kill. The leader of a rebellion that had cost too many lives.

"Go up and say Rian ordered another round and you've been summoned. I'll stay close by."

"You're not coming with me?" I nearly choked.

"It'll look too suspicious if I follow you, I'll be right down the hall if you need me."

I did as he asked and was surprised that the guard had no qualms about a pretty girl. He was too focused on Frederick as he passed.

The room was awash in candlelight, casting flickering gold against the deep crimson walls. Silk sheets tangled in a mess of limbs, two women and a man draped lazily across Rian's broad frame, their bodies slick with sweat and wine. He lay sprawled in the center, his golden-brown hair damp against his forehead, lips parted in lazy amusement as he trailed his fingers along the curve of a woman's hip.

It took a second for them to notice us. The first woman—dark-haired, bare but for a sheer wrap hanging off her shoulders—gasped, scrambling for a blanket to cover herself. The other woman twisted in alarm, pushing away from Rian's chest, while the man sat up, cursing.

"Out," I said with an air of authority. "It's my turn."

The dark-haired woman hesitated, looking between me and Rian as if waiting for approval. Rian, for his part, simply smirked, running a hand through his hair as he propped himself up on an elbow.

"Now," I added, stepping forward, my patience already thin. I didn't have time for this.

That was enough. The man grabbed his trousers from the floor and stumbled past us without looking back. One of the women followed in a rush, but the dark-haired one lingered a second longer, eyes darting to Rian before she finally slipped out, slamming the door behind her.

Silence settled over the room, thick and heavy.

Rian stretched lazily, completely unbothered by my presence. "I don't recognize you, you're not one of Miss Liza's girls." He dragged a hand down his chest, feigning boredom. "So, what is it, then? A warning? A bribe?" He grinned. "An invitation to join whatever cause you lot are pushing now?"

I ignored the smirk, ignored the cocky arrogance that dripped from every word. My hand itched for my blade, but I held back, my mind suddenly latching onto something else—something important.

He knew things.

He had been a key player in the rebellion for years, moving in circles of power I had only begun to uncover. And if he was as deeply entrenched as we suspected, then he might know something about the night my parents were murdered.

My fingers curled into a fist at my sides.

"Who gave the order?" The words left my lips before I could stop them. "Which rebel deserves a blade through the heart more than you do?"

Rian arched a brow. "What order?"

"Don't play games with me." I stepped closer, the fury rising like a storm beneath my skin. "The massacre. My parents. Who was behind it?"

Rian chuckled, dragging himself upright until he was sitting at the edge of the bed. "Ah. So that's what this is about." His gaze flicked over me, assessing, amused. "I've been accused of many things, but I'm afraid you'll have to be more specific."

I unsheathed my dagger in one swift motion and pressed it beneath his chin, forcing his head up. His smirk faltered.

"Tell me." My voice was low, edged with something raw and vicious.

Rian's lips curled, his breath warm against my blade. "And if I don't?"

The answer was easy. I pressed harder, a thin line of red welling at his throat. "Then you'll die slower."

His smirk returned, though there was something harder in his gaze now, calculating. "Then I guess I have nothing to lose."

Wrong answer.

I lunged, straddling him and pressing my blade against his throat. I tried to ignore the bulge under the blanket and focused on my task. I came here to kill him, but no one said anything about getting answers.

"Two men were murdered in a small home. They had two daughters, one blonde and one red. They once worked for the King and Queen and—"

Rian laughed. "Malakai and Viktor? Those two hooligans were always bound for death, but it wasn't I who ordered their hit. Now, if you don't mind, remove yourself from this room before I kill you myself. It would be such a waste to let a pretty thing like you bleed out."

I felt a sharpness at my side and looked down to see a blade pressed against my skin.

A sharp, bitter growl scraped its way up my throat, but I swallowed it down, gripping Slayer so tightly my fingers ached. Rian thought this was funny. A joke. Like he hadn't spent his miserable existence crawling over the bodies of better men just to sit on his filthy little throne.

Something flickered inside me, white-hot and electric. It surged up my spine, curled behind my eyes, a pressure so sharp I thought my skull might crack open from the force. The room dimmed for the briefest moment, the candlelight trembling, shadows stretching unnaturally along the walls.

Rian's smirk faltered. His fingers twitched on the blade at my side, but his grip slackened. His breath hitched, eyes narrowing as he took a step back.

"Wh-what the hell?" His voice wavered, edged with uncertainty. "Your eyes . . . what's wrong with them?"

I stiffened, but before I could demand what he meant, something in the corner of the room caught my attention. Behind him, the tarnished mirror hanging on the wall reflecting both of us—Rian's growing panic, the tension in my shoulders—but it was my eyes that froze me.

Lightning crackled within my irises, bright, electric veins of white-blue energy flickering and arcing like a storm trapped in a bottle.

I sucked in a breath, but the power inside me didn't fade—it pulsed, an undeniable presence thrumming beneath my ribs, coiling in my chest like it had always been there, waiting.

Rian must've seen the shift in my expression, because he scrambled back another step, lips parting like he wanted to say something else—but he never got the chance.

I lifted Slayer without hesitation, the blade singing through the air as it met flesh.

Rian choked, eyes going wide as his hands flew to his throat, blood spilling between his fingers. He staggered, knocking into the table, sending bottles crashing to the floor.

I watched him, my chest rising and falling with measured breaths. "You talk too much," I murmured, voice steady. "Consider this me shutting you up for good."

His body slumped to the floor, twitching, his own blood soaking the boards beneath him. I stepped over him, wiping Slayer clean before sliding it back into its sheath.

The mirror behind him still shimmered faintly, the storm in my gaze refusing to die.

I let him fall forward, the sound of his body hitting the floor barely registering over the roaring in my ears. The fury simmered, unresolved, unsatisfied. But the mission wasn't over. Not yet.

Unclasping the necklace, I clutched the purple stone in my hand and focused on the energy within me. Gemma hadn't been forthcoming with how to do this, so I had to trust my instincts. I inhaled deeply, letting myself relax before I held out my hand over Rian's body.

Nothing happened.

A flicker of frustration curled in my chest. My fingers tightened around the stone as I tried again, pulling at the power I *knew* was there. But it was like reaching into the dark, grasping at smoke—formless, slipping through my fingers before I could seize it.

I ground my teeth, forcing myself to breathe past the rising doubt. I had done this before. I had taken a soul. The power was *mine* to wield.

The stone remained cold against my palm.

A sharp pang of anger spiked through me. *No.* I wouldn't fail here. Not now.

I thought of everything Rian had done. The people he had betrayed, the lives he had destroyed—including mine. TI fed that simmering rage, let it coil around my bones, let it breathe.

And then, like a dam breaking, the magic *rushed* through me, searing-hot and electric.

The stone in my palm pulsed.

Tendrils of black energy snaked outward, writhing through the space between us before latching onto Rian's chest. His body—lifeless and slack only moments ago—twitched violently, his limbs jerking as though some unseen force was trying to wake him from death itself. The movement wasn't his. It was the soul, struggling, resisting, trying to claw its way back into the flesh it no longer belonged to.

A deep, unnatural groan echoed through the room—not from his lips, but from somewhere beyond, the sound of something ancient and wrong being torn apart. The tendrils burrowed deeper, sinking into his ribs to wrap around what remained of him like living shadows with minds of their own. His skin crackled, dark veins rupturing beneath the deathly pale flesh as an eerie blue-gray mist curled from his gaping mouth, wisps of energy flickering in and out of visibility like a dying flame.

The stench of charred flesh thickened in the air, acrid and suffocating, as the power devoured him from the inside out. His muscles spasmed once, twice, before locking in place, frozen in the final, horrific expression of something that had once been human but was now a mere shell. The mist stretched, tangled, and then with a final, shuddering pull, unraveled completely, siphoned into the waiting stone like water through a cracked vessel.

Heavy silence rang in my ears.

Bile curled in my stomach.

This—this was monstrous. Stealing a soul, forcing it into this cursed relic, trapping it for eternity. No afterlife. No peace. Just imprisonment.

It was horrifying.

And yet...

Rian had deserved it.

I told myself that over and over, gripping the stone so tightly my knuckles ached. He had murdered, enslaved, ruined lives without a second thought. He had profited off pain. He had laughed in my face when I demanded justice.

And yet, the feeling wouldn't go away.

I closed my eyes, forcing breath into my lungs. *The end result is what matters.* That's what I had to believe. That's what I *needed* to believe.

Because if I didn't... what did that make me?

15
LIGHTNING STRIKES
ARIE

The following morning came draped in the muted hush of steel against steel, the sharp clang of blades echoing through the courtyard as the sun clawed its way over the high stone walls. The training yard was alive with movement —bodies twisting, dodging, striking. Breathless curses cut through the cool morning air, accompanied by the steady thud of boots against packed earth.

I stood at the center of it all, my pulse hammering as I faced Frederick. His stance was relaxed, his sword gripped with the kind of ease that only came from years of experience. He smirked at me, rolling his shoulders, the morning light casting ominous shadows across his face.

"Come on, then," he taunted, tapping his blade against mine. "I won't go easy just because you're new."

"I'd be offended if you did," I shot back, lunging.

Frederick deflected my strike with an effortless twist of his wrist, sending my momentum veering sideways. I caught myself just in time to block his counterattack, our blades ringing out like a bell tolling in the crisp air.

I tried to focus on the fight, but my mind had been reeling since last night's mission.

The smooth flow of the magic when I took Rian's soul had come too easily. It felt wrong, like a part of me crossed a line I shouldn't. A quieter part of me was certain it was the right call. I had to, didn't I? Rian was a threat, and if I didn't do it, someone else would. He may not have killed my parents, but he'd been part of the chaos that had been inflicted on this kingdom. Still, the ease of it . . . it felt too natural, too comfortable. Almost as if I'd done it before.

I bit my lip, pushing the thought away. That wasn't the only thing that bothered me. My memories, *my damn memories*, were still elusive. The Queen had told me they would come back eventually, but it had been too long, and nothing had returned. Not the smallest detail. Not the faintest recollection.

It should've happened by now, shouldn't it? Especially with all the tonics I'd been drank.

Maybe there was something else—something more that could help. Maybe after this I'd ask Frederick if he knew of anything. I was tired of not knowing, of feeling caught in a constant out of body experience.

I dodged another of Fredericks attacks.

The other assassins trained around us, but their eyes lingered longer than they should. A quick glance confirmed it— two men stood off to the side, their attention locked on me.

They weren't subtle about it.

One was broad-shouldered with cropped dark hair, his stance casual but predatory. The other was taller, leaner, with sharp eyes that tracked my every movement waiting for the perfect moment to strike. Their expressions weren't ones of curiosity, but of scrutiny. Challenge.

I ducked beneath Frederick's next swing, rolling out of the

way before jerking my chin toward the pair. "Who the hell are they?"

Frederick barely spared them a glance as he circled me. "Antonio and Rex," he muttered. "Some of the more . . . hardcore brothers. They don't take kindly to outsiders."

"Ah," I said dryly, shifting my grip on my sword. "And here I thought they were just admiring my footwork."

Frederick snorted. "More like waiting for an excuse to carve you up."

"They're welcome to try."

"Be careful with them. Word has spread that you worked alongside Dom and Sienna. Those two have been trying to get into that position for months."

I shrugged. "I don't really give a fuck what they want. As long as they mind their own business."

He grinned at that, but before he could respond, a sharp whistle cut through the yard. Tibault, ever the taskmaster, stood near the steps, arms crossed. "That's enough for today. Rest up. You're no good to me if you're dead on your feet."

We both lowered our blades and stepped back, taking a breath to steady ourselves. The adrenaline from the sparring match lingered in my chest, my pulse still hammering as I wiped a bead of sweat from my brow. The tension between us, the unspoken challenge, hung in the air for a moment before vanishing on the soft breeze when we both sheathed our swords.

Frederick was the first to break the silence, his voice quiet and probing. "I've been meaning to speak with you about last night. How are you doing?"

I glanced at him, meeting his gaze, but found myself unsure how to answer. There was a weight pressing down on me—a weight that started the moment I'd taken Rian's soul. I ran a hand through my hair, trying to make sense of the confusion swirling inside me.

"I'm . . . confused," I admitted, my voice softer than usual. "I don't know how to explain it. I didn't expect my magic to come so easily, but it did. I was able to take his soul without even thinking about it." I stopped, desperate to find the right words, but they remained distant. "It felt. . . almost natural, like I'd done it a thousand times before. But it wasn't. I know it wasn't."

Frederick's brow furrowed slightly, his concern evident as he gave me space to process. "It must have been . . . unsettling."

"Unsettling doesn't even begin to cover it," I murmured. "It felt wrong, but at the same time, it felt necessary, like I had no choice. But it wasn't even hard. Just. . . it just happened." I looked at my hands as if I might find some explanation there. "I didn't even have to think about it. I just . . . took his soul."

He studied me carefully, his eyes narrowing with something like understanding. "And how did that feel?"

A cold shiver ran down my spine, and I exhaled, trying to push past the knot in my throat. "Wrong," I whispered. "But it was the right thing to do. Does that make sense?"

He didn't answer right away. He simply watched me, like he was seeing something deeper than my words. "It does," he said, finally.

I took a deep breath, trying to gather the fragments of my thoughts. But it felt like they were slipping through my fingers. "It's not just that," I said, my voice tight with frustration. "I don't know why, but something about it feels off. Like I'll lose pieces of myself if I do that again." I swallowed hard, the weight of the admission heavy in my chest. "And that's not even the worst part."

Frederick's expression softened, and he stepped closer. "Then what is?"

I met his gaze, unable to keep the uncertainty out of my voice. "I can't remember them. My parents." The words tasted bitter on my tongue. "I don't remember them at all. I see flashes and fragments of a dream I can't hold onto. How they taught me to fight, how they cared for me. But that's it. And I don't even remember their names." I looked away, feeling a lump form in my throat. "Gemma's the only reason I even know they're dead. And it's like . . . I'm losing them all over again, but I don't know how to stop it."

Frederick didn't say anything at first. I wasn't sure what I expected him to say, but the way he looked at me, like he wasn't judging, was more than enough.

"I don't know how to fix this," I muttered, shaking my head. "Every time I think I'm getting a piece of it back, it's like it's gone again. Like trying to hold water in my hands."

Frederick took a step closer, his voice quiet but steady. "You don't have to fix it alone, Arie. Whatever this is, we'll figure it out. Piece by piece."

I nodded, grateful for the reassurance, even though part of me still felt lost. But for the first time in a while, I didn't feel completely alone. Maybe that was enough for now.

As the other assassins dispersed and the clang of blades died down, I found myself standing alone for a moment, the chaos of the yard fading to a distant hum. My gaze flicked over to where Antonio and Rex stood sentry, eyes sharp, like wolves waiting for the kill.

I forced myself to push away those thoughts, to focus on the here and now. I wasn't here to solve the mystery of my past—I was here to get stronger, to prove I belonged. The rest could wait, at least for a while.

Then came the sound of approaching footsteps.

I turned just as Antonio and Rex flanked me, their expressions carved from stone.

"Well, well," Antonio drawled, arms folding over his broad chest. "The Queen's new pet."

I exhaled through my nose, already unimpressed. "That's original."

Rex tilted his head, his grin slow and cruel. "We've been wondering, sweetheart—whose dick did you suck to get into the Elites?"

A sharp, ugly heat flared through me, curling in my stomach like a coiled snake. The sheer audacity of it would've been laughable if it didn't make my fingers twitch for the blade at my hip.

I met his gaze with cold amusement, refusing to let him see anything else. "Yours, obviously. How else do you think I got the stomach for this job? I mean someone had to take care of such a small . . ." I held out my pinky.

Antonio barked out a laugh, but Rex's eyes darkened, jaw tightening. "You think this is funny?"

"I think it's hilarious that you're threatened by me. Now, if you don't mind. I have places to be."

Antonio stepped closer, his presence looming, his voice a low, venomous murmur. "You're not going anywhere. The only way you got in with them is if you proved yourself. Which from where we stand, is nothing."

Rex grunted. "I think it's time you prove you belong here, *Rose*. We don't like little girls walking in and acting like they belong."

I barely resisted the urge to shove a knife between his ribs just to see the surprise bloom in his eyes. Instead, I smiled, slow and sharp. "Then you're really going to hate what happens next."

Rex's fingers flexed, curling into fists. Antonio's nostrils flared.

In the next instant they were on me—Antonio lunging with

a brutal swiftness that left no room for hesitation, Rex moving in on my other side. I parried Antonio's first strike, the metal ringing in my ears, but Rex was quick, his blade glancing off my shoulder as I turned to meet his attack.

I gritted my teeth, the sting of the cut sharpening my focus. My sword clanged against Antonio's, but the force behind his blows was like a hammer, relentless and unyielding. My feet slid back in the wet mud as Rex closed in, both of them moving with the lethal precision of seasoned killers.

"Don't expect us to go soft on you," Rex barked.

"Wouldn't dream of it," I grunted back.

"Good, because you're not making it out of this alive," Antonio added.

Their attacks came faster, each one forcing me to retreat, to defend rather than counter. My muscles screamed, fatigue creeping into my bones as I parried and blocked. They were relentless, their movements synchronized in a dance of death I hadn't expected. My breathing grew ragged as I struggled to hold my ground. Each breath tasted like iron, my heartbeat echoing in my ears. I couldn't keep this up. I was going to die here.

The storm overhead blowing in rumbled ominously, dark clouds swirling like they sensed my desperation.

A cold shiver ran down my spine, seizing me in an icy grip that wasn't from the rain. Something stirred within me, deep and foreign. It was a sensation I couldn't quite name, but it felt too familiar, too dangerous. It curled and writhed, a raw pulse of power coiling beneath my ribs, pushing insistently against something that wasn't a wall but felt like one—like I was being held back by an invisible hand.

It felt like the magic I'd used to rip Rian's soul from his body, but it was different, sharper, more insistent. The sensation wasn't just inside me; it *was* me. It was as though a part of me had been lying dormant, waiting to awaken, and now that it stirred, it refused to be ignored.

My breath hitched as the force pressed against my chest, its weight making it hard to think, to focus.

What the hells?

I tried to recall what this feeling was, but nothing came. There were fragments, splinters of memory, but they slipped through my fingers like sand. This stupid fucking memory loss was going to be the death of me . . . if Antonio and Rex didn't get to me first.

The rain pelted us harder, and the frantic sounds of my struggle against the seasoned assassins filled my ears, but the feeling inside me swallowed it all.

The rush of power inside me grew stronger, clawing its way out like a beast wanting to be freed.

Unleash it, a voice demanded, and I understood. It wasn't a suggestion. It was a command. A side of me I hadn't dared acknowledge came alive, something that called to the storm and the sea.

I could feel it, deep inside, a presence that felt both foreign and familiar.

Exhaling sharply, my sword slipped from my fingers as the energy in my chest swelled, growing, until it erupted from me with a force that split the sky. I threw my arms wide, my breath catching in my throat as the storm answered my call. Lightning flashed, bright and jagged, tearing through the clouds with a deafening crack.

I wasn't prepared for the power, for the way it felt to become a part of the storm, to feel the lightning as it surged through me. It was like a wild current running through my veins, and I let it take me.

A blinding flash of light erupted from me, too fast for even Antonio and Rex to react. Electricity crackled violently, dancing across the ground and up into the sky, and in an instant, both men were thrown back. Their bodies hit the ground with sickening thuds, lifeless. Their weapons clattered to the earth, forgotten.

The storm raged above, relentless, as if the world itself had exhaled, its fury spent. But all I could do was stand there, my breath ragged, heart pounding, staring down at the two bodies lying still in the wet mud. The rain continued to pour, but it felt distant now, almost as if the storm had already claimed everything I needed.

I had done it. I had unleashed it.

But now, the echoes of the power still vibrating within me, sickening realization crept in: I'd killed members of the Brotherhood. Fellow assassins.

"What the fuck did I do?" I whispered, too afraid to speak louder.

A pulse of energy thrummed against my throat, sharp and insistent, like something stirring beneath my skin. The stone.

It *called* to me.

Take them. Consume them. Grow your power.

I shuddered, blood roaring in my ears. Why did that sweet womanly voice sound familiar?

The bodies before me lay twisted and broken, their souls hovering in the air, translucent wisps of blue-gray light caught between death and oblivion. They *belonged* to me now. The stone knew it. And it wanted them.

I swallowed hard. I *should* resist. I *should* fight it.

But the hunger inside me . . . gods, it felt *good*.

My fingers tightened around the stone, and before I could think, before I could stop myself, I *pulled*.

A sudden rush of darkness flooded through me, thick and suffocating, swallowing me whole. It burned through my blood, ice and fire colliding in a storm of raw, unrelenting power. The world around me dimmed, the rain, the wind, the very *air* twisting in on itself, warping to fit the darkness I embraced.

The souls screamed.

I gasped, my knees buckling as something inside me expanded, stretching wide like wings unfurling from a cage. My vision blurred, shadows curling at the edges, and for a moment, I wasn't sure where I ended and the power began.

Then—

"Gods above, *Rose*."

A voice cut through the haze, sharp and familiar, yanking me back to reality.

Tibault.

I blinked, the darkness retreating just enough for me to see him stalk toward me, his chest heaving, rain dripping from his dark curls. His eyes were wide, wild with something caught between awe and horror.

He slowed before reaching me, gaze flicking between my face and the bodies at my feet. "Are you okay?" he demanded, his voice rough with disbelief. "*How* did you do that?"

I stood there, shocked and confused, unable to say anything. Instead, I stared at the two bodies and tried not to notice the burnt flesh filling my nostrils.

Tibault blocked my view of them, and I silently thanked him.

Tibault took another step closer, his gaze flicking between me and the bodies, then to the stone still clutched in my trembling fingers. His brows furrowed, rain dripping from his jaw as he studied me with a mix of caution and something else—understanding.

"Did you just—" He swallowed, his voice low, hesitant. "Did you take their souls?"

I sucked in a sharp breath, the weight of what I had done pressing down on me like a crushing tide. My fingers curled around the stone, as if letting it go might somehow undo what had already been done. But nothing could erase the raw truth, the power still thrumming inside me, the wisps of blue-gray light now fully absorbed into the gem at my throat.

"Yes," I whispered, barely able to say it aloud.

The moment the word left my lips, the last of my composure shattered. A sob ripped from my chest, sharp and jagged, and before I could stop myself, I sank to my knees, my body wracked with shaking breaths.

"I—I didn't mean to," I choked, my fingers digging into the mud as if I could ground myself in something real, something solid. "It just *happened*. I could feel them—I could *hear* them, and then the stone—" I squeezed my eyes shut, pressing the heels of my palms against them, trying to block the memory of power flooding through me, the sheer *rightness* of it even as it horrified me.

Tibault didn't speak right away. I half expected him to recoil, to back away like I was some kind of monster. He didn't.

He crouched beside me, his hand settling firm and steady on my shoulder. "Hey," he murmured, voice softer now. "Breathe, Rose."

I shook my head violently. "No, you don't understand. I *took* them, Tibault. Their souls. I—" My voice broke, my hands clutching at the wet fabric of my shirt as if I could tear away the guilt, the weight of what I'd done. "What if I can't stop it next time? What if—"

He grabbed my wrists, pulling them gently away from my chest, forcing me to look at him. "*We will figure this out.*" His tone was firm, unwavering, but not unkind. "You're not doing this alone."

I let out a shaky breath, my vision blurred with tears.

He exhaled, giving my wrists a gentle squeeze before letting go. "Come on," he said, shifting his stance, offering me his hand. "We can't stay here. We'll figure the rest out later, but right now, we need to get you inside before anyone finds us out here."

Hesitating, I glanced down at the bodies one last time. The rain had already begun washing the blood into the mud, as if the earth tried to erase what happened. But the memory would linger. The power still coiled in my veins, whispering, waiting.

I sighed. Tibault's words didn't help the sick feeling in my stomach—nothing could. My mind was a whirlpool of unanswered questions: *who was I? An assassin, a woman with soul reaping powers who could command the skies?*

That was the final straw. If Gemma's tonic wouldn't help me remember. I was going to have to find a different way.

"I know I have absolutely no right to ask since you're saving my ass already, but I need a favor."

Tibault narrowed his eyes but nodded.

"I need to know who the fuck I am and the only way I can do that is if I remember. Gemma has been trying to help but it's not working. There must be someone else who can help me."

"And you want my help?" Tibault asked, his brow furrowing as his jaw clenched. He crossed his arms, his gaze sharpening as he took a step closer to me.

My lips pressed into a thin line, my posture tense as I met his gaze. "Can you?" I asked, my voice steady despite the uncertainty I felt.

Tibault exhaled slowly, resignation crossing his features. He uncrossed his arms, one hand coming up to rub the back of his neck as he sighed. "I'll see what I can do. For now, you need to get back inside." His eyes flicked over my shoulder, taking in the scene around them, before returning to me. "I'll take care of this."

I nodded, the corners of my mouth pulling into a grateful smile. "Thank you, Tibault. I owe you." My shoulders eased, but the heaviness of our situation weighed on me, lying in wait for the moment it could strike again.

He let out a soft laugh, shaking his head with a wry grin. "You owe me nothing, Rose." His gaze softened, the edge in his tone gone as he took a step back. "Just remind me to not get on your bad side, eh?" He gave me a teasing look, trying to lighten the mood despite the tension in the air.

16
FRACTURED
ARIE

What the hells was wrong with me?

I buried my face in my hands, trying to quiet my storm of thoughts but it was like trying to tame a raging tide with a flimsy net. The weight of what I had done pressed into my ribs like iron shackles, dragging me down, down, down into a darkness I wasn't sure I could crawl out of.

And then there was Tibault.

Of all people. *Tibault.*

I never expected him to be the one to pull me back from the brink. He had never been cruel, but he had never been particularly kind either. We had always circled each other like wary predators, neither friend nor foe, bound by circumstance rather than choice. I wasn't sure if he distrusted me or simply didn't care to get to know me. Then again, I had never really tried with him either.

I collapsed onto the bed, my mind a jumbled mess of fragments. Every thought, every memory felt like shards of glass, scattered and impossible to piece together. It was too much—too fast. The night had been a blur of blood and power, of things I wasn't sure I was ready for. I had killed a man. Stolen his soul. *Three souls.*

A shudder wracked my body. I felt *sick*. My chest tightened, my breath coming in quick, shallow gasps. Tears, hot and heavy, slid down my face, tracing paths of confusion and fear. The weight of it pushed me deeper into the bed, as though I could bury myself beneath the covers and escape from what I had become. The pounding in my head only made it worse, a constant, insistent throb that threatened to drown me.

"Fuck!" I cried, my voice raw. Anger, confusion, and frustration churned inside me, twisting in my gut. How had everything gotten so out of control? Why couldn't I just—*understand*? My power, my past, my place.

Tomorrow was the masquerade ball. The one where I had to take more souls, but how could I? I couldn't even trust myself. How was I supposed to pretend everything was fine when I had no idea who I was or what I was capable of?

I wanted to scream. To shatter something. Anything.

A vase sat on the bedside table, the ceramic cool against my heated palm and I chucked it across the room. It hit the adjacent wall with a crash.

This was exactly why I needed Tibault to come through for me. If there was another way to get my memories back, I'd take it. I couldn't move forward until everything was in place, until I could see the whole puzzle again.

I wanted to *feel* something that made sense. But instead, all I felt was overwhelming *emptiness*.

The soft knock at the door was a welcome interruption. Though, at this point, I wasn't sure I could face anyone. I just wanted to be left alone in the silence, in the chaos of my thoughts.

"Go away," I called out, my voice shaky with the strain of holding it together.

The door creaked open, and in walked two servants—not Ana or Cala—one holding a steaming bucket, the other a towel draped over her arm. Their presence hinged on comfort, but it didn't erase the heaviness in my chest.

"The Queen has asked us to take care of you, miss," the first servant said, her voice gentle and soothing. She set the towel on the bedside table, moving with practiced grace. "We're nearly done drawing you a bath. Her Majesty insists that you rest before the ball tomorrow."

"Fine," I said absently, too tired to respond properly.

I undressed, my body riddled with cuts and bruises from Antonio and Rex, not including the lingering ones from the Pits. The women around me didn't seem to notice.

As they eased me into the bath, the warm water enveloped me, and I let out a shaky breath. The tension in my shoulders eased a little. But when I closed my eyes, the images of those I'd killed flooded my mind.

The two women spoke softly between themselves as they worked, chatting about the upcoming ball and their excitement to serve the Queen. Their voices were polite, almost rehearsed, as though they had done this many times before.

I kept my thoughts to myself, but I couldn't stop the question from bubbling up.

"Do you . . . do you like serving the Queen?" I asked, my voice a little raspy, though I didn't know why I cared about their answer.

They nodded, too quickly, too enthusiastically.

"Yes, my lady," one of them replied. "Queen Gemma is kind and fair. We are happy to serve her."

I nodded, but something about her expression felt off. It was subtle—nothing anyone not paying attention would have noticed—but I watched for it. Her smile didn't quite reach her eyes and there was a flicker of hesitation in her gaze.

A lie? Or maybe just . . . doubt?

Another glance passed between them. And again, that slight, almost imperceptible hesitation. They were lying to me, but I didn't know why. Was I being paranoid?

I stared at them, watching their expressions carefully, as they bathed and cared for me. But I couldn't shake the feeling that something more lurked beneath their polite smiles. Something I couldn't quite place.

And that, more than anything, made me uneasy.

They left quietly while I glanced at my reflection.

At first, a stranger was stared back at me.

I froze.

This face was mine, but it felt . . . foreign, like I was looking at someone else entirely. There was a softness in my features that I couldn't recall, a certain weariness that didn't belong. My eyes were red from tears, but there was something else there now—something cold, something distant.

I leaned closer, each shaking exhale fogging the surface of the looking glass. There had to be a connection, something familiar in my gaze, but the woman who stared back at me, wasn't entirely . . . me. Wet hair clung to my face in heavy ropes—it was still me physically but this woman? She had never known peace, a haunted look in my green/brown/blue/color eyes.

I hated it.

A cold shiver ran down my spine.

I squeezed my eyes shut, trying to push the image of that foreign reflection out of my mind. But it lingered, haunting me like an unwanted shadow.

The bedroom was quiet when I returned, save for the rhythmic sound of my breathing, but the silence became suffocating.

After dressing, I paced the room, trying to focus on

anything other than the unease that settled deep inside me. The feeling that there was something I wasn't being told. A truth that danced just out of reach. I had to know what it was.

The scent of roasted meat and spiced vegetables drifted through the air, and my stomach twisted with hunger. On the small table near my bed, a silver tray had been set with dinner—succulent lamb, buttered greens, and a hunk of fresh bread still warm from the oven. My stomach growled, but my attention was drawn elsewhere.

Beside the plate sat a familiar chalice, filled with the thick, red liquid Gemma had given me for days now. The tonic.

I hesitated.

Gemma claimed it would help and maybe it had. But something gnawed at me now, the unease roiling through my gut like a coiled snake. My memories were still shattered, small pieces of me swept under the run no matter how desperately I tried to piece them together.

What if the tonic wasn't helping me at all?

What if it was doing the opposite?

I didn't have a reason to not trust that Gemma was trying to help but then why hadn't the tonic done its job by now?

I picked up the chalice, swirling the thick liquid, watching the way it clung to the sides. My heartbeat drummed in my ears. Would I even know if I was being drugged every day? My mind was already a mess—fragments of a life I couldn't piece together, emotions that felt both foreign and familiar, and now a power inside me that I barely understood.

I brought the chalice to my lips. The scent was slightly sweet, almost floral, but something about it turned my stomach.

No.

I wouldn't drink it. Not tonight. What's the worst that could happen? After all, I *still* didn't remember anything.

With a slow exhale, I stepped toward the nearest plant, a lush, leafy fern in the corner of the room. I tipped the vial, letting the liquid spill into the soil. The red tonic soaked into the dirt, vanishing within moments.

A sharp knock came at the door.

I stiffened, my fingers curled around the empty chalice. My pulse quickened as I turned toward the sound.

Another knock, firmer this time.

Steeling myself, I set the empty chalice back onto the tray and crossed the room. With a measured breath, I pulled the door open.

Tibault stood on the other side.

The candlelight from the hall cast deep shadows across his face, sharpening the angles of his features. His dark eyes flicked over me, taking in my damp hair, my loose tunic, the tension wound tight in my body.

"You're awake," he said simply.

I arched a brow. "Obviously."

He didn't smile. Instead, he shifted his weight slightly, glancing past me into the room. "May I come in?"

I hesitated. I wasn't sure I wanted company but something about Tibault's expression gave me pause. "Fine. But if you're here to lecture me, I'd rather you save your breath."

Tibault let out a low chuckle as he stepped inside. "Wouldn't dream of it." He crossed his arms and leaned against the edge of the table, his dark eyes scanning me with something unsettlingly close to concern. My stomach twisted, and I shifted where I stood.

"I came to check on you," he said simply, his voice smooth but careful, as if testing the waters before stepping in.

Rolling my eyes, I said, "I don't need a babysitter."

A flicker of amusement ghosted across his face, "I know that, I just wanted to make sure you were okay after what happened." Tibault watched me carefully. "You won't be punished for what happened. I spoke with the Queen. She knows how important your mission is. Those men provoked you and you defended yourself."

I let out a slow breath, though it did little to ease the building tension in my shoulders. "Is that supposed to make me feel better?"

Tibault's mouth quirked slightly. "It should. Robin's rule is simple—anyone who harms recruits outside of training is executed on the spot. You did him a favor."

His words settled over me like a heavy cloak. I didn't know if it was meant as reassurance, but it didn't feel like it.

I ran a hand over my face, trying to push past the weight pressing at my skull. "There's something really wrong with me, Tibault," I admitted, my voice quieter now. "Something feels off."

His expression shifted, the amusement and sharp remarks gone. His brows knitted slightly as he studied me. "It's probably just stress," he said, though doubt lingered in his voice.

"You've been through a lot."

"I suppose."

"But the memory loss—it's getting worse, isn't it?"

I hesitated before nodding.

Tibault exhaled through his nose, thoughtful. "I will help you, but we'll wait until after the ball. Then we go to Gemma together."

The mention of the ball barely registered. Something else clawed its way to the surface, a whisper of a memory threading through the haze. A man. His voice curled around me like smoke. *I can help you. All you have to do is say my name three times.*

But what was his name?

I squeezed my eyes shut, grasping at the pieces before they could slip away, but the memory was already gone.

Tibault must have noticed something in my face because his voice softened. "Rose?"

I blinked, clearing my throat. "Just tired."

He didn't look convinced. "You sure that's all?"

"I feel like I'm losing pieces of myself. I can't remember things I know should be there. And the worst part is—I don't even know what I've forgotten. It's like my past has been carved out of me, and all I'm left with is the emptiness where I used to be."

Tibault didn't speak right away. Instead, he watched me with an expression I couldn't quite place, something heavy yet unreadable.

After a moment, he pushed off the table and walked over, stopping just a foot away. His voice was quieter when he spoke. "I've seen people lose themselves before." His jaw tightened slightly. "The mind can break just as easily as the body. Maybe easier."

I didn't know what to say to that. For once, he wasn't making a sarcastic remark or shrugging things off with his usual air of detachment. This was something real, something close to him.

"Sounds like you've dealt with this too," I said, voice softer than I intended.

He exhaled a slow breath, dragging a hand through his dark hair. "Yeah." A pause. "And I know that it doesn't happen in an instant. It's slow. Subtle. Like water wearing down stone." His gaze flickered to mine. "You're not there yet. I won't let you get there."

Something in my chest tightened, something too raw to name.

"You can't promise that," I said, forcing a half-hearted

smirk. "Besides, I'm stubborn. You might be stuck with me forever."

Tibault chuckled, the warmth of it catching me off guard. "Wouldn't be the worst thing."

I blinked. He must've realized what he'd said because he cleared his throat, shifting slightly as if shaking off the weight of the conversation.

"How did you come back from it?" I asked.

"The Brotherhood. Being part of something more than just myself. I took all that anger and uncertainty and turned it into discipline and purpose."

The candlelight caught in his eyes as he turned toward the window. "They gave me targets instead of ghosts to chase. Taught me how to carve purpose from chaos."

"There's something you're not saying, isn't there?" I saw it, in the tells of his face, the same tells Frederick pointed out when he taught me how to play poker. The slight tick of the jaw, the distant look in the eyes.

"Sometimes I wonder if I'm doing the right thing, if being here is the right path for me."

"Like you're missing something?"

Tibault shrugged. "Not sure, but right now the brotherhood is all I have."

"So did joining help you?" My whisper hung suspended like cobweb strands.

His laugh tastes bitter. "Better than drinking myself dead."

The admission lingered like gunpowder smoke between us. Moonlight fractured across his cheekbones, as I counted each shallow breath but that didn't quite steady my pulse.

He turned abruptly. "You're not broken yet." Callused fingertips graze my wrist—a spark where skin met skin—before retreating.

"Get some rest, Rose," he said, stepping back toward the door. "Tomorrow will be a long day."

I watched as he pulled open the door, pausing briefly before looking back. For a moment, I thought he might say something else. But instead, he just gave a small nod before disappearing down the hall.

I exhaled, sitting at the edge of the bed, staring at the flickering candlelight.

That night, I dreamt.

Sunlight filtered through the thick canopy of a towering oak tree, dappling the ground in golden patches. The air smelled of warm earth and ripening apples, the lazy hum of summer bugs thick around us. I was small, cradled between my fathers as tears streaked my cheeks, hot and frustrated. Blood trickled from a gash in my knee, stinging where the jagged bark had bitten into me. Twigs and brittle leaves clung to my tangled hair, souvenirs from my latest adventure.

My father's arms tightened around me, his deep, steady presence grounding me. "Do you see now why we told you climbing trees and trying to fly isn't something you can do?" His voice was gentle, but amused, the corners of his mouth twitching with suppressed laughter.

I sniffled, scrubbing at my face. "But, Papa Malakai, I wasn't trying to fly! I was climbing my ship to get to the mast. I have to keep watch for pirates."

His laughter rumbled through me, warm and rich like the scent of woodsmoke. The kind of sound that made the world feel safe.

"We've talked about that too, sweetheart," my other father chimed in, his tone more exasperated but filled with affection. "Pirate ships are no place for little ones."

"But I'm not little anymore, Papa Viktor!" I huffed, sitting up straighter in his arms, as if sheer will alone would make me grow taller. "I can reach the apples off Mr. Radley's apple tree without even having to climb it now!"

Papa Malakai chuckled, ruffling my hair before pressing a kiss to my forehead. "Don't you ever lose that spunky attitude, little fish. You're going to do great things."

Papa Vik scooped up baby Frankie, rocking her against his chest as he turned toward the house. "But first, you need to get washed up for dinner."

I pouted but let Papa Malakai take my hand, his calloused fingers warm around mine. His voice softened, turning serious. "Make sure you take care of her, okay? You're her big sister now. It's our job as the older ones to protect the young ones."

I nodded, straightening my spine with newfound determination. "I'll keep her safe, Papa. I'll keep us all safe."

He grinned, squeezing my hand. "I know you will, little fish."

The world shifted.

The warmth of summer vanished, replaced by a suffocating chill. The oak tree disappeared. I stood in the dim glow of the fireplace, the familiar scent of my childhood home replaced with something acrid—something wrong.

Malakai and Viktor sat in their chairs laughing and smiling at one another.

No. No, no, no.

The door burst open with a deafening crack. Shadows spilled in like living ink, faceless figures moving with deadly precision. Malakai was the first to stand, hands raised, his voice calm but urgent as he pleaded with them.

Steel flashed.

Blood splattered across the room.

I came awake with a choked gasp, drenched in sweat, and my breath coming in sharp, ragged gulps. My pulse thundered in my ears, the horror still clinging to me like a phantom, refusing to fade even as the dim glow of reality settled around me.

I wasn't sure if the first part of my dream had been real or just the desperate longing of a shattered mind.

But the second part—I knew.

I had seen it with my own eyes. I had lived it. And I knew what I had to do. I clenched my fists, my heart pounding with purpose. My fathers' deaths would not go unanswered.

Gemma was right. I had a duty.

The souls of the lost needed to be cleansed. My fathers deserved justice.

And I would be the one to deliver it.

17

BENEATH THE MASK
ULRICH

THE SUIT ITCHED. NOT IN THE WAY WOOL CHAFED OR saltwater stung, but in a deeper, more visceral way—like my own skin rejected it. Like it knew I didn't belong here.

I tugged at my cuffs, exhaling slowly through my nose as I stared at my reflection in the dim candlelight. A nobleman's mask stared back, his sharp edges softened by civilization, by control. But beneath it all, I was still the same man. Still the same pirate who had crossed seven seas for her.

Arie.

My gut twisted at the thought of seeing her again. She would be there standing beneath the golden chandeliers, possibly draped on another man's arm. The thought curdled in my gut, bitter and seething. She wouldn't know me. Wouldn't remember the nights we spent whispering secrets beneath star-strewn skies, wouldn't remember our time at Seven Falls, and how badly I'd wanted to kiss her when her back was pressed against the kitchen counter.

Damn Queen Gemma.

Damn whatever spell had taken her from me.

I needed tonight to go smoothly. We had one shot at this—

one chance to get in, to find her, and to remind her who she really was. And if she didn't remember?

I reached into the inside pocket of my suit jacket and pulled out Slayer—Arie's dagger. The weight of it was familiar, grounding, like holding a piece of her in my hands. It was large, the curved blade wickedly sharp. I ran my thumb along the edge, feeling the deadly promise it held.

The hilt had been carved into a dragon, I continued to run my thumb along its tail until it reached the base. With a soft click, a hidden compartment slid open, revealing an even smaller blade nestled within. A final trick, a last resort—because Arie always believed in having a way out.

I snapped it shut and exhaled slowly, tucking the dagger back into my jacket. Maybe, just maybe, this would remind her of who she was.

What we were.

Squaring my shoulders, I forced down the nerves coiling in my gut. We had to get this right.

"Hells, Hook." A sharp slap landed between my shoulder blades, jolting me forward. I grunted, more annoyed than surprised. Frankie grinned at me, all teeth and trouble, her eyes flickering with mischief beneath the low candlelight.

"If you weren't in love with my sister," she mused.

I rolled my eyes. "Good thing I am then."

She sighed dramatically, leaning against the vanity beside me. "Shame. I do love a man in a suit."

"Wait," she gasped, and her jaw dropped. "Did you just admit—"

"Have all the preparations been handled?" I asked quickly. I had no intention of talking about my feelings with Arie's sister. It should be obvious how I felt about her but to openly admit it to anyone but Arie felt wrong.

Frankie groaned, shoving off the vanity with a huff. "Yes,

Captain. Everything is in place. Hansel will handle the distraction, Tink and I are on guard duty, and the rest of the rebels will be stationed outside the castle walls, ready to storm the gates the moment we give the signal." She folded her arms. "You don't need to triple-check everything."

I met her stare in the mirror, my reflection a ghost of the man I used to be. "I like things to go right."

She snorted. "Since when has *anything* gone right?"

She had a point.

But this time had to be different.

I adjusted the black mask on my face, ensuring it sat snugly before surveying my reflection. The man staring back was nearly unrecognizable. Gone were the wind-tangled locks that usually framed my face; now, my hair was slicked back, civilized, controlled. The beard I'd grown over the months at sea had been shaved clean, leaving sharp angles and sharper eyes.

And the suit—hells, I could barely stand it. Black, tailored to fit, not a wrinkle in sight. It felt more like a costume than attire fit for a ball. Like I'd stepped into the skin of someone else entirely.

Frankie whistled low. "Damn, Hook. You clean up too well. Almost makes me forget you're a pirate."

"That's the point."

Something unrecognizable passed through her gaze before she schooled her features. "You sure about this?"

No. Not at all.

I nodded anyway. "I have to be."

Because Arie would be there. And whether she remembered me or not, I wasn't leaving without her.

"Have you checked on the *Dutchman*?" I asked.

Frankie nodded. "Yes, Keenan says they're still doing okay, though more of the crew is falling to the illness. The sooner we get Arie back the better."

Now that was something Frankie and I could agree on.

The masquerade was in full swing by the time we arrived. The grand ballroom of Queen Gemma's castle was a masterpiece of excess, a world away from the rough wooden decks and salt-stained sails I was used to.

Golden chandeliers hung high above, their flickering candle light reflecting off the marble floors, casting ever shifting patterns of shadow and light. The vaulted ceiling stretched endlessly, painted with celestial murals—constellations and gods frozen in time. Massive arching windows revealed twinkling stars and a beautiful, bright crescent moon.

The scent of spiced wine, roses, and warm beeswax filled the air. Laughter, low murmurs, and occasional clinks of crystal goblets blended seamlessly with the music. The nobility moved through the gilded space, each figure adorned in rich fabrics, elaborate masks obscuring their faces—peacocks, foxes, ravens, and creatures of myth long forgotten..

Frankie, dressed in deep blue with a silver mask that curled like waves over her cheeks, nudged my ribs with her elbow. "Enjoying yourself, *your lordship?*"

I didn't answer. My focus was elsewhere.

"Leave him be, Frankie." Tink scolded, then looked at me. "You can do this. Come on, dance with me until we find Arie."

"All right," I agreed, leading her out to the dance floor.

I wrapped my arm around her and placed the other in hers. It was weird seeing her this way, in her full human body, and not hearing the twinkling bells when she spoke.

"You look very beautiful, Tink."

Her face flushed. "Why, Ulrich, did you just say something nice?"

I groaned and she laughed.

All around, people danced while my heart hammered against my ribs, drowning out the hum of violins and murmured conversation. Every carefully laid plan—every calculated step—shattered the moment I saw her.

Arie stood amidst the swirling dancers like a flame come to life. She was a vision of fire and shadow, standing beneath the glittering chandeliers—her hair a wild cascade of crimson curls, each fiery strand catching the light as if it burned with a life of its own. A black mask obscured half her face, an enigma of silk and lace that only heightened her allure, drawing the eye to the sharp curve of her jaw, the full lips painted a daring shade of red.

The dress clung to her, the midnight fabric sculpting every graceful curve of her tall, commanding frame. Each step she took was deliberate, a siren's call wrapped in silk and barely refined beauty. Eyes followed her—some filled with intrigue, others with envy—but none could look away. Me included. She was the kind of beauty that left men breathless and woman in awe, a storm wrapped in elegance poised to strike.

Dropping Tink's hand, I moved before I could think better of it, my purpose for being here slipping through my fingers like sand. The dance floor swirled around her, dozens of people lost to the haze of candlelight and music, but all I saw was her.

I stopped just inches away, pulse roaring, and held out my hand.

"Dance with me?" My voice was rougher than I intended, more plea than command.

For a breath she hesitated—then slowly, her lips curled into a smile as she placed her hand in mine, sealing my fate with a single touch.

Her fingers slipped into mine, warm and steady.

She didn't recognize me.

A flicker of something sharp twisted in my chest, dark and

hollow, but I shoved it down. This was what Queen Gemma had done—ripped away her memories, stolen every moment we had shared, leaving her standing before me as a stranger.

But even without recognition, she looked at me like I was worthy of her attention.

The music swelled, violins sweeping into a haunting waltz, and I guided her into the dance. The moment our bodies aligned, heat bled through the silk between us, and for a second, I swore she felt it too—the pull, the familiarity buried deep within her lost memories.

Her gaze flicked to mine, sharp and searching. "You don't look like the type to ask a stranger to dance."

A ghost of a smile tugged at my lips. "And you don't look like the type to say yes."

Her lips curled, but there was something guarded in her expression, like she wasn't sure whether to be amused or wary. "Maybe I was feeling reckless."

My grip on her waist tightened instinctively. *You have no idea how reckless this is.*

Then again, that was Arie. The embodiment of recklessness and danger. She'd taken everything I'd ever known and thrown it off the *Black Betty* and into the Seven Seas. I never dreamed I'd find someone as magnificent as her and yet I came here risking everything to save her. To help her save herself.

As the music carried us deeper into the dance, her body molded to mine, her touch steady despite the uncertainty in her eyes.

She didn't remember. But maybe—just maybe—I could make her feel.

I tightened my grip on her waist, guiding her across the marble floor, the weight of what I had to say pressing against my ribs like a violent beast. But I had to do something, it was my job to convince Arie that this was wrong and not who she really was.

"You shouldn't be here," I finally said.

Arie arched a delicate brow. "Where else would I be?"

"Anywhere but at her side." I spun her, the candlelight catching the gold woven into her midnight dress. "The Queen is using you, Arie."

Her eyes widened when I said her name. She tried to back away, but I held her tighter.

"You. You're the man from the fighting pits."

"Yes, and I'm trying to warn you that the Queen is twisting the truth. You're fighting for a cause that isn't yours, fighting for a corrupt queen who would see you dead once her mission is over."

She scoffed, barely missing a step. "You don't know what you're talking about."

I leaned in, my breath warm against her ear. "Don't I?"

Her fingers tensed in mine. "The Queen has given me purpose. She's given me a chance to make a difference. To stop the rebels who want to burn everything down."

A flicker of uncertainty passed over her—her jaw tensed, her brows drew together for the briefest of moments, as if she doubted her own words. Her gaze darted away before settling back on me.

I exhaled sharply. "The rebels are fighting for their freedom."

Her jaw tightened, something flashing behind her mask—another, deeper flicker, quickly smothered. "And yet they leave destruction in their wake."

"They aren't the ones spilling innocent blood." I searched her face, hoping and praying that she could feel the truth buried inside her stolen memories. "She's lying to you, Arie. The things she's told you about the rebels is a lie. This—" I squeezed her hand. "*We* are real. I promised you I would prove to you that we are meant to be, that I'm not the bad guy. I swore to help you put the pieces back together. You have to remember, Arie. I'm here pleading with you to see reason."

A shadow passed over her expression, her steps faltering for the first time.

I pressed on, desperate now. "Tell me—have you ever seen the rebels do the things she claims? Have you ever questioned what she's asked of you?"

Arie's lips parted, but no words came. A hesitation, a further crack in the foundation of whatever false truths Queen Gemma had built around her. It wasn't much, but it was enough.

I softened my voice, dipping my head slightly so my lips almost brushed the shell of her ear. "You used to fight for something real. You used to fight for *us*."

Her breath caught.

For a second, just a second, I swore something shifted behind her mask. A distant familiarity. A pull in the way she looked at me, in the way she moved—not as a stranger, but as someone who had once known the rhythm of my steps as well as her own.

Then, just as quickly, it was gone. Her expression steeled, her grip turned rigid.

"I don't remember you," she said, but her voice lacked conviction.

I smiled, slow and knowing, my thumb brushing over the back of her hand in a way I knew—*knew*—drove her mad. "But you feel it, don't you?"

Her pupils dilated, a sharp inhale betraying her.

I spun her again, but this time, I didn't let go, pulling her back into my arms, my grip firmer, my hold unwilling to let her slip away again. Our bodies aligned in a way that felt too natural to be coincidence. The music swelled around us, the masquerade blurring into meaningless shapes and shadows.

"You were never meant to be a pawn in someone else's war," I murmured. "You were meant to be free."

Her mask hid whatever war waged in her mind, but I saw the way her breathing hitched. The way her knuckles whitened. She stepped further away from me.

I tried to move toward her, but the crowd surged in response to the new music, the sea of masked bodies shifting between us.

I cursed under my breath, shoving through the throng, but it was too late.

I hadn't given her Slayer.

18
A PAWN NO MORE
ARIE

The ballroom glowed in golden light, the chandeliers painting shifting patterns across the polished marble floor. The air was thick with the scent of crushed roses and spiced wine, a cloying sweetness that clung to every breath. Silk and velvet swirled in hypnotic motions as masked figures moved in elegant rhythm, their laughter blending seamlessly with the waltz. It was a night of beauty and illusion, a carefully crafted dream where identities were hidden, and truths could be bent to fit the moment.

And I was dancing with a stranger.

Yet . . . he didn't *feel* like a stranger.

The man's hand was firm against the small of my back, guiding me through the steps with effortless grace. His other hand clasped mine, warm and steady, his fingers a whisper of something *familiar* against my skin. The moment he had asked me to dance, something in my chest twisted. Something I couldn't name.

Now, caught in his hold, I felt it tightening.

Yet his declaration that the rebels weren't the ones in the wrong, that it was Gemma . . . no, he was wrong. The Queen had nothing to do with the destruction, she wanted to fix it. My mind flicked back to our discussion about the rebels, how they'd burned and overtook villages in the Enchanted Forest. The look in her face, the sadness that crept to her eyes, there was no way she'd lied about that. I was sure of it.

Wasn't I?

But it wasn't that alone that had me so confused. *We are real. I promised you I would prove to you that we are meant to be, that I'm not the bad guy. So, I'm here pleading with you to see reason.*

What did he mean by this? I had no idea who this man was. I barely remembered who I was for sea's sake. Something tightened in my chest and I stepped back. I almost asked him to take off his mask but he spoke first.

"You were never meant to be a pawn in someone else's war," he murmured. "You were meant to be free."

Thankfully, the music stopped and I wrenched myself from his grip as the crowd dispersed, giving me the distraction I needed.

I turned, slipping back into the throng of nobles before he could stop me. I had a mission. A duty. And I would not *fail* her.

Even if the ghost of that strange man's voice followed me as I disappeared.

The grand halls of the castle whispered with old secrets, their shadows curling against the cold stone. The faint strains of music from the masquerade barely reached these corridors, muffled by the weight of history and the sins committed within these walls.

I moved soundlessly, my blade an extension of my arm, my pulse steady despite the gravity of my task. The names Gemma had given me were etched into my mind, each one an enemy to the kingdom, a threat to the peace she had built. I believed in this. *I had to believe in this.*

The first target was exactly where the Queen said he would be.

Elder Sinclair sat hunched over his desk, candlelight flickering against the lined creases of his face. A man of power, stripped down to nothing but ink-stained fingers and weary eyes. He never heard me approach.

In one swift motion, I drew my blade across his throat.

A wet, gurgling gasp. His hands clawed at his desk, knocking over papers and ink as he choked on his own blood. His mouth opened and closed in silent protest, his eyes wide with the last flickers of fear. I caught him before he hit the ground, my grip unyielding as I pressed a hand to his chest and drew out his soul.

The effect was immediate, much faster than it had been the last few times.

The soul surged forward as if it knew where to go, sinking into my palm like liquid fire. My breath caught, the shock of it thrumming through my veins, cold and electric, seeping into the marrow of my bones.

Sinclair's soul writhed against my skin, pulsing with its last echoes of existence. A tattered thing of memories and regret, clinging to the last vestiges of the man it had belonged to.

I could *feel* him—his fear, his desperation, the final flickers of a life wasted on wealth and power that now meant nothing. I could end it here. Send him where he was meant to go.

A woman's voice slithered through my mind, dark and familiar, dripping with something both seductive and *terrifying.*

Or—you could take him for yourself. Consume it, little one.

I froze. My heart slammed against my ribs.

That voice.

I knew it.

Didn't I?

A whisper of something old, something buried deep in the marrow of my bones, curled around me like a phantom tide.

You were made for more than this. You were made to take. To devour. Just like I was.

The soul twisted in my grip, writhing with newfound urgency, sensing—*knowing*—that another force reached for it. A deeper pull, something more insatiable than death.

Take it. The voice coiled closer, breath against my ear, velvety smooth. *You are more than flesh, more than mortality. You were born for power, for dominion. Do you not feel it? The hunger? The ache?*

And gods, I *did*.

It crackled beneath my skin, something vast and untamed, a force clawing its way out of the depths of me. A second heartbeat, an ancient rhythm thrumming in sync with the pull of the soul in my palm.

I shuddered.

Another flash of memory—salt, thick and suffocating in my lungs. A shape rising from the depths, monstrous and endless, the ocean curling around it like a worshiping lover.

Teeth. Eyes like burning gold. A hunger that had no end, only *need*.

The Leviathan.

The soul curled tighter, drawn toward my core, its fading energy latching onto mine like a parasite. I felt its memories shifting, breaking, becoming *mine*—a life unlived pressing against my ribs, a second consciousness forming in the back of my mind. If I let it in, if I consumed it, I would be more. Stronger.

You could be a god., daughter of mine. Be a god.

The voice was a knife to my chest.

No.

This wasn't who I was. All my memories could be lost until the end of time, but I would always *know* the person I was. Consuming souls was not it, becoming greater—becoming a god—wasn't who I wanted to be. It was one thing to take souls and want to make them better, but it was another to consume them. I already felt the darkness that clung to these wicked souls. Blood stained my hands, but I'd be damned if it stained *my* soul.

Gritting my teeth, I ripped my other hand forward, clutching the violet stone at my neck. The pulse of its magic flared at my touch, resonating with my own power, waiting.

You're a fool. Just like your father.

The soul screamed.

It writhed, desperate, fighting to escape, to run.

I forced it downward.

A guttural noise tore from my throat as I shoved the soul into the stone, watching as the swirling tendrils twisted violently, resisting, until—

A final, piercing wail.

The stone *drank*.

The light inside it pulsed, violet veins of energy curling through its depths as the soul was sealed away. The pull of it left me all at once, the absence of it almost enough to send me to my knees.

Silence.

Cold sweat dripped down my spine. My hands trembled and my breath came in sharp, ragged pulls, but I was still *me*.

The voice in my mind had gone quiet.

I wiped my blade against his cloak and turned—

"Fucking hells, Arie!" A furious voice snarled. A woman's silver mask leaned slightly askew, her wild blonde curls tumbling from their pins. "What are you doing?"

I gritted my teeth, my muscles tense. "Who are you?"

The woman faltered, a look of hurt flashed in her eyes I didn't understand. She stumbled back but didn't loosen her grip on her blade. "Did you kill this man? This isn't you! Gemma has twisted your mind, and you don't even see it."

"Are you with the man I was dancing with? I'll tell you the same thing I told him, you don't know what you're talking about."

The woman let out a bitter, humorless laugh. "Don't I? You're standing here, in a dead man's study, stealing his soul, and you want to tell me this is who you are?" Her eyes burned with something dangerously close to grief. "You used to fight monsters like her, Arie."

"This man deserved it. He killed my family."

Well, he may not have given the blow but he ordered it. As had the other rebels.

The woman stilled. "What?" She gave Sinclair a look. Anger? Why would she care about this man?

"How do you know me?" I asked, curiosity getting the better of me.

The woman tore her mask away, the silver fabric fluttering to the floor. Beneath it, her face was illuminated by the faint candlelight.

"I have known you my entire life. You were the first friend I'd ever had. You carried me three miles after I'd fallen from Mr. Riddler's apple tree. You're the one who sat next to me and promised that everything was going to be okay as our fathers lay dead in the next room."

She took a step closer, and I could hear the tremble in her breath. "*You are my sister, Arie.*"

The world narrowed.

I stood rooted to the spot, every muscle locked, every breath shallow. Her words cracked something inside me, splintering across the surface of my thoughts like a hammer against glass.

Sister.

That wasn't right. That wasn't *true*.

I had no sister.

The Queen had saved me from a life of nothingness. Had given me purpose when I had none. If this woman had been my sister, if she had ever truly *mattered* to me, wouldn't I *remember*?

And yet—

A flash. Laughter in the trees. The scent of crushed apples and damp earth. A small hand gripping mine, covered in dirt and scraped raw at the knuckles. Tears, so many tears and a voice that sounded like my own: *I won't leave you. I promise.*

I stumbled back a step as if I could physically shake the memory loose but it was out of reach. Only a dream. This was what the Queen had warned me of. A trick by the rebels. A *lie*.

"No." Rage flared hot beneath my skin. "My family is dead."

Then, I lunged.

Steel clashed against steel in a flurry of movement, the corridor filled with the sharp *clang* of our blades meeting. She fought like wildfire—fast, reckless, untamed—but I had been trained for precision. I met her strike for strike, anticipating her movements before she made them.

"I don't want to hurt you." She pleaded, a single tear sliding down her cheek.

As if she could.

She feigned left, but I caught her arm, twisting it behind her back. She hissed in pain, but instead of faltering, she slammed her elbow into my ribs, forcing me to release her.

"Damnit, Arie, listen to me!" She panted, her chest rising

and falling. "You've been lied to. Manipulated. The people you're killing? They aren't the villains in your story."

I tightened my grip on my dagger, my heart thundering against my ribs. "I don't believe you."

Heavy footfalls echoed from around the corner. The woman tensed.

"Shit," she muttered under her breath.

Before I could react, she turned and fled, vanishing out the open window.

"Rose?" Frederick stopped in the doorway with Dom at his side. "Are you alright?"

I pushed aside the weird feeling in my chest and swallowed. "No, there are rebels in the castle."

Frederick shook his head. "There's no way. The Queen's guards have every entrance sealed and we have assassins all over the grounds. We would know."

Obviously there was a flaw in their security.

"I—"

Dom held up a hand. "The Queen wants you in the ball. There are more targets to eliminate. We'll take care of the cleanup and search for rebels."

My shoulders relaxed. "Understood."

I left the corpse behind and started down the hallway, my steps soundless against the cold stone. The weight of what I had done settled in my bones, but it was nothing compared to what I now carried.

I clutched the stone around my neck, its surface smooth and deceptively cool beneath my trembling fingers. But inside... inside, it *burned*. The power it held thrummed against my palm, pulsing in a rhythm that was not my own, an ancient echo that whispered beneath my skin.

I swallowed hard, my throat dry. Should anyone wield something like this?

Gemma had said this was necessary. That she would *fix* them. But something about this didn't sit right. Could a soul truly be changed? Bent into something new and returned as if nothing had ever happened?

Or would they be something else entirely?

A chill slithered down my spine.

The stone pulsed again, almost . . . *eager*.

Ancient.

Wrong.

I tightened my grip, as if I could crush the feeling out of existence. Whatever unease slithered through me, I had to bury it. Doubt was dangerous.

Doubt got people killed.

And I still had work to do.

Music swelled from the orchestra, the haunting melody weaving through the air, curling around the murmurs of conversation and the clinking of crystal glasses as I entered the ballroom.

No one here knew the truth.

No one knew that blood had been spilled in the castle's halls while they laughed and waltzed beneath Gemma's careful gaze. No one would know that the lord they spoke with or the lady they danced with would die tonight. The rebellion leaders had to die.

A flicker of doubt rushed through me, and I faltered. What if the strangers were right? What did I really know about the Queen? Sure, she'd given me a place to stay, and had helped me find purpose again. She had agreed to help me find my parents' murderer. But my memories? The fog was slowly clearing, more flashes of an open sea, dozens of men and women working tirelessly, a man with blonde hair and a . . . scar along his face.

His name, a flicker of recognition flowed through me. It started with a D... no, a P.

"There you are." Queen Gemma looped her arm in mine and tugged me closer, pulling me out of my thoughts. "Sinclair?"

I nodded, and my heart hammered in my chest.

"Good. Ranta just left to take a stroll in the gardens. See to it that he enjoys the flowers, will you."

Without answering, I moved through the throng of people until I stepped out into the cool night. I sucked in a deep breath, my head dizzy and my stomach in knots.

I needed to remain diligent. An assassin who lost their focus ended up on the other side of death. And I had no plan to die tonight. I had to remember that I'd watched rebels tear down my fathers. This is what I fought for now.

The night air was a sharp contrast to the warmth of the ballroom, crisp and cool against my flushed skin. The scent of roses and damp earth curled around me as I stepped onto the stone pathway, my heels clicking softly against the ground. Lanterns lined the garden, their golden glow casting long shadows against the hedges and statues. The quiet hum of insects filled the space between rustling leaves, but beyond that, all was still.

Ranta was out here somewhere.

I flexed my fingers, steadying my breath as I moved deeper into the garden. The weight of my dagger was a reassuring presence at my hip, a reminder that I was not defenseless, that I was not weak. And yet... the flicker of doubt lingered, whispering like a phantom at the back of my mind.

I slipped through the shadows, my steps silent as I followed the faint scuff of boots. There—just beyond the fountain, where the moonlight barely reached—a figure stood with his back to me.

Ranta.

The rebel general was older than I expected, his shoulders slouched with the weight of years spent fighting a war I only just joined. He stared down at a silver pendant in his hands, running his thumb over its surface as though lost in thought.

He didn't hear me approach.

I could end this now with a blade to the throat. A final breath lost to the wind.

I drew my dagger and—

"Arie."

I froze.

The voice wasn't Ranta's.

It came from behind me.

The stranger from earlier stood at the garden's edge, only this time his mask was gone, revealing blue eyes and a face that . . .

"Listen to me. I know a part of you knows me. A part of you must remember saving me from sirens, killing the Leviathan, taking on Wendy." He moved closer, his steps slow and deliberate. "Tell me you haven't forgotten about the falls, the promises I made to you."

He stood dangerously close now. My heart was a thunderous beat in my chest as my body refused to move, as though it needed him closer.

He leaned in, his breath hot on my ear. "Don't you remember the way your body reacted to me in the kitchen?"

My stomach whirled.

Something hard slipped into my palm, and I instinctively curled my fingers around it. The weight was familiar—solid, grounding. A piece of me.

I stepped back, my breath shallow as I lifted the dagger, my fingers tracing the grooves of the ornate hilt. The carved dragon coiled around the grip, its tail curling down to the butt, where I knew a hidden compartment lay sealed within. *My* carving. The craftsmanship was unmistakable. I had shaped this weapon with my own hands, once upon a time.

Slayer.

The name rippled through my mind like a drop in still water, sending fractures through the fragile walls that held my memories at bay.

Flashes. Blood dripping from the curved edge, catching the light like molten rubies. The first time my fingers had curled around the hilt, the way it had settled into my grip as if it had always belonged there. The whisper of steel slicing through flesh. The rush of power, the certainty of purpose.

Every kill. Every moment.

The last strand snapped and recognition slammed into me like a tidal wave. All of my memories unraveled, a roar like a tidal wave flooded my mind.

I looked up at the man who I saved all those months ago. The man who had promised me things, who had helped me in ways he couldn't even begin to imagine.

The man that I *loved*.

"*Hook*," I whispered.

"Arie, come back to me. Gods, I can't bear losing you again. Please, I love—"

"Hey!"

I spun around only to be met face-to-face with Ranta.

"You're the Queen's newest assassin." The weathered man held out his arm. "Accompany an old man back inside, will you? As long as your friend here doesn't mind?"

"Actually, I do—"

"It's no trouble at all." I glared at Hook—*Ulrich*—and then my face softened. "Sir Ulrich, we can finish this discussion later."

Ulrich stumbled back, his eyes wide in shock, a single tear sliding down his face. But I couldn't focus on him. I couldn't focus on anything except the cold weight of realization settling in my chest like a stone dropped into deep, black water.

I left him standing there, frozen in place, and tightened my grip on Ranta's arm, escorting him back into the ball. The sounds of music and laughter swelled around me, a stark contrast to the storm tearing through my mind.

I remembered.

Not just flashes, not just pieces—everything.

The cell. The chains. The damp stench of rot in my lungs.

Jameson, whispering promises of pain in my ear, his hands and blades slicing at my defiance.

Saving Hook from sirens, helping Pascal get away from his abusers, killing Wendy.

And then Gemma. The chalice that was placed before me, the way the wine warmed my throat as my vision blurred, the way she laughed over me as I sank into darkness.

It had been the *tonic* all along.

I'd been drinking my own destruction, swallowing my memories, sip by sip, until she had molded me into exactly what she needed.

A weapon.

A killer.

A pawn in a war that had never been mine.

My pulse roared in my ears as my fingers twitched toward the stone at my throat. The souls trapped within, their power thrumming beneath my fingertips like a miniature heart.

Gemma had told me I was cleansing the world of rebels, but she had been lying. She had always been lying. She'd wanted me to finish what Ursa had started.

Oh Gods, I was going to be sick.

"So tell me," Ranta smiled up at me, his voice light, almost amused, as if he didn't just witness my entire world crash down.

"Did I just save your life?" He gestured back toward Ulrich. "Or did he save mine?"

I forced a smirk, trying to push down the bile rising in my throat. "That depends," I said coolly. "Are you planning to do something that would require saving?"

Ranta chuckled, but his gaze sharpened, seeing *too much*. "Oh, I think we both know I already have."

I kept my grip on his arm as we wove through the ballroom, the weight of Slayer comforting against my hip, of the stone pressing against my throat.

"You remember now, don't you?" Ranta asked and I narrowed my eyes. "No time to ask questions now. There's a few things you need to know. It was Gemma and Ursa who sent assassins to take out your fathers. They needed to and the only way to get to you was through them. *They* sent you on this mission, Arie."

Gemma had ordered my father's death.

"Why are you telling me this? How do I know you're not lying?"

Sadness came and went in Ranta's face. "I understand why you're hesitant, but I assure you. Malakai and Viktor would kill me themselves if they knew I let their daughter go down this path without stepping in. The Elders and I play a part, a part we don't like but it's important nonetheless. Gemma believes she has allies but the only allies she has are the assassins in the Brotherhood who blindly follow her. It's time for a change, my dear and I think we're about to get just that."

I swallowed, doing my best to take in this new information. Gemma had twisted everything, pulled the strings, turned me into the thing my mother had once been—a collector of souls, a force of destruction.

I reached for the necklace, my fingers brushing the stone's surface. I had taken lives, stolen their souls, poured them into this cursed relic—finishing the work my mother, Ursa, had started.

I wanted to tear it from my throat.

"Keep it safe," Ranta murmured.

I snapped my gaze to him. "What?"

"The stone," he said, voice lower now, unreadable. "Whatever Gemma has planned, it hinges on *that* and if you're not careful, she'll use it to turn you into something you can't come back from."

His words sent a shiver through me.

Because somewhere deep inside, I already knew—

She nearly had.

Before I could respond, a sharp voice rang through my mind.

Arie!

Holy hells, Tink. I can hear you again.

The biggest weight lifted from my shoulders and if I was anywhere else I might have wept.

Your memories are back.

They are. Where are you?

Here, in the ballroom. We have a plan to get you out of here and—

Tink's voice was drowned out by another voice sending a hush over the crowd.

"Ladies and gentlemen."

Queen Gemma.

She stood from her throne at the head table, a vision of regal elegance in deep violet silk, her golden mask glinting under the chandelier's glow. Her smile was poised, serene.

"As we celebrate this most *opulent* of nights, let us remember the order and peace we have all worked so hard to maintain."

Her gaze swept the gathered nobles, lingering—for the

briefest of moments—on me and then on Ranta. A flicker of anger on her face came and went before she continued. "But peace is not so easily kept. It is not born of mere *wishes* or *good intentions*. It must be cultivated, upheld by those who *understand* the weight of power. The burden of leadership."

She stepped around the table to stand at the front, the sound of her heels a crisp staccato against marble.

"There are those who would see this peace undone," she said, her voice darkening. "Who whisper rebellion in the shadows, who spin *lies* to poison the minds of good men and women. They do not wish for freedom. No—what they crave is *chaos*. Anarchy disguised as revolution."

A murmur rippled through the crowd, unease shifting in the air like a gathering storm.

"But we will not be fooled," she declared, her voice rising, filling every corner of the hall. "We will not be swayed by traitors and thieves who seek to dismantle all that we have built."

Her lips curled in a smile—cold and knowing.

"Because here, in *my* kingdom, justice is not blind. It is swift. It is absolute."

She lifted a hand, her jeweled fingers catching the light. "And so, we drink tonight not just to revelry, but to *order*. To the strength of our reign."

The nobles raised their glasses in eager compliance, but my grip tightened on my dagger's hilt.

Her reign.

Her order.

A slow, insidious feeling curled in my gut.

"No, my Queen."

A voice rang out, cutting through the silence like a blade.

The entire room shifted, a breathless pause before the world cracked open.

Robin and a tall woman stood near the banquet table, their

masks discarded, their eyes burning with purpose. What were they doing?

"There is no peace," Robin continued. "You've built your throne on the bones of better men. You've ruled through manipulation and fear."

I reached for my dagger, but Ranta grabbed my wrist.

"Wait," he murmured.

I wrenched free, but my feet remained rooted to the floor.

"You spent decades spewing lies about your intent, about what you're doing behind the scenes, and most of all about what happened to the VonWhite's."

The crowd burst into murmurs and gasps.

"What are you doing?" Gemma hissed. "You know what will happen to her if—"

A blond haired man laughed . . . *Pascal*? "Your little pet is dead and her beasts are free."

Robin continued. "And now I'm doing what I should have done a long time ago." He turned toward the crowd. "Gemma has you believing that the VonWhite family perished at the hands of rebels. We're here to tell you she's wrong."

A figure stepped forward, shoulders squared, chin high.

Clayton. What was Ulrich's brother doing here? He'd been headed to Khan last I knew.

"The true heir to the throne," Robin said, voice carrying over the stunned silence. "The youngest son of King Charles VonWhite. Clayton VonWhite, second heir to the throne."

A breath of disbelief swept through the nobles. Some recoiled. Some whispered. Others watched with unreadable expressions, their gazes flicking between the Queen and the young man standing before them.

Beside Robin, the woman parted her lips, a flicker of something cold and lethal flashing in her eyes before she schooled her expression into a smile.

"How quaint," Gemma drawled, stepping forward. "Do you actually think these people are going to believe the lies of rebels? The VonWhite family are dead."

"There is no lie here, Gemma." Next to me, Ranta walked toward the middle of the room. "Only yours."

"You're one of them?" Gemma shouted. "A filthy rebel who killed our beloved king and queen."

Elder Wulf moved to the middle of the ballroom. "You ordered me to kill the children, but I refused. So, I sent them away and now they've returned to take their place."

Fury like I'd never seen before radiated from Gemma. "You dare defy me, Wulf? You betrayed *me?*

Queen Gemma's voice sliced through the air, sharp as steel.

"Assassins. Seize them."

The ballroom erupted into chaos.

19
An Assassin's Word
Arie

The moment Gemma's command left her lips, the ballroom descended into hell.

A deafening explosion rocked the castle, shaking the very foundation beneath my feet. Glass shattered somewhere behind me, and screams filled the air as shards rained down like deadly stars. The chandeliers swung violently, their golden light casting chaotic, twisting shadows over the panicked guests scrambling to flee.

Then the rebels stormed in.

The heavy doors at the entrance burst open with a deafening crack, the wood splintering beneath the force of a battering ram. Smoke curled into the air, thick and acrid, curling around the invading force like living tendrils. Men and women clad in dark leathers surged forward, their weapons gleaming under the flickering candlelight. Their eyes burned with purpose, their movements sharp and practiced, like wolves unleashed on unsuspecting prey.

Swords clashed as guards met them head-on, but the rebels were faster, more determined. They struck with precision, weaving through the nobility like ghosts of vengeance. Tables overturned, goblets of wine crashing to the marble floor, staining it like pools of blood.

Another explosion roared through the night, shaking the stained-glass windows until they gave way, fragments raining down as flames licked at the sky outside. The gardens—once pristine and perfect—were a battlefield, fire consuming the hedges, smoke curling toward the heavens like an omen.

I stood frozen amidst the chaos, my pulse roaring in my ears.

I remembered.

I remembered everything.

The sirens. The Leviathan. The way the wind had tasted of salt and storm as I had fought for my life beside Hook. I remembered the desperation in Pascal's voice when he begged me to run, the gleam of my blade as I struck down Gregory to escape.

I remembered the pain. The rage.

And yet—

A piece of me, dark and hungry, whispered that I was not done. That I had a purpose to fulfill. That Gemma's dream was not yet realized.

The souls in the necklace pulsed, their trapped energy throbbing like a second heartbeat. Power curled beneath my skin, a part of me now, an extension of who I had become.

I knew what was right. Gemma was the enemy.

But the draw remained.

Even as my memories slotted into place, a hollow ache bloomed deep in my chest, as if I had been carved into something else, reshaped by her hands.

Gemma had made me into a weapon, but I had allowed myself to be wielded.

A scream ripped through the ballroom, and I snapped back to the present just in time to see a flicker of movement to my right. I ducked, twisting to the side as an assassin slashed where my head had been moments before. My instincts kicked in, honed from years of training—*training they had given me.*

I blocked his next strike with Slayer, the curved blade catching the candlelight as I shoved forward. The assassin grunted, stumbling back enough for me to strike. I drove my dagger deep into his ribs, twisting once before pulling free.

A hand gripped my shoulder.

I whirled, blade ready—

Robin.

"Don't hesitate," he snapped, shoving me out of the way as another assassin lunged for me. He met the strike himself, parrying with lethal precision. "They won't"

I sucked in a sharp breath and nodded, gripping Slayer tighter.

"You're going to die for this treachery, Robin." One of the assassins grunted as his sword swiped close to Robin's face. "You and your Hoods are finally going to get what's coming for you."

"Enough, Branson. It's time you all see the Queen for who she truly is."

I left Robin to finish taking care of Branson and searched the room. Pascal fought near the banquet table, his blade catching the light as he deflected a strike from an assassin. Hook —Ulrich—fought toward me, his mask torn away, revealing storm-tossed blue eyes filled with raw emotion. Behind him, Tink and Frankie were back-to-back, taking on as many of Gemma's assassins as they could.

For all their skill, we held our ground.

But we were outnumbered and something had to give.

From the corner of my eye, Queen Gemma whispered something to one of her assassins before slipping through a side passage, her expression calm—*smug*. She was leaving her men to do her dirty work. *Coward.*

My stomach churned.

She wouldn't run. Not without the stone.

I lifted my hand to my throat, feeling the cool weight of the Obsidian Heart Stone pressing against my skin.

"Ulrich!" I yelled as he reached my side. "We have to go after her."

Ulrich shook his head. "Robin and Gretel will take care of her, we have to get you out of here."

"The fuck we do! She killed them, Ulrich. My fathers are gone because of her."

Ulrich nodded without hesitation. "All right then, let's go."

"Really? Just like that?" I asked. I'd never known the man to *not* object to something I wanted to do.

"Yes, Arie. Just like that," he said seriously.

We sprinted through the side corridor, the sounds of battle roaring behind us, my mind still trapped in the ballroom, still trapped in the weight of everything that had crashed down on me. My breath came fast, my pulse hammering against my ribs as the shattered pieces of my past slotted themselves together with violent clarity.

A sharp voice cut through the noise.

"Rose!"

I whirled just as Frederick stepped out from the shadows of an adjacent hallway, his dark leathers stained with blood, his expression hard as flint. He still held his blade at his side. He didn't raise it—yet.

"Give me a second Ulrich," I left him standing at the end of the hallway and met up with Frederick.

"You need to come with me," he said, his voice low but commanding.

I shook my head, stepping back. "No, Frederick. You don't understand."

"I understand that the rebels are getting away and we need to stop them," he said sharply. "You and I both have orders."

The words twisted something sharp in my chest. The "Rose" he knew—the one he had fought alongside, trained with, bled with—would have followed those orders without question. She would have driven her blade into any throat Gemma told her to, believing it was justice, believing it was right.

But I wasn't *her* anymore. I never really had been.

"They aren't the enemy, Frederick," I said, my voice firm despite the shake in my hands. "Gemma is. She's the one who's been lying to us this whole time. The rebels—they've been fighting *for* the people, not against them. She took away my memories and forced me to help her. My name isn't Rose. It's Arie Lockwood."

His expression flickered—just for a second. But then his jaw tightened.

"You're wrong," he said, his voice quieter this time, but no less lethal. "After everything they've done? The cities they've burned? The people they've killed?" His grip on his sword tightened. "Don't stand here and tell me they're innocent."

Guilt slammed into me.

Because I *had* believed that once.

Had believed it with everything I had.

But now—

Now I *remembered*.

I swallowed hard, forcing myself to meet his gaze. "They didn't kill my father, Frederick," I said. "Gemma did. I was made to believe it was an Elder, someone from the Brotherhood. It may have been a Brotherhood assassin who wielded the blade, but I think I've known it was Gemma who gave the order for a while."

A muscle in Frederick's jaw twitched.

Frederick exhaled sharply, shaking his head as he took a slow step forward. His expression hardened, but there was something else behind his eyes—something cold, calculating.

"You're a fool, Arie," he said, voice low, measured. "After everything you've been through you *still* haven't learned your lesson."

I stiffened.

"This isn't about right or wrong," he continued. "It never has been. You think the rebels are your allies? That they're fighting for the people? You *really* believe that? Gemma can give you everything."

I clenched my fists, my heart hammering against my ribs. "She took away my memories. She manipulated me. killed my fathers and then forced me to—"

"To become something *greater* than yourself," he cut in sharply. "You were nothing before her. A scared little girl playing pirate and chasing ghosts." He tilted his head, a cruel smirk playing on his lips. "So, tell me, do you want to continue this never-ending pain, this cycle of doubt and suffering? Or will you finally understand that the Queen is merciful? She will end your suffering here and now."

Something about those words—

End your suffering here and now.

The world tilted.

A flash of cold steel.

Leather biting against my wrists.

Pain—sharp, unrelenting.

The sound of my own screams echoing in my ears.

A room.

A table.

The scent of blood and damp stone.

I jerked my gaze back to Frederick—no, *not* Frederick.

His smirk deepened as realization dawned, my eyes widening.

Jameson.

A shimmer, so subtle but unmistakable, rippled over his skin like heat distorting the horizon. It started at the edges, warping the contours of his face, his features flickering between what I had known and something more familiar—*too* familiar.

I blinked, my stomach twisting, my grip on Slayer tightening. The illusion magic wavered again, the fabric of the lie unraveling before my eyes. His hair darkened, the sharp lines of his face redefined, and those familiar, ice-blue eyes met mine with a gleam of amusement.

Frederick was gone.

Jameson stood in his place.

My breath hitched, my body tensing with the weight of the realization.

"You," Ulrich growled, he surged forward but the other assassins surrounding Jameson stepped forward.

"No," I whispered, my voice barely audible over the pounding of my heart.

Jameson tilted his head, a slow, mocking grin spreading across his lips. "Oh, but *yes*, little siren."

I stumbled back, bile rising in my throat.

"Surprised?" he asked, stepping forward like a predator savoring the moment before the kill. "I'd hoped you'd figure it out sooner, but watching you flounder in the dark has been . . . *entertaining*."

The breath whooshed from my lungs as memories crashed into me—his voice whispering in my ear, his laughter threading through my nightmares, gripping my wrists, pressing me down, and breaking me piece by piece.

"You're a fucking dead man," Ulrich spat, rage burning in his eyes. I could see the fire in him, the raw fury ready to explode, and without thinking, I grabbed his arm, my fingers pressing into his skin.

"Let me handle this, Ulrich. Please."

He paused, his body rigid, a storm of anger flashing across his face. His eyes—those intense, burning eyes—locked onto mine, and for a moment, the world around us seemed to stop. The fury inside him was palpable, threatening to consume us both.

I saw the internal battle waging behind his gaze. He wanted to lash out, to tear into Fire with everything he had. I could feel the heat of that urge, the tension in his muscles, but then something shifted. It was almost imperceptible, but his jaw tightened, and the fire in his eyes dimmed just slightly.

He let out a sharp breath, his fists unclenching, but the anger still simmered beneath the surface. With a silent nod, he backed off, stepping to the side, allowing me to take control of the situation. His gaze never left mine, but there was a raw trust in it, an unspoken understanding that, for once, this fight was mine to fight.

Swallowing hard, forcing myself to meet Jameson's gaze, to push past the suffocating weight of my past.

"Why?" I demanded. Rage clawed its way up my throat, my hands trembling with the need to *tear* him apart. "Why go through all of this? Pretending to be someone else? Lying, manipulating—"

"Because the Queen demanded it. Do you know how insufferable you are? More importantly, do you know how easy it was to get you to trust me? You really should work on that."

Behind me, Ulrich surged forward. "You're a dead man."

Jameson's smirk didn't falter. If anything, it grew, sharp and cruel, like a blade honed just for me.

Hook's rage was a tangible thing, pulsing in the air between us, but I lifted a hand, stopping him before he could charge.

This was *my* fight. Jameson had stolen too much from me—I wouldn't let him take Hook, too.

I tightened my grip on Slayer, my knuckles aching. "You really think this is funny?" I asked, my voice a dangerous whisper.

Jameson tilted his head, eyes glinting with amusement. "*Incredibly*," he drawled. "The little siren, so desperate for a place to belong, that she walked right into the lion's den. *Again*." He tsked, shaking his head. "You never learn, do you?"

A sharp, burning heat spread through my chest, but I refused to let it show. Instead, my lips curled into a smirk of my own. "You know, for someone so damn proud of his lies, you seem awfully pressed about me getting away."

His gaze darkened, the smug veneer cracking for just a moment.

Good.

I pressed forward. "What's wrong, Jameson? Did I ruin your fun? I bet it *kills* you that I got out—*that I survived*."

His nostrils flared, his grip on his sword tightening. "I don't *lose* my marks," he seethed. "*Ever*."

I let out a humorless laugh. "Then I guess I'm your first."

A flicker passed behind his eyes, a sharp change in his expression that was almost imperceptible, but it was there. His jaw tightened, his brow furrowing enough to notice.

"You think this is over?" he murmured, voice deceptively soft. "You think you've won?" His fingers flexed around the hilt of his sword, and his smirk returned, this time edged with something more sinister.

My stomach clenched at those words, a sickening echo of a past I'd fought so hard to bury. His voice, that same dark amusement, had taunted me in the dark. Had been the last thing I heard before the pain. Before the chains. Before the screams.

Hook took a step closer, his rage barely contained. "If you

ever touch her again, I will gut you from groin to gullet," he growled.

Jameson flicked his gaze toward Hook, lips twitching. "Ah, yes. Captain Hook. Tell me, does it bother you? Knowing that no matter how hard you try, you'll never *really* be able to save her?" His eyes cut back to me, glinting like a predator in the dark.

Something inside me snapped.

I lunged.

Slayer sang through the air, aiming straight for his throat, but he dodged at the last second, the blade grazing his cheek instead. A thin line of red bloomed against his skin, and for the first time since he revealed himself, his smirk faltered.

"Bitch," he hissed.

Not giving him time to recover, I pressed forward, forcing him back with each swing, each strike laced with all the rage, all the pain he'd ever inflicted upon me.

I *wanted* him to feel it, to *know* what it meant to suffer.

He blocked my next strike, our blades locking, and leaned in close, his breath hot against my skin. "You. Are. Weak."

I snarled, twisting my blade against his with all my strength. "And you're predictable," I spat.

With a sharp jerk, I wrenched Slayer free and struck again, forcing him back step by step. The clash of steel rang through the hallway, each impact a violent echo of the storm raging in me. He parried fast, but he wasn't fast enough. I was done hesitating, done letting my past hold me back.

Feinting to the left, I pivoted and slashed deep across his ribs. He cursed, stumbling, but the smug glint in his eyes never wavered.

"Remember," he rasped, bracing himself as he raised his blade. "The more you fight, the more fun this is for me."

My blood turned to ice.

For a split second, I wasn't here—I was back in the darkened chambers of the castle, shackled to a table, his voice purring in my ear as steel bit into my flesh.

The memory sent white-hot rage tearing through me.

I drove forward, knocking his sword aside. My knee slammed into his gut, forcing a sharp gasp from his lips. He staggered, but I didn't let up. I spun Slayer in my grip and drove the blade straight into his chest.

His mouth parted, a wet, strangled sound slipping free. He looked down, eyes widening as if he couldn't believe what had just happened.

I twisted the blade deeper.

Jameson's body convulsed, his knees buckling as blood spilled from his lips.

I leaned in close, my voice a whisper against his ear. "Who's the weak one now?" Then I wrenched Slayer free.

His body crumpled to the ground.

Somewhere close by, a sharp, piercing cry split through the night. The sound tore through the air like a blade, so loud and sharp it sent a shockwave through the hallway. The window beside us trembled—then shattered. I flinched, shielding my face from the shards as they rained down.

Outside the shattered window, perched on a nearby roof, beady black eyes locked onto mine, wings spread wide as if caught mid-flight. The massive bird shrieked again, the mournful sound wrapping around my bones like a curse.

The Morrigan.

"Arie, we need to go. Now." Ulrich grabbed my arm, and we raced down the hallway.

Robin and Gretel caught up with us at the end of the corridor, their breath labored but their weapons ready.

"Where's Gemma?" I demanded, scanning the empty hallway. There were no guards here, no sign of the Queen's presence—just the eerie stillness of the abandoned wing.

Robin wiped a smear of blood from his cheek, his expression grim. "She has to be inside still. There's no way she slipped past us."

I exhaled sharply, tightening my grip on the necklace. "She wouldn't leave without this."

I unclasped the chain and held the stone up to the candlelight. The deep purple gleamed, nearly black in the dim hall, pulsing with unnatural power. A storm of trapped souls swirled just beneath the surface, their whispers curling against my skin like invisible fingers.

Gretel stilled beside me, her breath hitching. Her green eyes flickered between me and the stone, horror creeping into her expression. "That stone . . ." She swallowed, taking a hesitant step forward. "That's the *Obsidian Heart Stone.*"

Robin's head snapped toward her. "The what?"

Gretel didn't look at him. Her gaze was locked on the necklace, her jaw clenched so tightly I thought she might crack her teeth. "I've been searching for that stone ever since I killed its last owner," she whispered, barely audible. "I wondered what had happened to it. I should have known Gemma probably had it."

A chill slithered down my spine. "Who did you kill?"

Gretel's hand curled around the hilt of her dagger as if grounding herself. She finally looked at me, something raw and haunted behind her eyes. "My foster mother. The woman who raised me." Her lips pressed into a tight line. "Esme."

Robin stiffened beside her. "You never told me."

Gretel nodded slowly, her expression unreadable. "There's a lot you don't know about me, Robin. The stone has powers to control an entire army to the point they become zombies. It drains people of their power and absorbs it, but apparently it can collect souls too." She looked at me. "It can create shadows and does more harm than good. It was created by witches before it was stolen and went missing, and by the time I learned of it, the giants had it. Originally, they intended to use it to win the war against the humans. Though once they realized how dangerous it was, they hid it within a mine in the Enchanted Forest. They didn't have the necessary power to destroy it so hiding it was their only option. Though, I suspect they hadn't expected the humans to take over so much of their land."

I looked down at the necklace in my hand, my grip tightening. It *hummed* in response, as if sensing recognition, as if *thriving* on its own legend.

"I had no idea," I admitted, my voice low. "Gemma gave this to me, and said it was meant to hold the souls of the rebels we executed." My throat tightened. "I thought . . ." My stomach turned violently. "She said she was *fixing* them."

Ulrich stepped closer until his body met mine and I wanted to melt into him. He leaned in and said, "Gemma stole your memories and manipulated you. She did this."

Gretel let out a sharp, humorless laugh. "She did, and I can tell you for certain there's no fixing a stolen soul, Arie. There's only taking, breaking, and consuming."

My pulse roared in my ears and my stomach heaved at the thought. "I know that now," I muttered.

It had never felt right, the way the stone absorbed the souls. But I had convinced myself that Gemma's purpose was noble, that it was for order—for the kingdom.

But now, with Gretel's words, I knew the truth. Now that my memories were back, I knew this wasn't about *fixing* anything.

This was about control.

I turned to Robin. "We need to find her."

"We will," he promised, but his voice was tight. His gaze

flickered back to the stone, then to me. "But right now, we need to get out of here. If this is true and Gemma needs that necklace, then we have the upper hand. We need to leave before we get pinned down—"

A shrill whistle cut through the air.

Robin stiffened, his eyes darkening as he reached for his weapon. "Shit."

A beat later, the sound of booted feet echoed through the halls, followed by the gleam of metal as figures emerged from the far corridor.

Dom and Sienna.

"Well, well," Dom drawled, his voice thick with amusement. "Look what we have here, Sienna. Turns out you were right about her."

Sienna smirked. "It will make killing her all the sweeter."

"You two need to back off." Robin stepped forward.

Dom's smirk widened, his grip shifting on the twin daggers in his hands. "Back off? Now, Robin, that doesn't sound like you." His gaze flicked between us, predatory and assessing. "Come on now, be honest. Didn't you see this coming? Though I never thought I'd say that Queen Gemma made a mistake in making you an Elder. She never should have trusted you. And she's sent us to clean up the mess."

Sienna tilted her head, dark amusement glinting in her eyes. "And we do so love cleaning up messes."

Robin's hand tightened around his blade, but it was Gretel who moved first, stepping beside him, her stance wary but unyielding. Blood stained the fabric at her side, but she didn't seem to notice—or if she did, she wasn't going to show her weakness.

"I'd love to see you try," she said, voice laced with steel.

Dom let out a sharp laugh, tilting his head back as if this was a grand joke. "Oh, sweetheart," he sighed, twirling one of his daggers between his fingers, the movement effortless. "I was hoping you'd say that."

"Call her sweetheart one more time." Ulrich gritted his teeth.

Before Dom could respond, Sienna lunged, her blade slicing through the air. Robin parried, steel crashing against steel. And just like that, the others followed.

Blades flashed. Shadows twisted. Shouts and the sharp clash of metal filled the corridor.

I barely had time to react before an assassin lunged toward me, a dagger aimed for my ribs. I twisted at the last second, bringing Slayer up to block the strike. The impact jarred my arm, sending a shockwave through my bones.

Ulrich was beside me in an instant, taking on two assassins at once, his movements fluid and deadly. Robin fought Dom with a ferocity I had never seen before, his strikes precise, relentless.

A sudden scream cut through the noise.

I spun just in time to see Gretel stagger backward, her hand pressed against her stomach, blood seeping between her fingers.

No.

Something in me snapped.

I tore forward, shoving Sienna off balance before dropping to my knees beside Gretel. Her face was pale, her breath shaky.

"We need to get her out of here," Robin snarled, knocking an assassin away with the hilt of his blade.

I pressed my palm against Gretel's wound, trying to stem the bleeding. "Hold on, you're going to be fine."

Behind me Sienna laughed, "Is she though?"

Sienna stalked forward only for a blade to slice through the back of her neck, blood spurting across the floor in front of her.

Her body dropped to the floor and Tibault stood in her place.

"*NO!*" Dom screamed, but it gave Robin the distraction he needed. He swung with all of his might, his sword slicing through Dom's neck with ease, severing bone. His head rolled away from his limp body.

"Where's Tink?" I asked frantically.

"We need to get her to the underbelly," Robin said as he helped Gretel up. She groaned.

"Let's go," Ulrich agreed. "We have to hope the rest of our people made it out alive."

I sure hoped he was right.

"Where are we?" I asked as we stepped out of the sewers and into an underground city. We ran along a rickety bridge as floating balls of light buzzed by. My heart raced in my chest at the sight of such an expansive place below Chione.

"We're in the Underbelly," Robin called from ahead of me as he led us forward.

The city blurred into the background. My focus needed to remain on Gretel, her weight heavy against my side, each unsteady step sending a bolt of worry through me.

She was losing too much blood. Frankie and Tink had been fighting in the ballroom when we'd called for a retreat. I hoped to all the gods they'd made their way back.

"Keep your damn feet moving," Gretel murmured, though her voice was weaker than I wanted it to be. "I can walk."

"Sure," I shot back, adjusting my grip on her waist as she sagged. "That's why I'm basically carrying you."

"Let me take her," Ulrich said, more demand than request. Since we'd left the castle, he'd been watching me—not with suspicion, but with something heavier. Like he feared that if he looked away, even for a second, I might disappear.

Not that I blamed him.

Everything had unraveled so fast—my mind, my memories, the battlefield of the ballroom still burning in my thoughts. I wasn't even sure if I was really here. I felt like I moved through layers of reality, trying to piece myself back together with hands heavily stained from the things I had done under Gemma's thrall.

Ulrich's presence grounded me, even if I wasn't ready to admit that. But right now, my focus was Gretel.

I hesitated, my arms aching from holding her upright for so long. She had gone pale, her fire dimmed by blood loss soaking through the torn fabric of her dress. Every time I looked at her face, my stomach twisted—she had a hand in saving my life tonight, and now she might lose hers.

Swallowing hard, I nodded, relinquishing my grip as Ulrich slid an arm beneath her legs and lifted her effortlessly. Gretel groaned as her eyes slid shut, her head lolling against his shoulder.

I flexed my fingers, suddenly missing the weight of her against me. "We need to move faster."

Robin nodded. "Not much farther,"

We continued, but my gaze caught Tibault as he walked beside me.

I hadn't expected *him* to help.

Tibault had always been sharp-edged, unreadable, standing just on the fringes of where I thought my enemies and allies divided. He was *Brotherhood*, trained and bred for his loyalty to Gemma's cause. And yet, back there, he had chosen to fight beside me.

Why?

The question burned at the back of my mind, twisting around my heart like something alive. Was it just the tides of war shifting? Had he seen something that made him doubt

Gemma's rule? Or was this just another game—another calculated move?

I didn't know.

And I hated that.

I stole another glance at him through the dim torchlight, the flickering glow sharpening the lines of his face. He was focused, every muscle taut like a drawn bowstring, his grip tight on his weapons as though expecting another fight at any second. But there was something else too—something almost *unsettled* in the way his jaw clenched, the way his eyes darted to me, then away.

"Why are you here, Tibault?" I asked.

Tibault's gaze snapped to mine, something flickering behind his eyes. "I'm helping."

That was all he said.

We moved quickly through the underground, the air thick with damp earth and the lingering scent of smoke. People darted between alleyways, whispers of the battle above already spreading like wildfire. I barely took in the details—I couldn't afford to. The past and present crashed together in my mind, but none of it mattered. None of it compared to the weight pressing against my chest—the suffocating realization that *Jameson had fooled me.*

I had trusted him . . . well, I trusted *Frederick*. Hells this was so messed up. It was like Pascal and Peter only worse. I knew in the deepest part of my soul that Pascal would never do the things Frederick—Jameson—had.

Even without my memories, even with the warnings, and the nagging feeling that something wasn't right—I should have known.

My stomach twisted and my hands curled into fists, fingernails biting into my palms.

He had played me. Manipulated me. *Tortured me.*

And I—

I had let him.

Bitterness flooded my mouth.

Ulrich must have noticed because he glanced back at me. "Are you hanging in there?"

No.

But I wasn't about to say that.

"We just need to get to wherever the hells it is we're going," I muttered.

He gave me a long, searching look before nodding and adjusting his grip on Gretel.

Robin stopped at a small house and rapped his knuckles against the wooden door in a quick, deliberate pattern. A moment later, the door creaked open, and Kaelryn's sharp gaze swept over us.

"Kael?" My mouth dropped. Hells, I'd nearly forgotten about him.

"Good to see you made it out alive, Arie. I suppose that means my job here is done." His gaze flicked to Gretel. "Shit." He stepped aside without another word, motioning us in.

Ulrich carried Gretel inside, disappearing into another room with Kaelryn on his heels.

I lingered in the doorway, my pulse still hammering in my skull. The warmth of the underground hideout should have been comforting, but my insides felt frozen.

Robin touched my arm lightly. "You couldn't have stopped it"

"What?" I asked.

"Gemma has had many people in her grasp for so long. Her power has been unmatched. She trapped me a long time ago and took away someone important from me just to prove a point. What she did to you was wrong but it wasn't something you could have stopped."

I swallowed, my throat raw. "Why does it feel like I ripped myself apart?"

"You weren't just breaking free from Gemma," he answered, voice quiet, but unwavering. "You were breaking free from the person she made you. From everything she forced you to become. And you didn't just leave that behind, Arie—you had to tear yourself away from it, piece by piece."

"We are going to end this. Together."

I closed my eyes, inhaling deeply. I wasn't sure if I would ever feel whole again. I had killed for her, taken their souls for her. I looked down at the stone hanging from my neck and blinked back tears. No matter how comforting Robin's words were, I had to put it all aside.

I had a war to win.

20
Never Let Go
ULRICH

Jameson was dead, and Arie had been the one to kill him.

I should have been satisfied. I *should* have felt some sense of victory, knowing the bastard who had betrayed her, who had tortured her, who had laughed while she suffered—was nothing more than a corpse cooling in the dark.

But I wasn't satisfied.

Because *I* hadn't been the one to kill him.

I hadn't been the one to drive Slayer through his gut, to watch the light drain from his eyes, to make him feel *fear* the way he had made her feel.

And worse? I hadn't been there to *stop* it from happening in the first place.

I watched Arie across the room, her hands curled around a cup she wasn't drinking, her fingers white from the grip she had on it. She had told us everything when we got back—every bloody, twisted detail. She hadn't sugar-coated it. She hadn't tried to soften the edges. She had laid it bare, and every word had sunk its claws deeper into me.

The rage in my chest was a living, breathing thing. It coiled beneath my ribs, simmering hot and dark, my fingers twitching with the phantom sensation of wrapping around Jameson's throat. *He should have died screaming.*

But it wasn't just anger.

It was *fear*.

I had never seen her like this. Never seen that *look* in her eyes. Cold. Hollow. As if something in her had cracked wide open and she hadn't figured out how to put it back together.

It wasn't just Jameson's death. It was *all of it*.

The torture. The manipulation. The way she had looked at her own hands after pulling the Elder's soul from his corpse, as if she wasn't sure if they were still *hers*.

I tightened my jaw, forcing myself to exhale slowly, to push back the darkness slithering in the back of my mind, whispering for blood, for the need to kill all those who had harmed her.

I leaned against the wall, waiting a moment before speaking. "You've been quiet."

She didn't turn, didn't react right away. Just a slow inhale, then, "So have you."

I huffed a small laugh, though it lacked any real amusement. "Thought you could use some space."

Silence stretched between us, thick and heavy, but I let it. Rushing her wouldn't do either of us any good. She was like a storm on the horizon, caught between calm and destruction, and I wasn't sure which way the winds would take her.

Finally, she exhaled and turned just enough to look at me. "Frankie and Tink . . ." she trailed off, her brows knitting together. "You think they're still out there?"

Pascal and I had discussed it earlier. There was no doubt in my mind that Frankie was alive. I'd seen her scrape by impossible odds many times, and if Tink was with her, she had an even better chance. But the fact that Arie was only asking now told me just how far away her mind was.

"They're alive," I said, keeping my voice steady. "And Frankie's got some explaining to do when we find her."

Arie's lips pressed together, but she didn't ask.

Didn't demand answers.

Didn't say much of anything.

It wasn't like her.

I pushed off the door and stepped closer, watching her carefully. "What's going on in that head of yours, Sea Witch?"

Her fingers twitched where they rested against the windowsill, but she didn't look at me this time. "I don't know," she admitted. "I should feel. . . different. I should feel angry or —" She exhaled sharply. "Something."

I knew that tone. That hollow, detached edge, like she was slipping away even though she stood in front of me.

"You've been through hell," I reminded her, keeping my voice low. "Give yourself a damn minute to catch up."

She laughed softly, but it was the kind that made my stomach twist—one with no humor, no warmth. "A minute won't fix this."

I reached for her before I could stop myself, my fingers brushing against her cheek. "Then let me."

Finally, she looked at me, and my heart clenched at the exhaustion in her eyes.

"I don't know how."

I swallowed, stepping closer until I could feel the warmth of her body through the chill clinging to her skin. "Then let's figure it out together."

Her breath hitched, but she didn't pull away. Didn't move at all.

I didn't know if I was getting through to her, but I wasn't letting her slip away. Not again.

Not ever.

I trailed my finger lower, her soft skin sending chills through me. My fingertip looped around the necklace, cupping the stone in my palm.

"I have something for you," I murmured. "Something much better than this."

Arie didn't say anything as I turned, reaching into my jacket and pulling out a small chain. The trident pendant glinted in the dim light, silver and familiar, time-worn but whole.

The second she saw it, her breath hitched. She stiffened, tremors racing through her arms.

"Where did you get that?" Her voice was quiet, but there was something sharp underneath it, something raw.

"Frankie found it after you were taken," I said, turning the pendant over in my fingers before offering it to her. "Slayer and this were all that remained."

Her eyes didn't leave the necklace, like she was afraid it might disappear if she blinked.

"The chain was broken," I continued. "Ace had it replaced. I kept it safe."

Her fingers twitched at her sides, hesitation flickering across her face.

"You kept it," she whispered.

It wasn't a question.

I nodded. "I couldn't let it fall into the wrong hands. And I knew what it meant to you." I swallowed, pressing the pendant into her palm. "We all did."

Her fingers curled around the trident, gripping it tight. "I thought it was gone," she admitted, her voice barely above a breath. "I thought—"

"You didn't lose it," I said softly. "It's always been yours."

She let out a shuddering breath, her knuckles whitening around the chain. She didn't move to put it on, didn't say anything. Just stood there, staring down at it like it was a piece of herself she hadn't expected to find.

She swallowed hard, then looked up at me. "Why?"

I exhaled, brushing my fingers over hers where they clutched the pendant.

"Because it belonged to you," I said simply. "And because I swore that when I found you, I'd give it back."

Her lips parted, but no words came. Her eyes shimmered with something I couldn't place, like this moment had cracked something open inside her, something too fragile to name.

For a long second, neither of us spoke.

Then, just above a whisper— "Ulrich."

Not Hook. Not Captain.

Ulrich.

My name in her voice sent something electric down my spine, grounding me in a way I hadn't felt in years.

"I'm here," I said, voice rougher than I meant it to be.

She pressed the pendant against her chest, fingers trembling slightly. I lifted my hand, brushing my thumb over her jaw, feeling the warmth of her skin beneath my touch.

She glanced at my lips, her breathing uneven.

"Arie," I murmured, barely more than a breath.

Her hesitation lasted all of a second before she surged forward, closing the distance.

Her lips met mine hesitant at first, soft and searching. Then something shattered between us, something raw and desperate, and she pressed closer, like she was afraid I'd disappear if she let go.

I groaned, wrapping my arms around her waist, pulling her flush against me. She fisted my jacket in her hands, anchoring herself, and I held onto her as tightly.

This wasn't just a kiss.

It was everything.

Every stolen moment, every whispered promise, every unspoken word.

And I'd be damned if I let her go again.

21
ALL OF YOU
ARIE

THE MOMENT MY FINGERS BRUSHED AGAINST THE trident, something inside me cracked. The cool metal, worn smooth from years of touch, pulsed against my palm like a heartbeat. My father's heartbeat. A memory buried beneath lies, beneath the lies Gemma had fed me.

A sickening wave of guilt washed over me, and I had to fight to stay grounded. The faces of those I had killed came rushing back, their eyes wide in terror as I struck, as I stole their souls. And I hadn't even known who they truly were, whether they were good people or not. Sure, the two assassins had tried to attack me, but the Elders? For all I knew, they had been innocent, caught in the game Gemma had been playing from the beginning. The horror of it made my chest tighten, the guilt choking me until it felt like I couldn't breathe. I didn't want to think about it. I couldn't think about it—not now, not when everything was falling apart around me.

But I knew I would have to face it eventually. I would have to confront the fact that I'd done unspeakable things, taken lives, all because Gemma had twisted my mind with her poison.

I curled my fingers around the pendant, my breath hitching

as a rush of images flashed through my mind—my birth father's warm laughter, his strong hands securing the chain around my neck, the way his voice had rumbled as he told me, *this will always bring you home, my little tide.*

Home.

I lifted my gaze to Ulrich, my pulse roaring in my ears.

He stood before me, watching, waiting, his jaw tight, his blue eyes filled with something dark. Something wrecked. Something that had been waiting—aching—inside my chest.

Everything between us snapped.

I reached for him, dragging him to me in a violent kiss. Our mouths clashed, his breath hot against my lips, but I didn't care. I *wanted* this, wanted to drown in the fire between us, wanted to feel *everything*.

His hand gripped my hip, fingers digging into my flesh like he was trying to anchor himself. He kissed me back just as fiercely, but then—he stopped.

His forehead dropped to mine, his breaths ragged, uneven. His grip on me turned bruising before he loosened it, stepping back just enough to look me in the eyes.

"I don't think I can be gentle," he rasped, his voice raw, laced with dangerous promise. "Not with you. Not with this. I can't be what you need."

I exhaled sharply, heat flashing through me—not just from frustration, but from the challenge in his words.

I grabbed his face, forcing him to look at me, my nails digging into his jaw.

"You think I need *gentle*?" My voice was sharp, edged with demands. "I don't want soft. I don't want careful. I want *you* —in every form. I want your hands on me, your weight against me, your teeth at my throat. I want to feel you, Ulrich. *All* of you. So, if you think you need to hold back for my sake, don't."

A muscle in his jaw ticked, his hand flexed at his side like he was holding himself back.

I shoved at his chest. "Give me everything you have. *Break me.*"

Something snapped in him.

He moaned my lips before his teeth grazed my throat, his tongue soothing the sting a second later.

My gasp was raw as he pushed me back against the bed, the weight of his body pressing me down, his grip unyielding as his fingers slid into my hair, pulling hard enough to sting. The hard, unforgiving ridge of his cock rested against my thigh, a pulsing, throbbing promise of what was to come.

"Open for me," he growls, his voice low and gravelly, a command that makes me clench in response. I did as he asked. My thighs fell apart, and he settled between them, his hips nudging mine, the head of his cock brushing against my soaked entrance.

"Gods," I choke out, my fingers clawing at his back as his girth split me open, filling me until I was gasping for air. Thick and unrelenting, the stretch was almost too much, but it was exactly what I needed. He paused, letting me adjust, his breath hot against my neck.

"You feel so fucking good," he murmurs, his voice husky and strained from the effort to took him not to lose control.

His thrusts were slow at first, teasing, but then the rhythm grew faster, more desperate. It was a wild ride, a rush of pleasure that bordered on pain, making my body tremble under his touch.

His teeth nipped at my earlobe, sending shivers down my spine. "Say it again, tell me what you want, little mermaid."

I arched into him, needing more. "Break me, Ulrich."

His silver hook glinted in the dim light as it trailed down my ribs, cold metal contrasting with the burning heat of his skin. I moaned—the cruel edge that could flay me open, the careful precision with which he avoided drawing blood. His mouth followed the path, teeth scraping my hip bone, and I realized with dizzying clarity that every touch was a confession. This man who commanded ships and slayed monsters mapped my body like uncharted waters, murmuring ancient sailor's prayers against my thigh.

His breath hitched when my hips rolled against him. "Look at you," he smirked, dragging the blunt curve of his hook down my sternum. "So eager to be ruined."

I laughed—a sharp, broken sound—and dug my heel into the small of his back. "You're the one trembling."

A lie. We both were.

He pinned my wrists above my head with his forearm, the hook now buried in the mattress beside my face. A warning. A surrender. His free hand slid between us, fingers dragging through slick heat before pushing inside me with a growl that vibrated against my throat.

"Still think you can handle this?" he asked, curling his fingers in a way that made my vision blur.

My answer dissolved into a wordless cry as he added a third finger, the stretch bordering on pain. His eyes locked onto mine, blue fire consuming every twitch of my features. And when his thumb found that swollen bundle of nerves, I shattered—back arching off the bed as white-hot pleasure ripped through me.

He didn't let me come down.

The moment my muscles stopped clenching he shifted. His weight pressed me deeper into the mattress, his breath heavy and ragged against my throat. His fingers withdrew from me, leaving behind a slick emptiness that made me whimper in protest. Though it only lasted for a second as his grip tightened around my wrists, keeping me pinned beneath him as he lifted his other arm, the gleam of silver slashing in the dim light.

I stilled, my breath caught somewhere between fear and anticipation.

His hook traced the curve of my hip, the cold bite of metal against my fevered skin sending shivers through me. He dragged it lower, teasing, the blunt edge ghosting along my inner thigh.

"Ulrich," I breathed.

"Shh," he murmured, his voice laced with something possessive. "Let me have you."

The sharp tip of his hook traced over my slick folds, teasing, spreading me open without pressing in. I gasped, my body twitching against him, the contrast between the ruthless steel and the molten heat of my core a dangerous, sinful sort of pleasure. He dragged it through my wetness, slow and deliberate, coating the metal in my arousal.

My head thrashed against the pillow as I clenched around nothing, desperate for more, but he smirked, watching me squirm beneath him. The bastard enjoyed this.

"You like that, don't you?" His voice was velvet over iron, smooth and unyielding.

I glared at him, my lips parting to argue, but he pressed the hook against my clit, not enough to hurt—just enough to make me *feel* it. My protest dissolved into a strangled moan.

"Thought so," he murmured, his own breath shuddering as if restraining himself was as torturous for him as it was for me.

He brought the hook to his mouth.

My stomach clenched at the sight of it, my nails digging into his forearm as I watched, spellbound.

Ulrich's tongue flicked over the metal, tasting me. He groaned, the sound guttural, almost pained, before dragging his tongue along the curve of his hook, lapping at my arousal with slow, deliberate licks.

"Sweet as sin," he muttered, his voice husky, ruined.

I swallowed hard, my thighs clenching, my body a live wire of need.

But he wasn't done with me.

His grip on my wrists loosened enough for me to move, and I barely had time to brace myself before he replaced the hook with his cock.

A sharp thrust—deep, unrelenting—knocked the air from my lungs. The fullness stole my breath, his groan of satisfaction mingling with my choked gasp. For a heartbeat, he stilled, forehead pressed to mine, the vein in his neck pulsing.

"Ulrich." My nails bit into his back, my legs wrapping around him instinctively.

"Tell me," he growled, his mouth at my ear. "Tell me you belong to me."

I gasped as he pulled out and slammed back in, stretching me open, filling me completely.

"Say it," he demanded, his voice raw.

"I—I belong to you," I choked out, my entire body trembling beneath him.

A dark sound rumbled from his chest. His mouth met mine in a kiss that was more claim than affection, his tongue sweeping against mine in a battle for dominance he never intended to lose.

"Good girl," he murmured against my lips.

Each snap of his hips carved my name into my fractured soul. I raked my nails down his back, and he rewarded me with a deeper angle that made stars burst behind my eyelids.

When his teeth closed around the trident pendant resting against my throat, something primal surged between us—ancient magic sparking where silver met skin. The room filled with the scent of lightning and sea brine, our curses singing to each other through joined flesh.

"Yours," he gasped against my lips, the word raw and fractured. "Mine."

The claiming tore another climax from me, violent as a riptide. Ulrich followed with a roar, his release spilling hot and endless as he crushed me to the mattress.

He collapsed beside me, chest heaving, his hook glinting where his fingers still tangled in my hair. We didn't speak.

Ulrich's thumb brushed the pendant now resting between my breasts, his touch lighter than moonlight. When I looked up, I found him watching me—that shattered look in his eyes edged with something dangerously like hope.

"What's going on in that handsome head of yours?" I asked.

He pulled me closer until our noses touched.

"That you're here, with me." He ran his fingers through my hair. "And no matter how far you go, no matter what monsters you take on, I will be there."

My breath hitched.

"To love you." He kissed my cheek. "To support you." Then my forehead. "To tell you you're being a pain in my pirate ass." Then my lips.

His eyes locked onto mine, all seriousness in his tone. "I will never let you down, little mermaid. I will never turn my back on you. Never stop fighting for you. Never stop coming for you."

I swallowed, my stomach flipping in unsettling waves.

"Because you are mine. And no force on land, sea, or sky will ever change that."

I didn't have the words—for the weight of what he'd just said, for the way it settled deep in my chest like an anchor, steady and unshakable. I hadn't been ready to face how I felt for this man, but now that it was here, staring back at me, I couldn't ignore it.

There was no need for words, no grand confession. I could feel it in the way my heart raced when he was near, in the way every glance, every touch, held more weight than it ever had before. It was in the way my body responded to him, instinctively, without question. And as I looked at him, something shifted again, more subtle this time but just as powerful.

I didn't need to say it. I knew it. And somehow, I was certain he did too.

So instead, I smirked. "Who knew a pirate could be such a poet?"

Ulrich chuckled, the sound low and warm, curling around me like the promise of home.

"We'll get through this," he said, his voice softer now, laced with something resolute. "We'll find Gemma, we'll end this. Get some rest, little mermaid. Come morning, we'll figure it out." His fingers traced a gentle line along my jaw before dropping away. "And if Frankie isn't back by then, we'll tear this damn city apart until we find her."

I nodded, too afraid to say anything. Too afraid to admit my feelings or admit how the slightest touch from him made all the pain go away. That alone scared me more than anything.

But it was okay, he didn't expect an answer. His lips met mine again. We didn't get much sleep that night, and I was more than fine with that.

22
DUTCHMAN'S CURSE
ULRICH

Arie's breath was a soft, quiet rhythm in the stillness of the room. The kind of sound that made a man forget the world outside. That made me want to pull her closer, bury myself in her warmth, and let the world burn if it meant keeping her here—just like this.

I lay still for a long moment, watching the way the moonlight curled around her, painting silver over the wild tangle of crimson curls. She looked . . . peaceful.

Her lips were slightly parted, soft snores slipping past them as she shifted, curling deeper into the sheets. I wished it were my arms instead.

I exhaled through my nose. I should stay. Gods knew I wanted to.

But a sound pricked at the edge of my awareness—muffled voices, hurried footsteps.

I frowned, shifting slightly. Careful not to wake her, I slowly pulled away, cursing the loss of her warmth. Even after everything we had been through, everything that had torn us apart, she had ended up here, tangled in my sheets, in my arms. And yet, deep down, I knew this peace was only borrowed.

Reaching for my trousers, I slid them on, then my shirt, moving quietly as I fastened the buttons. Arie's scent clung to my skin—salt and spice, something distinctly her—and it made me pause.

There had been a time I thought I'd lost her for good. That she would never know me again.

And now...

I turned back toward the bed, unable to stop myself from drinking in the sight of her.

Her body was half-covered by the sheets, her bare shoulder glowing in the dim light, her fingers curled slightly against the pillow.

I could stay and wake her slowly, drag my lips across that golden skin, kiss away the shadows that lurked around her eyes even in sleep. But another sound—louder this time—snapped my focus back to the door. I pushed down my frustration, knowing there was far too much to do.

I finished dressing, grabbed my belt and weapons and made my way toward the door.

With a sigh, I left.

The second I stepped into the main living space, I knew something was wrong. The air was thick with tension, the kind that settled in the bones and warned of coming storms. And standing in the middle of it all—bloodied, furious, and pacing like a caged beast—was Frankie.

I stopped, eyes flicking from her, to Nathaniel, and lastly, Wulf. All of them looked like they had crawled tooth and nail out of hell.

"What happened?" I asked, my voice low, sharp.

Frankie turned, and the moment our eyes met, I knew the answer was going to be bad.

She looked like hell. Her clothes were torn, a streak of blood dried against her temple, her knuckles bruised and raw. But worse than that was the look in her eyes— hollow bitterness, and news that would gut me.

"Ambush," she spat, her breathing still uneven.

Nathaniel chimed in. "Those bastard assassins cut us off near the eastern dock. We barely made it out alive."

"I should have taken more of them down." She exhaled sharply, fingers curling and uncurling at her sides like she was working up the nerve to speak. Then, finally, she lifted her chin and faced us head-on.

"You would have died, kid." Hansel patted her on the back and she winced. He snatched his hand away. "Oh shit, sorry. The Brotherhood is no joke."

"She knows all about the assassins, Hansel," Robin said.

"That was a long time ago," Frankie started, voice clipped but steady, "but yes, I was one of them."

Hells, my jaw dropped.

Silence slammed into the room.

Pascal didn't move. Didn't even blink.

Nathaniel slammed his fist on the table. "Hells, I owe Hector twenty coins." Frankie shot the big beastly man a look and he shrugged. "A debt is a debt. But don't worry kid, we still love ya."

I had suspected Frankie had her secrets. Hell, everyone in this room did. But this? The Brotherhood? Pascal's one good eye flicked to me, searching my face for something—maybe anger, maybe betrayal. But all I could do was stare at Frankie, trying to piece together everything that suddenly made too much sense.

The way she fought—precise, efficient, always one step ahead.

The way she could read people—anticipate their next move before they even made it.

The way she'd always kept to the shadows.

I clenched my jaw, swallowing the sharp twist of emotions in my chest.

"I hoped," she continued, voice thick, "hell, I prayed that I could convince some of them to come with us. To fight against Gemma. To see that she's the real enemy." She exhaled sharply. "But then Dom and Sienna..."

She trailed off, shaking her head. Her anger masked something else—deeper than regret.

"They know how to twist the mind to their favor," a voice cut through the thick silence.

Tibault.

He stepped out of the shadows, arms crossed, his sharp eyes flicking between Frankie and the rest of us. "It's why Gemma considers them her Elites."

Frankie scoffed. "That's one word for it." And then she got a real look at the man standing before her. Her face paled. "Tibby. What are you doing here?"

"Yeah, why *are* you here?" Nathaniel asked. "Aren't you one of them?"

Tibault's gaze softened just a fraction. "It's good to see you're still alive, Frankie."

"Answer him," Frankie said. "You have always been about the Brotherhood. Always."

"Yeah, well, when you find out you've been lied to from the moment you started working with them, you see things from a different perspective. My eyes are open now."

"What are you getting at, Tibault?" Robin crossed his arms over his chest.

"Rose—er—Arie, said the tonic Gemma was giving her wasn't helping her memories, that something was off. So, I went to speak with the Queen." Tibault exhaled sharply, his gaze shifting to me, something unreadable in his expression. "I overheard her talking with Frederick," he continued, his voice quieter now, hesitant. "At least, I thought it was Frederick, but the way he spoke . . . it didn't sit right. I stayed hidden and listened. Gemma told him they had to stick to the plan. That once they had the souls they needed, Arie—" his eyes locked on mine, "—would be disposable."

A chill ran down my spine.

"She planned on getting rid of her," he said, no hesitation now. "The whole time. She never intended to let her walk away from this, no matter how well Arie served her."

I clenched my jaw, my hand curling into a fist at my sides. Of course she had.

Tibault's expression darkened. "She was . . . pleased with him. That once it was all done, once she had everything she needed, they'd deal with the *real* Frederick. They had used an illusion spell to make Jameson look like him and to take his entire persona."

Silence fell.

Tension crackled like a storm ready to break.

"Frederick's alive?" Robin asked, voice cautious, measured.

"He is," Tibault confirmed. "I had to be certain what they said was true, so I searched the castle. They had him in the same prison where they kept Arie in. He was a shell of who he once was. That's when I decided. So, I got him out and went to the ball in time to hear Robin tell everyone about the VonWhite prince."

"Decided what?" I asked.

"That I had been on the wrong side of this the whole time."

"This is what she does," Wulf chimed in. "She is smart, she is calculated and precise. Nothing she does is not thought out. What she didn't expect was you and your brother to come back." He looked at me.

"I have to admit, I'm surprised to see you here, Elder Wulf."

Tibault narrowed his eyes. "How did you manage to stay so close to her and not get exposed?"

Wulf shrugged. "I had no other choice. I had to ensure I played my part too."

Frankie sighed, "Look, we have all been scorned by the Bitch Queen, but can we focus on something a bit more time sensitive?"

"What is it, Frankie?" Pascal asked.

"Gemma has Tink." Arie walked into the room, dressed and looking far more refreshed than she had the day before.

"She spoke to you?" Pascal turned to Arie, and she nodded.

"For a brief moment. Jameson told Gemma that we were bonded, that the best way to get to me was through her. Tink tried to say more but our connection is blocked again."

I swore, sharper this time. It dawned on me then that she hadn't been with Frankie. I should have known the second I didn't see her here with the others.

Wulf exhaled, stepping forward. "She's making demands."

Frankie's eyes burned with barely contained fury.

"How do you know she's making demands?" Robin asked.

"It's being spread among the assassins, hoping it will get back to Arie." Frankie looked at me then, something unreadable in her expression. "She wants to trade Tink for the necklace."

And that's when I felt it—the shift in the air.

Arie looked at Frankie. "Where?"

"Neverland."

"Then we'd better get a move on," Arie said, her tone firm and determined. "We'll set sail as soon as we ensure everyone is ready. I'm guessing the rest of the crew is waiting for us on the ship you sailed here on?"

I winced, the weight of the moment pressing down on me. I knew this time would come, but I had hoped we'd have some kind of plan, some way to break the curse before we had to tell her. But there was no time for plans now.

The thought of what lay ahead twisted in my gut. The truth hung in the air, thick and suffocating. I didn't want to be the one to tell Arie. How could we explain that we'd sailed here on the *Jolly Dutchman*, and our entire crew was now cursed? The words felt too heavy, like a burden I wasn't ready to share.

But there was no turning back. Not now.

23

SEVEN DOCS
ARIE

SALTY WIND WHIPPED THROUGH MY HAIR AS WE approached the docks, the silhouette of the *Jolly Dutchman* looming in the distance like a phantom. The *Jolly Dutchman*. Of all ships.

As a kid, I had been captivated by the stories of it—the cursed ship, the daring escapades, the way it could sink into the sea and then shoot across the waters with an unnatural speed. I'd thought those tales were the kind of wild fantasies every pirate told to make their ship seem invincible. And maybe some of them were. But the *Dutchman*? That wasn't just another legend. The curse—no one had ever been able to break it, and as far as anyone knew, there was no way to.

The worst part wasn't the speed, or the stories, or even the eerie reputation it had gained. It was the fact that the curse still clung to it, unbroken, unyielding. I could feel that same chill creeping up my spine as we drew nearer, the weight of what that meant sinking in with every step. This wasn't the grand adventure I'd imagined as a child. This was something far darker, and I wasn't sure I was ready for it.

But I had to be, we had to save Tink and now the crew. There was time for sulking later.

Tightening my grip on Slayer, I tried to ignore the gnawing feeling in my gut. Ulrich walked beside me, his expression hard, his strides purposeful. The weight of his presence pressed down on me, though he said nothing.

Last night had been more than amazing—it had been *everything*. A collision of fate and fire, a moment carved out of chaos where nothing else existed but the two of us. I never thought I'd find someone like Ulrich, someone who could match me blow for blow, a man who could rival me in any monster hunt, challenge me without hesitation, and still look at me like I was the most important thing in the world.

Fierce not only in battle, but in the way he felt, how he cared—how he *fucked*. No hesitation, no second-guessing. He had taken on a curse, risked himself completely, just to come after me. Without a second thought. Without a doubt.

And for the first time in a very long time, I felt safe. Loved.

The docks were quieter than I expected when we approached but the moment we stepped closer to where the *Dutchman* was anchored, raised voices carried over the sea breeze.

"What in the seven hells is going on?" Ulrich muttered.

A small crowd had gathered near the gangplank, voices overlapping in heated arguments. I recognized one of them immediately—Doc. I nearly dropped to my knees and wept. Knowing that Doc was here, helping our men, sent warmth pooling through me.

After taking another glance . . . six people stood around Doc, and they all looked like him. Every single one.

"Are they . . .?" I trailed off, blinking rapidly as I took in the scene before me.

Some taller, some broader, a few with longer hair, and one

of them was female but the resemblance was uncanny. They all wore the same half-exasperated, half-smug expressions, and they were all currently locked in a very heated argument, waving their hands wildly as they talked over each other.

"You've been gone for *years*, you sack of shit!" one of them snapped, pointing an accusing finger at Doc.

"Oh, like you care, Edgar," Doc shot back. "You were always too busy stuffing your face to notice when someone left."

"I notice plenty," Edgar snapped.

Another—slightly taller, with dark eyes that flickered with exasperation—snorted. "Yeah, like you noticed when Darla came home with a new puppy last week. It only took you four days to notice *that*."

Edgar opened his mouth. Paused. Closed it.

The others groaned.

"Point proven," the taller one muttered.

"I *knew* I shouldn't have come back," Doc grumbled.

"You're damn right you shouldn't have!" Another crossed his arms. "You abandoned us! Left us to deal with the Brotherhood's mess. You think you can just *waltz* back like nothing happened?"

"I didn't abandon you—"

"You ran off to play doctor while the rest of us stayed here, fighting for our lives," the only woman of the group cut in. "Do you know what it's been like?"

"Do you know how long we waited for you to come back?" Edgar said.

Doc threw his arms up. "You're acting like I left because I wanted to! I had no choice—"

"Oh, she's *pretty*," the tall one blurted, completely derailing the moment as his gaze locked onto me.

The shift was instant.

The whole group turned toward me like a pack of wolves scenting fresh prey.

I raised a brow. "Excuse me?"

Another one waggled his brows. "She smells like magic."

And then they each spoke at the same time, confusing the hells out of me.

"I think I'm in love."

"She's mine."

"She's not *that* pretty."

"I want to take her home."

"She's way out of your league, Edgar—"

Ulrich groaned, rubbing his temples like he was moments away from strangling them all. "For the love of—*stop* that."

I crossed my arms. "Okay, enough of this." I looked at Ulrich, my expression softening. "Are these Doc's siblings?"

It hadn't hit me until then. Back in Neverland, Doc had told me about the family that had looked after Ulrich and Clayton before sending him with Pascal. I knew very little about Ulrich's past.

But now I knew that he wasn't just a pirate. He wasn't just my reckless, infuriating, brilliant captain.

He was the heir to Chione's throne. A prince raised in shadows, torn from the life he might have had, only to carve out something entirely different for himself. And somehow, standing in the darkest night on a dock surrounded by family, with the weight of that truth settling over him, he looked like he was happy. Truly happy.

"They're the only family I have outside of the lost boys and our crew," Ulrich finally answered.

"What? We don't know you!" Edgar raised a brow.

Doc groaned. "Of course you do, dummy, that's Ulrich."

The entire group of Docs narrowed their eyes at Ulrich before their brows rose in shock. Edgar and another man approached first. They poked and prodded and asked dozens of questions about how he was doing, where Clayton was, and if he was finally home. The others soon chimed in and I simply stood there gaping.

Ulrich had so many people who cared about him.

"Easy, settle down." Ulrich laughed. "I'd love to explain but right now we have some important business to handle. I promise, once this is over, I will come back and we can have family dinner. Now, let me introduce you all." He looked at me and then pointed to the tallest one, the most serious looking of the bunch. "The tall one here is Finn. He thinks he's in charge, but he's not."

Finn smirked. "That's exactly what someone *not* in charge would say."

Ulrich ignored him and moved on. "That's Edgar—don't listen to anything he says, ever. Unless it's about food."

Edgar grinned. "What! I don't only care about food."

Ulrich pointed to a man flipping a coin in the air. "That one's Rupert—he'll try to sell you something, don't buy it."

Rupert winked. "Unless you're in need of rare—"

Ulrich moved on. "Tobias, generally the smartest but also the most annoying."

Tobias pushed his glasses up. "Intelligence is a burden, but someone has to carry it."

Ulrich sighed. "Samuel—you won't hear him much, but when he *does* talk, it's usually something you don't want to hear."

Samuel gave a two-fingered salute but said nothing.

"And lastly—" Ulrich gestured to the only woman of the group. "Darla. Watch your pockets around her."

Darla gasped, placing a hand on her chest. "How *dare* you—"

Ulrich leveled her with a glare.

A low voice cut through the moment.

"Look who it is." Pascal grinned as he approached, his sharp gaze sweeping over Ulrich's chaotic family before landing on Doc with a smirk. "Only the rowdiest bunch of misfits to ever walk the streets of Chione. Thought you'd all gotten yourselves killed by now."

One of the brothers—Tobias, if I remembered correctly—clapped Pascal on the shoulder with enough force to make a lesser man stumble. "Takes a lot more than a few close calls to get rid of us."

Darla laughed. "Though if we're being honest, Doc here has had more close calls than the rest of us combined."

Doc shot her a withering glare. "At least I'm not the one who mistook a siren for a barmaid."

The group erupted into laughter, slapping backs and exchanging jabs like no time had passed. Even Ulrich relaxed, though his gaze flickered to me now and then, as if ensuring I hadn't run in the opposite direction.

Pascal let the camaraderie settle before he cleared his throat. "I'd love to stand here reminiscing all day, but I do need your help."

That caught their attention.

Pascal sighed, shaking his head with a dramatic expression of reluctance. "It's not an easy ask. I know you all probably have better things to do than clean up a crumbling city in the middle of a war, but . . ." He trailed off, eyeing each of them before delivering the final blow. "Kaelryn needs help, and I suppose I could look elsewhere, but I figured you lot would be up for the challenge."

Silence.

Then Tobias crossed his arms. "What kind of challenge?"

Pascal tilted his head, feigning nonchalance. "Oh, nothing much. Just, you know, protecting the Underbelly, keeping innocent people from getting slaughtered, making sure the place doesn't fall into absolute ruin." He shrugged. "But if it's too much trouble—"

Darla scoffed. "You're manipulating us."

Pascal smirked. "Is it working?"

They exchanged looks, muttering amongst themselves before Edgar exhaled heavily. "Fine," he grumbled. "We'll go."

Pascal clapped his hands together. "Knew I could count on you."

"But I have to stay," Doc added quickly, squaring his shoulders, he kept his gaze forward and away from his siblings. "The ship needs me, and I'm showing signs of the curse."

Doc lifted up his shirt and I clamped my hand over my mouth. Doc's pale skin flaked as his shirt rose and dark bruises covered his torso."

Before his siblings could comment, Ulrich chimed in. "He's right, he'll need to sail with us for now. But once this is over, you need to return to your family."

Doc nodded, then looked at his family. "I promise."

The six brothers and sister ran up and hugged Doc, tears streamed down their faces and one hiccuped uncontrollably as he sobbed, though I couldn't tell which one.

A strange feeling swept over me. The conversation faded into a dull hum, indistinct words lost to the wind as I stepped toward the water's edge. The scent of salt thickened in the air, the sway of the waves against the *Jolly Dutchman* lulled my thoughts, sending the chatter behind me to the back of my mind. Their easy banter sent an ache deep in my chest at the loss of my bond with Tink. Somewhere out there, she needed me.

Their endless arguments about whether Doc stayed behind or came with us was useless. A waste of time we did not have.

I clenched my fists at my sides, nails biting into my palms as I stared at the endless expanse of water stretching before me.

The waves rolled in a steady rhythm, uncaring of the war raging beyond their horizon, of the lives hanging in the balance. The salt stuck to my skin, my lips, the very air I breathed—it reminded me of Neverland, of what was at stake, of the promises I had yet to keep.

I should have been strategizing, thinking of the next move, figuring out how we were going to stop Gemma. But for a moment, for just a breath, I let myself feel the burden of it all.

I had felt Tink's pain through our bond, had sensed the exhaustion creeping through her like a sickness. Until the connection dulled and I lost her constant presence. I suspected that was Gemma's doing. And I had let it happen.

Exhaling sharply, I shook my head. No. No, this wasn't the time for guilt. I had spent too long drowning in my failures. I wasn't going to let her slip away.

A warm presence settled beside me. I didn't have to look to know it was Ulrich. He said nothing at first, only stood there, close enough that I could feel the heat of him against the cold night air.

"Arie?" Concern threaded his voice.

I turned, managing a small smile. "I'm fine. Just thinking about Tink."

"She's strong," he said at last, his voice low and rough like the tide scraping against jagged cliffs. "Stronger than any of us give her credit for."

I nodded, swallowing past the lump in my throat. "I know."

He hesitated. "But that's not all that's got you looking like you're about to tear the ocean apart, is it?"

I let out a hollow laugh, my gaze locked on the horizon. "No. It's not."

His hand found mine, warm and steady, anchoring me in a way I hadn't realized I needed. "Then talk to me, love. You know you don't have to do this alone."

I nodded, though doubt gnawed at the edges of my resolve. "It's not that."

"Then what?"

I hesitated, watching the horizon blur with distance and mist. "What if I can't stop Gemma? What if I can't break this curse?"

He was silent for a long moment, choosing his words with care. "You will," he said with so much confidence that warmth bloomed in my chest, pushing back the chill of fear. The others were gathered now at the end of the dock, waiting with eager impatience.

"Don't think you're getting out of here without us."

I rounded at the familiar voice and three shadowy figures strode up the docks toward us. My heart raced.

Robin, Hansel, and Gretel.

I raised a brow. "Shouldn't you be worried about your home and getting your people to safety. "

Gretel, still slightly pale and limping from her run in with assassins, said, "Kael can handle things while we're gone. We want to see this through until the end."

Hansel laughed. "The only reason these two want to go is because they have people on Neverland they need to find."

Pascal stilled at that. "No, I only take Lost Ones to Neverland for a reason—"

"They weren't children when they were taken, they aren't Lost Ones," Robin stepped closer until he stood in front of Pascal. "Gemma's beasts, the ones who fight in the cages at the Pits, were people we loved and cared about."

"People we need to get back," Gretel said.

"Hells. I understand why you'd want to join, but this ship is cursed and—"

"I know about its curse, pirate." Robin gritted his teeth. "And I don't give a flying shit. I will not go another day without seeing her. Without knowing I fought to get her back."

"Technically it'll take us more than a day to get to Neverland." Nathaniel grinned and Frankie nudged him in the stomach.

"Shut it," she hissed. "You ruined a really cute moment, you ass."

"Look, Robin." I sighed. "If you're willing to take on a curse to save the one you love . . ." I forced myself not to look at Ulrich, already feeling his eyes on me. "Then who am I to stop you. You, Gretel, and Hansel are always welcome aboard our ship."

Robin cleared his throat. "Thank you."

"Well, now that that's over with, let's board this cursed piece of flotsam and get to Neverland," I said.

Except now we had to stop a soul sucking, wicked queen from destroying the Celestial Plains and one of the Gods.

And break an unbreakable curse.

No big deal.

"Ready?" Ulrich asked, holding his hand out for mine.

I grabbed it and squeezed. "As ready as I'll ever be."

"Hey, love birds," Nathaniel called from the ship. "If you two are done making kissy faces, we could use you up here."

The gangplank groaned under our weight as we stepped aboard the *Jolly Dutchman*, its deck slick with salt and time-worn by the endless stomping of sea misted boots. Doc ran past us, presumably to check on his patients. The scent of damp wood and brine filled my lungs, mingling with something worse —something I recognized instantly.

Decay.

Men and women emerged from the shadows like ghosts, their movements sluggish, their bodies frail and hollowed by the relentless grip of the curse. Skin, once bronzed by sun and salt, had turned sallow and papery, flaking away in thin patches as if time itself were peeling them apart. The curse had stolen the vitality from their flesh, leaving their fingers bony and trembling, their lips cracked and colorless. Their eyes, sunken and rimmed with dark circles, carried the weight of sleepless nights.

Hair, once thick and wild from the sea air, now hung in limp, some losing patches altogether where their scalps showed raw and irritated beneath.

Those who still had their strength stood at attention, their spines stiff with discipline, but even they bore the signs of slow decay creeping through their veins. Some shifted uncomfortably, as if their very bones ached with each movement. Others merely stared, their gazes locked on me with something between hope and wariness, as if I carried their salvation in my hands.

And I did.

A sharp breath, a few steps forward—and then Keenan was there.

"Arie!"

He practically knocked the air from my lungs as he pulled me into a crushing embrace. His grip was strong, but I could feel the tremor in his limbs, the deep, shuddering inhale against my hair. He smelled like home. Like salt and steel and the storm-worn resilience of a man who had survived too many battles to count. And to my relief, the curse hadn't done much to him. His eyes were sunken and his skin flaky in spots, but for the most part he was still intact.

For a moment, I melted into the warmth of his embrace, into the familiarity of someone who had been at my side through every war, every hunt, every impossible storm. And then, just as quickly, he pulled back, turning his head and coughing violently into his sleeve.

A deep, wracking cough, the kind that didn't belong to a man like Keenan.

A thread of unease curled down my spine.

When he looked back at me, there was something haunted in his gaze.

"Half the crew is down, Arie," he admitted, his voice raw. "And the rest? We're holding on, but . . . we don't have much left. Food's low. Water is worse. Doc did what he could before he left, but we're bleeding resources faster than we can find them. No one in Chione wants to sell anything to the crew of the *Dutchman*."

Half the crew.

The weight of it pressed into my chest, heavier than the sea itself. I had been gone too long.

"It doesn't matter," I said firmly. "We're leaving now, and we'll figure it out."

Keenan frowned. "We don't have the numbers—"

"We have enough to get her out to open sea," I cut in. "I'll handle the rest."

Before anyone could respond, the sound of footsteps echoed from behind us, and I turned just in time to see Calypso and Clayton step onto the deck. Frankie had given me a lot of information on Calypso and how she seemed to weasel her way onto Clayton's ship—King Roland's ship. She stood barefoot, the hem of her flowing blue-green gown damp as though she had just stepped out of the sea. Her hair, wild and untamed, curled around her shoulders. But it was her eyes—deep, fathomless pools of black—that made my breath catch. There was something in them, something knowing, something that sent a slow curl of unease through my stomach.

I stiffened at Ulrich's side, the tension radiating from him in waves. He looked between Calypso and Clayton, then back to me, confusion and frustration warring in her gaze.

Calypso's gaze swept over Ulrich, slow and assessing, before she shifted her attention to me. A knowing smirk ghosted across her lips, but there was no humor in it—only the sharp gleam of something ancient and unshakable.

"Don't tell me they're sailing with us," Keenan groaned. "That's all we need is to have Frankie moping around the ship again.

"I heard that you ass," Frankie huffed, though a small smirk tugged on her lip."

"Having me on this ship will save you and your crew." Calypso hooked her arm through Clayton's.

I squared my shoulders, cooling my expression. "This ship is cursed, and anyone here with it."

Calypso's smirk remained in place, but there was a subtle shift in her posture, she was more guarded, like a mask slipping into place. Her eyes gleamed with something unreadable as she locked her gaze onto mine. "Oh, I know about the curse," she said, her voice smooth, almost too calm. She tilted her head slightly, as though studying me, sizing me up, like I was a puzzle she was trying to solve but couldn't quite fit together. "And I know that breaking it won't be easy."

"And you know this how?" Ulrich's voice cut through the air, sharp and demanding.

Calypso didn't flinch. "Considering I sailed with the original crew, I'd say I know this ship better than anyone here." There was a knowing edge to her tone, like she'd lived through the torment the curse had wrought. And for some reason, the weight of her words settled uneasily in my chest.

Gods, how old is this woman?

Ulrich's eyes narrowed, his suspicion creeping through. "You're responsible for the curse, aren't you?"

The question hung in the air, thick and accusing. I raised a brow, taken aback by the sudden leap he'd made, but the cold intensity in his eyes told me he wasn't just guessing. There was a depth beneath his suspicion—an uneasy certainty, as if he already had proof, or at least thought he did. It was a risk to make such an accusation, yet he threw it out without hesitation.

I trusted him. More than I'd trusted anyone in a long time outside my crew. I trusted him with my life, and I'd trust him in this too, no matter what happened next. Even if the answers weren't clear yet, I knew I wasn't alone in this. Not with him by my side.

For a brief moment, I allowed myself to breathe through the weight of that thought, the confidence it gave me, before turning my attention back to the situation at hand.

Calypso turned to Ulrich, her gaze sharp as a blade. "Do not mistake me for a villain in this story, Captain." The title rolled off her tongue like a mockery. "The original crew of the *Jolly Dutchman* deserved what they got. Their greed, their arrogance—it cost them everything."

I clenched my jaw. "Then why does the curse still stand? The original crew is long gone."

Calypso's expression turned unreadable. "Because the debt remains." She exhaled softly, almost as if she pitied me. "The *Dutchman's* fate was sealed long ago. It is bound to the sea, bound to the Red Moon, and those who sail it will always pay the price."

"Then how do we break it?" Pascal asked.

Calypso's lips curled, but it wasn't a smile. "To undo a curse as strong as this one?" She let the words linger in the air before delivering her final blow. "You'll need to gain the favor of a god."

Silence settled between us, thick as the humidity pressing against my skin.

Ulrich crossed his arms, his jaw tightening. "Well, that's convenient." He shot me a glance, a flicker of amusement warring with the frustration in his eyes. "We just happen to know a few of those."

Calypso chuckled, shaking her head. "You are full of surprises, Captain Hook."

Ulrich turned to me, stepping closer, his expression shifting —no longer just determined, but something more. He reached for my hand, lacing his fingers through mine like an anchor, grounding me when the weight of the curse felt too heavy to bear.

"We'll figure this out, Arie." His voice was softer now, but just as fierce. "I swear it. I won't let this curse take you, or our crew."

I swallowed hard, gripping his hand a little tighter, because gods, I wanted to believe that. I needed to.

Nodding, I said. "We can get to Neverland, stop Gemma, and then I will beg Kai or Pan to break the curse. I will do whatever it takes, give her whatever she wants." My thumb brushed against his knuckles, "I've lost too much already," I murmured. "I'm not losing you, too."

After a moment, I exhaled, pulling myself back to the task at hand. "How long do we have?"

Calypso looked to the sky before answering. "You have four days before the Red Moon."

My lips pressed into a thin line. "Damn it. Even with my magic, it'll take at least two to get to Neverland."

"That's too close," Pascal muttered, rubbing at his jaw. "If anything goes wrong, if we hit a storm, or—"

"I can get you there faster."

Calypso's voice cut through the room, smooth as rolling waves.

I turned sharply toward her, brows knitting together in suspicion. "And why would you do that?"

Calypso smiled, slow and knowing. "Because the sooner you find what you need, the sooner I get what I want."

Ulrich looked down at me. "She speaks the truth. She's not

offering out of kindness, Arie. But she's not lying either." His gaze flicked back to Calypso, "She'll get us there."

I studied Ulrich for a long moment before finally nodding. "Fine," I said, voice even. "Do it."

Calypso's smirk deepened. "With pleasure."

"What about Chione?" Clayton cut in. "What about the chaos we started? The assassins aren't going to stop just because Gemma is gone."

I knew what he was asking. Knew that Chione was on the verge of collapse. That the war hadn't ended when Gemma fled. Her assassins were still out there, cutting down anyone who dared rise against them. And the people—the ones who had fought, who had believed—were now scrambling for their lives, fleeing into the Enchanted Forest like rabbits running from a fox.

And yet, my mind was already elsewhere. On the Dutchman. On our crew. On Ulrich.

"I agreed to take the throne," Clayton continued, stepping closer to his brother, his jaw tight with barely restrained frustration. "I agreed to do what you wouldn't. But you don't get to just walk away. Not this time. You owe Chione more than that. You agreed to help."

Ulrich met his stare, and I couldn't help but notice the internal battle playing out behind his eyes. There was a tension there, something deep and conflicted, like he was weighing two impossible choices. I could see it—the pull between his duty to Clayton, to Chione, and the need to leave with me, to follow the path we'd started together.

His brows furrowed, the muscles in his jaw working as if each word Clayton spoke was another piece of the weight he was already carrying. It was clear that no matter what he chose, someone would be left behind, and the burden of that decision was heavy enough to make his gaze flicker with something more than just frustration—guilt, perhaps, or regret.

Finally, he said, "If we don't stop Gemma, if we don't break this curse, none of it matters, Clay. I will be stuck on this ship for gods knows how long and that won't be good for anyone. I want to help. I do. But right now, I need to see this to the end."

For a long moment, Clayton didn't speak, but it was easy to see that he knew what the right choice was. Finally, he sighed, running a hand down his face. "Fine. But when this is done, you come back." His gaze flicked to me, cold and expectant. "*Both* of you."

"Don't you have to stay on the ship?" Frankie asked. "Everyone who sails on the ship is cursed, yes?"

Calypso rolled her eyes. "The curse is of my making and Clayton is one of mine. We will not be harmed. Clayton can stay in Chione and take care of what he needs to while we sail to Neverland."

Clayton shifted his weight, clearly uncomfortable by Calypso's claim. Frankie's tightening of fists and soured look said she felt the same way. There was no way I was touching or getting anywhere near that triangle of trouble.

Frankie opened her mouth to speak but Calypso beat her to it. "I have no desire to explain what I mean. The only important thing to know is that Clayton will be safer here and Chione needs him."

"How did you know where we were going?" Pascal stepped closer to Frankie who had gripped her sword a little tighter.

"Do we have time for this?" Calypso asked. "As I said, you only have four days to finish what you've started."

No matter how much I didn't trust a thing Calypso said, I sighed, "She's right. We need to get moving."

Ulrich stepped up beside me. "You heard the captain." His

voice carried across the deck, low and commanding. "Prep the sails. Get whatever rations we have left stored."

"I'm not the captain, Ulrich, you are."

Ulrich shook his head. "You have always been the captain, Arie. No one is better suited for it than you."

I sighed. "Fine."

I reached up, fingers brushing the trident necklace at my throat. It hummed beneath my touch, power curling in my veins like a rising tide, eager—demanding—to be used.

The sea would answer me. And I would make damn sure we got there before it was too late.

"Alright," I said, turning back to my crew, my voice steady and strong. "Let's get this damn ship moving."

"Yes, let's," Calypso purred as she walked past me, not giving a damn as Ulrich called after her. "I do think we'll want to leave soon. I overheard assassins in the port village asking about a red-headed rebel responsible for the explosions the night of the ball."

I cursed and tugged Ulrich along as I walked up the plank. Assassins were the last people I wanted to deal with. We had more important things. Like breaking a curse, saving a fairy and winning a godsdamn war.

24

TANGLED TIDES
ARIE

The *Jolly Dutchman* creaked beneath my feet, its wooden bones groaning against the weight of the curse, against the unnatural force driving it forward.

My force.

I stood at the bow, fingers curled around the worn railing, eyes fixed on the horizon, on the ink-black waters stretching endlessly before us. The sky had begun to shift, the deep navy of night peeling away to soft hues of violet and ghostly blue, but no sun broke the darkness—not yet.

My pulse thrummed in time with the sea's song, the low, unrelenting pull of magic curling through my veins, sinking into the water, pushing the *Dutchman* forward at impossible speeds. It answered me. It obeyed me.

And still, it wasn't fast enough.

I swallowed, gaze drifting back to the deck behind me.

My crew looked awful.

I had walked among them earlier, weaving between hammocks and makeshift bedding in the cargo hold, between the bodies of men and women who had once been vibrant and reckless with life. Their groans still echoed in my ears, the hacking coughs and fevered mutterings, the desperate glances when they realized I was back. I did my best to give them hope but it wasn't enough.

I had spoken with Keenan, had tried to reassure him—but what could I say? That I'd fix this? That I'd make it right? That I wouldn't let them slip any farther?

I could promise all of that, but I didn't know if I could keep it.

None of this would have happened had I stopped Jameson before he kidnapped me.

Thank all the gods he was gone, though the only regret I had was that he hadn't suffered like I had.

Keenan's voice cut through my thoughts. "Arie."

I turned to find him standing just a few steps away, exhaustion carved into every line of his face, but his eyes—his warm, steady eyes—held something else entirely. Relief.

"You're really here," he murmured, his lips twitching into something that almost resembled a smile. "I was starting to think I hallucinated you earlier."

"I'm here," I said softly.

His gaze searched mine, looking for something—assurance, maybe, or the pieces of me that had been missing for so long. Then, without another word, he stepped forward and pulled me into a hug. I exhaled, sinking into the familiarity of him, the quiet comfort of a friend who had stood by me longer than most.

"I've missed you," he admitted, his voice rough. "And we need to talk. About everything."

I nodded against his shoulder, but he must have felt the tension coiled in my body because he pulled back with a knowing look. "But not tonight," he added, giving me a wry smile. "You need rest, Captain."

The title made something flicker in my chest, but I didn't argue. I wasn't sure I had the energy to.

Before I could act, my gaze flicked to Calypso, who lounged against the mainmast with an air of practiced indifference, her arms crossed lazily over her chest as if the events unfolding around her was nothing more than an amusing spectacle. The sea breeze toyed with her wild hair, strands of it curling like tendrils of ink against her sharp, unreadable features.

Ulrich had made it abundantly clear—Calypso wasn't to be trusted. I agreed. She was an unknown, a force of nature bound by no loyalty but her own. There was an unsettling fluidity to her, something shifting and untethered, like the tide itself—impossible to pin down, impossible to predict. She had helped us, yes, but I couldn't shake the feeling that every move she made was for her own amusement, her own agenda.

Her dark eyes met mine, a slow smirk curling at the edges of her lips, as if she could hear my thoughts, and she relished the uncertainty twisting in my gut. I clenched my jaw

"Do me a favor Keenan, keep your eye on that one will you?" I murmured.

"You got it, Cap."

I turned toward the captain's quarters, my feet moving of their own discord. Exhaustion dulled the edges of my mind, and without thinking, I pushed the door open.

And froze.

Ulrich stood near the desk, the warm candlelight casting shadows over him. When the door creaked, he turned. His sharp blue eyes locked onto mine, his expression unreadable, his body still tense from whatever thoughts occupied him.

It didn't occur to me until just then that technically, I wasn't the captain of this ship.

Ulrich was.

The thought hit me with a strange crushing force, one I couldn't quite name. I should have looked away.

But I didn't. Because standing there, caught in the dim glow of candlelight, he wasn't just the man who had fought beside me. Wasn't just the pirate who had taken on a curse to come save me. He was something more. His presence alone made my pulse stutter, made my breath catch, made my fingers twitch at my sides.

I swallowed hard, my throat suddenly dry.

His lips parted, as if he was about to speak. I beat him to it.

"I—" I cleared my throat, dragging my gaze back up to his face. "I didn't realize . . . I mean, I'll find somewhere else to sleep."

A muscle in his jaw twitched. "It's your cabin," he said, voice low.

Something about the way he said it made my stomach flutter.

"This isn't the *Black Betty*, Ulrich."

He moved around the desk and stopped in front of me. He spoke, but the words came out strained. "It's fine, you deserve to be here. I'll sleep elsewhere—"

Before I could stop myself, I reached out and grabbed his arm. His skin was warm beneath my fingers, the muscles taut with nervous energy.

"Don't," I said, the word slipping out before I could think better of it. "Will you . . . will you stay? You deserve to be here too, after all."

Ulrich stilled, his eyes searching mine, and for a moment, neither of us moved. The air thrummed with an electric tension, a fragile thing that could shatter at the slightest touch. My heart pounded against my ribs, each beat echoing with uncertainty and something dangerously close to hope.

We'd slept together back in Chione, but this felt different, this felt intimate whereas before it felt like need, a desire to touch and kiss and feel him against me. This time I wanted comfort.

He didn't pull away.

Instead, he let out a slow breath, the sound close to surrender. "If that's what you want."

It was more than that. More than want.

But I couldn't bring myself to say it.

I nodded, releasing his arm slowly, the imprint of him lingering on my skin long after my hand fell back to my side. We stood in silence, the weight of unspoken words pressing down until it became suffocating.

Then Ulrich exhaled, running a hand through his already tousled hair. "Gods, Arie. When I think about everything that's happened the last few months . . ." He shook his head, half in disbelief, half in exasperation. "You really have a knack for throwing yourself into chaos."

I scoffed, crossing my arms. "Oh, please. You're the one who sailed a cursed ship. If anything, you're the reckless one. Who does that?"

His lips twitched. "And yet, somehow, I'm still the sane one."

I smirked, stepping closer. "Sane? You're a pirate, Ulrich. That word doesn't belong near either of us."

He laughed, the sound rough and warm, like the crash of waves against the hull of a ship. "Fine. But at least I have self-preservation. You, on the other hand, would probably dive headfirst into the mouth of a kraken if it meant saving someone."

I arched my brow. "Umm . . . I did that, remember? And don't deny it, you'd dive right in after me."

His smirk softened into something quieter, real. "Yeah," he murmured. "I would."

My voice changed, seriousness in my words. "I've missed this."

Ulrich reached out, fingers brushing against mine before he caught my wrist, tugging me close enough that I could feel the warmth radiating from his skin. "As have I. I'm glad you're safe, Arie. That you're here." His voice dipped lower, rough with unspoken emotions, ones I wasn't ready to name.

"I couldn't have done any of this without you."

His fingers tightened around my wrist, like he was grounding himself in my presence. "You would've found a way. You always do."

"I'm not so sure this time."

His gaze flicked to my lips, and a slow, knowing smirk curled across his face. "Are you implying you need me?"

I rolled my eyes. "I'm saying I—"

His hook pressed to my lips. "No more words, little mermaid. I'm going to kiss you, so shut up and let me."

My breath hitched and I gave a slight nod. Ulrich's mouth devoured mine, fierce and demanding, and I kissed him back just as hard, pouring everything I couldn't say into the heat of it.

His hook lowered to my side as he pulled me closer, the cool metal a stark contrast to the fire spreading through my veins. My fingers tangled in his hair, tugging him down, desperate to erase every barrier still between us.

He groaned into my mouth, low and rough, and the sound sent a jolt straight through me. I gasped for air as he broke the kiss, trailing his lips down my neck, leaving a path of fire in their wake. The room spun around us as he backed me against the wall with a controlled urgency that made my heart race faster.

"Arie," he breathed against my skin, my name a promise and a curse all at once.

I didn't trust myself to speak. Instead, I reached for him

again, dragging him back to me with a need that bordered on desperation.

The kiss broke on a breathless sigh, my lips tingling, swollen from his intensity. But I wasn't done. Not even close.

I seized him by the front of his shirt and turned, pushing him back until his shoulders hit the wall with a dull *thud*. His chest rose and fell in quick, shallow breaths, his pupils blown wide with ravenous darkness, but he didn't stop me. Didn't try to take control. He just watched, heat simmering in his gaze, as I reached for the first button of his shirt.

Slowly. Deliberately.

I dragged my fingers along the fabric, down the column of his throat, feeling the way his pulse leapt beneath my touch. The buttons came undone one by one, revealing inch after inch of bare, warm skin. I smoothed my hands over his chest, trailing them over hard muscle and old scars, savoring the way his body responded—every flex, every twitch beneath my touch.

When the last button slipped free, I pushed the shirt off his shoulders. It slid down his arms and pooled at his feet, forgotten. My lips followed the path of my fingers, pressing soft, open-mouthed kisses down the curve of his throat, across his collarbone, tracing the map of old wounds like they were something sacred.

Ulrich groaned, his head tipping back against the wall.

I kept going.

Down his chest, over the hard ridges of his stomach, until I knelt before him, my breath heavy against his skin. I could feel the way he trembled, how his fingers curled into a single fist at his side like he barely held himself together.

I reached for his belt, sliding my fingers beneath the leather. A slow, dragging pull. The clasp came undone with a soft *snick*, and I yanked it free, the motion sharp, the sound of it snapping through the air like a promise.

I tossed it aside without a second thought.

His breath hitched, sharp and uneven, as I undid the button of his pants, fingers dipping just beneath the fabric to drag them lower. His muscles tightened beneath my touch, anticipation thrumming between us.

Ulrich exhaled a rough curse, his voice raw.

Gods, I wanted to ruin him.

My fingers curled around him, the heat of him branding my palm, impossibly hard yet silky-smooth beneath my touch. The thick weight of him lay heavy in my grasp, pulsing with every teasing stroke.

A sharp inhale hissed through his teeth, his hips jerking ever so slightly as I dragged my hand up, my thumb sweeping over the sensitive tip, gathering the bead of pre-cum there.

Gods, he was big—almost too big—but that only made me more eager, more desperate to take my time, to savor the way his body tensed beneath my touch.

I stroked him, watching the way he bit his lip, and his muscles flexed, rippling under his skin. He was beautiful like this—wild and restrained all at once, caught between the urge to let go and the desire to make me suffer for drawing it out.

The deep, guttural groan rumbled from his chest as I flicked my tongue against his tip told me everything I needed to know.

Lowering my lips over the swollen head, I flicked my tongue across the sensitive ridge again, savoring the taste of him—salt and heat, intoxicating and entirely him. A strangled groan rumbled from deep within his chest, his fingers twitching at his side as if he barely restrained himself from grabbing my hair and guiding me the way he wanted.

I teased him first, hollowing my cheeks as I took him inch by inch, dragging my tongue along the length of him, letting the desire coil tighter between us. His breath hitched again when I finally pushed myself lower, stretching my lips around him as I took him deeper.

My fingers dug into his thighs for balance, nails biting into taut muscle as I pressed forward, until he grazed the back of my throat. The heat of him, the sheer size, made my throat tighten, but I relaxed, breathing through my nose as I took him to the hilt.

A violent curse tore from his lips, his hips jerking despite his restraint, pressing deeper for a moment before he wrenched himself back.

"Fuck, Arie," he groaned, his voice thick.

A satisfied hum vibrated through me, sending a shudder through his body as I pulled back, sucking gently before sliding down again, my tongue tracing every curve, every vein, committing him to memory.

"Gods," he rasped, his voice strained. "You're going to ruin me."

I looked up, meeting his stormy gaze through my lashes, and hollowed my cheeks as I sucked him back in.

His restraint snapped, his fingers tangling in my hair with a rough, demanding grip that sent a shiver down my spine. His breath came ragged, his hips jerking forward as he guided me, setting the rhythm—slow at first, savoring the drag of my lips around him, then faster, more frantic.

A strangled groan tore from his throat. His grip tightened while his hook dug into the wall behind him. His control slipped as he thrust deeper, hitting the back of my throat. I gagged, my eyes watering, but I didn't pull away—I wanted this, wanted him to take from me, to lose himself in me.

"Fuck," he ground out. His entire body tensing. I could feel it—the barely contained need, the storm raging inside him, barely leashed.

And then, as if he couldn't take another second, he

wrenched me back. My lips left him with a sinful pop, my breath coming in sharp, uneven gasps. Before I could recover, he hauled me up, his strength effortless, turning us in a dizzying blur.

My back slammed against the wall, the cold stone a sharp contrast to the fever burning between us. He pinned me, his body pressing into mine, trapping me beneath the full weight of his need.

I gasped as his hook caught the fabric of my shirt, tearing it open with a single, savage motion. His mouth was on me before I could speak, trailing heat along my collarbone, teeth grazing, tongue soothing. My skin hummed under his touch, and I arched into him, desperate for more.

He growled against my neck, a primal sound that sent shivers cascading down my spine. "You want this?" His voice was rough, almost unrecognizable.

"Yes," I breathed, my fingers tangling in his hair, pulling him closer.

His hand—the one still intact—slid down my side, firm and demanding. It settled on my hip, pulling me tighter against him. I could feel everything: every inch of his need pressing into me, the raw intensity of his desire. He shifted slightly, his thigh pushing between my legs, making me gasp and cling to him harder.

The effect was instant. He attacked my mouth with renewed urgency, the kiss wild and consuming. My head spun as he devoured me whole, each stroke of his tongue claiming more than the last. My own need rose to meet his, fierce and unrelenting.

His hook found the waist of my pants next. The metal was cold against my skin as it caught beneath the fabric and pulled —hard. The pants gave way with a satisfying rip, leaving me exposed to him.

"Fuck," he muttered again, pulling back just enough to look at me. His eyes were dark and hungry as they raked over me. "You're perfect."

I opened my mouth to protest—to tell him how wrong he was—but then he moved again, silencing me with another bruising kiss that left no room for doubt or denial.

The wall scraped against my back as he lifted me higher, positioning himself with ruthless precision. I wrapped my legs around him instinctively, anchoring myself to him as if letting go would mean falling forever.

There was a moment—a brief pause where time seemed to stretch impossibly thin—and then he thrust into me with a force that shattered the world around us. I cried out at the sudden fullness of it all; at how right it felt; at how much I needed this—needed him.

"You have no idea," he rasped, lips trailing down my jaw, his breath scorching my skin, "how badly I need you right now."

"Then take me," I breathed and locked my ankles together behind his back as he captured my mouth again, kissing me like it was some kind of battle he refused to lose.

My head fell back against the wall as he shifted his attention lower, teeth grazing along my collarbone. His hot mouth returned to my bare skin, lightning dancing under my skin at the contact.

Tightening my grip on him, my fingers dug into his shoulders as I tried to hold on—to sanity or control or maybe just consciousness. But it was useless; he was everywhere at once, overwhelming every sense until there was nothing left but him.

And then we were moving again—away from the wall toward the bed in a dizzying blur of motion. He laid me down with surprising gentleness considering how fast my pulse drummed beneath his touch. Light flickered across his face as he hovered above me for one breathless moment before closing the distance again.

I tilted my head back as his lips moved lower, tracing the line of my jaw, the column of my throat. His stubble scraped against my skin, sending sharp jolts of pleasure through my frayed nerves. I gasped when he nipped at the sensitive spot beneath my ear, his teeth sinking just enough to make my stomach clench before his tongue soothed the sting.

"You feel like fire," he rasped, his voice rough. "Burning me alive."

I let out a breathless laugh, my nails raking down his back, the heat between us unbearably feverish. "Stop holding back."

"As you wish," he grinned sheepishly before trailing kisses lower. His warm breath fanned across my exposed skin, sending shivers down my spine as his stubble rasped against the soft flesh of my belly.

"Ulrich—" His name left my lips on a desperate cry.

His grip on my hip tightened, holding me firmly in place as he hovered over me, his eyes darkening with desire. Just when I thought I couldn't take any more, he continued downward. His lips followed the curve of my navel, warm and teasing, before his teeth grazed the sensitive skin. My breath hitched as he lingered there, savoring my reaction, before he dragged his mouth lower.

I barely had a second to catch my breath before his tongue flicked out, a slow, languid stroke that made my spine arch off the bed. A strangled gasp escaped my lips, my fingers clutching the sheets so tightly that my knuckles whitened as molten heat surged through my body. I cried out, my voice breaking the silence of the dimly lit room, and he gently lifted my legs, draping them over his broad shoulders. The cold press of the silver hook against my thigh sent a shiver through me—a delicious warning of danger that heightened my senses. I whimpered, hips bucking instinctively, but his grip tightened, holding me in place, forcing me to take everything he gave.

"Not so fast," he murmured, the warmth of his breath sending another wave of need crashing through me. "Let me enjoy you."

His words, low and commanding, sent fire licking up my spine. Then he sucked—*hard*—and I shattered, a broken moan tumbling past my lips. He didn't stop. He lapped at me like a man starved, before he slipped his fingers in, curling, stroking, filling me as my body trembled beneath him.

I barely registered the shift in movement before he rose above me, his weight pressing me into the mattress. My legs fell to the side, and my core pulsed with unmet desire as I clenched on nothing. The thick, teasing press of his cock against my clit sent another jolt rippling through me.

His forehead rested against mine, his breath ragged, his body taut. His lips brushed mine in a tormenting stroke, his voice a husky rasp. "Tell me you want this."

I shivered, my nails digging into his shoulders as I whispered, "I want this."

A low growl vibrated through his chest, and he thrust into me, stretching me, filling me, stealing the air from my lungs. A strangled cry escaped, but he caught it with his mouth, swallowing the sound as his lips consumed mine. The slow, deliberate drag of his hips sent pleasure rippling through my veins, claiming every inch of me.

He devoured me with a ravenous hunger, as if he had been deprived for an eternity, craving every part of me with a ferocity that bordered on desperation, and I met him with the same wild desperation. Every stroke, every shift of his body against mine, felt like something sacred—something neither of us could ever take back.

His teeth scraped along my jaw, his breath hot against my ear. "Mine."

And I knew, down to my very bones, that I had never belonged to anyone else.

His body pressed flush against mine as he drove into me, deep and unrelenting. With each punishing thrust of his hips, heat licked up my spine, winding tighter and tighter until the tension in my core was unbearable.

I was burning. Drowning—

I shattered.

Pleasure crashed over me in a violent wave, ripping through me like a storm tearing through the sails of a ship. My body arched, my nails dug into his strong back as I cried out his name, lost in the pleasure he pulled from me so effortlessly.

But he didn't stop.

He chased me through the aftermath, dragging me higher, wringing every last bit of pleasure from me until I was trembling beneath him, boneless and wrecked. His lips found mine again, this time softer, lingering, and I felt the emotions behind the touch. This wasn't a claiming.

It was something neither of us dared put into words.

His rhythm faltered, his breath coming in ragged gasps—he was close.

And I wanted to be his undoing.

With what little strength I had left, I pushed at his chest and flipped us over before he could protest. A sharp curse escaped his lips as he landed beneath me. My moan nearly drowned out his as he slid deeper with this new angle and his heady gaze darkened.

I smirked, straddling him, relishing the impossible stretch of him.

"My turn."

A shuddering breath left my lips as I settled deeper onto him, my nails digging into his chest. His head fell back against the wall with a guttural groan, fingers clenching around my waist, his hook flat against the base of my spine, urging me on.

"Fuck, Arie," he rasped.

I rolled my hips slowly, teasing, savoring the way he twitched inside me, the way his muscles tensed beneath my touch. His eyes snapped open, dark and dangerous, locking onto mine with an intensity that sent a thrill down my spine.

"You're playing a dangerous game, little mermaid," he warned, his grip tightening.

I smirked, dragging my nails down his chest. "Then stop me."

A muscle ticked in his jaw, his patience hanging by a thread, but he let me move at my own pace, let me take my time driving him to madness. I rose up, nearly letting him slip free, before sinking all the way down, reveling in the sharp hiss he let out, the way his fingers flexed against my skin.

I set a rhythm, torturously slow at first, making him feel every second of it. Pleasure built, winding tighter and tighter, until his control finally snapped.

His hand moved, fisting my hair while his hook pushed harder against my back as he took over, slamming up into me with a force that sent a strangled cry from my lips.

I clung to him, the world splintering as pleasure crashed over me in waves, his name tumbling from my lips in broken gasps. He drove into me relentlessly, each thrust sending sparks of heat curling through my veins, my body unraveling under his touch.

I gasped, barely able to form words as he drove me higher, closer to the edge.

"Gods, yes," I finally choked out.

And as he followed me over the edge, his body shaking beneath mine, I knew there was no going back.

I was his.

He was mine.

And I would make sure he never forgot it.

25
HOME
ULRICH

I woke to the feeling of being watched.

A slow, lazy grin curled at my lips before I even opened my eyes. I could feel her gaze—Arie—like the heat of the sun against my skin, her presence a tangible thing, warm and intoxicating. When I finally cracked one eye open, she was beside me, sheets pooled around her waist, her red curls a wild mess from the night before. And gods, she was magnificent.

I stretched, muscles sore in the best possible way, and turned toward her, my grin widening. "See something you like?"

She lifted a brow and smirked. "Not really. Just wondering how someone with such a pretty face can be such a pain in my ass."

I chuckled, reaching out to tug her down onto the bed with me, but she dodged, moving just out of reach. "Cruel, love. Wounding my delicate heart first thing in the morning."

She rolled her eyes, but there was laughter hidden behind them. "I didn't take you for the delicate type, Captain Hook."

I propped myself up on my elbows, watching her, drinking

her in. The soft golden light filtering through the cabin windows made her ethereal, and for a moment, I let myself exist in this space—the quiet, the warmth, the knowledge that she was here, safe. With me.

"You're beautiful," I said, voice rougher than I intended.

That caught her off guard. She blinked, her lips parting slightly before she schooled her features, but I caught the way her cheeks reddened.

A sharp voice from above deck cut through the air, shattering the moment. "Land!"

Arie's head snapped toward the sound, and she was already moving for her clothes before the lookout's voice finished echoing.

I groaned, flopping back against the mattress. "Gods, we can't even have one morning of peace."

"Oh, quit whining and get dressed." She tossed my shirt at me.

I caught it, grinning as I tugged it over my head. "You sure you don't want to stay here a little longer? Let the others handle the *land* situation?"

She shot me a pointed look as she pulled on her boots. "Do you really want to take that risk?"

I winced. "Point taken."

Arie smirked, shaking her head as she threw open the cabin door. I followed her up to the deck, squinting against the sunlight as the salty breeze hit me.

Neverland.

The jagged cliffs in the distance rose like teeth from the sea, dark and looming against the sky. The dense, green foliage beyond was wild and ancient. An ach pressed in on my chest, a lump forming in the back of my throat. Neverland was the only home I remembered and while it would always hold a special place in my heart—I looked over at Arie—but she was the one who felt like home now. Her presence was like a quiet anchor, a comfort I hadn't realized I needed until she was by my side. No matter where we went, no matter what happened next, she had become my constant. And that, in a world as unpredictable as this, meant everything.

I heard Arie exhale softly beside me, her fingers gripping the railing.

"It looks . . . different," she murmured.

I glanced at her. "Different how?"

She shook her head, a flicker of something unreadable in her eyes. "I don't know. Maybe it's just the thought of what awaits us."

Pascal strode up beside us, reaching into his coat pocket. "I've got the dust we need to pass the protection spell," he said, holding up a small vial filled with shimmering gold. "But only enough for essential people. We'll need to get Tink back before we can get everyone on the island."

I frowned, jaw tightening. "So, we're just supposed to leave the rest behind?"

Pascal exhaled, running a hand through his dark hair. "We don't have a choice, Hook. The island's protections will rip apart those who try to cross without it, you know there isn't a soul here that is pure of heart, or a child for that matter. We've all done things to survive. So, it's either we go now, get Tink, and come back for the rest, or we waste time trying to find another way and lose whatever chance we have to save her."

My fists clenched at my sides. He wasn't wrong, but it didn't sit right with me. The thought of leaving the others—especially the sick—to fend for themselves made my stomach churn.

As if summoned by my thoughts, Keenan appeared beside

me, his face drawn and pale. "You don't have to worry about them anymore," he said, voice hoarse but steady.

I turned to him, eyes narrowing and heart lurching. "Why's that?"

Keenan hesitated before glancing toward the lower deck. "Calypso says she can put the infected into a slumber. They won't feel anything. Won't suffer." He swallowed hard. "She says they'll be comfortable until we get back."

My gut twisted.

Calypso. Again.

I bit back a curse, my jaw working as I fought the urge to argue. I didn't like it. Didn't like how she kept inserting herself into our problems with a solution wrapped up in an ominous little bow.

Still... the alternative was letting them suffer.

Arie shifted beside me, watching me closely. "Ulrich."

I turned to her, exhaling sharply through my nose.

"We don't have a better option," she said softly, but there was steel in her voice. "You know that as well as I do."

I rubbed a hand over my face. "It doesn't sit right."

Pascal shrugged. "Not much does these days."

I shot him a glare, but Keenan stepped in before I snapped. "Look, I don't trust her either," he admitted. "But the crew—*our crew*—needs help now, not later. And unless you have another way of keeping them from suffering until we can fix this, we need to take the offer."

I hated it. Hated that he was right. I glanced at Arie, who watched me carefully, waiting for my decision.

With a sharp exhale, I nodded. "Fine. But Keenan, keep an eye on her. I don't trust she's here for good reasons. Tell Doc we'll have one of the Lost Boys bring more supplies, too."

Keenan nodded before making his way below deck to inform the others. I turned back toward Neverland, the jungle stretching before us like an open mouth, waiting to devour us whole.

"Let's get this done," I muttered.

Arie nodded, reaching for the vial in Pascal's hands.

And with that, we stepped toward the edge of the ship, ready to descend into whatever hell awaited us.

26
Never Again
ARIE

The moment my boots hit the sand, the familiar weight of Neverland settled around me. The thick, humid air carried the scent of damp earth and salt, a mix of jungle and sea that had once felt like home.

But something was wrong.

The wind howled through the trees, rustling the dense canopy like a whisper of warning. The island was always unpredictable—but this? This felt... unnatural.

Ulrich landed beside me, his stance defensive as he scanned the shoreline, his weight balanced for a fight. Pascal followed, his usual smirk absent as his gaze flicked toward the treetops. Frankie adjusted her weapons, rolling her shoulders like she could feel the shift, too. Nathaniel, Robin, Gretel, and Hansel joined us seconds later.

A figure stepped out from the jungle.

Ace.

He looked like shit. "Ace, what the hells happened to you?" Pascal shoved people aside until he stood in front of Ace.

"About time you got here," he said, his voice a low rasp. "We've got a problem."

Ulrich crossed his arms. "No warm welcome?"

Ace's lips twitched, but it wasn't a smile. "I'd say 'good to see you,' but I'm not sure if it is yet." He flicked his gaze toward me. "You're back. *That's* interesting."

I frowned. "Interesting how?"

"Interesting because I don't think it's a coincidence that you showed up at the same time shit went sideways."

I exchanged a glance with Ulrich before stepping closer. "What do you mean? What's happening?"

Ace exhaled sharply, dragging a hand through his already disheveled hair, his fingers trembling slightly before he curled them into a fist. "The island isn't right. The waters are restless, tides pulling in ways they shouldn't. The jungle's too quiet. And my boys—" He broke off, shaking his head. "—They're seeing things. Shadows that move when they shouldn't, whispers in the dark when no one's there."

Robin stiffened. "If they're seeing shadows, then Gemma brought assassins with her. More than likely her, which means we'll need to be extra careful."

Gretel's brows furrowed before her eyes widened in horror. "Shadow magic?" She turned to Robin. "But I thought only you had that. That's why she wanted you so—" Her words cut off, her expression twisting as realization hit her like a crashing wave. "Holy fucking gods above. She didn't."

Robin's jaw tightened, his face grim with something close to shame.t. "It took her a while, but she figured out how to use my blood to give others my shadow magic. It doesn't work as well, and it doesn't last long—and forget about controlling it like I can—but it works. Not good for us," he added.

"Shit," Gretel muttered, running a hand over her face.

Nathaniel stepped forward, his expression tight. "Care to explain what you're talking about?"

Robin glanced around before exhaling heavily. "It's easier if I show you."

The air around him darkened, shifting like mist catching the wind. Then, in the span of a single breath, his form coalesced, warping into a mass of near-transparent iridescent smoke, the color flickering between shadow and nothingness.

It wasn't like the usual illusions of magic. This wasn't a trick of the light. Robin had become the air itself, shifting in a way that made my stomach twist.

A slow chill curled down my spine as I took a step back.

Ace's fingers twitched toward the dagger at his hip. "That," he said, voice quiet but laced with steel, "is not normal."

I swallowed hard, forcing myself to keep my expression neutral. "No. It isn't."

Ulrich's hand brushed against mine, grounding me, but his posture had stiffened as well.

Robin shifted back, his body snapping into solidity like a blade unsheathing. His expression was tight, wary. "Now imagine a dozen of them, moving unseen, with the sole purpose of killing anything in their path."

A dense, oppressive silence fell over the group.

Gretel exhaled sharply. "We're fucked."

"Let's get to the treehouse before any of them find us," Pascal said.

It took us a while, but we made it without incident, even if it took hours, dodging and weaving from tree to tree for cover. It hadn't changed much since I'd first been here, and as we neared the entrance, the sounds of activity inside soothed some of my fears. The Lost Ones were alive and well, their home brimming with life despite the dangers lurking in the shadows below.

Ace led the way, shoving open the broad wooden doors

with little ceremony. But the moment we stepped inside, the room stilled.

For a breath, silence fell, heavy and thick, before the Neverbeasts—previously scattered among the Lost Ones—suddenly stilled, nostrils flaring as they caught my scent.

Then, in a blur of movement, they shifted.

Hulking forms melted into human shapes—tall, lean bodies covered in faded scars and painted markings; their sharp eyes locked onto me as they surged forward. My muscles tensed instinctively, prepared for a fight, but before I could reach for Slayer, I was surrounded.

Warm, strong arms wrapped around me, nearly knocking me off my feet as they pulled me into a crushing embrace.

"Arie." The voice was deep, rough with emotion, and I barely had time to process it before another set of arms joined, and then another. The Neverbeasts—these fierce warriors, these creatures of Gemma's making—held me, murmuring words of gratitude, of relief.

A woman with long, curly black hair gripped my shoulders, her amber eyes shining. "You saved us," she whispered, voice thick. "Freed us from that hell. I never got the chance to thank you."

A man with sharp cheekbones and a scar running across his nose clapped a hand against my back. "We thought we'd die in Wendy's hold," he admitted. "But you, gods, you got us out."

One by one, they murmured their thanks, their voices layering over one another, their gratitude a force so palpable it nearly knocked the air from my lungs.

I swallowed hard, overwhelmed. "You don't have to thank me," I said, though my voice came out uneven. "I did what needed to be done."

"You did more than that," another Neverbeast interjected,

his dark, calloused hand squeezing my forearm. "You gave us back our lives."

Ulrich shifted beside me, his presence solid and steady, but when I glanced at him, his expression was unreadable.

"Well, if it isn't the mermaid," Marian pushed her way through the crowd of Neverbeasts and pulled me into a tight hug.

"Maiden," I laughed and hugged her.

She stepped back and smiled. "I'm glad to see you're okay. Though I'm a little disappointed you brought a shit storm with you. Didn't we just get rid of a monster?"

I shrugged. "I slay monsters daily. What's one more?.."

Marian snorted. "Right."

Before Marian could say more, the air around us shifted. The quiet murmurs of the Lost Ones and the Neverbeasts settled into something more hushed—expectant.

Slow, deliberate footsteps approached from behind.

I turned, my breath catching in my throat as Robin stepped forward, his face pale beneath the grime and exhaustion of the past few days. His expression was unreadable, his dark eyes fixed on Marian with the kind of intensity that sent a ripple of unease through the air.

Marian stiffened beside me, her entire body rigid.

"Marian?" Robin's voice was a hoarse rasp, like he had just seen a ghost.

A curse ripped from Marian's lips, barely above a whisper as she strode toward him.

Robin didn't move. He just *stared*.

Marian stopped inches from him, her breaths sharp and uneven. "You absolute *ass*," she hissed.

Then, before anyone could react, she launched herself at him.

Their bodies collided, and Robin stumbled back with the

force of her, his hands coming up just in time to catch her before she crushed them both to the ground.

And then she kissed him.

Hard.

Robin froze for a split second before his arms tightened around her, one hand tangling in her wild hair, the other pressing her flush against him like he never planned to let go. The way he kissed her wasn't careful, wasn't hesitant—it was desperate, claiming, *relentless*, like he had been starving for this moment for years.

The entire treehouse fell into stunned silence.

Then Ace let out a low whistle. "Well, shit."

Pascal muttered something under his breath, shaking his head. Gretel raised an eyebrow, crossing her arms, but there was a hint of amusement in her expression. Only for a second before her eyes wandered, searching for something—or someone—in the crowd.

I glanced at Ulrich, watching the scene unfold with his arms crossed, an unbothered smirk playing on his lips. When he noticed me looking, he leaned in slightly. "I take it they've got history?"

I huffed a small laugh. "Seems like it."

Robin and Marian finally broke apart, breathless and staring at each other like they had shattered the laws of nature.

Robin exhaled shakily, his forehead resting against hers. "Gods above, I thought I lost you."

Marian punched him in the shoulder. Hard. "You *did* lose me, you idiot."

Robin winced, rubbing his arm, but deep fondness colored in his expression. "You hit harder than I remember."

"You're damn right I do." Marian swallowed hard, her walls cracking just enough for the emotion to seep through.

"What happened?" he asked.

She reached up, tracing her fingers lightly over his cheek as if still trying to convince herself he was real. "A lot happened and you're not going to like hearing it," she admitted.

Robin's jaw tightened, but his grip on her didn't loosen. "I don't care. I just—I need to know. I need to know everything."

The weight of the moment settled between them, and I could feel the way it cracked open something a raw, buried thing. It was—

"Giantsbane?" Another voice rumbled through the crowd. A woman, much taller than those around her, stepped forward. Her silver hair cascaded down mossy-green skin and her golden eyes pierced through the room.

"Ymira," Gretel dropped the dagger she'd been holding, the blade clattering to the ground as she moved. "I'd hoped like hell I'd find you here."

They embraced, though not as abrasive as Robin and Marian, but that was loveblooming between them. The look of lost lovers who found each other again. Warmth spread through me.

"Sounds like Wendy and Gemma took a lot of loved ones," I said.

"She did." Robin grabbed Ymira by the shoulder. "It's good to see you again, Ymira. I wasn't certain Gemma would have brought you here after everything but we hoped."

Ymira pulled Robin into a hug. "Thanks for taking care of her while I was gone."

Gretel huffed. "No one needs to take care of me, I do just fine on my own."

The bickering between old friends continued until—

A voice erupted through my mind.

Arie.

I stumbled back.

Arie, are you there? I can feel you. Shit you are here, aren't you?

Tink.

The moment her voice whispered through my mind; my knees buckled. A strangled gasp caught in my throat, my hands hitting the wooden floor of the treehouse as my vision blurred with the force of our connection snapping into place. The tether between us had been weak, nearly severed by distance and time, but now, it burned through me with the sharpness of a brand.

Ulrich was at my side in an instant, his voice tight with concern. "What's wrong?"

I shook my head, barely able to form words.

Tink, seven hells, it's good to hear your voice. I was so worried about you. Where are you? Where's Gemma?

A pause. A shudder in our bond.

She's here. With me. I'm supposed to tell her the second you step foot in Neverland. I'm also supposed to tell you that you and you alone need to come to the entrance of the Celestial Plains for the exchange.

I stiffened, my nails digging into the wood beneath me. *Of course* Gemma wouldn't just hand Tink over. *Of course* she would try to control the situation, dictate the terms, make the rules bend to her will.

You can't though, Arie, there are assassins everywhere and—

I clenched my jaw, my thoughts spiraling. To get past the assassins with only a handful of our crew would be next to impossible and the gods knew what Gemma would do if I didn't go alone. But the idea of leaving Tink there, with *her*—it made violence boil my blood.

I can't just leave you there, Tink. You die, I die, remember?

The weight of those words settled between us, the unbreakable truth of our bond.

We'll come up with a plan. Don't tell her I'm here yet. Give me twenty-four hours to figure out a plan. I'll reach out when we're ready.

A sharp exhale, like she had been holding her breath. *Okay, but be careful, Arie. She has her assassins all over the place. If they catch on that you're here and I haven't told her...*

She didn't have to finish.

I already knew how that would end.

It'll be bad, I acknowledged. *I get it. We'll stay safe for now and won't go anywhere until we're ready to come get you. Be careful, Tink.*

I will.

And then, just like that, she was gone.

I sagged forward, pressing my forehead against the floor, my pulse a frantic drum against my ribs. My whole body trembled, my muscles tense with the need to *do something*, to *move*, to tear through the trees and storm to the entrance of the Celestial Plains.

But I couldn't.

Not yet.

Ulrich's hand brushed over my back, his voice softer now. "Arie."

"What's happening?" Frankie asked frantically.

I swallowed hard before lifting my head to meet Ulrich's gaze. His eyes searched mine, filled with the patience and understanding I didn't deserve.

"Tink," I whispered.

"Did you say Tink?" A frown drew Pascal's brows low. "I thought you couldn't get through to her."

I nodded. "She's alive. She's with Gemma. And she's supposed to tell the Queen the second we step foot in Neverland."

Ulrich exhaled through his nose, shaking his head. "Of course, she wants the upper hand any way she can get. I'm sure she has a plan."

My fingers curled into fists. "Yeah. But so do we."

The others watched, waiting. All of them knew something had happened, but they were letting me catch my breath, allowing me time to *process*.

But I didn't need time.

I needed action.

I stood , rolling my shoulders, the weight of responsibility settling into place like an old, familiar wound.

"She gave us one day before she'll be forced to tell Gemma we're here," I said, my voice steady now. "That's how long we have to come up with a way to get Tink back and keep Gemma from getting into the Celestial Plains."

Ace crossed his arms, nodding slowly. "Then we better get to work."

The room shifted with a renewed sense of urgency, as if the very air thickened with the weight of what was to come. Conversation buzzed around me, a whirlwind of anxious voices blending with the sharp clink of metal and the rustle of preparations. The Lost Ones, along with the Neverbeasts, moved with purpose, their every action deliberate. Maps were pulled from their hiding places, the edges crinkling as they unfolded, revealing the twisted paths of Neverland

But beneath the movement, beneath the planning, a tension lingered. Because this wasn't just about getting Tink back. This was about stopping Gemma before she got what she wanted, before she reached the Celestial Plains and did something none of us could undo.

Pascal leaned over the map, his fingers drumming against the frayed edges. "The entrance to the Celestial Plains is hidden in the deepest part of Neverland. I can get us there, but it's not going to be easy. My guess is she'll have her assassins all over the area. If they see that you're not alone, it'll be bad. But I have a way to get us there where not even the assassins will notice."

Ace leaned back slightly, his brow furrowed in thought. "Question," he chimed in, his tone laced with skepticism. "Gemma has Tink, right? And fairy dust. So why doesn't she just use it to enter the Celestial Plains? Why go through all this trouble for the souls?"

Pascal's eyes darkened. "My guess? She doesn't have enough. Wendy harvested a lot of fairy dust for Gemma, but she also used a significant portion for herself and to control the Neverbeasts. Fairy dust is powerful, but it burns fast, and we don't know how much Gemma has left."

"It's more than that," I cut in, crossing my arms, a sinking feeling settled in my gut. "The souls aren't just her ticket in. They're her disguise."

Ace scoffed. "Disguise?"

I nodded. "Everything we've learned about Gemma tells us one thing: she never makes a move without layers of contingency. Ursa didn't just steal souls—she consumed them, twisting herself into something more powerful, something unnatural. Wendy took the fairy dust and experimented, pushing it beyond what anyone thought possible. All of this—everything Gemma has done—has been building to something bigger."

Fairy dust was very useful, not just to get into Neverland but it also had a way of getting through the Celestial Plains. Souls and fairy dust were the key. Wendy had managed to take so much of it, killing all the other fairies in the process. Tink never talked about the loss of the other fairies often, but I knew it was hard for her, and saw it in the pain flickering in her eyes.

"Oh, fuck." Frankie's eyes widened. "She used Ursa and Wendy as her test subjects."

Ace's expression tightened, but it was Pascal who spoke. "She plans to consume the souls within the stone," he confirmed. "It's not just about gaining power; it's about deception. My father would sense her if she tried to enter the Celestial Plains with fairy dust alone. But if she absorbs the souls, she can use them as a cloak, warping her presence, masking her true identity. Like Ursa, she'll become—"

"A monster," Nathaniel muttered.

"Exactly," Pascal said. "One capable of slipping past the wards undetected."

A heavy silence settled over us, the weight of the revelation sinking in. I couldn't be certain everything was true but it made sense. I'd thought about it during our trip here and it all led back to this. To the fact that Gemma had one goal in mind. Complete and utter destruction. We already knew what would happen if the gates were opened and the souls left the Celestial Plains. I had no idea what Gemma's true goals were or why she was doing this. All I knew for certain was that she needed to be stopped.

Losing your family was never easy.

But this just confirmed that Queen Gemma had no plans to give Tink back in exchange for the Obsidian Heart Stone. This was a trap, and everyone at this table knew it.

Stay safe, Tinkerbell. I'm coming.

Ace and Pascal continued working out a plan. We'd take to the treetops, using what little fairy dust we had left to fly above the trees where the shadows wouldn't see us. I would drop down and use my trident to take down Gemma while the others focused on getting Tink back. Ace and some of the Lost Ones had managed to scout the area and found weak spots we could use to get in without being ambushed by assassins. The entire thing was a risk, but we had to take it—I had to take it.

But as I looked around at the faces of my friends—Ace, Pascal, the Lost Ones—I felt a heavy weight in my chest. They were risking everything for me, putting their lives on the line for a cause that wasn't even theirs. The thought twisted in my gut, and I couldn't shake the nagging feeling that it wasn't right. They might die for me, and that... that didn't sit well at all.

"None of you should be doing this. This is my fight. It started with me so it should end with me."

Beside me, Pascal scoffed. "Started with you? I'm certain it started with me and Hook, too. We told you from the start, we were in this together. We started it here and we will end it here together."

"He's right," Frankie agreed. "You can't go at it alone. Gemma and her assassins will eat you alive. We all deserve to be there and we're better as a team anyway."

Damn if she wasn't right, but that didn't mean I liked it.

"All right, but you all need to stay out of sight unless things go sideways. Find a way to get to Tink and I'll keep Gemma occupied. This feels like a trap so we need to tread carefully," I said.

"Come on." Frankie smiled. "Careful is our middle name."

Though everyone in the room laughed, I only shook my head.

Ace cracked his knuckles. "Then we have a plan."

I looked around the room, taking in the faces of my friends. The people willing to walk into hell with me.

"One day," I murmured. "That's all we have."

Robin's gaze hardened. "Then let's make it count."

The night was unnervingly quiet. The jungle that usually buzzed with the sounds of Neverland's wilds—crickets, distant animal calls, the occasional rustle of the trees as the wind whispered through their branches—had fallen silent. As if the island itself held its breath. Waiting.

Just like me.

I sat on the worn wooden steps of the treehouse, staring into the dark as I turned the Obsidian Stone in my hand. The others were inside, resting as best they could before the chaos that would unfold tomorrow. But sleep wouldn't come for me. My mind was too restless, too tangled in the pending doom.

A twig snapped behind me.

I didn't turn, didn't reach for my blade because I knew who it was before she sat down beside me.

"Can't sleep?" Marian asked, her voice soft but laced with exhaustion.

I shook my head.

Frankie plopped down on my other side, stretching her legs in front of her. "Yeah, well, me neither," she admitted, dragging a hand through her tangled curls. "I figured if we're going to be insomniacs, it might as well be together."

A hint of a smile ghosted my lips, but it faded just as quickly. Silence stretched between us, heavy with unspoken thoughts.

Marian was the first to break it. "Tomorrow's going to be hell."

I exhaled, pressing my hands against my knees. "I know."

"You ready for that?" she asked, her tone careful but firm.

"No," I answered honestly. "But I don't have a choice."

Frankie huffed out a quiet laugh. "Yeah, well, you and the right choice don't exactly get along."

I nudged her with my shoulder, and she smirked, but her

eyes searched my face, looking for the things I wasn't saying. She must've found them because her expression softened.

"Whatever happens tomorrow," Frankie said, "we've got your back. No matter what."

Marian nodded, staring straight ahead. "And we'll make it out of this. All of us."

I wasn't sure if she was saying it for me or herself. Maybe both.

I swallowed, staring at the darkened treeline. "I used to think I was better off alone," I admitted, my voice barely above a whisper. "That it was safer that way. Easier."

Frankie snorted. "Yeah, well, that's a dumb thought."

I huffed out a breath. "Yeah."

Marian's fingers toyed with the hem of her sleeve. "But you don't feel that way now, do you?"

I shook my head. "No."

Because I had them. I had all of them—Frankie, Marian, Ulrich, Pascal, Robin, Hansel, Gretel, the Lost Ones, the crew. And gods, I didn't realize just how much I *needed* them until now.

Tomorrow, I'd be walking into a trap. We all would. And I didn't know if we'd all make it out, but for the first time in a long time, I wasn't doing it alone. For that, I was grateful.

"I'm glad you're here," I said, glancing between them.

Frankie scoffed. "Please. Like you'd survive without us."

Marian smirked. "She has a point."

I rolled my eyes, but a warmth settled in my chest.

I leaned back, staring up at the night sky, the weight of everything dawn would bring pressing on my shoulders. The plan was set. All we could do now was wait. The thought alone sent an anxious energy humming in my veins, but I forced myself to exhale, letting it go. For now.

Frankie nudged my arm. "You're too quiet. That's dangerous."

I huffed a soft laugh. "Not everything has to be about me." I shifted my gaze to Marian, a smirk tugging at my lips. "Speaking of which, what's going on with you and Robin?"

Marian stiffened slightly, her fingers twitching against her knee before she sighed, rolling her eyes. "Nosy much?"

Frankie grinned, leaning in. "You should know by now that's part of the package."

Marian shook her head but didn't deflect. Her gaze drifted toward the firelight flickering in the distance, something unreadable passing through her expression. "He helped me once," she admitted. "Saved my life."

That caught my attention. I sat up straighter. "Robin did?"

She nodded, exhaling slowly, as she chose her words carefully. "I was already with Gemma when he found me," she admitted, her voice quieter now. "He saved me. Saved a lot of people. But she was too strong. It didn't matter how far I ran or how well I hid. She found me, and dragged me back." Her fingers curled against her knee, knuckles white. "I barely remember what happened after that. One day, I woke up in Neverland, and everything I'd felt—everything I'd known—was gone."

Her voice dropped to a barely audible whisper. "I didn't even remember him, at least not until you broke her hold on Wendy. Then everything came rushing back."

I swallowed, understanding all too well what it felt like to have stolen memories resurface. "That must have been a lot."

Marian gave a dry chuckle. "Understatement." She paused, then shrugged. "I wouldn't call what I feel for him love—not yet, anyway. But I've never felt this way about anyone."

Frankie whistled low. "That's saying something."

Marian smirked. "Shut up."

I nudged her shoulder, offering her a knowing look. "You don't have to put a name to it. Just... let yourself feel it."

Her smirk softened into something more uncertain. "Yeah. I guess."

We fell into silence again, but this time it felt lighter, like the night's weight had shifted just a little. The fire crackled, distant laughter carried through the trees, but we sat there, side by side, waiting for morning. Together.

27

FLYING ABOVE
ULRICH

I REALLY HATED THIS PLAN.

I'd spent the night next to Arie and my mind refused to settle down. Arie and all the horrible things that could go wrong had kept me up into the small hours of dawn. While nearly everyone was accompanying us, I worried about what we were walking into.

Every step felt heavier than the last, the weight of memories pressing down on my chest like a phantom anchor. The last time we were here, I lost her.

Arie walked beside me, her steps precise, calculated, but I could feel the tension pulsating off her. The same tension I carried in my bones. Neither of us had forgotten.

The trees closed in around us, the air thick with the scent of moss and rotting wood, but all I could smell was blood. Her blood. The ghost of it still lingered in the cracks of my mind—the way it had stained the rocks when Jameson dragged her away, the way she fought until the very end. How I wasn't fast enough.

The memory of it gnawed at the back of my mind—the helplessness, the rage, the sheer agony of watching Jameson drag her away while I could do nothing but bleed and scream her name. That moment had burned itself into my bones, an open wound that never quite healed.

I clenched my jaw and forced the memory back.

Not this time.

I kept my hand near my sword, muscles coiled, every nerve on edge. I didn't trust the silence. Not here. Not after everything.

Arie's hand flexed at her side, and I didn't miss the way her fingers twitched toward her weapons. She felt it too.

I slowed my pace, scanning the trees, the undergrowth, the shadows that pooled in the crevices of the jungle floor. I didn't trust any of it. The last time I had walked this path, I had been running. Running after Jameson. Running after her. I swallowed hard and tore my gaze from my surroundings, looking at Arie instead. She was different now. Sharper. Stronger.

But was she whole?

I didn't know. And I hated that I didn't know.

Arie caught me staring, her brow furrowing slightly. "You're quiet."

I smirked, masking the storm inside me. "Enjoy it while it lasts."

She rolled her eyes but didn't press.

Good. Because I didn't want to tell her I was afraid. Afraid that this was another trap. That we were walking into the jaws of something we couldn't claw our way out of. Afraid that if I lost her again, I wouldn't be able to pull myself back from the edge.

"Stay close," Arie murmured, her voice barely above a whisper, but steady. Determined.

I huffed beside her, forcing something akin to amusement into my tone, even as my stomach twisted into knots. "Not a problem, love. Just try not to get yourself killed before we get there."

A wry smile ghosted across her lips, but there was something else behind it. A flicker of something fragile she would never admit to. "No promises."

"All right," Pascal called out. "This is the end of the treehouse's territory. Beyond here is where the assassins will be watching. Take some fairy dust, sprinkle it over your head, and rise straight above the trees."

As the shimmering grains of fairy dust settled over us, weightlessness took hold, lifting us into the sky.

Nathaniel let out a strangled yelp, flailing as he shot upward. "Oh, *hell no*—this is *not* natural!" He twisted midair, eyes wide with panic as he desperately tried to control his ascent. "How the *fuck* do you steer this thing?"

Pascal sighed. "It's not a thing, it's *fairy dust*. Just relax and let it guide you."

"Relax?" Nathaniel's voice pitched higher. "I'm floating in the *bloody sky* with nothing keeping me from plummeting to my death, and you want me to *relax*?"

Meanwhile, Frankie hovered just a few feet away, her face tinged green. "This is worse than the time I drank that bad batch of moonshine," she muttered, pressing a hand to her stomach. "I think I'm gonna be sick."

"Try not to vomit midair," I drawled, watching her with mild amusement. "It doesn't tend to fall straight down."

She shot me a withering glare, but she was too busy holding it together to come up with a proper retort.

The rest of our group, however, handled the flight with ease. Arie flew with practiced grace, adjusting her movements with the wind. Pascal and I barely spared a thought for the height, our focus ahead as we guided everyone forward. Even

Robin, who always carried an air of tension, didn't seem the least bit rattled by the flight.

For a moment, I forgot about the danger snapping at our heels. I forgot about the assassins lurking below, their smoke magic curling through the trees like spectral hands reaching for us. There was only the wind, cool against my skin, threading through my hair like a lover as I rose higher and higher.

It had been years since I'd felt this—since I'd truly flown. Not in a ship, not tethered to the mast of responsibility, but *really* flown. As kids, we didn't get to do it often—fairy dust wasn't something we could waste. But on the rare occasion we did, it felt like freedom. Pure, untouchable, *boundless* freedom. Back then, it was a game, a race to see who could fly the fastest, fly the farthest, who could dart between branches without getting caught in them.

Now, it was survival.

Still, for a split second, I let myself savor this. The weightlessness. The rush. The way the world stretched out below, vast and untamed.

Then my gaze dropped to the trees beneath us, and the moment shattered.

Shadows moved in the underbrush, flickering between the trunks. The assassins were there, waiting to devour anything in their path. I'd never heard of shadow magic where beings turned into smoke but watching Robin change had left me on edge. He'd explained the things he could do and was certain the other assassins weren't as skilled, but I wasn't so sure.

"Faster," Arie ordered, her voice sharp.

We pushed forward, the wind cutting across our skin as we soared over the treetops. At first, it was more endless forest, the dark canopy stretching in every direction. But in the distance, something caught my eye—a glimmer of cascading water, splitting the cliffs into vibrant streams of color. The sight tugged at something familiar in the back of my mind, a memory just out of reach.

As we drew closer, recognition hit me like a punch to the gut. *Seven Falls.*

I twisted toward Pascal. "Wait—this is Seven Falls?"

Pascal nodded, his expression unreadable.

"What the hell are we doing here?" I demanded.

His gaze flicked toward Arie, then back to me. "Because the pool at the bottom of the falls—it's the entrance to the Celestial Plains."

I stared at Pascal, my brow furrowing in disbelief. "You're joking."

Pascal shook his head. "Not in the slightest."

I let out a sharp breath, my gaze flickering between him and the cascading water below. "You expect me to believe that *this*—" I gestured toward the shimmering pool at the base of the cliffs, "—is some kind of gateway? I've been swimming in these pools for years."

Arie hovered beside me, arching a brow. "You grew up in Neverland, Ulrich. You've seen mermaids that can sing men to their deaths and fairies whose dust makes you fly—but *this* is where you draw the line?"

My jaw tightened. "That's different."

She lifted a brow and smirked. "Is it?"

I opened my mouth to argue but snapped it shut as a gust of wind carried us higher. How had I not known this?

"Come on," Pascal called, already veering toward the tallest of the seven falls. "We'll land at the top. It's the safest place to regroup."

Without another word, I followed, the air turning cooler as we ascended. The highest fall loomed ahead, its water shifting in red hues. As we landed, the roar of the falls filled the air, mist curling around us, dampening our clothes.

I took a steadying breath, but my mind reeled. A gateway. A hidden entrance to the Celestial Plains.

Frankie ran to the cliff and let the contents of her stomach spew over the side.

Arie stepped forward, her gaze locked on the shimmering pool below. The wind caught the loose strands of her hair, but she didn't waver. She looked almost eerily calm—too calm for what she was about to do.

"I'll go down first," she said, her voice steady. "I have to face Gemma alone. We don't know what we're walking into, and if she sees all of us, she'll know we aren't playing by her rules. She might disappear and take Tink with her, or she might spring whatever trap she's set."

I huffed, glancing between them. "So the plan is just to let you waltz into danger alone? I fucking hate this plan."

Arie smirked, but there was no humor in it. "That *was* the plan, yes."

Frankie wiped her mouth and groaned. "I hate that plan."

Arie turned back toward the falls, already bracing herself. "If I need you, I'll signal. You'll be close enough to intervene. I'm not doing this alone. I have my family at my back."

She met my eyes, something softer flickering beneath her guarded expression. Without a word, she stepped closer, her fingers brushing my cheek before she leaned in, pressing a quick, gentle kiss to my lips. It was brief, but the warmth of it lingered, a silent promise that we were in this together.

With that, she gave me a final, knowing look and, with a nod, stepped off the ledge and dove toward the water below.

28
WICKED SOULS
ARIE

The wind howled in my ears as I plummeted from the waterfall, the roar of cascading water a deafening rush around me. My stomach clenched, every instinct screaming that I should brace for impact, but the lingering effect of fairy dust held me in its grip. Instead of crashing into the pool below, I drifted down like a feather caught in the breeze, my descent controlled, almost too easy.

I landed lightly on the slick rocks at the water's edge, my boots barely making a sound against the stone. Mist curled around me, cool against my skin, and for a moment, all I could hear was the rhythmic pounding of the falls.

Clap. Clap. Clap.

Slow, deliberate applause echoed through the cavernous space, each measured beat cutting through the mist.

"Well done," came the smooth, silken voice I loathed.

I turned, my jaw tightening as Gemma emerged from a small rock formation, her figure sharp against the shimmer of water reflecting off the stone walls. She stood with effortless poise, clad in dark silks that seemed to shift like smoke around her frame. Her hair was pinned back, a few loose tendrils framing her face.

"You sure know how to make an entrance," she mused, her lips curling into something that might have been amusement—if not for the unmistakable edge twisted through it.

I squared my shoulders, forcing myself to steady. "You knew I'd come."

She tilted her head, feigning innocence. "Of course. You've always been predictable, darling."

My hands clenched at my sides, nails biting into my palms. Predictable. She taunted me, as if I were still the same girl who had blindly followed orders, who had trusted the wrong people. But I wasn't that girl anymore.

I lifted my chin. "And yet, you don't seem surprised to see me alive."

Gemma exhaled a soft laugh. "Should I be? Jameson played his part, but I never expected him to finish the job. You, of all people, are far too stubborn to die." She took a step closer, eyes gleaming in the dim light. "And look at you now. Free from his torment, free from my grip. Tell me, Arie, what does freedom taste like?"

My jaw tightened. "I wouldn't know. Not until you're dead."

She sighed, shaking her head like a disappointed parent. "Still so dramatic. But I suppose that's why I've always liked you."

Her words slithered over me like oil, thick with manipulation, but I refused to let them sink in. I'd been under her spell before. Never again.

I forced a smirk, tilting my head. "Then you must *really* love me now."

Gemma's smile faltered for all of a breath—a flicker, barely there—before she masked it with amusement. "Oh, darling. You have no idea."

And then, with a snap of her fingers, the mist around us stirred, shifting with purpose. And I knew—I wasn't alone with her.

The trap had been sprung.

Gemma's eyes gleamed, sharp and expectant. "Let's not waste time with pleasantries, Arie. Hand over the stone."

I didn't move. My fingers twitched at my sides, aching to curl into fists, but I kept my stance firm. "Where's Tink?"

Gemma exhaled an exaggerated sigh, as if indulging a petulant child. "Really, must we do this? You don't have any leverage here, darling. Just give me the stone, and I'll consider letting you all leave in one piece."

I lifted my chin. "I want to see Tink first."

For a moment, she watched me, her expression unreadable. Then, she flicked a hand, and from the shadows, a tiny, flickering glow emerged.

Tink fluttered into view, her wings barely carrying her, her small body trembling as she hovered in place. I sucked in a breath. She looked—wrong.

Her iridescent wings, once vibrant and full of life, were dulled, the edges frayed and uneven. Her glow flickered, weak and sputtering, like a candle on the verge of going out. Her usually bright eyes were heavy-lidded, her movements sluggish.

Cold rage slithered down my spine.

"Tink," I murmured, reaching toward her. But the second I did, something inside me shifted.

Like a floodgate breaking open, the block between us shattered.

The bond, severed for what felt like an eternity, snapped back into place, and I staggered under the weight of it. Under the weight of everything I felt from her. It wasn't warmth, or comfort, or anything I had hoped for.

It was *agony*.

Exhaustion pulsed through her, sharp and unrelenting. She was running on the last dregs of magic she had left. And, without a doubt, I knew why.

Gemma had drained her. Used her like a damn well to siphon magic until there was barely anything left.

"You took almost every last drop of fairy dust she had to offer," I seethed.

Gemma didn't even have the decency to look ashamed. She only smiled, tilting her head. "Of course I did. Did you really think I'd waste such a precious resource?"

Tink let out a small, pained sound, her wings faltering, and I bit back the scream building in my throat.

I clenched my fists so tightly my nails dug into my palms. My heartbeat roared in my ears, a steady, deafening drum of fury.

"You're going to regret that," I whispered, my voice laced with quiet fury.

Gemma's smirk deepened, full of condescension. "I highly doubt it." She flicked her wrist, and the assassins around us moved in, shifting like dark phantoms. "You have nothing to leverage. No one to help you. You came alone, Arie. And that was your first mistake."

Before I could react, a sudden force wrenched my arms behind my back. A sharp gasp left me as a vice-like grip pinned me in place. One of her assassins—a towering brute with cruel eyes—had me locked in an iron hold.

"Let go of me!" I snarled, twisting violently, but his grip tightened, sending a jolt of pain through my shoulder.

Gemma stepped forward, her eyes flicking to my fist where the stone rested, warm and pulsing against my palm.

She snatched my hand, her fingers prying mine open so she could grab the stone, a pulse of energy radiating outward. Shadows flickered, twisting unnaturally around her as the air rippled.

"It's funny that you actually believe those up on the cliff were the only ones I brought with me." I said, my voice steady despite the storm raging in my chest. Then, I whistled.

The sound cut through the night like a blade.

A moment of silence. Then—chaos.

A guttural roar echoed from the trees. Dark figures burst from the shadows, howls and shrieks filling the air. The Lost Ones. Their ragged clothes and fierce eyes gleamed with the promise of battle as they descended upon the assassins.

And then came the Neverbeasts, led by Robin and Marian.

"It changes nothing. You have failed, Arie." Gemma quickly pressed the stone to her mouth.

"No—!" My protest was drowned by the sound of the souls inside shrieking.

She inhaled.

A rush of dark energy burst from the stone, and dozens of souls were drawn into her through a vortex of power. The wind howled, swirling around her as her body convulsed. Her eyes rolled back, a shuddering gasp leaving her lips as the magic took hold.

I had to stop her.

I had to—

A slow, eerie smile curled Gemma's lips as her gaze snapped to mine, glowing with an unearthly energy. "Too late."

My heart pounded.

I didn't hesitate. I couldn't.

I lunged.

Slamming into her with all the force I had, I sent us careening into the pool of water s. The current was merciless, dragging us deeper. I kicked furiously, fighting against the swirling darkness, but hands—Gemma's—wrapped around my throat.

Bubbles burst from my lips as she shoved me down, her grip unrelenting.

We fought beneath the surface, our limbs entangled as the water thrashed around us. I managed to break free, ramming my knee into her stomach, but she recovered too quickly. A sharp burst of pain exploded at the back of my skull.

The last thing I saw was Hook and Pascal diving into the water—before everything went black.

A voice, deep and commanding, wove through the darkness.

"Wake up, Arie."

The words echoed in the vast emptiness that cradled me, rolling like distant thunder. The water should have swallowed them, but they rang clear, cutting through the murky blackness.

"Finish what you started."

A warmth—faint but familiar—wrapped around me, as if unseen hands steadied me, even as I drifted further into the abyss.

"Use the trident. Find your way."

The weight of those words sent a shiver through me.

My fingers twitched.

Fire burned through my lungs. My body lurched, desperate for air.

With a violent gasp, I surged forward. Cold night air wrapped around me as I coughed up water, my body convulsing from the force of it. Each breath was a ragged, painful drag, my chest aching as I sucked in air.

The world blurred, shifting between shadow and moonlight.

A figure loomed over me.

"Arie."

Ulrich's voice, rough with concern, reached me first. Then, his face sharpened into focus—his silver eyes stormy, his jaw set tight with worry. Water dripped from his dark hair as he knelt beside me, his broad frame blocking out the night sky.

"You almost didn't come back." His voice was quiet, but the accusation in it was unmistakable.

I tried to answer, but another cough wracked through me, more water spilling from my lips.

Ulrich didn't hesitate. He braced a hand against my back, steadying me as I fought to regain control of my breath. His grip was firm, grounding, even as tension rippled through his body.

I blinked rapidly, my mind catching up to what had happened—Gemma, the souls, the falls—

The trident.

My *father's* voice.

I inhaled sharply, the memory slamming into me with the force of a wave. My fingers dug into the wet earth. "I have to—" My voice was hoarse, but the urgency in it was clear.

Ulrich's brows furrowed. "Take a second."

"No time," I rasped. My father's voice had been clear. *Use the trident. Find your way.*

I had no idea how, but Gemma had to be stopped.

"Where did she go?" I rasped, my throat raw from the water.

"She was gone when we surfaced," Pascal answered grimly, shaking droplets from his soaked sleeves. "My guess is she consumed the last of the souls."

A cold dread slithered down my spine.

"Wait . . . does that mean we're—" My voice faltered as I finally took in our surroundings.

The breath left my lungs.

The sky stretched in endless, rippling waves of color—deep blues and purples swirled together, shifting like liquid fire, streaks of green and silver threading through them. It was like the northern lights had been spilled across the heavens, casting an eerie, dreamlike glow over everything.

But the light didn't touch the ground.

The field around us stretched vast and endless, but the grass beneath our feet wasn't green—it was black. Not charred or burnt, but an unnatural, inky void, swaying in a phantom wind that didn't touch my skin. The soft blades curled and uncurled like reaching fingers, whispering quietly as they moved.

A weight settled over my chest, thick as the air itself. It wasn't dark here—it was *hungry*.

I swallowed hard, my pulse thundering as Ulrich helped me up. "Is this . . . ?"

Pascal nodded. "I've only been here once with my father, but yes, Arie. We are in the Celestial Plains."

The name sent a shudder through me.

As we walked, the silence felt heavier than the air itself. It wasn't just quiet—it was suffocating, pressing in from all sides.

A soft whisper brushed against my ear, sending a sharp chill racing down my spine. I turned sharply, scanning the landscape. But there was nothing.

No . . . not quite nothing.

I squinted, catching movement in the corner of my eye. A shape lingered in the distance, hazy and shifting, not quite solid, but not quite gone.

"Did you see that?" I murmured.

Pascal barely spared it a glance. "Ghosts."

"Ghosts?" I raised a brow.

Pascal nodded, his expression blank, unreadable. "The ones that haven't let go. Those with unfinished business." His voice was distant, detached, like he had made peace with the strangeness of this place.

As if to prove his point, another figure flickered in the mist ahead. It was clearer than the first—more defined, more human. A woman with long, flowing hair, her face turned away from us. She stood still, as if listening, before vanishing into the darkness.

I swallowed hard, gripping the trident at my side.

"And those?" Ulrich asked, glancing up at the glowing orbs drifting lazily above us. Some flickered dimly, others pulsed with gentle radiance.

"Souls," Pascal answered. "The ones who have already passed but haven't moved on yet."

"Why not?" My voice was tight, uneasy.

"Because Pan hasn't guided them yet," Pascal said. "He takes them one by one."

"So they just . . . wait?" I asked, watching one drift out of reach.

"Yes," Pascal said. "They have nowhere else to go."

The thought sent a shiver down my spine.

A sudden wail carried through the stillness—a distant cry so full of sorrow and longing it sent goosebumps prickling along my arms.

Robin stiffened beside me, his hand twitching toward his sword. "And that?"

Pascal didn't turn toward the sound. "That's one of the Nexius."

"The what?" Ulrich pressed.

Pascal finally stopped walking and turned to face us fully. "Not every soul gets the chance to cross over," he said. "Some are too twisted or broken. They lose themselves here, unable to move forward, unable to go back." His jaw tightened. "The Nexius loosely translates to—"

"The wicked death." I gaped.

Seven hells, just great. That's all I need are fucking wailing balls of wicked death.

"Yes, and they don't like visitors."

A heavy silence followed his words.

I exhaled, pressing my fingers against my temple. Exhaustion clung to me like a second skin, but I forced myself to keep going. There was no turning back now.

Pascal gestured ahead. "Pan is waiting just beyond the next ridge."

We walked on, past the lingering ghosts and waiting souls, past the whispering shadows that danced at the edge of our sight.

And somewhere in the distance, the wailing continued.

The air grew hotter before we saw the flames.

The old house came into view first—a massive structure, weathered by time, with a gnarled tree jutting out from its center. Its roots had cracked the foundation long ago, twisting through the walls and floors as though claiming it for themselves. The branches stretched high into the shimmering darkness of the Celestial Plains, their charred tips glowing red from the fire that devoured them.

The house burned.

Flames licked hungrily at the walls, black smoke curling into the sky like the fingers of a giant beast. The crackling roar filled the air, drowning out everything else except for the voices—raised, furious.

Pan and Gemma.

The two of them stood just beyond the flames, their figures silhouetted against the inferno. Pan, tall and steady, his expression unreadable, his golden eyes burning with something ancient. And Gemma—gods, Gemma.

I had seen her twisted before, had seen her cruelty, her obsession with power. But this—this was something else.

Her irises were slitted like a serpent's, glowing faintly in the firelight. The veins along her neck and arms bulged dark and unnatural, her skin no longer smooth but textured, scaly. Her fingers curled into claws, sharp and black, and when she sneered, her teeth were wrong—too long, too pointed, like something that had never been human at all.

"What the hell is happening to her?" Ulrich muttered beside me.

"She's changing," Pascal whispered. "The souls, the magic she's stolen—it's twisting her into something else."

"Just like Ursa," I said.

I searched for Tink, but Gemma stoodalone. What had she done with her?"

Gemma pointed a clawed finger at Pan, her voice seething with fury. "Give him back."

Pan didn't move. "He was never yours to keep."

A snarl ripped from Gemma's throat, raw and full of pain. "You stole him from me! You took what was mine and left me with nothing!"

"You lost him long before I took him," Pan said, his voice steady. "You chose power over love, Gemma. You made that choice, not me."

The fire flared higher as if drawn to her rage.

Gemma tensed, her clawed hand shaking at her side. "I will burn this place to the ground," she hissed. "I will tear this entire realm apart if you don't give him back."

Pan exhaled slowly, shaking his head. "You don't even remember who you were before all this, do you?"

She flinched.

Just slightly.

But I saw it.

She turned her head slightly, and her slitted eyes found mine.

A slow, wicked smile curled across her lips. "You'd be wise to turn around and go back to Neverland, witch."

I forced myself to stand my ground, my heart hammering against my ribs. The sight of her sent something cold slithering down my spine, but I refused to look away. Instead, I unclasped the necklace and called upon the power thrumming through my veins. A surge of energy crackled beneath my skin, raw and electric. The trident charm pulsed against my palm, warmth spreading up my arm like liquid fire.

I gritted my teeth, focusing. Channeling.

Light burst outward, swallowing the tiny pendant in a storm of gold and sapphire hues. The air vibrated with a deep hum that resonated through the Celestial Plains, and then the weight in my hands changed. Metal formed in my grasp, solid and ancient, as the trident materialized in full. The haft was long, forged of gleaming gold and etched with swirling patterns that glowed faintly, pulsing like a heartbeat. The three prongs gleamed, sharp and deadly, crackling with veins of blue lightning that danced between them. The power it wielded was intoxicating, familiar in a way I didn't fully understand.

Gemma's smirk faltered, just for an instant. Her slitted eyes flicked from the weapon to me, her clawed fingers twitching at her sides.

I spun the trident once, letting the weight settle comfortably in my grip before resting it against my shoulder. I met Gemma's gaze head-on and smirked.

"Oh, I'm sorry," I drawled. "Did you think you were the only predator here? That was your first mistake."

A low growl rumbled from Gemma's throat, her scaled fingers curling into fists. "You have no idea who you're messing with."

"Funny," I said, twirling the trident effortlessly. "I was about to say the same thing to you. Where's Tink?"

Gemma laughed. "You think I brought the fairy here? Foolish child, I took what I could from her and left her in Neverland to die. Do you think I intended to hand her over? I know the two of you are bonded."

"She's surrounded by those ready to kill her the moment I give the word. Just like you're connected to your precious fairy, I'm connected to my assassins. Only the ones truly loyal to me, of course."

The fire crackled around us, embers swirling from the sky like tiny fallen stars. The twisted tree at the heart of the house groaned under the force of the flames, its branches stretching toward the heavens as if pleading for mercy. But there was none to save it—not in this battle, not between these two.

Pan stood in the threshold of what I could only assume was his home, a silent sentinel against the backdrop of swirling cosmic light. The eerie glow of the Celestial Plains framed him in ethereal hues, casting shadows that shifted like living things around his towering form. His expression was unreadable—calm, composed—but there was an undeniable power to his presence, an ancient authority that pressed against the very air, cutting through the cosmos like a blade honed over centuries.

He looked so much like his son. Not just in the striking blond hair or the piercing eyes that seemed to hold entire lifetimes within, but in the way he carried himself—steady, unyielding, a force of nature in his own right. Yet, where Pascal carried the flightiness of youth still shaping itself, Pan stood eternal, as though time itself bent around him rather than touching him.

And being a god, I suppose it had.

"Gemma," he said, his voice steady. "This is a foolish decision. You need to stop before you take this too far."

Gemma's slitted eyes burned with fury as she bared her teeth. "Too far?" she spat, the shadows coiling around her shifting like restless serpents. "You dare speak to me of going too far?"

I tightened my grip on the trident. "Why are you doing this?" I demanded. "What do you gain by attacking him? What is this even about?"

Gemma turned her gaze on me, and for a moment, I thought she might strike. But then, something flickered in her expression— something broken and filled with ages old heartache.

"I came here to take what was stolen from me," she said, her voice sharp but trembling. "I came to take back my husband. The man *he* took too soon."

Pan exhaled softly, shaking his head. "You abandoned him, Gemma," he said, his voice heavy with something I couldn't quite place—regret, perhaps? Pity? "He was sick, dying, and instead of staying by his side, you left. You left him in search of dark magic, in search of a cure that didn't exist."

Gemma's body tensed, her claws flexing at her sides. "And what would *you* have done?" she snarled. "Watched him wither away? Watched him slip through my fingers while I did nothing? You stand there, judging me, but you've never had to make that choice!"

Her voice cracked on the last word, and I saw it then—the deep, festering wound hidden beneath all her hatred.

Pan's expression softened, slightly. "You've always blamed

me, haven't you?" he murmured. "For everything. Not just for him."

Gemma's breath hitched, her entire frame trembling. "You *always* take from me," she whispered, the rage now barely masking the grief threatening to swallow her whole. "My parents. My love. My *child*."

The last word struck like a thunderclap, reverberating through the plains.

I sucked in a sharp breath.

Gemma . . . had lost a child?

A haunting silence settled over us.

Pan's expression was unreadable. "Gemma—"

"Shut up!" she roared, voice breaking, her shadows exploding outward.

The flames roared higher, the sky itself darkening in response to her fury.

Ulrich stepped forward, his jaw tight, his hook gleaming in the flickering firelight. His blue eyes were ice-cold as they locked onto Gemma, his disgust plain. "And what about all the lives *you've* taken?" he said, voice sharp as a blade. "The innocent people you butchered. The families you tore apart. What about them, Gemma?"

She sneered, head tilting as though he had said something amusing. "*They* were necessary sacrifices," she said. "Everything I've done—every life I've ended, every soul given to me—was to bring me here. To *this* moment."

"To *what*?" I shot back. "To vengeance? To taking more innocent lives? To watching the world burn?"

"To *saving* those who deserve it," Gemma spat, eyes flashing. "To giving power to those who have *suffered* while the gods play with our lives as if we are no more than toys to them! Do you not see it, Arie? The gods will never change the world. But I will. I told you I was going to fix the souls of villains and I'm going to start with his." She pointed at Pan.

I clenched my fists. "You're insane."

"No," she said, shaking her head, her smirk widening. "I am inevitable. And when I consume *his* soul," she turned back to Pan, her lips curling in satisfaction, "I will become *a god*."

A chill crawled down my spine.

"You don't have to do this, Gemma." Pan's voice was calm, level. "Consuming me will not make you divine. It will only make you into a monster."

Gemma's gaze darkened. "And I will still be greater. I will take your power. And when I do, I will *reshape* the Celestial Plains and the other realms into a world where the strong do not *suffer* under the weight of the weak."

I took a step forward, raising the trident. "I won't let you."

She tilted her head, eyes gleaming with wickedness. "Oh, but you *will*." She smiled, slow and venomous. "Because I have something you want."

I tensed.

Her voice dropped to a taunting whisper. "When I kill Pan, you'll take his soul for me, I will bring your fathers back."

The world stopped.

The trident in my hand trembled.

Malakai. Viktor. *Alive.*

The thought nearly shattered me.

The sheer *thought* of having them was intoxicating—to hold them again, to hear their laughter echo through the halls, to spend nights playing cards like Frankie and I had as kids. The yearning curled deep in my chest, a temptation as strong as the sea itself. But as much as I wanted it, as much as the ache threatened to consume me, I knew the truth.

They were gone.

I had started this journey on a warpath, vengeance burning

like a brand in my veins. But seeing Gemma stare her past in the face, watching how revenge had twisted her, how it consumed her until all she wanted was destruction—it was a warning, a reflection of what I would become if grief guided my every move. That wasn't the story I wanted to tell my children.

I wasn't her. I wasn't my mother.

I was a goddamn monster hunter, a sea witch who grew fins and called storms, a direct descendant of Atlas himself. And I would write my own story.

"No."

I didn't realize I had spoken until I heard my own voice—quiet, but firm.

Gemma's smile fell, the flicker of amusement in her eyes vanishing, replaced by a cold, calculating look. The air between us seemed to crackle with tension, heavy and oppressive.

My fingers curled tighter around the trident, the wood pressing into my skin as if it were the only thing that could keep me steady. The weight of the decision bore down on me, but I didn't falter. "I won't trade one soul for another. Not even for them."

The fury that twisted across her face was unlike anything I had ever witnessed. It was raw, uncontrollable—her entire demeanor shifted, and I saw the mask of control slip, revealing the rage beneath. Her lip curled into a sneer, the sharpness of it making her look more like a predator than a queen. Her nostrils flared as her breath came faster, a faint tremor in her hands as they balled into fists, the tendons in her arms straining with barely contained violence.

"You stupid girl," she hissed, the words laced with venom that cut through the air. The sound sent a shudder down my spine, but I didn't move. My resolve only hardened in the face of her anger. I would not yield.

Before I could react, she *whistled*.

The shrill sound sent a shudder through me.

Shadows poured in through the burning wreckage of the house, darting through the trees, leaping over flames. Dozens of them.

Assassins.

My stomach plummeted.

"But . . . how?" Pascal's voice was tight with disbelief.

Gemma smirked, tilting her head. "I came prepared." She let out a soft, taunting laugh. "The fairy dust Wendy procured for me allowed them to slip in while I distracted Pan."

My hands clenched around my weapon as the assassins fanned out, encircling us.

Beside me, Ulrich pulled out his—I blinked, gaping. "Where is your sword?"

Ulrich pulled out the cutlass at his side as assassins grew closer. "Here."

"No, that's not yours. I've spent months fighting alongside you, and before that, fighting *against* you. I know what the hells your sword looks like."

"Is this a necessary conversation right now?" Pascal bit out, his voice sharp with frustration.

"I had to give it up," Ulrich said, his words flat, as if he were trying to keep the weight of them from sinking in.

I blinked, confused, trying to grasp what he meant. "What do you mean?" The words felt thick in my throat, each syllable heavy with the fear of what was coming.

Pascal sighed, exasperation dripping from his tone. "He had to give it up to Kaelryn so he would help at the masquerade ball. To save you."

My breath caught in my chest, the air around me suddenly feeling too thin. *Give it up.* My mind raced, trying to understand what Ulrich had sacrificed, what it was that he had given away. For me. His sword, his *life*. The thought hit me like a physical blow, my heart skipping a beat as it processed the weight of his words.

"Now, let's focus on what matters," Pascal said.

I cleared my throat, tearing my gaze from Ulrichs, and peered back at the assassins. I drew Slayer in my open hand. Dual-wield and ready to kick some assassin ass, I tilted my head from side to side and rolled my shoulders.

"Kill them," Gemma ordered, her voice a low growl.

Everything exploded into chaos.

Ulrich was the first to react, his instincts sharp and immediate. His sword flashed in the dim light as he lunged at the nearest shadowy assassin, the blade cutting through the air with a deadly grace. The man's eyes widened, and he barely managed to raise his weapon in time to block the strike. But Ulrich was relentless—his follow-up a swift, lethal motion that forced the assassin back. The sound of steel ringing against steel echoed through the chaos, and Ulrich's eyes burned with the fury of battle.

Pascal was right beside him, moving with a fluidity that matched Ulrich's. A strike came from one of the other assassins aimed at Ulrich's side, but Pascal was there, his blade meeting theirs in a clean parry, sending the would-be attacker stumbling. Pascal wasted no time—he countered with a vicious swipe that sliced across the assassin's arm, blood spraying in the air like a warning.

I barely had time to react before two assassins lunged at me, their blades whistling through the air with a sickening promise of death. My heart skipped, adrenaline surging through me as I swung my trident into position. I ducked just in time, feeling the rush of air as the first blade slashed where my neck had been seconds before.

Without hesitation, I twisted, the trident spinning in my hands. With one smooth motion, I swept the first assassin off their feet, the end of the pole catching their legs just below the knee. They hit the ground hard, their head slamming against the stone with a sickening thud.

The second assassin didn't hesitate—he was faster, more determined. His blade slashed toward me again, aiming for my ribs. I twisted in the air, my body low, and with a quick, calculated movement, I drove the blunt end of my trident into his side. The impact was sickening—bones cracking beneath the pressure. He let out a strangled scream, crumpling to the ground, clutching his midsection as blood poured from his mouth.

Screams echoed around us, a chorus of agony mixed with the clash of steel. The air was thick with the metallic scent of blood, the heat of battle rising with every passing second. I barely registered the movement to my left—another assassin coming at me, but I reacted without thinking. My trident moved like an extension of my body, blocking his blade with the shaft before bringing it up into his throat. The man gurgled, his eyes wide with shock as he dropped to the ground.

The sounds of blades clashing, bodies slamming against stone and dirt, filled my senses, drowning out everything else. My heart pounded in my chest, but I couldn't stop moving. I couldn't hesitate. Every swing, every step, was about survival. About staying alive long enough to see the end of this fight.

And then—

The air crackled with energy as Gemma tilted her head back, her lips parting in a cry that shattered through the Celestial Plains. I faltered, and so did the assassins.

A low hum vibrated through the ground, then the wailing began.

One by one, the Nexius responded, their glowing forms flickering like dying embers before twisting violently toward her. The moment they reached her outstretched hands, she tore them from the air, ripping them free of their fate. They screamed as they were pulled into the vortex of her power, their shimmering essence twisting and writhing before vanishing into her.

Pan's eyes went wide, horror flashing across his face. "No!" he bellowed, stepping forward, his hand raising as golden energy surged from his palm. A gust of wind rushed outward, aiming to sever her connection to the souls—but it was too late.

Gemma's head snapped back, her mouth stretching open in a scream that didn't belong to this world. The sound was raw, primal, filled with the echoes of the Nexius souls writhing inside her. They coiled beneath her skin, dark tendrils of energy pulsing through her veins like ink spilling through water.

Scales rippled along her arms, shifting colors like oil slicks—black, violet, hints of molten gold that shimmered before settling into a deep, abyssal hue. Her limbs twisted unnaturally as her nails clawed into the earth, fingers stretching into hooked talons that dug deep into the ground. The bones in her neck cracked, stretching as her face elongated and shaped into something neither dragon nor human, but an abomination caught between.

Then came the wings.

Huge, leathery, and wrong, they erupted from her back in a spray of torn fabric and shredded flesh, dark as a storm-torn sky. The webbing between them glistened, translucent like Tink's wings, threaded with eerie, pulsating veins of violet light. She unfurled them with a snap, the force sending gales of wind ripping through the air.

Her spine arched, bones snapping and reforming as two massive, jagged horns curled from her skull, branching outward like the antlers of a great beast, their edges gleaming like sharpened obsidian. A thick tail lashed behind her, ridged with spines, slamming against the ground with a force that split the very earth beneath her.

But the worst part—the thing that made my breath seize in my throat—was her feet.

Not claws. Not talons.

Webbed.

A grotesque mix of reptilian and aquatic, the flesh between them was thick and sinewy, slick with an unnatural sheen, each step leaving damp, slithering imprints in the dirt. It was as though the transformation had not only corrupted her but had dredged something ancient and from the deepest trenches of the sea and forced it into the shape of a monster.

Gemma turned her glowing, slitted eyes toward me, her pupils thin as blades, and smiled—baring rows of jagged, needle-like teeth.

And then she took to the sky.

29

DEATH'S GRAND ADVENTURE
ULRICH

A FUCKING DRAGON. *A DRAGON.*

Why in all the Seven Seas did it have to be a dragon?

I'd fought sea serpents, krakens, and creatures that didn't have names—things with too many teeth and too many limbs that lurked in the darkest parts of the ocean. But flying beasts? Those were the ones I hated the most. A predator with wings had every god's damn advantage. The only way to ground it was to take out its wings and that was no easy task. Keeping it pinned was also a feet. And this one? This was worse than any creature I'd ever faced.

Gemma—if the beast before me could even be called that anymore—towered before us, her grotesque form stretching impossibly tall, her wings casting shifting shadows across the burning wreckage of Pan's home. Her elongated skull turned slowly, eyes flickering between us with eerie intelligence, as if deciding who to devour first.

A gust of wind slammed into me as she shifted, sending a blast of heat and energy through the field. The air itself vibrated with the wrongness of her presence, thick with the stench of brimstone and something that smelled like the deep, rotting belly of the sea.

To my left, Arie continued her fight against the assassins, her grip on the trident white-knuckled, her chest rising and falling in short, sharp breaths.

"Arie," I said, voice low and steady.

She didn't look at me. Her focus was locked onto the monster before us.

"Arie," I tried again, stepping closer.

Still nothing.

I swore under my breath. "Oi, little mermaid."

That got her attention. She blinked, and for a moment, I thought I saw fear flicker across her features before she shoved it down, replacing it with cold, hard resolve.

I grunted as I shoved my sword through another assassin. "Tell me you've got a plan, love."

"Working on it." She grunted as she dodged an oncoming attack.

Fantastic.

"Alright," I said, adjusting my grip on my sword, "someone tell me we're not just standing here waiting to get eaten."

"Ulrich," Arie's voice was sharp. "No sudden movements."

My lips twitched. "Think she'll eat me slower if I stay still?"

Arie shot me a look. "Not the time."

"Never is."

Dragon-Gemma loomed over us, her massive wings beating against the air, sending gusts of wind that flattened the blackened grass. The glow of the Celestial Plains flickered and pulsed like the entire realm responded to her transformation.

But she wasn't the only danger.

An assassin lunged at Arie, but she was faster, dodging with an elegant twist and driving her trident straight through his gut. He crumpled, but there were more—too many.

Another came for me.

I barely managed to twist out of the way before his dagger sliced across my ribs, hot pain blooming along my side. I swore, grabbed him by the wrist, and slammed him to the ground, my hook tearing across his throat.

To my right, Pascal's knives danced, his movements fluid as he dodged and struck with practiced precision.

"We're getting overwhelmed!" Arie's voice carried through the chaos as she pressed her back to mine.

Gemma let out a deafening roar, her massive, webbed feet crushing the earth beneath her as she surged forward, her serpentine neck snapping toward us. A wave of dark power rippled through the air, sending a deep, unnatural chill straight through my bones.

And then, Pan spoke.

His voice wasn't loud, but it was everywhere, sinking into my skin, into the ground, into the air itself.

"Spirits of the Fallen, hear me."

The ground shuddered.

One by one, ghosts materialized out of thin air, their presence a sudden weight pressing against the battlefield. There was no rise from the ground, no slow drift from the sky—one moment they were nowhere, the next, they were here.

Their eyes burned like silver fire, their faces set in grim determination. Some held weapons formed from their energy, while others bore the scars of past battles, their spectral armor gleaming with an unnatural brilliance.

Then, they moved.

"Aid the living. Protect the realm." Pan's voice commanded.

Beside me, Arie faltered. The trident and slayer clattered to the ground, and she fell to her knees. Tears streamed down her cheeks as she sobbed. In front of her stood two men, their spectral bodies faded and flickered as they each grabbed hold of an assassin. Their eyes burned like silver flames, their hands grasping weapons conjured from pure energy. With one swift motion they plunged the weapons into the assailants.

I dodged another oncoming attack, doing my best to protect Arie as she stared at the souls coming closer. Two men who I suspected were Malakai and Viktor. I had never seen them before, but the way they all looked at one another and the way she'd dropped to her knees made me think these were the men she'd fought to avenge for years.

"My little fish," One of the souls with graying hair stepped forward, knocking another assassin out of his way. "It's good to see you, but now's not the time for tears. Use your trident."

Arie didn't move. She stayed frozen on her knees, her breath coming in ragged gasps.

I could see it in her eyes—the battle raging inside her. Disbelief. Hope. Fear. Like if she reached for them, they'd vanish into nothing.

"M-Malakai? This—this isn't real," she whispered, her voice barely audible over the chaos.

The one she'd called Malakai turned toward her fully now, the silver glow of his form flickering slightly. His expression softened, but his stance remained firm, unshaken.

"We don't have time for that, little fish," he said gently, but there was steel beneath his words. "We are here. That is all that matters."

Arie sucked in a sharp breath, her fingers twitching toward the trident lying in the dirt.

"But how?" Her voice cracked, eyes darting between them, searching for something—anything—that would make sense of what she was seeing.

The other, presumably Viktor, took a step closer, his spectral form barely disturbing the grass. A soft flicker of warmth passed through his gaze, the same kind I'd seen on Arie's face so many times before.

"Because you needed us," he said.

Arie pressed a hand to her chest, as if trying to keep her heart from shattering apart. "I—I don't—"

Another assassin lunged, but Malakai was faster. With the ease of a man who had wielded a blade his entire life, he intercepted the attack, twisting his sword and driving it straight into the man's gut. The assassin gasped, his body jerking before collapsing in a heap at Malakai's feet.

Viktor turned, slicing down another before glancing back at Arie.

"We'll handle them." His silver eyes burned as he looked toward the assassins pouring into the clearing, his grip tightening on his energy-forged blade. "But you need to do your part."

Arie's fingers curled into fists, still shaking—but then she exhaled. A slow, shuddering breath.

She reached for the trident.

Just beyond her, I saw . . . "Hector?"

The pirate beamed at me. "Hook, fancy meeting you here."

I shook my head, but the grin on my face slipped away when two others appeared.

A man and a woman.

They stood apart from the others, their spectral forms flickering, but they weren't looking at the battle.

They were looking at me.

Something inside me twisted painfully.

I didn't know them, not really.

I didn't have memories of my parents. No faces to recall, no voices to remember, no bedtime stories or whispered reassurances in the dark. That part of my life had been stolen from me before I had the chance to hold onto it.

But this? This was different.

I knew them. Somehow, someway—I knew.

The man's eyes, the sharpness of his jaw, the way he held himself. I'd seen those same traits in the mirror.

And the woman . . . her golden hair caught the celestial glow, wavy and wild. Her lips parted slightly, trembling, like she wanted to say something, but the words wouldn't come.

The tender pain in her gaze unraveled something inside me, something I didn't realize I had been holding together with a fraying thread.

I took a step forward.

She did too.

And for a split second, it was just us.

A boy who had lost everything.

A mother who had never stopped searching.

The man beside her—my father—watched me like he was committing my face to memory, his throat bobbing as he swallowed hard.

He lifted his hand.

Aching, desperate, like he had spent years reaching for me.

But before he could—before either of them could—they turned.

Their expressions shifted from longing to battle-hardened focus.

A group of assassins closed in from the left, blades gleaming beneath the eerie celestial sky. The two ghosts moved as one, stepping between me and the threat without hesitation.

My mother— gods, my mother—drew twin daggers from her spectral belt and drove them into the first assassin's ribs.

My father swung a massive blade, cutting through another like a force of nature.

I stood there, stunned, unable to move, unable to breathe.

They were fighting for me.

For us.

For what was left of their son.

Something thick and foreign swelled in my throat, but there was no time for this.

Another assassin charged toward Arie from behind, and I forced myself to move.

I met him halfway, my cutlass slicing through his shoulder as he let out a strangled cry.

I couldn't fall apart.

Not yet.

Because Gemma roared again, and this time, she launched herself forward.

Her massive tail swung through the battlefield, a blur of dark scales and raw power. Her jaws snapped shut with a sickening crack, missing Pan by mere inches as he twisted away. The wind from her bite sent dirt and debris spiraling outward, tearing up the blackened grass beneath them, blinding all in the vicinity including her assassins. The ground trembled as her claws followed through, slashing deep trenches into the earth where he had stood only moments before.

Pan barely had time to breathe before she came again—relentless, vicious, a force of destruction given form. His jaw clenched, and he threw up a hand. The air itself seemed to shudder. The souls lurking near—the ones that had been watching, waiting—screamed. Their forms blurred into tendrils of energy, spectral light peeling from the air, twisting, writhing as they surged toward him.

The glow of them wrapped around Pan's fingers like living mist, coiling into his palm, brightening until the space around him crackled with raw, unfiltered divinity. His silhouette burned with a golden radiance, his eyes flashing as he turned toward her.

Then—he struck. The power lashed forward like a divine bolt of lightning, splitting the sky with its brilliance.

It hit Gemma mid-flight. A deafening shriek erupted from her throat as her massive form spasmed, twisting violently. Her wings convulsed, the edges catching fire from the totality of the magic. The massive dragon form jerked, her wings faltering. Her body twisted, spiraling down in a tumble as the force of the blow tore through her. She crashed into the ground, sending a shockwave rippling through the battlefield.

The battlefield lay in eerie stillness, the air thick with dust and the acrid scent of scorched earth. Smoke coiled through the darkness in twisting ribbons, obscuring everything in a shifting haze.

For a moment—silence.

Then, the crater stirred.

A sound like grinding stone rumbled through the space, low and guttural, vibrating through the shattered ground beneath our feet. The dust parted in wisps, revealing the monstrous form at its center.

A deep growl, low and menacing, rattled through her, a warning that sent chills prickling down my spine. Her eyes snapped open, glowing like embers in the dark.

The ground fractured beneath her weight as she propelled herself skyward, her enormous wings snapping outward in a blur of motion. The force of her ascent sent a powerful gust tearing through the battlefield.

She rose high above us, an ominous silhouette against the darkened sky.

And then—fire.

Dark flames churned from her throat, coiling and surging, an inferno barely contained. The air around her darkened, warping with heat. Then she unleashed it. The roar of flames tore through the space, a tidal wave of searing heat and pure destruction. The firestorm swallowed the distance in mere heartbeats, turning the night into a hellscape of molten gold and black smoke.

But Pan did not move. The god of life and death stood his ground, unflinching. At the final moment, he lifted a hand. A ripple spread outward from his fingertips—a pulse of unseen energy, calm yet absolute. The fire met its barrier. The collision shook the plains, sending shockwaves rippling outward, rattling the ground beneath us. Flames clawed at the invisible wall, writhing and searing, desperate to consume him.

But they could not break through. Pan's expression remained unreadable, his form untouched, his power an immovable force against her rage.

Above, Gemma let out a snarl that sent vibrations through my very bones, a sound both primal and furious. Her massive wings beat against the sky, each powerful stroke stirring up a whirlwind of dust and embers. And then she dove again.

Pan barely had a moment to counter before they struck.

Her claws tore into his chest, sinking deep with a sickening crunch of flesh and bone. Dark, inky blood erupted from the wounds, spilling down his torso, seeping into the ground beneath him. His body twisted under the sheer force of the impact, his breath escaping in a sharp, guttural exhale.

Pascal's anguished cry rang through the battlefield as he pushed forward, sprinting toward his father with reckless desperation.

"Father!"

Pan swayed, his divine form flickering, his wounds seeping into the charred ground. His breath came in ragged gasps, his chest rising and falling unevenly as he fought to remain standing. The god of life and death was on the verge of collapse, and Pascal knew it.

Pascal's knees hit the ground beside Pan in time to catch his fall, Pascal's hands trembling as they pressed against his father's wounds.

"Stay with me," Pascal pleaded, his voice cracking. "Please, don't—don't leave me."

Above, Gemma hovered like death itself, wings outstretched against the storm-lit sky. Her eyes burned with something beyond rage now, inching closer to madness. Her chest swelled as she inhaled deep, preparing to finish what she started.

I turned, searching, knowing only one thing could stop her now.

And then I saw her.

Arie.

She had stepped away from the others, her trident clutched tight, her face a mask of unwavering determination. How had she gotten so far from me? She didn't falter. She dug her feet into the earth and lifted the trident above her head. The sky split apart. A deafening crack ripped through the heavens as black clouds churned, swirling into a violent storm that hadn't been there moments ago. Wind roared, lightning flashed in vibrant colored strikes, and the very air itself charged with raw, electric power. The weight of it pressed down on my skin, sharp and humming, setting my every nerve on edge.

And Arie—she was at the center of it.

Her eyes blazed, no longer just glowing, but alive with streaks of pale blue electricity, flashing like the heart of a storm itself. Energy rippled along her arms, coiling through the trident.

Gemma's golden eyes snapped toward her, widening slightly. Not in fear. Recognition.

Arie gritted her teeth and slammed the base of the trident into the ground.

The sky roared in answer.

A jagged bolt of lightning tore from the storm, striking the trident like a divine conduit. For a moment, Arie was no longer herself—she was power incarnate, bathed in blue-white light, her form outlined in raw energy.

And then, with a snarl, she thrust the trident forward—straight at Gemma.

The lightning obeyed.

It shot forward in a blinding arc of destruction, crashing into the dragon midair with a force that sent shockwaves across the battlefield.

Gemma screamed.

Her massive form convulsed as the electricity tore through her scales, searing through flesh and bone. Her wings spasmed, failing her. The dragon plummeted toward the ground, trailing smoke and the scent of burning flesh.

I barely had time to brace for the violent landing before the earth trembled with the force of her impact.

Her monstrous form twitched, muscles spasming as she struggled to rise. The lightning had burned deep, leaving charred black streaks across her iridescent scales. One of her wings hung limp, torn, but not completely useless.

I took a step forward, cutlass at the ready. She was weakened. This was our chance.

But just as I moved, she did too.

Faster than I could react, her head snapped up, her eyes locking onto Arie. Gemma lurched forward, her massive form propelling toward her like a beast desperate for a final kill.

I didn't think.

Didn't hesitate.

Didn't let myself consider the consequences. I'd be damned if I lost her again.

I ran, shoving Arie out of the way just as Gemma's talons slammed into me.

A searing pain shot through my shoulders, the unholy strength of her grip piercing through muscle and bone as her claws clamped down.

And then the ground vanished.

Wind roared around me, the battlefield shrinking as Gemma's wings beat against the storm-ridden sky, lifting us impossibly high.

I could hear voices shouting—Arie's among them. But they were far away, muffled.

Gemma's grip tightened, her claws digging in deeper, and I gritted my teeth against the pain.

Through the haze of agony, I managed to lift my head, just enough to meet her gaze.

And she grinned. A wicked, jagged thing—sharp as her talons embedded in my body.

"Let's see her save you from this."

Gemma's voice slithered through my mind like a dagger between my ribs before she let go.

The wind shrieked past my ears, ripping through my hair as I plummeted, weightless, untethered—a falling star with no sky left to burn in.

The battlefield below rushed up to meet me, the shattered earth stretching wide, hungry, ready to consume me.

Somewhere, far below, voices screamed my name.

But I couldn't focus on them.

The sky twisted, the storm clouds spiraling into a blur as the wind roared, howling, deafening, drowning out everything else.

The pain in my shoulders was nothing. I barely felt it. Because Arie would finish this.

The only thing that mattered now was the fall.

The inevitable end rushing up to meet me.

And then—

Nothing.

30
A GOD'S OFFER
ARIE

No.

The word remained trapped in my throat as Ulrich collapsed onto the muddy battlefield, his body hitting the ground with a sickening crunch. The noise of his fall reverberated across the chaos, louder than the thunderous storm, louder than the howling wind that whipped through the air, louder than the blood pounding in my ears.

I fractured, splintering like glass under pressure. An anguished sound erupted from deep within my chest, a raw, primal scream that tore through the din of battle. A cry infused with rage, with piercing grief, with unyielding fury that ripped through the very atmosphere.

Through the cacophony, Gemma's laughter sliced through like a taunting knife, echoing in the storm's ferocity. My vision narrowed, and all I saw was her. The raging storm above seemed to bow to my wrath, its swirling dark clouds mirroring the tempest inside me.

Electricity danced over my skin, tracing intricate patterns along my arms and weaving through my hair like a living current. My body began to rise, hovering just above the battlefield, as raw, untamed power surged in the charged air between me and the ominous sky above.

Gemma stumbled back, her eyes wide with a mix of awe and fear. She could feel the energy radiating from me.

"Not so fun when you're the one being hunted, is it?" I spat, lightning still crackling along my skin. My voice was hoarse and rasping, laced with fury and something deeper—something final.

Gemma's lips curled, but it wasn't her usual smirk. False bravado. She was afraid.

I hovered closer, the storm shifting with me, the air heavy with static.

"You wanted to play god," I continued. "But you forgot one thing—gods can die too."

I hoisted the trident high above my head, its metallic surface glinting in the dim light. The sky responded with a violent rapture, clouds splitting as if torn by an invisible hand. Bolts of white-hot lightning tore from the gaping abyss, illuminating the darkness with a blinding fury. They snaked and danced, forming a chaotic web across the heavens, all converging with a crackling intensity on the tip of my weapon. The ground trembled violently, rattling loose stones that clattered and skittered across the barren earth. The sheer pressure of the storm made allies and assassins alike flinch, recoiling instinctively from the elemental onslaught.

Gemma's wings beat in a desperate, frenzied rhythm, her monstrous face twisting as she snarled, a look of uncertainty flickering in her fierce eyes for the first time. But it was too late for her to reconcile or negotiate.

The storm heeded my call.

With a swift, decisive motion, I swung the trident downward, channeling the fury of the tempest through its gleaming prongs.

A pillar of pure, blinding light exploded from the clouds, descending with the ferocity of a vengeful deity upon Gemma. Her body contorted violently, her muscles spasming as if under the command of an unseen puppeteer. Her defiant roar transformed into a piercing shriek as tendrils of lightning surged through her, engulfing her in a brilliant, electric storm.

The moment Gemma collapsed, her body unmoving and lifeless, I was moving.

My breath came in sharp, uneven gasps as I landed on the ground and sprinted toward him, my limbs shaking, my entire body screaming at me to move faster. The battlefield blurred, the ringing in my ears drowning out everything except the pounding of my broken heart.

"Ulrich!" The sound of his name ripped from my throat, raw, broken, desperate.

I fell to my knees beside him, hands trembling as I reached for him. He was too still. Too silent. His body lay twisted on the cracked ground, his skin pale beneath the streaks of blood that painted him.

"Gods, no," I whispered, my fingers brushing over his cheek. His skin was still warm. Still warm. That meant—he couldn't be gone. *He couldn't.*

"Ulrich," I tried again, my voice shaking, pleading. "Come on, love, open your eyes."

Nothing.

My chest heaved as I gripped his shirt, shaking him—gently at first, then harder. "You promised," I choked out, my vision blurring with tears. "You fucking promised you'd come back to me."

Still, he didn't move.

A sob tore from my throat, and suddenly I couldn't breathe. My whole body felt like it was splitting apart, the grief so vast, so all-consuming that it swallowed me whole.

"No, no, no"'" I gasped, pressing my forehead against his. "You can't leave me. Not like this."

My hands fisted into his clothes, clinging to him like I could hold him here, like I could will him to stay. My heartbeat too fast, too wild, the bond between us stretching thin—so thin I swore I could feel it tearing.

Around me, voices blurred into indistinct noise. The battle had stopped. The world had stopped.

Because without him—without Ulrich—

It might as well have ended.

How had I let this happen? How had I failed him when he had always stood by me, always fought for me, had taken on so much for *me*? And now, he was gone. Gone because of me. I had promised him we would survive, that we would make it through whatever came next, but I couldn't keep that promise.

"I love you," I whispered, my voice breaking apart like shattered glass, each word splintering as I forced it out. "Please, come back to me." I trembled as I reached for him, my fingertips brushing against his face, the coldness of his skin a cruel reminder that it was too late.

But there was no response. No warmth, no life. Just silence. The silence of everything I had lost, the silence of the future we would never have.

It was all my fault and nothing mattered anymore. Not the distant cries of battle. Not the eerie, flickering souls that still lingered in the air. Not even the fact that we had won.

Because without Ulrich, none of it meant anything.

Then, warmth. A firm but familiar weight pressed against my shoulder.

A hand.

I turned, gasping through the agony of grief, and found myself staring into a pair of silver eyes—my father's eyes.

Malakai.

And beside him, Viktor.

Gods, I had almost forgotten. In the chaos of battle, in the sheer devastation of losing Ulrich, I had pushed everything else aside. But they were here. Really here.

A sob wrenched free from my throat as I staggered upright, throwing myself into their arms. Malakai caught me first, his embrace strong and steady, his familiar scent wrapping around me like the warm memory of childhood summers. Viktor followed, one hand pressing against the back of my head, the other gripping my shoulder in quiet reassurance.

"My little fish," Malakai murmured against my hair, his voice thick with emotion. "You were never supposed to carry this much alone."

"I tried," I choked out, gripping his shirt like he might vanish if I let go. "I tried so hard, but I couldn't—I couldn't save him."

The words tore through me like shards of glass lodged in my throat. My body trembled, exhaustion and grief warring within me, twisting like twin serpents.

He never should have jumped in the way.

I wanted to scream at him. To rage at the gods, at fate, at the cruel fucking world that thought it had the right to take him from me.

Didn't he understand?

Didn't he know by now that I didn't need his protection? That I could fight my own battles? That I didn't need a hero—I just needed him?

Viktor leaned back enough to look me in the eyes, his expression unreadable yet so full of something I couldn't quite place. "Arie, listen to me. This isn't over."

I shook my head, the words bouncing around in my skull, meaningless against the tidal wave of grief rising inside me. "He never should have jumped in the way," I whispered, voice cracking under the weight of it all.

Malakai's grip on my arms tightened, steady, grounding. "And yet he did. Because he loves you."

I let out the sob clawing its way up my throat. "And now he's gone."

A heavy silence hung between us, thick as the air after a storm. Then, a shuffling sound—footsteps, slow and labored.

Forcing myself to turn away from Ulrich's still form, I faced Pan. His skin was pale, his usual celestial glow flickering dimly, but there was no mistaking the power that pulsed within him. He stood, braced by Pascal's support.

"Are you okay?" My voice was hoarse.

Pan exhaled, rolling his shoulders like he was testing their strength. The wound across his chest was already closing, the flesh knitting itself back together before my eyes. "I will be," he said, his voice steady despite everything. "I am already healing."

A wave of exhaustion hit me, my body still humming from the storm of power I had unleashed. I wanted to collapse, to let the weight of everything crash over me, but I knew that wasn't an option. Not right now, but soon.

"Arie," Pan said. "You have done a great service to the realms, something even a god could not accomplish. You stopped Gemma before she could tear apart the balance of life and death." He paused, standing straighter as he walked over to stand in front of me. "For that, I owe you a great debt."

I blinked. "What?"

Pan smiled faintly, "For your service to this realm, I will grant you what you wish. You may choose *one* person to bring back from death."

The words rang through me like thunder, the weight of his offer, crushing. I sucked in a sharp breath, my heart stammering in my chest. "Anyone?"

Pan inclined his head. "Anyone."

I turned instinctively toward Malakai and Viktor. My fathers. They stood together, still flickering with the ethereal glow of the dead, their spectral hands clasped.

"Do my fathers count as one?" I asked, hoping more than anything that he would allow such a thing. There was no way I'd be able to choose between them.

Pan studied them for a long moment before nodding. "I would not split up a family," he said solemnly before glancing to his son. "Yes, they will count as one."

I stared at Pan, my heart pounding so violently against my ribs I thought it might crack them open.

I could bring them back. My fathers who raised me, who had died protecting me and Frankie, who I had spent years aching for.

But just as I opened my mouth to speak, Pan lifted a hand.

"Choose wisely, Pirate Queen. You have others to consider, too."

Pascal looked up at Pan, his brows furrowed. "Why are you only allowing her to choose one? She saved the world, she deserves her *entire* family back."

"This isn't fair." His voice cracked, raw and trembling. He turned to Pan, his fingers clenched into shaking fists. "You're the god of life and death! Why can't you bring them both back? You can fix this. You have the power, so just do it!"

Pain carved deep into Pascal's face, his normally carefree expression shattered into something I'd never seen before. Desperation. Loss. Fury. His hands trembled at his sides, his body shaking with the effort of keeping himself together.

"It's not that simple, my son."

Pan's gaze settled on me, the weight of it pressing down like the entire sky had collapsed onto my shoulders. The god of life and death was offering something that should be impossible.

"I do not grant this lightly," he said, his voice carrying the depth of centuries, as if each word had been carved from the bones of time itself. "Restoring life is not something I can do so easily. It is not how the world is meant to work."

His golden eyes flickered, unreadable. Ancient. Heavy with a burden I couldn't begin to understand.

"I have only ever granted this gift to a few people. It is not a power I wield freely, nor is it something I can be called upon to do again."

Pascal stilled. "But you're willing to do it now?"

"For the price Arie has paid, it is the least I can do."

I looked at them—the two men who had raised me, who had loved me beyond measure. The ones I had spent years mourning, aching for, driven by vengeance.

Then I looked at Ulrich. The man who had fought beside me, bled beside me, died for me.

The man who walked through hell and back, who had risked everything again and again to bring me home. Who had held me when I was too broken to stand and seen me at my worst and never once wavered.

The man who had become my future.

The weight of the choice crushed my chest, an unbearable pressure that made it impossible to breathe.

I wanted both. But I could only choose one.

It didn't escape me that my friend also stood in the fray. He'd kept quiet but when he saw me watching him, he smiled.

"I always knew death would come for me some day, Captain. Don't you worry about me, this isn't any sweat off my back. You know I can handle it." Hector winked and I laughed.

"I love you, my friend." I smiled at him.

"I know." He beamed back.

"He'll be okay, I give you my word." Pan pressed a closed fist to his heart and bowed his head.

"Thank you,"

I turned my attention back to my fathers—to Ulrich.

A sob built in my throat, hot and raw, my fingers digging into my palms so hard that my nails cut into the skin. My eyes burned, my vision swimming, but I squeezed my eyes shut anyway because looking at them hurt too much. This was impossible. How could I choose between my past and my future?

A gentle hand cupped my cheek, warm and familiar.

"Little fish," Malakai's voice was deep, warm, and full of love. I opened my eyes, finding him smiling at me.

Viktor stepped closer, his touch warm and grounding as he squeezed my shoulder, his fingers pressing just enough to remind me that, for this fleeting moment, he was *here*.

"We have always wanted one thing for you, Arie." His voice carried the weight of a lifetime of love, of quiet sacrifices, of memories I clung to in my darkest moments. "Your happiness."

His thumb brushed against my arm, a touch so painfully familiar it broke me.

Malakai nodded, "That's all we've ever wanted. Not vengeance. Not war. Just for you to live—really live."

"And we can see now," Viktor added, tears brimming in his eyes, "where your happiness truly lies."

I sucked in a shaky breath, my fingers trembling as I reached for them, as if holding onto them could somehow make this moment last forever.

They were telling me to choose.

To choose Ulrich.

My chest constricted, a sob lodging itself in my throat. "No," I whispered, shaking my head. "I can't—I can't lose you again."

Malakai's expression softened, his silver eyes crinkling at the edges. "Arie," he murmured, brushing his knuckles against my cheek. "You were never meant to hold onto us forever."

Viktor squeezed my shoulder, grounding me when I felt like I was falling apart. "We are happy, sweetheart. Truly. There's nothing left unfinished for us, nothing left to regret. But you—you have a life to live."

"But Frankie—" My voice broke.

Malakai smiled, warm and patient. "We will watch over her. Over you both. Always."

My body ached with the choice I had to make, with the unbearable weight of knowing this was it. The last time I would see them.

But Ulrich had fought for me. Died for me. He had walked through fire for me without hesitation, without question. He had been my anchor, my home.

I let out the sob I'd been holding back and threw myself into their arms, my body wracked with renewed grief as I clung to them. They held me just as fiercely, whispering soft reassurances, their hands running through my hair, pressing against my back.

"We love you, little fish," Malakai murmured.

"And we are so proud of you," Viktor added, his voice thick.

I squeezed my eyes shut, breathing them in, memorizing them—this warmth, this love—because I knew when I let go, it would be the last time. I swallowed hard and stepped back, my chest hollow, my limbs trembling. I turned to Pan, my heart pounding so hard it hurt.

"I choose Ulrich. Bring him back."

The words barely passed my lips before I was falling to my knees beside Ulrich's body, clutching his hand as if I bring him back myself.

Pan's power surged around us, and for one agonizing moment, the world held its breath. A shimmering light flickered in the air above Ulrich's still body, barely more than a wisp at first. Then it grew, shifting, swirling, pulsing like a heartbeat.

The edges of the glowing mass curled inward, folding in on itself as if it were being pulled—drawn back to where it belonged.

The soul drifted downward, tendrils of light stretching toward Ulrich's chest. The moment they touched, the glow exploded, a pulse of power rippling through the air. The force nearly knocked me back, but I clung to him, my fingers digging into his cooling skin.

Seconds passed, before a sharp, gasping breath tore from his lips.

His body jerked violently, his chest rising as if he'd been yanked from the depths of the sea. His fingers twitched, then clenched. A deep, ragged cough wracked through him, his shoulders shuddering as he sucked in lungfuls of air.

My breath hitched.

He was alive.

I flung myself at him, arms wrapping around his neck, holding him so tightly I was sure I'd crush him.

Ulrich let out a breathless laugh, the sound rough and disbelieving. But his arms came around me just as fiercely, as if he could keep me there forever. His body was warm, solid, real—and I could feel his heartbeat beneath my palm, steady and strong.

"Gods above, Ulrich," I choked out, my fingers digging into his skin. "You absolute bastard."

He huffed a weak laugh against my hair. "Good to see you too, little mermaid." He looked past me to Pascal. "Good to see you, old friend."

"Next time you try something like that, I'll kill you myself," Pascal joked.

I loosened my grip just enough to pull back, my hands framing his face. His eyes met mine, dazed, but clear. Alive.

A breath of a second passed, and then I confessed. "I love you."

The words tumbled from my lips before I could stop them, raw and unguarded, unburdened by fear or hesitation. I let them fill the space between us, let them be the only truth that mattered.

Ulrich froze, his lips parting slightly as if he hadn't heard me right. As if the words weren't sinking in.

I swallowed, my voice trembling. "I love you," I said again, softer this time, but no less fierce.

A slow, crooked smile spread across his face, something warm and real and home. "Took you long enough."

And then he kissed me.

A sharp throat clearing shattered the moment.

I blinked, reluctantly pulling back to find Pan standing over us, his arms crossed, his expression entirely too amused.

"I hate to interrupt," he mused, "but there is still one last thing we need to address."

Pan's golden gaze flicked down to Ulrich, his expression unreadable, ancient and knowing. Then, he spoke. "Rise."

Ulrich's breath hitched. He braced his hand and hook against the ground, his arms trembling as he pushed himself up. I slipped my arm around him instinctively, steadying him as he struggled to his feet. He leaned into me for a moment, his body still weak from death's grasp, but that didn't stop him.

When he stood tall, Pan nodded in quiet approval.

"I have watched over my son from the moment he was born," Pan said, his voice carrying over the Celestial Plains like rolling thunder. "And in all that time, you were there."

Ulrich's body went rigid beside me.

"You sailed the seas in search of him. You fought, bled, and sacrificed more than most ever would. And when the time came, you brought him home." Pan's gaze softened, but only slightly. "You saved his life. Both of you did."

I swallowed hard, gripping Ulrich's arm tighter.

Ulrich said nothing, but I could feel the weight of Pan's words pressing against him. The tension in his shoulders, the way his fingers twitched at his sides—he wasn't used to this. Being acknowledged, being seen.

Then Pan exhaled, a sound full of something heavy, something final.

"And because of that," he continued, "I offer you this."

A hush fell over the plains. The air shifted, charged with something ancient and powerful.

Pan lifted his hands, and the space before him rippled—like the surface of a lake disturbed by a single drop of water.

A pair of souls stepped forward, manifesting from the very air itself.

My breath caught in my throat.

Ulrich went still.

They weren't just any souls.

They were his parents—King John and Queen Sydney.

Ulrich stood frozen, his body taut with an emotion I had never seen before. His eyes were locked onto the two figures emerging from the ethereal glow, their forms flickering like dying embers in the wind.

I didn't need him to say it—I could feel it in the way his breath hitched, the way his fists clenched like he was afraid this moment would slip through his fingers.

The resemblance was undeniable. His mother stood poised with effortless grace, her golden hair tumbling over her shoulders, her eyes the same shade of piercing silvery blue that I had drowned in so many times before. His father—tall, broad shouldered, and a presence that demanded attention—carried the same sharpness in his gaze, though softened now by something warmer, something regretful.

They had never gotten to see him grow up.

But they were here now.

"They have been waiting," Pan said. "And now, if you so choose, you can bring them back."

"Really?" Pascal raised a brow. "Didn't you just say bringing people back from the dead was difficult."

Pan nodded. "Arie saved the world, Ulrich saved mine."

Ulrich took a step forward, hesitant, like he wasn't sure if what he was seeing was real. Then his father moved first, closing the distance and pulling Ulrich into his arms. I expected Ulrich to stiffen, to resist, but after a brief hesitation, his arms came up, gripping his father just as tightly.

His mother was next, cradling his face between her hands, her thumb tracing over his cheek as if memorizing the features of the son she never got to watch become a man. Her lips parted like she wanted to say something, but no words came—just a soft, choked sound before she pulled him into her arms, holding onto him like she would never get the chance again.

My throat tightened.

His entire life, he had lived not remembering them. Not knowing where he had come from. Not having the chance to say goodbye.

Ulrich pulled back just enough to look between them, taking in their faces, the love in their eyes, the hope they carried.

Ulrich inhaled sharply. His voice came out thick, raw, burdened with the weight of an impossible choice.

"As much as I wish I could save you," he said, his tone uneven, cracking under the weight of grief. "As much as I want to get to know you, to have a life with you, I can't choose you."

The words felt like blades to my skin. My heart stuttered in my chest.

"What?" The word slipped past my lips before I could stop it. My eyes widened. What the hells was he doing?

Queen Sydney let out a small, shuddering breath, but the smile that graced her lips wasn't one of sorrow. Her eyes shimmered—not with sadness, but with pride.

King John's chuckle was a low, rumbling sound, as he shook his head before he stepped forward and clapped a firm hand on Ulrich's shoulder.

"We never expected anything else, my boy." His voice was warm and steady, as though he had known Ulrich's choice before he had spoken it. "Besides, Pan already knows we are better off here than anywhere else."

Sydney nodded, her grin soft, full of something deeper than acceptance. "That's right." A flicker of something almost playful danced in her expression. "We've been helping souls cross to the other side."

Ulrich's throat bobbed with a hard swallow, his fingers twitching at his sides. "You're not upset?" His voice was quieter now, hesitant, a child's fear over disappointing their parents.

His mother laughed softly, the sound like a winter breeze dancing through an empty valley. "Of course not, my little snow." She reached forward, brushing a stray lock of hair from his forehead, the touch so light yet filled with the promise of a lifetime of love. "We love you and your brother, but you have friends here—people who need you out in the real world. We were already on borrowed time."

King John nodded, his expression full of understanding. "The countless trips, the war councils, the sleepless nights—" he sighed, shaking his head "—they left us tired. It's clear to me that you are already a better leader than I ever was."

Ulrich sucked in a breath, his jaw tight, his eyes glistening with unshed tears.

Queen Sydney reached out, her fingers grazing his cheek, light as the snowfall he was named after. "We are so proud of you."

"Clayton has taken the throne, not me. I'm not a ruler." Ulrich shook his head.

"You are a leader in your own right, as is your brother." Sydney looked over at me then. "Take care of him for us, yes?"

I nodded.

Then, they stepped back, fading into the celestial glow, returning to the place they had always belonged.

Ulrich watched them go, his entire body rigid, unmoving.

I took a step closer, reaching for his hand, offering him something solid in this moment of impossible loss.

He took it.

"You okay?" I asked, still trying to comprehend why he hadn't saved them.

"I am, because now I can do what I'd hoped to do when we got here." Ulrich turned to Pan, ignoring my confused face, and said, "I choose Malakai and Viktor."

We emerged from a large oak tree, the same one I remember finding Pascal at last time we'd been in Neverland. I kept peering behind me, as though Malakai and Viktor would fade and I'd lose them all over again but there they were, walking hand in hand behind me.

Ulrich's fingers tightened around mine, his grip steady, grounding. I glanced up at him, seeing the raw emotion flickering in his deep blue eyes—a storm of relief, exhaustion, and something tender. He had been given a second chance, and the weight of it clung to his features, but he was here. He was alive.

Pascal and Pan trailed behind us, their steps quieter but no less significant. Pascal's expression was unreadable, but there was something lighter about the way he carried himself, something softer in the way he walked. Pan, regal and commanding even in his weakened state, moved with quiet grace, his celestial presence humming in the air around us like the last notes of a fading song.

"The others are on their way," Pan said as he came through the tree next. "They'll meet you here but I'm afraid this is as far as I go."

Pan stepped forward, the echoes of battle lingering in the air between us. His outstretched hand revealed the Obsidian Heart Stone, the purple gem pulsating with a soft, eerie glow—a heart still beating.

I stared at it, my pulse quickening. "Why are you giving me this?"

"You're going to need it if you want to break your curse," Pan said simply, his voice as steady as the tide. No riddles. No ambiguity. Just the truth.

"Calypso said I needed to gain favor from a god to break the curse."

Pan laughed. "Ah, yes, Calypso and her games. Consider you slaying the dragon and freeing me and my people from her enough."

Before I could respond, he turned to Pascal. For the first time since I'd met him, the immortal god looked hesitant. A strange reverence passed through his expression as he reached into the folds of his robes and pulled out a crown.

But this was no ordinary crown.

It looked as though it had been pulled from the very heart of Neverland itself—woven from the branches of ancient trees, shaped by time and power. The dark wood twisted into an elegant circlet, thick vines curling through the gaps, their leaves deep emerald with the shimmer of eternal life. Antlers, sharp and proud, jutted from either side, their edges tipped with gold, gleaming in the dim light. The craftsmanship was seamless, as though it had not been created, but rather grown by the land itself.

Pascal's breath hitched, his fingers twitching at his sides. "What is this?"

Pan's lips curved slightly, almost wistful. "Something I once wore when I first became a god. But I am no king. No ruler. I was never meant to sit on a throne. My place has always been between realms, protecting the balance of the living and the dead." He studied Pascal for a long moment. "But you—you are different."

Pascal's eyes flickered with something unreadable. "I'm not a leader."

"You could be." Pan stepped closer, his gaze searching. "You are the last true son of Neverland. You have spent your life fighting for it, protecting it. And now, it needs you more than ever." He held out the crown. "Not as a symbol of power, but as a promise. A new beginning."

Pascal swallowed, staring at the intricate crown as though it might vanish if he blinked. His entire life, he had been searching —wandering, lost in the shadow of a father he could never reach. But now... now, he was being asked to become something more.

"You can lead Neverland," Pan continued, his voice softer now. "Make it a home again. Not just for the Lost, but for everyone who needs a place to belong."

Silence stretched between them, thick with unspoken meaning.

Pascal hesitated a moment longer before, finally, he reached out and took the crown.

Pan gave a final nod, his celestial glow dimming as he stepped back. The air around him rippled, the space between realms bending to his will. With a final glance at Pascal, then me, he vanished, dissolving into threads of light that wove themselves into the sky.

The weight of his departure settled over us, the silence stretching in his absence. It was over.

Or, at least, this part was.

The wind shifted. A rustling sound broke through the quiet.

I turned sharply, my muscles still coiled from battle. The movement in the underbrush was slight—barely noticeable—but my instincts screamed.

From between the trees, Frankie stepped out.

She opened her mouth to say something but stopped short. She looked like she'd seen a ghost.

Frankie's gaze was locked ahead, her eyes wide and unblinking. For a moment, she looked as though she might collapse, the strength draining from her limbs.

I followed her line of sight, my heart pounding in my chest.

Malakai and Viktor stood near me, their figures faintly glowing with the remnants of divine energy that still clung to them, like ghosts struggling to remain tethered to the mortal realm. The two men, the ones who had once been her world, her everything, turned in unison.

Their eyes found Frankie.

I could see the way her breath hitched, like she was trying to breathe but couldn't, as if the sight of them was something she had long buried, something she hadn't expected to ever face again.

Her mouth opened, but no sound came out. Her body stiffened, caught between disbelief and something deeper—pain, longing, regret. Her face, usually so composed, was now a mask of confusion and heartbreak, torn between the people she had loved and lost. The moments stretched on, heavy and full of unsaid things, and I watched as her eyes watered, threatening to spill over with emotion she didn't know how to process.

"Frankie," I whispered, my voice low, as I reached out, but she didn't move. She didn't even blink. She was still, as if frozen in time.

She couldn't speak, couldn't even seem to comprehend the weight of this moment. And I knew, without a doubt, she hadn't been ready for it—none of us had.

Frankie staggered backward, shaking her head so violently that her curls bounced. "No."

Malakai took a step forward. "Frankie—"

"No," she rasped, "This isn't real."

Viktor's expression softened. "It's real, baby girl."

Frankie choked on a breath, her entire body shaking. She looked between them like she couldn't decide if she wanted to run or collapse.

"How—" Her voice broke. "How is this possible?"

Tears slipped down her cheeks, her legs buckling, but Malakai was there in an instant, catching her before she hit the ground.

Frankie's hands fisted into his shirt, her sobs ragged, disbelieving, desperate.

"You're real," she whispered, her breath hitching. "You're really here."

Viktor knelt beside them, his hand sliding over her hair in the same way he had done when we were children. "We're here, sweetheart."

Frankie shook harder, her cries turning into something

more than just grief—relief, longing, the sharp sting of years lost.

I watched, my chest tightening as Frankie finally surged forward, her arms snapping around them both, holding on like she would never let go again.

And then, in a sudden blur of light and motion, Tink shot toward me.

Her tiny, fluttering form whizzed around my head in a dizzying, frantic display of energy. Bright, golden dust trailed in her wake, catching in my hair, sticking to my skin like tiny stars.

"You reckless, impossible, insufferable, stubborn, stupid—" Tink's voice hit my ears in rapid succession, a mixture of relief and exasperation as she zipped around me, her light pulsing in time with her emotions.

I laughed, blinking against the blinding flurry of her glow. "I missed you too, Tink."

She came to a sudden stop, hovering inches from my face, her tiny hands pressed against her hips. "Missed me? *Missed me?* You nearly got yourself killed! I was losing my mind, and then Gemma had me trapped, and then—"

I reached up and gently plucked her from the air, cupping her in my palms before she could spiral into another tirade. Her glow softened, and for the first time since I'd met her, her shoulders sagged as the weight of all that had happened finally caught up to her.

"It's over, Tink," I murmured, my throat thick with emotion. "We did it."

She blinked up at me, her tiny face a mixture of disbelief and wonder. "Yeah," she breathed. "You did."

Robin's voice broke through the moment, soft but steady. "Glad to see you're all still breathing."

I turned, spotting him leaning against a nearby tree, arms crossed, that familiar half-smirk tugging at the corner of his mouth. But there was something else there too—something tight, wary, his sharp eyes scanning each of us as if making sure we really were whole.

My heart hammered in my chest, the weight of everything pressing against my ribs. My fingers curled tighter around Tink, who now rested quietly in my palm. The warmth of her small body, the dim glow pulsing softly against my skin, was the only proof that she was really here—that we had made it.

Robin pushed off the tree and took a step closer, his gaze sweeping over me, Ulrich, and Pascal. "What happened?"

"Yeah you all look like shit." Nathaniel said and Gretel smacked him upside the head. Nathaniel laughed.

What *hadn't* happened? The battle, the souls, my fathers, Ulrich—*gods, Ulrich*. I squeezed his hand without thinking, grounding myself in the warmth of his palm against mine.

I glanced back toward the tree—the smoldering ruins of Pan's home had faded but power still crackled in the air, cascading down my skin. How could I possibly put into words what we'd been through?

"All that matters," I murmured, voice still hoarse, "is that Gemma is gone."

The words felt fragile, breakable, like if I spoke too loudly, the spell of reality would shatter like a dream. But they were the truth.

Robin exhaled slowly, a visible wave of relief passing over him. His shoulders loosened—just barely—but I could see the exhaustion there, the weight of everything we'd been through clinging to him like a second skin.

"Good," he said, nodding once. "Then we need to move."

Ulrich lifted a brow, his grip still tight in mine. "Why the rush?"

A rustle of movement answered him, and Gretel stepped

forward from the shadows, her expression grim. "Because the Red Moon rises in a few hours."

My stomach clenched. The curse. I had almost forgotten in the chaos. *How could I have forgotten?*

Tink stirred, her light flickering. "Then we don't have much time," she whispered, her voice barely more than a breath.

The moment slammed into me. We had destroyed one monster, but the curse still loomed over us like a noose, tightening with every passing second. My crew—*our* people—were dying.

Robin's jaw clenched, his usual smirk disappearing. "We need to get back to the treehouse. Now."

I forced myself to nod, to *move,* but my body was feeling the effects of everything I already survived—my fathers, Ulrich, the souls, *Gemma.*

The battle was over, but the consequences of it were unraveling fast.

And the worst part?

I wasn't sure we had enough time left to fix what came next.

As we began to move, my steps faltered. My hand drifted toward my chest, fingers brushing over the curve of the Obsidian Heart Stone resting against my neck next to the trident.

It pulsed faintly.

Pan's voice echoed in my mind, the memory still fresh from only moments ago.

You'll need it to break the curse

My thumb brushed over its surface as the weight of Pan's words settled in my bones.

My heart slammed once, hard, against my ribs.

"Gretel," I started, "What else can you tell me about this stone?"

But it wasn't Gretel who answered, it was Ymira. "An artifact created by witches, stolen by pirates, protected by mermaids, and hidden by giants. It's dangerous and a weapon that no one should wield. It can't be destroyed, not really, but I can guarantee that it will darken your soul the more you use it."

I thought about the way it had called to me, how badly it had wanted me to consume the souls I'd placed inside it.

"Pan said it was the answer to breaking the curse," I said.

"Then what the fuck are we waiting for?" Nathaniel swatted at a bug that flew by his face. "Let's save our people."

31

FOREVER AFTER
ULRICH

We made it back to the treehouse in record time. The moment my boots hit the wooden planks of the landing, I could already hear the low thrum of tension bleeding through the air. It coiled like smoke in my lungs, thick and heavy.

Keenan paced back and forth near the central table, worry carved deep into the lines of his face. His eyes flicked up the moment we entered, scanning each of us—his gaze lingering the longest on Arie. Relief flashed in his expression, but it didn't last. The weight of the curse hung too heavy in the room.

And there was Calypso.

She lounged like royalty in one of the wooden chairs, legs crossed, one arm draped over the back with her nails glinting like polished coral. Her eyes were half-lidded, studying the tip of her finger as if it held more importance than anything in the world. Like she hadn't just watched the near end of everything from the sidelines.

Arie strode forward, her jaw clenched tight. She didn't say a word as she reached into her coat and yanked the Obsidian Heart Stone free.

The dull, eerie pulse of it made my skin crawl.

Without hesitation, she threw it down on the table beside Calypso. The stone landed with a heavy thud, its surface flickering faintly with the echoes of the trapped souls it had consumed. The table groaned beneath its weight, as though even wood recognized its burden.

Calypso didn't flinch.

Didn't even glance at the stone.

"Well," she drawled. "Looks like you didn't die after all."

Arie's voice cut through the tension like a blade. "Is this it, the artifact that was taken from you?"

Calypso finally lifted her gaze—languid, deliberate. Her eyes shimmered like the ocean at dusk, ancient and fathomless.

A long silence stretched between them.

Then she gave a soft, almost amused hum. "Took you long enough to figure that out."

Keenan froze mid-step. "Wait—*what?*"

Arie took a sharp breath, stepping closer to the table. "You said something was stolen. Something sacred. And Pan... he called this the key."

Calypso uncrossed her legs, sat up straight, and finally—finally—looked at the stone. Her gaze turned sharp, calculating, as if she were reading it like a map drawn in suffering and smoke.

"Not stolen," she said quietly, fingers brushing the table's edge. "Ripped from the depths of the sea by those who had no right to touch it. Gemma used it to twist the natural balance, to feed herself and her army. It was never meant to be used like that."

"And now it's back," I said, stepping forward, my voice tight with everything that had led us to this moment. "Will you break the curse?"

Calypso's expression didn't shift. Without a word, she reached for the Obsidian Heart Stone, her fingers curling around it with inhuman grace. The stone pulsed once, recognizing its true master, before she tucked it into the folds of her cloak.

Then she stood, flicked her fingers—

Snap.

"Done."

A beat of stunned silence fell over the room.

Frankie's eyes widened. "*What?*" she barked, storming toward her. "That's it? A centuries-long curse that's been rotting people from the inside out, and you break it with a *snap* like you're casting out flies?"

Calypso turned to her with an expression that could've frozen all of the seven seas. "Would you have preferred a bloodletting? A sacrifice? Fire and storms and screams?"

"Yes!" Frankie threw her arms out. "Honestly, yeah, I think I would've preferred a little *effort*."

The goddess tilted her head slightly, her lips curling in the faintest smirk. "Mortal curses require mortal force. But divine ones? They recognize their maker."

"What does that mean?" Pascal asked, stepping between them.

"It means the curse was never tied to the ship alone—it was tethered to what was stolen from me. From *my* realm. Return the balance, and the sea obeys."

Frankie let out a sharp breath, clearly not satisfied but too drained to argue further. "So . . . everyone's okay now?"

"Those who still draw breath will recover. Slowly." Calypso's voice softened, just a fraction. "But the ones who teetered too long between life and death may need more time. Their souls have been frayed."

I exhaled, the knot in my chest loosening only slightly.

Arie moved beside me, her shoulders sagging with exhaustion. "That's it then. It's over."

"For now," Calypso said, turning toward the door. "But the sea always remembers. And balance never comes without a price. Now if you don't mind, places to be, stones to protect."

With another snap she was gone.

Frankie's jaw dropped, then she threw up her hands. "You have *got* to be fucking kidding me."

Arie made a strange sound—half gasp, half snort. Then she started laughing.

Not a soft chuckle, not the kind of laugh you offer at a bad joke. This was unhinged, full-bodied, head-thrown-back laughter that echoed off the walls of the treehouse like a storm breaking loose. She clutched her stomach, bending forward as the laughter kept coming, uncontrollable and wild.

I stared at her, unsure whether I should be alarmed or relieved. "Arie?" I said cautiously. "Are you . . . okay?"

She straightened slowly, tears glinting in her lashes, her cheeks flushed. "Yeah," she said, breathless between the fading tremors of laughter. "I'm fine. Gods, I'm better than fine."

"Didn't really sound like it," Frankie muttered.

"No, seriously," Arie said, wiping her eyes. "After everything we've been through—dragons, soul-eating stones, cursed ships, near-death, actual death—*she just snaps her fingers* and it's *done*. And now she's off? To do what? Run errands?"

Pascal groaned, flopping into a chair. "Who cares? It's over."

"Shall we go check on the crew?" I asked, running my thumb over Arie's hand that I still refused to let go of.

She beamed up at me, her smile brighter than I'd ever seen it before. "I'd like that."

Hand in hand, we stepped out into the night air. The scent of salt and rain lingered, but the sky had cleared, the storm passing at last. The Red Moon hung low in the sky, its ominous glow no longer a threat but a fading omen, one that would not claim us tonight.

Familiar faces gathered around a fire pit as we left the treehouse, sharing stories, laughter, relief. Marian leaned against Robin, exhaustion making her eyes heavy, but her usual sharp grin was still in place. Frankie sat between Malakai and Viktor, her hands gripping their arms like she couldn't quite believe they were real. Gretel and Ymira had gone off in the woods somewhere and I certainly wasn't about to ask where they were going. The way they looked at one another was telling enough.

As we approached the sea, The *Jolly Dutchman* swayed gently in the bay, its once-doomed crew free of their torment. The curse was broken, the weight lifted, and for the first time in a long time, the future didn't seem quite so grim.

Arie exhaled softly, her grip tightening in mine. "It's strange," she murmured. "I spent so long chasing revenge. So long wondering if there was a future beyond it. But now..." She trailed off, glancing up at me with a small, vulnerable smile. "Now I just want to *live*."

I brushed a strand of hair from her face, pressing a kiss to her forehead. "Then let's live, little siren."

She grinned, mischief glinting in her sea-green eyes. "As long as it's with you, Captain."

"Always."

The wind carried the sound of celebration through the trees, a reminder that we had won. That we had *survived*. And though there would be more storms, more trials, more impossible battles ahead—tonight, we had peace.

And for now, that was enough.

EPILOGUE

Two Years Later – Atlantis

My dress shimmered when I moved—like sunlight through water—fitted at the waist and flowing out behind me in soft, endless waves. Embroidered along the hem were swirls of silver and seafoam, delicate shells and coral patterns that glittered like they'd been stitched from moonlight.

It was the kind of dress fit for a queen.

And tonight, that's exactly what I would become.

After two years of rebuilding—of peace, healing, and rediscovering myself—my father decided it was time. He'd ruled long enough, guided Atlantis through war and suffering. He wanted to rest, to enjoy his final years watching and getting to know his daughter. And after a lot of soul-searching, I accepted the mantle he offered.

Not because it was expected of me.

Not because of blood or legacy.

But because I finally believed I could do it—that I deserved it.

Behind me, footsteps echoed through my room.

"You know," a familiar voice drawled, laced with teasing affection, "for someone who once swore she'd never wear a crown, you look positively royal."

I turned, a grin tugging at my lips before I even saw him. "Ulrich."

He leaned in the doorway like he belonged there—and maybe he did. Dark jacket open, shirt just a little too rumpled to be proper, his hair tousled like he'd run his hand through it too many times. Sunlight hit the silver rings on his fingers, the glint in his eyes matching the crooked smirk curving his mouth.

"You weren't supposed to be here," I said, trying to sound like I hadn't been upset when he told me he wouldn't make it today.

He had spent the better part of the last two years in Chione. Also rebuilding after Gemma's downfall. It had taken much longer than King Clayton—*still seemed odd to call him that*—would have liked, but it was way better than it had been. The ports were patrolled by Robin's men . . . well, Frankie's now.

Robin and Marian decided it was best to live in Neverland until the Neverbeasts were ready to join civilization again. So, Frankie, having been an assassin and showing her worth, was named the new Commander. She and Tibault spent a lot of time together as they worked to rebuild the Brotherhood but my sister was happy. Even if I missed her constantly.

Ulrich shrugged, sauntering forward. "Yeah, well, I didn't want to miss my chance to tell you how utterly, painfully stunning you are right now."

My face warmed despite myself. "Flatterer."

"Only when it's true." His fingers brushed my waist then settled against the curve of my hip like he'd done it a thousand times. "You nervous?"

"A little," I admitted. "I keep thinking about my life . . . how it can't possibly be mine."

"It always was," he said without hesitation. "You just had to fight like hell to claim it."

That made me smile.

Ulrich leaned down, his lips ghosting over my ear. "And for the record, if you change your mind, we can still run away and terrorize the seas together."

I laughed, leaning back into him. "You say that like we won't do it anyway."

I rested my head against Ulrich's shoulder, letting the quiet comfort of him settle around me like a warm tide. For a moment, we just stood there, breathing in sync with the sea.

"How's the crew?" I asked softly, my fingers brushing along the embroidery at my hip.

"Better than ever. Keenan's bossing everyone around while you've been away." He paused, then added more seriously, "They miss you."

I closed my eyes, feeling a pang of something bittersweet behind my ribs.

After the curse had lifted, the healing hadn't been instant. It took weeks—months—for the crew to recover. The toll of teetering between life and death had left more than just physical scars. But slowly, piece by piece, they'd come back to themselves. And in that time, everything began to change.

Keenan had accepted temporary captaincy again—reluctantly at first, then with steady resolve—and with my help, he'd started mapping a new path forward. We built a resource system that didn't just serve the sea, but the cities along its shores. Atlantis. Bellavier. Even the outer islands, and all those hidden like Atlantis.

For the first time in a long time, the world felt like it was growing instead of crumbling.

"We'll be back before they know it," I said, my voice thick

with emotion. "They deserve a little freedom to be pirates after everything they went through."

"They had you," Ulrich murmured. "That's why they survived it."

I shook my head, but the smile that curled on my lips wasn't denial—it was gratitude. The kind that came from knowing where you've been and were still standing to see where you went next.

"I just pointed them toward the light," I whispered. "They did the rest."

Ulrich took my hand, threading our fingers together. "And now look at you. About to become the ruler of Atlantis. Rebuilder of worlds. Not bad for a sea monster's nightmare."

I laughed, resting my forehead against his chest, letting his heartbeat ground me. "Let's just hope I don't trip on my gown in front of half the ocean's royalty."

He leaned down, his lips brushing my temple. "If you do, I'll blame the wind."

Ulrich lifted my hand until his lips pressed against the silver band around my finger. "I'm still so surprised you said yes," he chuckled.

The door burst open with a dramatic *slam*, cutting him off.

Frankie snorted as she stormed in. "So were we. Pretty sure that was the universe's greatest act of charity."

Ulrich blinked, caught off guard, then burst out laughing as the rest of the girls poured into the room behind her like a whirlwind of chaos and silk.

Marian swanned in with a jeweler's box in hand. "Girl saw the way he handled his sword and said, 'Yes, please.'"

"I figured it was the hook." Gretel arched her finger and Frankie snorted again.

Ymira ducked through the doorway last with Tink on her shoulder, tall and unreadable with a small smile playing at the corners of her mouth. "Or maybe—just maybe—she married him because she loves him, you deranged harpies."

Frankie scoffed. "Whatever. Doesn't change the fact that you, pirate boy, are now *very* much in the way."

Ulrich raised his hand and hook in surrender, grinning like a fool. "Fine, fine. I know better than to challenge a war council. But don't forget—she's *my* Queen, too."

"Only when she's not ours," Marian quipped, already reaching for the hem of my gown.

Ulrich pressed a kiss to my forehead and lingered for a moment, murmuring just for me, "You're going to be brilliant tonight."

Then he winked at the group and made a dramatic bow. "Ladies. Giant." His eyes flicked up to Ymira.

She lifted a brow. "Watch it, pirate."

He smirked, and slipped out just as Gretel shut the door behind him with a solid *click*.

"Right," Frankie declared, spinning me toward the mirror. "Let's get you crowned before you pass out or throw up."

"I vote throw up," Tink muttered as she adjusted the beadwork in my curls. "It'd be more fun."

"Let's avoid both," Marian said smoothly. "Tonight, Arie becomes Queen of Atlantis."

And just like that, everything in the room shifted.

They weren't just my friends anymore. They were my family. My *home*.

Even though placing a crown on my head today would make me a queen, it wouldn't change who I was—not truly. It wouldn't stop Ulrich and me from doing what we loved, from exploring the uncharted corners of the world, hand in hand, salt in our hair and laughter in our lungs. The crown was a symbol, yes—of duty, of power, of a legacy born from blood and magic —but it wasn't a prison.

We had fought too hard to carve out our freedom. To reclaim it from the jaws of fate, from the shadows of past lives and broken oaths. That crown didn't mean we'd be locked behind palace doors. It meant we'd carry our people, not behind, but beside us. It meant building something better.

And not just for Atlantis.

King Rylan had told me Atlantis wasn't just a single kingdom and the moment I accepted the crown, I became queen not just of a city—but of the sea itself. Every tide, every trench, every kingdom hidden beneath the waves was now mine to protect. Mine to nurture. I planned to ensure that each corner of the sea—no matter how deep or distant—was cared for, heard, and defended. The sea had given me everything: my heritage, my power, my purpose. Now, I would give back.

Ulrich and I would still sail, still chase sunsets and monsters, still argue over maps and steal kisses under moonlight. And we'd do it all with family by our side.

This coronation wasn't the end of anything.

It was the beginning of everything.

"Are you with us?" Tink asked, and I looked up at her flying form above me. Our bond had grown stronger each day—we could feel each other's emotions, could tell when the other wasn't being truthful, and when one of us carried too much alone.

"I'm here," I said softly, standing straighter as the full weight of the moment settled over me. My reflection in the tall mirror beside me caught my gaze. The woman staring back was familiar and foreign all at once—storm-touched, sea-tempered, crowned not by gold, but by everything she'd fought to protect.

Tink flitted down to my shoulder, her glow dim and warm. "Good," she whispered. "Because it's time."

Frankie peeked her head through the door with a dramatic

sigh. "You ready, Your Majesty? Or do you need one of us to carry you out there?"

"I mean, I wouldn't mind," Marian said with a wink, sauntering in behind her. "It's your coronation, after all. Might as well be dramatic."

Frankie snorted and pointed toward Ymira. "Forget Marian, let the giant do it. She's got the arms for it."

Ymira's brow arched as she crossed the room, towering above them all. "Say that again and I'll throw you off the balcony."

Frankie grinned, completely unfazed. "See? Only queens with big arms threaten their friends with bodily harm."

Without warning, Ymira gave her a playful shove. Frankie stumbled into Marian, who caught her with a laugh as the room burst into laughter. Even Gretel, who had been leaning casually against the wall, shook her head with a grin.

"Forget tripping," Gretel said. "If you don't walk out of here glowing, they're going to think we replaced you with a sea spirit."

I chuckled, warmth blooming in my chest. "I'll do my best to shimmer appropriately."

Ymira smirked. "Good. We didn't iron out a sea-wide alliance for you to fumble the aesthetics."

I turned back to the mirror one last time. My gown shimmered like moonlight rippling across the ocean's surface, and the soft curls of my hair had been woven with shells, pearls, and pieces of silver sea-glass.

"Let's do this." I grinned before pushing open the doors and making my way to the throne room.

The doors opened, and the hush that fell over the space was instant.

Light streamed through the coral-glass windows, scattering prisms across the polished floor like fallen stars. The room was packed—dignitaries from across the seas, creatures from all corners of the realm but most importantly, my family.

I passed Pascal first—his arms crossed, but his smile soft and proud, the weight of leadership still lingering in his stance. Nathaniel stood beside him, dressed in his finest, though the defiant glint in his eye hadn't dulled one bit. He gave me a wink, mouthing, *About time*. Keenan was just behind them, his expression unreadable until I met his eyes. Then he nodded, a rare flicker of emotion breaking through—the kind that said *you did it* without needing words.

Tink hovered just above the crowd, her light brighter than ever, a tiny beacon of everything we'd survived.

Across from them stood my fathers—Viktor and Malakai—watching me with pride that radiated through the very marrow of my bones. They were right where they belonged, no longer ghosts or memories, but a part of this moment in full.

And then I saw him.

Ulrich.

Waiting just in front of the throne, a vision in black with silver embroidery that traced the edges of his collar and cuffs like frost kissed by moonlight. He stood tall, hand clasped behind his back while his hook was tucked into his pocket, his storm-blue eyes locked on mine the second I appeared.

The breath left my lungs.

I had seen him in every state—bloodied, broken, laughing, in the throes of passion—but there was something about him standing beneath the vaulted shell-like canopy of Atlantis's throne room that nearly unraveled me.

He smiled. Just a small thing, but it lit something in my chest.

This was real.

Two years ago, I was a weapon, a memoryless siren drowning in someone else's war.

Now—I walked toward my future. My people. My crown. My kingdom.

And my love, waiting at the end of the aisle with that smile that made the whole sea turn calm.

As I reached the final steps before the throne, Ulrich waiting just ahead, a figure stepped out from the side alcove.

King Rylan.

My father.

He wore his ceremonial robes—deep indigo embroidered with silver kelp threads and symbols of the sea etched into the fabric with mother-of-pearl beading. The crown of Atlantis still rested on his brow, the same crown he had worn for as long as I could remember. But his eyes—they held something new tonight.

Pride.

He stopped in front of me, eyes sweeping over me with a reverence that stole the breath from my lungs.

"You look like your mother," he said softly, voice rough with feeling. "But stronger. Braver. And not deranged."

I tried not to laugh and instead said, "You really think I can do this?"

"I know you can." He stepped closer, placing his hands gently on my shoulders. "When I first held you in my arms, you were this tiny, squirming bundle of sea-salt and sunlight. I looked into your eyes and knew, even then, that you'd change the world."

A small laugh slipped from my lips, choked with emotion. "I've made mistakes."

"We all do," he said. "The difference is that you learned from them. You faced every impossible thing this world threw at you and still—still—you chose compassion. You chose love. That's what makes you a queen."

Tears welled in my eyes, but I refused to let them fall. Not yet. "You're really okay with stepping down?"

He nodded, a smile tugging at his lips. "I've had my time. My reign was spent rebuilding after a war, after loss. But you—Arie—you're meant to lead us into something greater. You've bridged worlds, broken curses, united kingdoms. You were never just my daughter. You were always Atlantis's."

He leaned in and kissed my forehead. "Make me proud."

I threw my arms around him before I could stop myself, wrapping him in a fierce embrace. He held me just as tightly, his steady heartbeat reminding me of everything I'd fought for.

When we pulled apart, he stepped back and lifted the crown from his head.

Then, with a smile and tears glimmering in his eyes, he turned toward the dais and gestured for me to follow.

King Rylan stood beside the throne, the crown of Atlantis in his hands—silver shaped antlers and sea-branches, woven with vines, tiny pearls nestled in the curves, ancient and powerful. He turned to me, voice strong and clear.

"Ariella Lockwood, born of sea and storm, blood of Atlas, heir of Atlantis," he said, the entire chamber holding its breath, "do you vow to serve not only the throne, but the people of these waters, to protect and guide them, to uphold the balance between the realms of sea and sky?"

"I do," I said, my voice unwavering.

He stepped forward, lifting the crown high above my head.

"Then with the blessing of the sea, and the goddess Kai, I pass this title to you."

As the crown settled atop my head, a hush rippled through the throne room. The weight of it wasn't in its gold and jewels—but in history, legacy, and duty. I turned slowly and stepped toward the throne, the sea of familiar faces parting in reverent silence.

With steady hands, I lowered myself onto the seat carved of coral and pearl, its edges gleaming like starlight beneath the chamber's lanterns. My heart thundered in my chest, not with fear—but with an ancient and powerful rising tide within me.

And then—

A shimmer rippled through the air.

No one else stirred, but I felt it—felt *her*.

A blinding light bloomed in the space above the crowd, soft yet commanding. Time itself seemed to pause as the figure took form, radiant and ethereal. Kai—the goddess of Sea and Sky.

She hovered in the space before me, her presence felt rather than seen by the others. Dressed in flowing robes of crashing tides and sweeping clouds, her eyes, storm-gray and endless, met mine.

A slow, knowing smile curved her lips.

She raised her hand in a graceful motion, two fingers pressed to her brow before sweeping outward in a gesture of blessing—a silent rite older than Atlantis itself. Light spiraled from her fingertips, wrapping around me like a protective tide, warm and electric.

Then, just as suddenly as she came, Kai faded.

A beat of silence.

And then a roar of voices, united and unshakable: "All hail Queen Ariella, Sovereign of the Sea, Guardian of the Depths!"

My heart swelled, tears stinging the corners of my eyes as I turned to face them—not just my people.

My family.

My future.

And this—this was only the beginning.

AFTERWORD

It feels surreal to finally reach the end of Arie and Hook's story. When I started this journey, I never imagined how much it would mean to me, or how much it would shape me as a writer. Watching this world come to life, feeling the characters grow and evolve, and seeing their triumphs and heartbreaks unfold— it's been a journey that has changed me. And through it all, I hope you've been able to feel that growth, that passion, and that love for storytelling that has fueled every page.

This series has been such a wild ride. It's been filled with unexpected twists, magical battles, heartbreaking moments, and thrilling adventures. We've explored the realms of mermaids, witches, monsters, and magic—and I couldn't have asked for a better group of readers to share it all with. Your support has been nothing short of incredible, and I can't express how grateful I am to have had you along for the ride. Each chapter we've shared together has been a testament to the bond we've formed through these pages, and I carry that with me every day.

But even though this story is coming to an end, don't think for a second that the world we've created is going away. Stories have a way of living on, waiting for the right moment to be told.

AFTERWORD

Who knows what other adventures and characters are lurking just beyond the horizon? For now, I'm shifting my focus to my Urban Fantasy series, *The Dark Mercenary*. If you haven't had a chance to check it out yet, it's available on Kindle Unlimited! It's a whole new world, and I can't wait for you to dive into it with me.

Thank you, from the deepest part of my heart, for being here. For supporting indie authors. For taking this journey with me, for reading, for sharing your thoughts and encouragement. You've made this dream of mine possible, and for that, I will always be thankful. You're the true champions, the ones who make stories like these come to life. I can't wait for what comes next, and I hope you'll join me as we continue this adventure together.

Also by Jay R. Wolf

Looking for what to read next? Try my Dark Mercenary series!

The Dark Mercenary Series

Of Flame and Fang

The Dark & Twisted Tales Series

A Sea of Unfortunate Souls

A Land of Lost Souls

A Kingdom of Cursed Souls

Novellas:

A Cage of Cursed Souls

A Forest of Rebellious Souls – Coming October 2025

Acknowledgments

There were SO many people who have helped me through this process of this book and series but just a few who really kept my ass in line.

Karissa – MY SAVIOR. Who spent a solid two weeks fretting over edits, critiques, and getting pissed at me for pulling on your heart strings. However, I cannot in good faith promise to not throw more bricks at you. Sorry, not sorry. But thank you for everything, I cannot wait until we are doing this together on our co-write!

Rae – This series would be still sitting in a google doc waiting for me to take the plunge to publication if it weren't for you. You helped guide me, push me to new heights, and encouraged me the entire way. You are a beautiful soul and I love you dearly.

Jared – My love, my rock, and my soul. Your constant belief in me is endless and never goes unnoticed. You may never read my books, or see this but you don't need to because you already know how special you are to me, and our boys. Love you always and forever FingDing.

Cassie – Your constant putting me to work helped fund this damn so you really should get the ultimate acknowledgement. Thank you for your support in so many more ways than just that. I appreciate you as a fellow author but even more as a friend.

About the Author

Jay R. Wolf is an author of dark and urban fantasy, a wife and mother of three, and a huge geek.
She is from a small town in Michigan and moved to Race City USA to pursue her dreams. Though her dream of racing cars is in the wind, she finds herself in a comfy lifestyle in the Mile High city where writing fantasy has become a passion.
Her other hobbies include long walks in ancient forests where the wild things roam, gaming against evil foes, and catching fish in the great lakes.

Want to know more?
Website:www.authorjayrwolf.com
Facebook/Instagram@authorjayrwolf

Made in United States
North Haven, CT
25 June 2025

70128423R00252